BEYOND THE
BLUE HILLS

Katie Flynn has lived for many years in the Northwest.
A compulsive writer, she started with short stories and
articles and many of her early stories were broadcast on
Radio Merseyside. She decided to write her Liverpool
series after hearing the reminiscences of family members
about life in the city in the early years of the twentieth
century. She also writes as Judith Saxton. For the past
few years, she has had to cope with ME but has
continued to write.

Praise for Katie Flynn

'Arrow's best and biggest saga author. She's good.'
Bookseller

'If you pick up a Katie Flynn book it's going to be a
wrench to put it down'
Holyhead & Anglesey Mail

'A heartwarming story of love and loss'
Woman's Weekly

'One of the best Liverpool writers'
Liverpool Echo

'Katie Flynn has the gift that Catherine Cookson had of
bringing the period and the characters to life'
Caernarfon & Denbigh Herald

KATIE FLYNN

BEYOND THE BLUE HILLS

arrow books

Published in the United Kingdom by Arrow Books in 2007

1 3 5 7 9 10 8 6 4 2

First published in Great Britain in 2006 by William Heinemann

Arrow Books
The Random House Group Limited
20 Vauxhall Bridge Road, London, SW1V 2SA

www.randomhouse.co.uk

Addresses for companies within The Random House
Group Limited can be found at:
www.randomhouse.co.uk/offices.htm

The Random House Group Limited Reg. No. 954009

A CIP catalogue record for this book
is available from the British Library

ISBN 9780099503132

The Random House Group Limited makes every effort to ensure
that the papers used in its books are made from trees that have been
legally sourced from well-managed and credibly certified forests.
Our paper procurement policy can be found at:
www.randomhouse.co.uk/paper.htm

Typeset by SX Composing DTP, Rayleigh, Essex
Printed in the UK by CPI Bookmarque, Croydon, CR0 4TD

For Pat Cox, who bore up nobly while Norman told
me all about life in a Lancaster bomber during
World War Two

Acknowledgements

First, my grateful thanks to Norman Cox, who explained with great precision how aircrew were selected and trained during the war. His experiences on bombing raids over Germany were a great help but if I've got something wrong that will be my fault and not his!

I'm also indebted to Joan Snelling, author of *A Land Girl's War* published by Old Pond Publishing, Ipswich. This is a lively and fascinating account of the Women's Land Army at work and play and the information it contains was extremely useful. I highly recommend it.

My thanks also to Deb McLeod of Pritchards Books, Formby, who obtained a copy of Joan's book for me.

And last but not least, my thanks to Alan Hague for telling me which Norfolk airfields were fighter stations and which flew bombers during World War Two.

'And beyond the wild wood again?' he asked. 'Where it's all blue and dim, and one sees what may be hills . . . or is it only cloud drift?'

Kenneth Grahame: *The Wind in the Willows*

Chapter One

July 1934

'Tina Collins, what the devil do you think you're doing? Oh, you're a wicked girl . . . look at the state of you! When our mam sees you she'll go raving mad. Come on, get up. It's back indoors for you, my lady, and a good scrub wi' soap and water.'

The small girl squatting on the cobbles in Blenheim Court raised round, innocent eyes to her sister's face, then glanced wistfully down at the neat array of mud pies she had just made, to the detriment of her blue gingham dress. 'I don't see why you're so cross, Tess; Mam said I could play out until it were time to leave and what's wrong wi' mud pies, anyway? And you swore, *and* you said I were wicked. Swearing's a lot wickeder than mud pies.'

Tess sighed and jerked her small sister to her feet, then began to pull her back towards the house. In a way, she knew she was at least partly responsible for her sister's state since she had been told to keep an eye on the younger girl. Indeed, when she had left Tina she had been sitting meekly on the step of No. 2 Blenheim Court, waiting for one of her cousins to emerge to play with her. It had simply not occurred to Tess that the kid might do anything as mucky as making mud pies, particularly since she was wearing

1

the only decent cotton dress she possessed. But that was Tina all over, Tess told herself as she pushed open the kitchen door; she always did the unexpected. Their mother frequently said that Tina should have been a boy – how right she was! Still, that did not justify Tess's nipping round to see her friend Sally, whose house was further up the court, to discuss the possibility of searching for a holiday job. She knew that Tina was a little monkey and could get up to all sorts of mischief when no eyes were upon her; she never should have tempted fate by leaving the smaller girl alone, even for a few minutes.

The kitchen was crowded with people, but by a great piece of good fortune no one took any notice of the sisters and Tess was able to give Tina a good clean down at the sink and to dry her on a handy tea towel. To be sure, Laura Collins did pause in the buttering and slicing of a loaf of bread to ask Tess why she was not already on her way to the city centre, but then she answered her own question. 'Of course, you'll be waiting for your cousins. They won't be much longer, but why not go on ahead and wriggle your way to the front? King George and Queen Mary might not come to Liverpool again and I would like you to be able to say that you'd watched the king opening the longest underwater tunnel in the world.'

Tess, who hated being conspicuous, said that she would doubtless be able to see everything if she made her way into the enclosure reserved for school-children, but this only made her mother laugh and rumple her smooth black hair affectionately. 'Get along wi' you,' she said. 'Look, I'm going to give you your carry-out because we'll likely not find each other and you'll want to have a bite to eat before the day's over.' She handed a small, greaseproof-wrapped parcel to Tess, then bent down to give another to Tina, but stopped short with a squawk of dismay. 'Oh my God, wharrever have you been doing? And your dress is all wet down the front! Folk'll think you've been playin' mud pies!'

'She has been playin' mud pies,' Tess said grimly. 'But she's pretty clean now, Mam, and it's a warm day. Her dress'll dry out before we reach the tunnel.'

'Tale-clat, tale-clat,' Tina muttered, as her sister towed her back towards the kitchen door, pushing cousins aside as she did so. 'You swore! You never told our mam that you said a swear. *And* you never told Mam you'd gone off to see horrible old Sally, leaving me all by meself with nothing to do but make a few mud pies.'

Tess opened her mouth to respond pretty sharply, then closed it again and gave her little sister a hug instead. After all, Tina had a point, for Tess was eleven, old enough to control a child of five, and since the two of them would have to stick closer than glue all day it would be foolish to start off on the wrong foot. She admitted to herself that, though undoubtedly extremely naughty, her sister was neither wicked nor spiteful; she had not told their mother that Tess had abandoned her to go and visit

3

Sally, for Tess appreciated that Tina's mutter had been too low for Laura to hear.

She had tucked her own sandwiches into her skirt pocket and now, as a peace offering, took her sister's packet and pushed that into her pocket as well. 'I'll carry your butties. Want a piggy-back?' she asked. 'I'm sorry I told on you; it were a mean thing to do. I say, look at the crowds!'

They had emerged from the court and turned right into Penrhyn Street to reach the Scottie, where they joined a great number of people, many of them children, all heading towards the city centre. Tess was a trifle daunted and hung back, though Tina would have pressed forward, but at that moment a voice hailed them and, turning to glance behind her, Tina saw four of her Moffat cousins hurrying towards them. The sisters stopped to let Bill, Fred, Annie and Emily catch up with them. 'You should've bleedin' well waited,' Bill said breathlessly, giving Tess a punch on the shoulder, which was meant to be playful but made her give a squeak of protest. 'You got your abnabs first 'cos you're spoiled lickle brats, whereas us Moffats had to wait till the whole lot were done and wrapped.' As he spoke, he pulled his packet of sandwiches out of his pocket, unwrapped them and folded back the bread to peer at the contents. 'Eh up, guess wharr I've got? Cheese 'n' pickle! Them's me favourites. Much better'n perishin' fish paste what we usually get for us carry-out.'

'We never get fish paste 'cos if we did we wouldn't

eat it,' Tina said, smugly, if untruthfully, for towards the end of the week they frequently found that their butties contained nothing but the merest smear of paste. 'I wonder if we've got cheese 'n' pickle too. Can we have a look, our Tess?'

'Oh, you'll have sliced ham or chicken,' Bill said, rather thickly, for he had already started to eat his first sandwich. 'Your mam can afford it 'cos she's only got two kids, not seven like our mam.'

'You've got Uncle Wally earnin' as well as your mam, and your Ellen's working, too,' Tina said swiftly, always keen to join battle. 'I bet that cheese is – is really chicken, but you just said cheese so's we wouldn't know,' she added lamely.

'Oh, shurrup, you two. Considerin' we was all in the kitchen and watched Mam and Auntie Laura makin' our butties between 'em, like on a factory line, even Bill must have known what was in 'em,' Annie said. She was thirteen and already looking forward to leaving school, as her elder sister Ellen had done. Ellen was working in the jam factory and Annie planned to join her there. The remaining Moffats ranged in age from Bill, who was twelve, down to Cyril, who was the same age as Tina.

'Where's the others?' Tina asked suddenly. 'Where's me pal Cyril?'

'He's comin' wi' Mam and Dad,' Bill said briefly. 'I don't think they realised the crowds 'ud be so huge 'cos they said to meet up on Dale Street – unless we got a place in the front, of course.' He grinned down at his young cousin. 'I know what you littl'uns are for wriggling through a crowd; no doubt you and Tess will have your noses pressed against the king's knees by the time Dad and our mams arrive.'

'I'm not little,' Tess said indignantly, although she knew that compared to Bill she really was quite small.

In the event, he was not far out. Tina thought nothing of forcing her way through the crowd which had already gathered and she was so small that people smiled and moved aside to let her through. Since she was clutching firmly on to Tess all the while, they both ended up right at the front. As they took their places, Tina jerked at her sister's arm. 'Can I have me butties now? I'm fair starved 'cos I were too excited to eat me breakfast. Aw, c'mon, Tess, it don't matter when we eat 'em. Mam never said we'd got to wait till the king came.' Tess looked rather guiltily behind her at the people who must have waited for hours, then produced the sandwiches and they both began to eat. They had finished and were turning their attention back to the scene before them when Tina gave a squeak of joy. 'Look, Tess, there's Dulcie from your class at the old school on Heyworth Street. Give her a shout and maybe she'll come over to us.'

Tess shouted but her voice could not penetrate the noise the excited crowd was making, so in the end it was simpler to make their way along against the ropes which separated the crowd from the roadway until they ended up, breathless but triumphant, next to Dulcie. She seemed pleased to see them and gave both sisters a broad grin. 'We've missed you ever so much, me and the rest of the class,' she said. 'Me mam said you must have left because your mam had lost her job in the pickle factory. But why didn't you tell anyone you was goin'?'

'We didn't know. Mam paid the last week's rent and then Auntie Millie – she's Mam's sister – asked us to move into Blenheim Court. It's just off the Scottie and there's heaps of shops there, and offices and little factories. Only this bleedin' Depression means wages have gone awful low so there's no tellin' how long we'll be wi' the Moffats.' Hearing her sister swear made Tina draw in her breath sharply, but Dulcie did not seem at all surprised; it was school-talk, Tess told herself a trifle guiltily, and hoped that her small sister would not repeat the word later.

'There's heaps of shops and that on Heyworth Street though,' Dulcie pointed out, ignoring the swear word as Tess had guessed she would. 'My mam always says there's nothing you can't get on Heyworth, from fresh fish to pet guinea pigs. Couldn't your mam try for work up there? Then you could come back to school and we could all be comfortable again.'

Tess sighed. They had been with the Moffats three months but she was still desperately homesick for Everton, where she had been born and brought up, and knew her mother felt the same. But she was beginning to understand quite a lot about earning one's living. Ever since their father had died, Mam

7

had had a struggle, but it had been not only the sudden loss of her job at the factory that had made a move necessary but the increase in the rent of their flat over the pet shop. Mr Papworth, who owned the shop, wanted to move into the flat himself and must have known that if he increased the rent Laura Collins would be forced to take her family elsewhere. He had been right, of course, and had it not been for the Moffats' kindness life would have been black indeed for the three Collinses. However, Tess did not mean to explain all this to Dulcie and merely said that her mam had a new job now, further along the Scotland Road. She did not add that it was a cleaning job in a big block of offices, but explained that living in Blenheim Court meant that her mother could walk to and from work, and even more important, perhaps, had no need to hurry home to give an eye to herself and Tina, since there was always a Moffat around to see that they did not get into trouble.

Dulcie, pouting a little, was beginning to say that surely Tess could look after her sister without help, when there was a commotion as folk began to turn towards the roadway and the cheering started. Immediately Dulcie's questioning ceased and she produced a tiny Union Jack from somewhere about her person, beginning to wave it enthusiastically and cheering at the top of her voice. The children watched, intrigued, as the royal party got out of the cars and mounted the steps on to the dais, though Tina tugged at her sister's arm. 'Which one's the bleedin' queen?' she demanded urgently. 'I reckon it's the pretty one in the pink hat. Course, I know who the king is; he's the one with the little beard.'

Tess, who was not too sure herself which of the beautifully dressed ladies was Queen Mary, was beginning to answer when Dulcie cut across her words. 'You little silly, don't you know nothing?' she demanded. 'The queen's the one in pale blue with a white fur wrap round her shoulders. I love the royal family, I do. I collect pictures from newspapers and magazines, cigarette cards . . . oh, all sorts. Me favourites are the little princesses – you know, the Duke of York's kids.'

Tess remembered hearing in school about the two princesses but had no idea whose children they were or what they looked like. However, before she could admit as much, the king stepped forward to the microphone and began to speak. Immediately, everyone fell silent, but as soon as she could do so Tina pulled her sister's head down to her own level. 'This is borin',' she whispered. 'We've seen 'em now, Tess. Can't we go back home? We could take Dulcie because the court's a real good place to play 'cos of there being no traffic. Oh, c'mon, do. I thought they'd be wearin' robes and crowns and golden jewellery, but they's just two old people and I'm bored.'

Privately, Tess agreed completely with her small sister; she thought that Queen Mary might at least have dressed a little more royally but felt she could scarcely say so. Instead, she told Tina in a hissing whisper that the speech would soon come to an end, and once this happened the crowds would disperse

9

and Dulcie could accompany them back to the court.

Almost as she spoke, the king stepped back from the microphone and the brass band began to play. The cars edged forward towards the steps, doors were flung open, the royal party climbed into their vehicles once more, and to the sound of cheering which quite eclipsed the music of the band the royal procession disappeared into the Mersey Tunnel.

The crowd began to disperse, though not as quickly as Tess had hoped, and greatly to her surprise, Dulcie agreed to return to Blenheim Court with them. Tess thought that this was probably because she had offered to let Dulcie share their tea, for it was an uphill walk back to Everton, and by the time she reached her home Dulcie would have been hungry. Furthermore, Aunt Millie was an easy-going soul and had made a great pile of butties in addition to those she had given the children, guessing that they would return ravenous after such an exciting day. Tess knew some parents would not have welcomed an extra mouth to feed, but Aunt Millie had prepared enough food for an army and anyway she never minded when her kids, or her nieces, brought in a pal now and then.

All the way back to Blenheim Court Dulcie talked about the royal family, and Tess had to acknowledge that the other girl seemed to know a great deal. It was strange, because three months earlier, when the Collinses had lived above the pet shop, Dulcie had never so much as mentioned the royal family, but when Tess remarked on this Dulcie explained that she had been given a book about the little princesses, and this had fuelled her enthusiasm. Tess thought wistfully how she would have enjoyed sharing Dulcie's absorption, for the girls had been good friends even though Dulcie lived in Desmond Street, a good way from the pet shop. Because Heyworth Street was so busy, however, Tess and Tina had usually played on the recreation ground down Mere Lane, which was a meeting place for most of the kids from the area.

The children waited until the crowd began to thin out, then turned their footsteps towards Scotland Road and the court. Dulcie, pleased with Tess's interest in her new hobby, began to chatter, linking her arm in Tess's and taking Tina by the hand. '. . . and one of these days I'm goin' to gerron a train and go to London, to see Buck'n'ham Palace, and when I'm real old I'll go to Scotland . . . can't remember the name o' the place . . . oh yes, Balmoral; I'll go and see Balmoral, where the Duchess of York lived when she were just plain Lady Elizabeth Bowes-Lyon. But most of all, I want to see them princesses for meself. Elizabeth – she's the older one what's her granddad's favourite – she's eight, and Margaret Rose, she's four.'

Tina, who had been thoroughly bored by the whole conversation at first, tugged at her sister's arm. 'I didn't know there were a princess what were younger than me,' she said excitedly. 'I bet she wears a golden crown; I would if I were a princess.'

'I would like to see 'em too,' Tess acknowledged,

11

turning to Dulcie. 'My mam very nearly called our Tina Elizabeth; I never thought before but I reckon it were because of the princess. Only in the end they called her Tina, after our great-grandmother.'

Dulcie stared at Tina. 'When's your birthday?' she asked abruptly. 'It 'ud be odd if . . .'

'Twenty-first of April,' Tina said at once. 'That's why Mammy thought she'd name me after the princess, 'cos it's her birthday on the twenty-first too!' If there was one thing no child ever forgot, it was his or her birthday. 'And Tess here is at the end of April. Mammy calls us her spring lambs.'

Spring 1935
It was a fine morning with the wind blowing off the Mersey, bringing with it a salty tang which made Laura Collins think wistfully of the seaside. In the old days, before her husband, Alf, had died, they had taken Tess to New Brighton on many a pleasant day, and they had planned to take the new baby once she was old enough to enjoy the treat. But Alf had been taken ill within weeks of the baby's birth – lung disease the doctor called it – and had died before Tina was twelve months old. That had put a stop to outings for it had taken Laura all her time and energy to feed and clothe her children, and to pay the rent; trips to New Brighton had been out of the question.

Laura reminded herself how good Millie had been to take her in, and as she walked briskly along the Scotland Road she felt guilty because she had not wanted to admit to Millie where she was going that day. She had said, truthfully, that she meant to buy Tess a birthday present, for her daughter would be twelve in a few days' time. What she had not said was that she was going up to Everton to see whether anyone had a room for a reasonable rent. The truth was that she was growing increasingly dismayed by the behaviour of her daughters, and she knew that the overcrowding of the small house in Blenheim Court was beginning to get all of them down. Millie, and her fat, good-natured husband Walter, seemed to take the difficulties of cramming so many people into No. 2 in their stride, but it made things so awkward! The kitchen was large but even so it was not possible for everyone to sit down to a meal at the same time. Walter's mother, Granny Moffat, and his Aunt Hilda had recently moved into the parlour since the old ladies could no longer look after themselves and were terrified that they might be sent to the workhouse. And then this very morning Millie had told her sister, almost casually, that she was expecting another baby. 'Our Ellen told me off good an' proper and said she'd move out as soon as she could 'cos the house were already crackin' at the seams, but I doubt she'll go. She can't afford a place of her own any more'n you can, Laura, me love. Besides, as I told her, babies don't eat much, nor they don't take up much space. We'll manage fine, I told her, and so we shall.'

But to Laura, the advent of yet another soul seemed like the last straw. She had felt guilty anyway because she had not bothered to search for either a better paid job or cheap accommodation throughout the long, cold winter. Now spring had come and she was going to do her best to find a room – and a room back in Everton, what's more. At the school Tess had attended on Heyworth Street she had made a number of friends and had been truly happy, but she had never really fitted into the school near Blenheim Court. And Everton was still home so far as the Collinses were concerned. Laura's mother had always said it was a village which happened to have become a part of Liverpool without ever losing its village identity, and it was this, most of all, that Laura and the children missed. You couldn't walk up Heyworth Street on a Monday morning without knowing almost everyone you met, and although Everton children congregated on the recreation ground and not outside their own front doors, Laura thought it was much healthier to play on green grass and in the fresh air. After all, the sun hardly ever penetrated the courts, even in high summer, whereas the Mere Lane playing field was open to the elements. However, she had not said a word of this to Millie because she did not want to hurt her sister, and she tried to forget that the previous day, when Laura had reprimanded Tina for 'unladylike language', Millie had said, robustly: 'Wharraload o' nonsense, our Laura! No harm in young 'uns talkin' a bit rough; mine do it all the time but that don't mean to say they're not decent kids.'

Laura had backed down, naturally, but she had felt guilty and had known, in that moment, that she and the girls would have to move out. She could not have her sister undermining what she and Alf had tried to do, and what she now struggled to do alone, which was to bring the girls up to be respectable. Furthermore, whilst in Heyworth Street, she had always seen that Tess attended school daily, but Tina was a different kettle of fish. Laura knew that Tess accompanied Tina to the gate of the primary school every weekday morning, but she was equally sure that her small daughter had got into the habit of sagging off whenever her cousin Cyril persuaded her to do so. Laura had always stressed the importance of education – though never in front of Millie – but knew that her sister had been a poor attender herself; knew also that the Moffats went to school when they felt like it, and dodged the Attendance Officer when they did not.

I should have done more and I should have done it earlier, Laura told herself as she made her way into Juvenal Street. The truth is, I don't think I really expected Alf to die, and when it happened the shock took all the stuffing out of me. Then I got the job in the pickle factory and began to pull myself together, until the boss decided school-leavers could do the work for half the wages and Mr Papworth kicked us out of the flat, and I seized Millie's offer like a lifebelt thrown to a drowning man. I simply clung on, let the water roll over me and depended on poor Millie to keep me afloat. I never meant to be here for more than a few weeks but somehow time passed and doing nothing seemed the easiest course. Lord, it's five years since my darling Alf went and just about a year since I moved in with Millie and Walter. Then she smiled to herself. I don't know why I didn't tell Millie what I was going to do today because the poor love must be as keen to get rid of us as I am to go – she's a darling, but she's only human after all.

Laura was a quick walker and was soon turning on to Netherfield Road, glancing around her with satisfaction as she did so. This was familiar and much loved territory. She passed George Lunt's and was tempted to go inside and ask the price of the beautifully iced birthday cake in the window, but decided against it; Lunt's was a big shop with branches all over the city and would charge accordingly, but the baker on Heyworth Street was in a smaller way of business and had known her all her life. If she explained that Tess would be twelve years old in a few days' time, she was sure he would price a cake according to her ability to pay. She passed the hairdresser and waved at a customer waiting her turn. She reached John Hunt's bookshop on the corner of Anthony Street and went inside, for she and Mr Hunt were old friends. When Alf had been confined to bed, reading had been his greatest solace and Mr Hunt had agreed to sell her books for a very fair price and to buy them back for a penny or two less when Alf had finished with them. Right now, he was dusting a number of books which he must have recently purchased, and beamed all over his face when he recognised his customer. 'Mrs Collins! Well now, what a treat! Gossip being what it is, I was told you'd moved away but that you meant to come back as soon as you could. Have you had any luck in your search for employment? This wretched Depression has hit Liverpool pretty hard. I expect you know that the pickle factory is laying off workers?'

'No, I didn't know and I'm really sorry,' Laura said sincerely. She liked her boss and had understood his dilemma when faced with falling orders for pickles. It had been only sensible to get rid of his better paid employees and to take on youngsters, since the fact that the girls would produce less did not matter when orders were down.

'Yes; Mr Roberts is a good employer and hates seeing his business dwindle,' Mr Hunt acknowledged. 'Now what can I do for you today, my dear?'

'I'd like a nice book, in good condition, suitable for Tess who's almost twelve years old; in fact, it'll be a birthday present,' Laura said. 'I mean to buy her a scrapbook too, because ever since the tunnel opening last year she's been very interested in the royal family, particularly the Duchess of York's little girls, and she wants to keep all her cuttings and picture postcards together, but as you know, Tess takes after her father. Reading is her passion.'

'Twelve years old, twelve years old,' Mr Hunt murmured, walking over to a section labelled *Children's Books*. He selected half a dozen and laid them on the counter. 'These are all suitable, but my personal choice would be either *Little Women*, by Louisa M. Alcott, or *The Railway Children* by E. Nesbit.'

Laura examined all the books carefully, though she put *Little Women* to one side, reminding Mr Hunt that she had bought a copy from him the previous year. Finally, she took his advice and went for the E. Nesbit, having surreptitiously checked in the front that it was reasonably priced. Mr Hunt beamed at her, took her money and wrapped the book in a piece of brown paper, then fastened it with some string. Laura thanked him and turned to leave the shop, remarking as she did so that she had a great deal to do, for she was hoping to find not only employment, but also a room to rent. Then, when her hand was actually on the doorknob, Mr Hunt called her back, indicating a pile of periodicals to the left of the door. 'If you care to look at those copies of the *Illustrated News* and *Woman's Magazine*, you might find something – photographs or articles – about the little princesses,' he said. 'Take anything that you think might interest your daughter and tell her it's a birthday present from Mr Hunt.'

'Why, thank you. It's awfully good of you, Mr Hunt,' Laura said gratefully, and presently selected two magazines, both of which contained photographs of the princesses. 'Tess will be made up when she sees these. I must remember to tell her to pop in and thank you herself. She's a good girl and loves books, as you know; when we lived in the area she often spent at least one of her Saturday pennies in here and I'm sure she will do so again if we manage to find accommodation in this area.'

Laura picked up her parcels and left the shop,

popped into the stationers and bought a large scrapbook, then strode up St George's Hill and turned into Cochrane Street, looking wistfully at the house in which she and Alf had been so happy. And then she was on Heyworth Street and, as she had anticipated, was soon the centre of a small group of friends and one-time neighbours who were doing their shopping, and were delighted to see her.

After telling everyone why she was back on Heyworth Street she went on her way and was presently hailed by someone coming up behind her. She stopped at once and turning to the speaker was delighted to see Ena Platt, who had worked on the bench beside her at the pickle factory and had been laid off at the same time as Laura. 'Why, Ena, it's grand to see you,' she said joyfully, for she and Ena had been good friends. Laura knew that Ena now had a job in a factory down by the docks and wondered if there was a vacancy there, though the work was said to be extremely hard. She opened her mouth to ask how Ena was getting on, but Ena was plainly bursting with news of her own and started to gabble as soon as greetings had been exchanged.

'Oh, queen, wharra bit of luck! I were plannin' to come round to Blenheim Court this very evening, but then I thought mebbe it wouldn't be tactful since you're livin' wi' your sister and mebbe happy in wharrever job you've got yourself. Only as I were comin' up the road I met Mrs Hibbert, what used to be your next-door neighbour, and she told me she'd just seen you and you was after work in Everton again, and somewhere to live, o'course.'

'That's true; I am hoping to make a move,' Laura said, rather cautiously.

'Do you remember my Tom's cousin Arthur, what owns Mitchell's greengrocery shop on Heyworth?' Ena asked. 'And do you remember the cobbler's next door? Well, it seems that Mr Threadgold, the man what owned the cobbler's, has retired, so he told Arthur he were puttin' his premises up for sale. It ain't huge but then he weren't askin' much for it and Arthur decided to take it on because his own place is doin' pretty well. I dunno what he means to sell but I don't think it can be just greengroceries else he could knock a hole in the wall and mek it into one. Any road, he come round to visit us last night and telled me he were lookin' for someone to manage his new premises, someone he could trust, and were I interested.'

'I say, queen! I guess it 'ud be a much better job than the one you've got at the cotton works,' Laura said enviously, but before she could go on Ena shook her head.

'No, there's one very big snag so far as I'm concerned. Arthur wants whoever takes the job to live in the flat above the shop and it's tiny, only two rooms.' She chuckled. 'Not much use for us Platts but I reckon it 'ud just suit you and the girls. The only entrance to the flat is through the shop, which was grand for Mr Threadgold, but it wouldn't do, Arthur says, for anyone who weren't connected with the business, so whoever gets the job must live in the flat. But look, can you get round to Mitchell's right away? I can't give you no more details but Arthur will fill you in, then you can decide whether you're interested or not. Only if I was you, I'd jump at it. He's a nice feller is Arthur, and would treat you right.'

'Ena, you're a real pal,' Laura said sincerely. 'But I wonder what rent he's asking for the flat? Still an' all, I'll soon find out, and if I get it – the job and the flat, I mean – I'll treat you to the biggest dinner you can eat at Lyons Corner House!'

Ena laughed and gave her an affectionate shove. 'Go on wi' you, and hurry yourself! Arthur means to put an advertisement in the *Echo* but I know for a fact he ain't done it yet.'

'Thanks, Ena. Are you going to walk up with me so as you can explain how I know about the job and how trustworthy I am?' Laura said hopefully, but Ena shook her head.

'Can't do that, queen; I were on me way to get me messages when Mrs Hibbert stopped me. Tell you what, though. I don't reckon you'll be above an hour wi' me brother-in-law, so what say we meet up at the Kardomah Café on Bold Street for a nice cup of tea and a bun while you tell me what's happened? Only I've got to go to Bold Street 'cos that's where me hairdresser, William Kerr, is. I had a marcel wave a fortnight back and they allus say it'll go frizzy if you don't return to the salon to have it set. Shall we say eleven o'clock? Me appointment's for ten which is why I can't come wi' you to Mitchell's.'

'Right; eleven o'clock it is, in the Kardomah,' Laura said gaily. What a bit of luck! But she had best not start counting her chickens before they were hatched. Nevertheless, as she hurried along the pavement in the bright spring sunshine, she thought how fortunate it was that she had almost always bought her fruit and vegetables from Mitchell's. She had been a good customer, and had liked Mr Mitchell and his handsome golden-haired wife, though Mrs Mitchell had stopped serving in the shop some years earlier.

Because it was early still, Mr Mitchell was only just beginning to load his pavement trestles with a tempting array of fresh fruit as she approached the shop, and for a moment she wondered, rather doubtfully, if he would remember her. Indeed, when she followed him into the shop his first reaction was to ask if he could help her, but then recognition – and a big smile – dawned on his face at the same moment. 'Mrs Collins, how nice to see you! Can I take it that you've returned to Everton? And how are the little girls?' He selected a couple of rosy apples, popped them into a brown paper bag and handed them across the counter. 'For the children,' he said. 'And now what may I get you?'

Laura felt her face grow hot and hoped that her cheeks were not now the colour of the apples he had just selected. 'I'm afraid I'm not a customer just yet, Mr Mitchell,' she said apologetically. 'I've come because I met Ena Platt ten minutes ago and she told me you were looking for someone to act as manageress in a new shop you'd just purchased; the one next door, in fact. I know you've not advertised the position yet, but I'd like to apply.'

Mr Mitchell had a round face, thick brown hair streaked at the temples with grey, and an enormous walrus moustache. When he smiled, he showed a number of large white teeth and his moustache sprang up in a manner both comical and friendly, Laura thought. 'Well, this is a pleasant surprise,' he said jovially. He half turned and shouted: 'William!' and presently a tall, skinny boy with a cowlick of toffee-coloured hair and a very prominent Adam's apple came into the shop from the back regions, hefting a sack of potatoes.

The boy dumped the sack on the floor and said, in a rather injured tone: 'I were just comin', Mr Mitchell, sir, only these blamed spuds weigh a ton, so they does.'

'It's all right, William, there's no hurry; I just want you to give an eye to the shop while this lady and meself have a chat,' Mr Mitchell said, reaching behind him to take a brown overall down from a hook. 'Pop this on, there's a good lad, and when young Wilf comes in tell him to give you a hand in the shop, 'cos our business may take a while.'

It was well after eleven o'clock by the time Laura reached Bold Street, though she had run most of the way and was breathless and clutching a stitch in her side by the time the Kardomah came in view. She would not have been surprised had Ena given up and left, but her friend was still there and beamed at her as she collapsed into a chair at the window table Ena had chosen.

'I were late meself,' Ena said. 'I've ordered a pot of tea for two and buttered scones . . . and by the look on your face, queen, I could ha' made it chocolate éclairs, as a celebration, like, 'cos I reckon you've got the job.'

'Yes; we've agreed that I'll give me present employer notice at the end of the week and start at Mitchell's in a month . . . only it's a bit more complicated than either of us thought,' Laura said. 'And I'm gaspin' for a cuppa . . . ah, here comes the waitress. I'll tell you everything when she's gone.' And presently, with the tea and scones before them, she was as good as her word. 'Mr Mitchell took me all over the shop he's just bought – Mr Threadgold has let him have the keys – and was very fair, I thought. The rooms upstairs are not large and there's no water laid on in the flat, though the big downstairs room which leads off from the shop has it all right. The thing is, Ena, that you were right in thinking your brother-in-law doesn't mean to sell greengroceries from his new premises, and when I asked him what he did mean to sell, he told me to guess. He said it was something Heyworth Street needed, but even so I couldn't think what it was he meant. I guessed hats, hardware, drapery, fish, sweeties for the children, and in the end I had to give up. But of course I should have guessed first go off, because of you and me meeting on Bold Street.'

'But there's plenty of hairdressers on Heyworth Street,' Ena was beginning, and then she gasped. 'Oh, Laura, don't say he means to start up a tea room! But no, it couldn't be that, because you'd need a kitchen and all sorts of other things like tables and chairs and a big oven . . .'

'Well, you're right. He does mean to start a café. He said it struck him years ago that it would be nice for local people if there was somewhere they could meet for a cup of coffee or a light lunch when they were getting their messages. He said he first thought of it because, on a Saturday, when the women are buying a whole week's greengroceries, the shop's full of customers simply waiting while the staff are weighing out their goods. If there was a nice little café next door, he could send them in there whilst their orders were made up.'

'But if the shop is full of people waiting, why can't they just leave their orders so Arthur's son, Michael, can deliver them?' Ena asked. 'I know the young feller does a deal of delivering already, 'specially on a Saturday.' She chuckled. 'His dad pays him to do it an' I know young Mike thinks it's a grand way of earning some pocket money,' she ended.

'Young Mike isn't magic; he can't get round to everyone at once,' Laura explained. 'And the more Mr Mitchell thought about it, the more he fancied branching out, doing something different. Oh, and by the way, I put me perishin' foot in it with a vengeance . . . I asked him why his wife wasn't interested in managing the café . . .'

Ena gasped. 'Oh, 'eck, what a fool I am! But I thought you knew! Arthur's wife ran off with a sailor several years ago, and he and the boy have soldiered on alone ever since.'

'I know now, 'cos he told me,' Laura said rather reproachfully. 'Mind, he didn't seem at all embarrassed, and since it was ages ago I suppose he's got used to the idea. But anyway, we talked about wages and conditions, and he explained that he didn't mean to charge us rent for the flat and that he wanted me to move in at once so that I could supervise the workmen who will be turning that storeroom at the back into a proper kitchen. He was ever so kind, Ena. I said I'd keep my job on until the place was up and running but he said that weren't necessary; he'd pay me the wage we had agreed from the moment we moved in, which is awful good of him because he won't have any money coming in until the place is all set up.'

Ena leaned across the table and gave Laura a smacking kiss on the cheek. 'You haven't said you've took the job but it's clear as daylight that you told him yes,' she said exuberantly. 'Oh, Laura, I'm that glad for you. And if you need a hand moving your stuff, then me and Tom and the kids will be round at Blenheim Court wi' a couple of handcarts as soon as you say the word.'

Laura thanked her but admitted that their removal would not involve even one handcart, let alone two. 'The truth is, queen, that I sold up completely when we left the flat over the pet shop,' she told her friend.

'There weren't no room at Millie's for so much as an extra chair, and I needed every penny I could get while I searched for work, so the little flat will be pretty empty. We're lucky in one way, though; Mr Threadgold left an old brass bedstead with a feather mattress in the back room, so me and the girls can kip down on that until I've saved up enough money to buy a few sticks of me own.'

Ena laughed. 'Tell you what, we've got an old paraffin stove what we only use in the winter; I'll lend you that so you've something to cook your breakfast porridge on. And I'm sure others will come up with bits and pieces. And now I'd best be going 'cos I've not done me messages yet and I've a list as long as me arm.'

The two women paid and left the café, heading in different directions. Laura, smiling to herself, thought that she had better buy a couple of sauce-pans, otherwise making porridge would be an impossibility, let alone anything more complicated. But at least she would be cooking for the three of them and not hovering guiltily around Millie whilst her sister used bought bread, tinned vegetables and anything else which was cheap and easy to feed her extended family. Poor Millie! She was now having to cater for the two old ladies as well as for her husband and children and Grandma Moffat had a weak digestion – or so she claimed – and could only eat very soft foods. Still, it ought to mean that Millie would welcome her news, Laura told herself hope-fully, turning her footsteps towards Blenheim Court.

And Tess and Tina would be tickled pink, for though Everton and their old haunts were within walking distance, she knew that neither child had ever gone back to their old stamping ground. Somehow they would have felt like intruders. But when they moved they would return to their old school, play with their old friends and become a part of Everton life once more.

Smiling to herself, Laura pictured her daughters' faces when she imparted her wonderful news. Despite the fact that they were sisters, they looked completely different. Tess was skinny, with black hair, straight as rain, just like her father's, and her dark blue eyes were fringed with long, black lashes. She had an appealing smile but was, on the whole, a serious child, though Laura thought that this was more because of her responsibilities than from any inbuilt lack of joy. Tina, on the other hand, was sturdily built with curly light brown hair, hazel eyes, and a round dimpled little face. Her cheeks were rosy and there was a wicked twinkle in her eyes. But they're both darlings, Laura told herself as she turned into Byrom Street, because though I won't deny that Tina is a handful Tess manages her very well, and they do their best to help me and to stay cheerful, no matter how hard things get. It'll be strange for them at first, with just the three of us in the flat, but at least I shan't have to look round for someone to give an eye to them during school holidays, because I'll always be on the spot. And there'll be a ready-made job for Tess in a couple of years' time, either in the kitchen or, more probably, waitressing. Yes, the more I think of it, the more I realise that my new job will be ideal, though I'm sure the girls will miss their cousins at first. Still, I know very well that Cyril has often led Tina into mischief, so it's as well to part them before my little girl gets completely out of hand. And Laura, hurrying as she neared the Scottie, began to sing beneath her breath; something she had not done for a long while.

'Come along, young Tina; it's your turn. And remember the stone must go into the first square but your foot mustn't.'

Tess and Tina had been sitting on the step of their aunt's house, waiting for their turn on the hopscotch pitch and discussing their favourite subject, which was the life of the two little princesses. Tina loved to pretend that she was Margaret Rose, but now she stood up and went over to where her cousin Annie was impatiently holding out the flat stone that they used for hopscotch. Tess saw her little sister straighten the imaginary crown on top of her head before throwing the stone carefully into the first square. The child gave a prodigious hop to clear the square, skidded, teetered for a moment, and then put her right foot as well as her left down, disqualifying herself. Tess sighed, expecting her to argue when Annie shouted 'Next', but for once Tina took her dismissal meekly, though when Annie turned away she pulled a face, crossing her eyes and sticking her tongue out as far as it would go. Tess guessed that this was because she thought hopscotch was a game far beneath the dignity of a royal princess, and preferred to return to her perch on the step so that she and Tess could continue their conversation. At least face-pulling wasn't too bad by Tina's usual standards, so Tess pretended to notice nothing.

'Phew!' Tina said, trotting over to her sister and carefully dusting the step before sitting down once more. 'Look, Tess, if we was to borrow next door's stirring cart, you could pretend to be one of those beautiful ponies what pull the royal carriage and I'd be Princess Margaret Rose, waving to the crowd on me way back home after a trip out.'

Tess smiled but shook her head. There must have been twenty children, of all ages and sizes, playing in the court, and she could just imagine the hoots of derision and rude remarks which would result if they played what most of the other kids would consider a sissy and snobby game. What was more, by pulling the cart round the court she would interfere with a game of footie, the hopscotch pitch, and a number of girls who were skipping to the well-known chant of *A house to let, Apply within, Next-door neighbour carry on*. She was opening her mouth to explain this to Tina when her mother appeared, hurrying into the court under the big stone arch, actually running, like a young girl. Tess's mouth dropped open; Mam was always so busy, so anxious, but right now she was smiling broadly. Her hair, which was curly like Tina's only very much darker, had not been pulled back as it usually was for work, and Tess remembered that it was her mother's day off, so she had chosen to wear her hair loose for a change. But it was plain that something really nice must have happened for Laura's large, velvet brown eyes were shining with excitement, and as soon as she reached them she sat down heavily on the step of No. 2 regardless of her best coat, and hugged them hard.

'Oh, my little loves, you'll never guess what's happened this morning,' she said, her voice rising. 'I'm so excited and so happy! Just wait till I tell you!'

'Mammy, I'm the Princess Margaret Rose, and you don't go squeezin' princesses, nor rumplin' their curls, nor makin' them sit down on dusty old doorsteps,' Tina said reproachfully. 'I bet you've knocked me crown all askew.' She put a hand up to her head, then gave a squeal of dismay. 'Oh, Mammy, you've knocked me bleedin' crown clear off. Now what'll I do?'

Tess waited for an eruption, for her mother hated to hear them swear, but instead Laura merely looked startled. 'Crown? What crown?' she asked. 'I didn't see no crown, queen.'

Tess gave a snort of amusement. 'You know what Tina is, Mam. It weren't a real crown, not even a paper one; it were just in her head, like.'

This remark made her mother giggle. 'In her head, not on her head,' she said, then gave Tess a smacking kiss on the cheek before standing up and pulling both girls to their feet. 'Sorry about the crown, Tina, me love, but I'm so excited I never gave a thought to

31

wharrever it was you were playing. I've got news for you, only I guess we'd better go indoors and find Aunt Millie, so I only have to tell my story once.'

As she spoke, she turned to go into her sister's house, but Tess said imploringly: 'Oh, Mam, tell us first! I know it's good news, so is it cakes for tea, or a trip to New Brighton? And it's my birthday quite soon – is it a party for all me friends?'

'No, it's better than all those things.' She lowered her voice. 'I've got a job in a shop on Heyworth Street and it includes a little flat above it. Oh, girls, I'm just so excited! You'll be able to go back to your old school, Tess, and of course Tina will go there too. It's right handy . . . and it will be grand to have a place of our own again. We shan't have much furniture at first, but I'll gradually buy some bits and pieces – second hand of course, from Paddy's Market – and Mr Mitchell says I can take the pair of you round any time, so you can see the flat for yourselves.'

'Oh, Mam, that's just so wonderful,' Tess breathed, feeling warmth rush into her cheeks. That very morning, she and Grandma Moffat had fallen out and poor Tess, who had been doing her best to carry a heavy tray through to the parlour for the two old ladies, had received a shouting at and a clack round the ear which had made her head ring. The slap had been delivered because she had not knocked on the door before entering the room; but how could I, Tess thought now, aggrieved, when both me hands were occupied with the tray? I did give the door a kick but Grandma Moffat didn't hear it – me plimsolls don't make much noise – and when she slapped me and the tea rocked out of the mug she told Aunt Millie that she had been cross because of the spilt tea, and never mentioned me not knocking. Tess had been dreading her next encounter with the old lady but now, she thought, she could put up with all sorts, knowing that escape was at hand.

She knew what had really annoyed Grandma Moffat was the fact that the old woman had been standing in the middle of the room in her long, lace-fringed drawers, pulling one of her many petticoats down over her head. Usually, her breakfast tray was delivered by one of the older cousins. It appeared that she did not mind them seeing her in her underwear, but for some inexplicable reason – inexplicable to Tess, that was – she had felt foolish being caught out by a younger child and one, furthermore, who was not related to her.

Now, however, Tess dismissed all thoughts of Grandma Moffat. They were passing the parlour door and entering the kitchen, where Aunt Millie was carefully pouring tea from the big brown pot into three enamelled mugs, one for herself, no doubt, and one each for the old ladies now firmly ensconced in the parlour. She looked up as the Collinses entered and pulled a face at her sister. 'You look flushed, queen. If you're goin' to say our gran had no right to give poor little Tess a clack round the ear, then I know it, and I told her so . . .' she was beginning, but Laura broke in.

'Millie, me daughter's not said a word because

33

she's been brought up not to be a tale-clat,' she said quickly. 'No, it's nothing like that. I've some news for you – and I think you'll be pleased for me if you'll listen just for a minute . . . oh, and since you're making tea, I'd be glad of a cup. I've run most o' the way back from Paddy's Market and I'm dry as a perishin' desert.'

'News?' Millie stood down the teapot and stared across at her sister. 'Go on then, spill the beans!'

The story was soon told and, much to Laura's relief, Millie was as pleased as could be. In fact, she asked if she might accompany the Collinses when they visited Heyworth Street. So it was a party of four which set out the next day. Mr Mitchell handed over the keys and Laura conducted them in through the front door. The shop was a fair size but the room at the back was even larger. 'Mr Mitchell and I think we'll get the builders to move the partition wall back about six feet – it's only flimsy, it's made of wood – and that will make the café quite a bit larger.'

Millie nodded. 'It'll make the kitchen smaller though,' she pointed out. 'But it's still a pretty big room, mind. Eh, our Laura, I reckon you've landed on your feet, 'cos you're a grand cook – but does Mr Mitchell expect you to do all the cooking for the café yourself?'

'We're going to take it very slowly at first, and buy in bread, cakes and such from the bakery up the road,' Laura said, throwing open the back door to reveal a tiny yard with a privy at the end, and a linen

34

line which stretched from the house to the old brick wall that bounded the property. 'There's a jigger along the back – see the green-painted wooden door? – but it's only wide enough for bicycles, so I don't think I'll be taking deliveries through there. That means that the kids will have the yard and the jigger to play in. Heyworth Street is too busy to be safe for games.'

'Aye, you're right there. I know the courts ain't the best place so far as the houses is concerned, them mostly being back-to-backs,' Millie admitted, 'but there's no through traffic, so the kids can play in them and be safe as houses.' She turned to the children. 'Well? What do you think so far?'

'It's grand,' Tess breathed. 'Is that privy just for us? And wharrabout a water tap? Is there a water tap?'

'Didn't you see it, you stupid girl?' Tina said scornfully. 'There were a low stone sink, just the right height for playin' paper boats, behind the back door, an' a huge old brass tap over it.' She turned to her mother. 'I dunno about the lavvy – if we has to share, I mean – but no one 'cept us can use the tap, can they, Mammy?'

Laura laughed but headed for the stairs. 'You're right about that – we shan't have to share anything,' she said joyfully, then glanced guiltily at Millie, but her sister was smiling and had obviously not taken offence. 'Follow me, everyone!'

The steep flight of wooden stairs ended in a small square landing with two doors leading off it. Laura threw open the nearer, revealing a reasonably sized room with a long window overlooking Heyworth Street. The walls were whitewashed, but Millie observed that they could do with another coat since the previous owner must have possessed a great number of pictures, judging by the faded squares. The window was extremely grimy and the window-sill, which was wide enough for a child to sit on comfortably, was covered in dead flies but otherwise the room seemed pleasant enough. 'This is our living room,' Laura said. 'A friend of mine – she's Mr Mitchell's cousin-in-law – has offered to loan us a paraffin stove, just until we get ourselves sorted out. I mean to buy some pots and pans and some plates and that, but apart from what we can cook over the stove, we'll just have to make do with cold food until the room downstairs has been made into a kitchen.'

'Oh, you'll manage grand,' Millie said cheerfully. 'I'll give you wharrever I can, chuck, but I reckon you'll soon find your feet. Now let's tek a look at the other room.'

'It's not very large,' Laura said rather apologetically, leading them back on to the landing and through the remaining doorway. This room over-looked the back yard, and was dwarfed at present by an enormous brass bedstead. 'There was a feather mattress but somehow I didn't fancy it,' Laura explained. 'Since we don't want to sleep on the springs, I laid out some money on a very cheap flock one, which will arrive tomorrow. I dare say it'll be a bit hard but we'll soon grow accustomed.' She looked hopefully at her sister. 'I know nearly all the bedding we've been using at the court is yours by right, Millie, but if you don't mind, I'd like to borrow it just for a few weeks.'

Millie turned and gave Laura a hug. 'What'll I want with that bedding now you ain't there to use it?' she said robustly. 'You can have it and welcome. And when we get home, I'll look out a few other things an' all. I'm not sayin' they're as good as what I'd like to give you, 'cos you're me dear little sister, but they're all I've got and they'll do until something better comes along.'

Laura returned the hug and felt tears form in her eyes, though she blinked them away resolutely. 'You're the best sister in the world, so you are,' she said, her voice breaking a little. 'Heaven knows what we would have done if you'd not taken us in. But it's time I shouldered my own responsibilities, dearest Mil. And now we'd best be getting back to Blenheim Court. Tell you what, when we reach Hodgson's I'll buy a big parcel of chips, enough for the whole family, then you won't have to bother about cooking.'

Millie chuckled. 'I weren't goin' to bother about cooking anyway,' she admitted. 'It would have been bread 'n' scrape 'cos it's nearin' the end of the week and I'm skint as usual.' The four of them trooped downstairs and Laura checked that the back door was locked, then led them out through the shop and back on to Heyworth Street. She started to go next door to give Mr Mitchell back his keys, but stopped when Millie tugged at her arm. 'Look, queen, it's awful good of you, but can you afford chips? There's fourteen gannets live at number two and chips ain't that cheap.'

Laura smiled at her, then handed the key to Tess. 'You and Tina take the keys back to Mr Mitchell,' she said. When they had disappeared, Laura turned back to her sister. 'Millie, love, I've not said anything to the kids because I don't imagine Mr Mitchell would want it talked about, but – but he has given me five pounds to help towards making the flat habitable. I never said I was hard up but he seemed to realise . . . well, when I said the bedstead would come in handy . . .'

'A fiver!' Millie said, her tone awestruck. 'That were real kind of him, queen. You can do a lot with a fiver.'

Laura nodded. 'Yes, I know. So you see I can certainly run to a parcel of chips!'

Chapter Two

Herefordshire, autumn 1936

It was a fine October day with the leaves already beginning to turn, and though the sunshine was warm there was still a nip in the air. Danny Brewster nudged Sophie, who was sitting beside him on the bus, as the village came in sight. Usually, he and his cousin Phil sat together but Phil had not been in school that day so Danny had gravitated to Sophie. The two of them moved along the central aisle so that they might be first off and could help Mrs Poulter to descend. Mrs Poulter was old and walked with two sticks; Danny had always been fond of her for he could still remember when she had come up to Manor Farm on a Tuesday to help his mother with the baking. She had often slipped him a little ball of raw pastry, or a few currants and sultanas, and now he and Sophie between them helped her to get down.

Having seen Mrs Poulter on her way, Danny slung his satchel on to his back and accompanied Sophie to the blacksmith's, where he and his cousin kept their bikes. Once, before they had got to know Sophie, they had kept them in the little yard at the back of Mrs Bailey's tiny general shop, but this had not been terribly satisfactory since when it rained the bicycles got sopping wet; there was no shelter in the yard apart from Mrs Bailey's hen coop, and they could scarcely shove their bikes in there.

Danny and Phil had started at the grammar school when they were eleven; Danny had passed the entrance examination and Phil had won a scholarship – and ever since then they had done the eight-mile journey by bike and bus to the grammar school in town. For two long years, he and Danny had been the only pupils catching the bus from the village, and though the drivers and conductors were always very friendly there had been occasions when Danny felt conspicuous sitting alone on the bus until it reached the next village, for Phil's father kept his son at home whenever he was needed on the farm. Then Sophie Cantrip had won a scholarship to the girls' grammar school and to Danny's immense relief there were now usually three of them waiting at the bus stop, and when Phil was absent Danny and Sophie sat together exchanging news.

Sophie was the blacksmith's only child and Danny and Phil liked her well enough, though Danny soon came to realise that appearances were deceptive; he had thought her a quiet little girl, afraid to say boo to a goose, but he quickly learned that she was simply shy and was both good company and amusing once she got to know you. Lizzy Pinfold, who got aboard the bus in the next village, was reckoned by the boys to be the prettiest girl in the area, with her yellow hair, bold blue eyes and curvy figure. Sophie, Danny thought now, glancing at her profile as they made their way up the village street, was not pretty at all, being thin as a hop pole, with straight light brown hair. Still, she was his friend, and he had never liked Lizzy Pinfold above half.

Shortly after Sophie had begun to catch the bus each morning, she had suggested that he and Phil might leave their bicycles in the Cantrips' big shed. 'Dad says there's plenty of room there and at least they'll be in the dry,' she had told them. 'He's seen you cycling off, getting wet as rats on your old bicycles, so he said I were to suggest you use our shed.'

Danny had been delighted to agree because, apart from anything else, it meant he had an excuse to visit the blacksmith's forge; a place which had intrigued him ever since Mr Fuller, his father's cowman, had first allowed him to accompany Magnum and Gemma, the two great horses which did most of the heavy work on the farm, to be shod. He had been five or six at the time, and when the blacksmith, with Magnum's huge foreleg between his knees, had picked up the hot shoe in his iron pincers, clapped it on to the hoof and begun to hammer it into place, he had winced, sure that Magnum must be in pain. But the horse had continued staring placidly before him and the small Danny had realised that what was new and strange to him was nothing out of the ordinary to the great black percheron.

Now Danny and Sophie had reached the yard behind the forge, and Sophie made for the back door of the cottage whilst Danny shouted goodbye and wheeled his bicycle on to the road. He waved to Mr

Cantrip hammering away at a cartwheel, then mounted his machine and began to pedal, thankful that it was Friday and that this was October, for though they were apple picking and cider making as well as doing all the other tasks necessary on a large mixed farm, at least the hops were finished. Danny hated hop picking and had once queried why the pickers his father employed from Birmingham should consider the hard work a holiday. 'They all live together in our big barn, and though Mum gives them free vegetables they have to buy and cook most of their food,' he had said. 'And they work on the hops day after day, and if the picking's easy they're paid less per bushel . . . it doesn't seem much of a holiday to me.'

He and his father had been sitting in the kitchen waiting for their meal whilst Deborah Brewster dished up. She had given a short laugh and said over her shoulder: 'Aye, I can see why you're puzzled. Maybe one of these days your dad will take you into Birmingham so you can see for yourself how the pickers live at home. Then I reckon you'll understand.'

Danny had looked enquiringly at his father. 'Understand what?' he had said plaintively.

His father had grinned at him and leaned across to rumple his hair. 'Heard of slums, Danny, my boy?' he had asked. 'The folk who pick for us come from an area where they live ten to a couple of rooms sometimes, with no running water and one WC shared by a dozen households. They work in factories where the noise and the smells are almost overpowering. Believe me, the time they spend at Manor Farm is heaven to them.'

Since then, Danny's father had taken him to Birmingham and shown him the area where many of the hop pickers came from and Danny had marvelled that people living in such conditions could be as cheerful and happy as the large families that camped out in their big barn appeared to be. But now the pickers had been and gone, and the work of drying the hops had begun in the two large kilns to one side of the farmyard. Drying hops was an expert business, carried out by old Fred Fuller, but though Danny never entered the kilns once the pockets of hops were safely stowed, he could not escape the sweetish smell which filled the air throughout the drying period. He could smell it now, even though he was still a couple of miles from Manor Farm, and grinned wryly to himself, knowing that other hop yards would be doing exactly as the Brewsters did, knowing also that his clothes probably smelled faintly but persistently throughout the drying period.

At this point in his pedalling, Danny turned right off the road into the rutted lane which led to his home, the cottages where the farmhands lived and, a mile further on, his Uncle Matthew's farm. Uncle Matthew was his mother's brother-in-law, and farmed sheep in the uplands as well as running a small herd of dairy cattle. His son Phil was fifteen, the same age as Danny; they were both only children and had been friends almost from the cradle, for

Daisy Ryland was on the best possible terms with her sister, and the two women saw to it that their boys were constantly in one another's company.

But though Uncle Matthew had agreed to his son's attending the grammar school, he had no qualms about keeping Phil off school whenever he was needed on the farm. That's why I'm so pleased to have Sophie as a friend, Danny mused now, standing up on his pedals as the lane grew steeper and more rutted. Phil got up early every other week, summer and winter, to milk the cows, and during the hop-picking season he came down to Manor Farm to help his uncle with the hops during the holidays. Sometimes he weighed them, sometimes he picked, but he always worked flat out.

Phil had a sort of maturity which Danny was aware that he himself lacked. Phil was interested in girls; would not dream of going to the cinema in town without inviting a girl to accompany him. He talked knowledgeably about all farming matters but had told Danny, quite seriously, that when he was old enough he intended to leave the farm. He had always been deeply interested in mechanical things and had announced when he was quite a small boy that one day he would be a pilot and fly aeroplanes. Even now, he despised Hilltop Farm for its position and his father's handling of his acres. 'If one must farm then the money's in the lowlands, not the hill pastures,' he had said. 'If I have to farm – and I don't believe I will because there are always openings for people with a mechanical bent – then I mean to make my father buy somewhere that's been neglected, perhaps left to grow wild because of the Depression. Then I'll make and mend, and plough and reap, and before you know it you'll be tugging your forelock to me, Danny Brewster, and asking me if I've any work for a good cowman. And as soon as the dibs are in tune, I'll buy me an aeroplane and start flying commercially, and if you're very good you can be my navigator.'

They had both laughed and Danny had fallen upon Phil, rolling him over and over and ending up sitting on his cousin's chest, all amongst the dust and chopped hay in the big barn. They had been cleaning the place after the pickers had gone home, conveyed, as always, for the first part of their journey by two of John Brewster's big hay carts, pulled by Gemma and Magnum. The boys took a wagon each and drove the great horses all the way to Hereford, proud of their ability to control the percherons, and saw the workers on to the train before treating themselves, at John Brewster's behest, to a bar of chocolate to eat on the journey home.

And almost as though thinking of him had conjured him up, Danny rounded a corner and saw Phil grinning at him from the centre of the lane with his sheepdog, Nell, at his heels. As soon as he saw the bicycle, Phil reached out and grabbed the handle-bars, effectively stopping Danny in his tracks, though he must have known that his cousin would not have dreamed of riding on past. 'Hey up, lad,' he said breezily. 'Thought I'd wander down and meet you off the bus, having nothing better to do.'

'Huh, a likely tale! But why weren't you in school today, and where'm you really going?' Danny asked.

Phil snorted and let go of the bicycle to grab him by his shirt collar, clearly hoping for a fight, but Danny was in his school uniform and knew what his mother would say if he returned home with his clothes in a mess after being tumbled flat on his back in the lane. Once, he and Phil had been evenly matched, but Phil spent a lot more time working on the farm than Danny did and was now both taller and heftier. So Danny did not attempt to shake his cousin off, but stood quite still grinning good-naturedly. 'Pax, Phil; Mum will go mad if I muck up my school uniform,' he pointed out. 'And now you might as well tell me what happened and where you'm bound.'

'Dad backed the Bentley out of the shed and hit my front wheel, making a good six-inch split in the tyre. He was on his way to Hereford and I had to stay 'cos the vet was coming to do some follow-up tuberculin tests on a couple of reactors.'

'Oh aye, any excuse to get out of a maths test,' Danny grumbled. 'You're a jammy bugger, you are.'

Phil grinned at him mockingly. 'Oh, and you're the sainted pupil, aren't you?' he said. 'You're just jealous, that's what. Well you don't fool me, Danny Brewster! You're just as keen to skip school as I am. And can't you guess where I'm bound, you great oaf?'

'Look who's talking,' Danny jeered. 'You just said your front tyre was buggered so I bet you're walking down to pick it up.'

Phil nodded and clicked his fingers to Nell, who was investigating the ditch. 'Come out o' that, old girl. It's a fair walk to the village.' He turned back to Danny. 'You're partly right; I'm going down to Cantrip's to pick up a new inner tube, but I'll put it on myself. It's cheaper that way.' He cocked an eyebrow at his cousin. 'Want to come down with me? Aunt Deborah won't be doing supper for hours yet; in fact, not until the light fails, 'cos your dad's got everyone apple picking as fast as they can go. He reckons the weather's going to break next week.'

Mr Cantrip had realised long ago that horses were being overtaken as a means of transport by motor cars and tractors and had set up a garage alongside his smithy. He was training up a couple of young lads as motor mechanics and Sophie had told Danny that her father spent most evenings poring over diagrams of combustion engines. And of course bicycles were simple to a man with a natural talent for anything mechanical. Danny was interested in such things himself, though not as interested as his cousin, who spent hours during his school holidays underneath the big red tractor which was slowly but surely taking over from Magnum and Gemma. Danny's father frequently said that his nephew was as good a mechanic as Mr Cantrip – high praise indeed.

'Well? You coming?'

Danny hesitated; if he accompanied Phil, he would probably see Sophie again. She loved Manor Farm and could easily be persuaded to spend the following day apple picking. When they had parted outside the smithy, he had not thought to suggest it, but if he went with Phil, he could do so.

'Well? You could give me a seater as far as the Cantrips', then we could walk back up together.'

'No, it'll take too long,' Danny said, making up his mind. His father was a good judge of weather; if he wanted the crop picked in a hurry then he, Danny, ought to get up to the orchard just as soon as he had changed into working clothes. He said as much to Phil, who nodded reluctant agreement and was beginning to continue down the lane when Danny stopped him. 'Hang on a minute,' he said. 'If you take my bike then you'll be down and back in half the time. And while you're there, do me a favour. Tell Sophie we're apple picking and say if she'll come up tomorrow and give a hand, she can have her dinner and tea with us.'

'Oh, you mean your girlfriend! Yeah, I'll pass the word along, though I don't know what you see in the skinny l'il maid. Still, I dare say she'll be another pair of hands,' Phil said rudely, taking the bike from his cousin and turning it to face towards the road once more.

'She's not my girlfriend, but I can tell you she'll be a lot more useful at the apple picking than that painted floozy you took to the flicks last week,' Danny said, with spirit. 'Silk stockings and no knickers, that's what Archie says.'

Phil guffawed. 'I should be so lucky,' he remarked. 'Shan't be long, and ta for the loan of the bike.' He straddled the machine and began to freewheel down the lane, holding his legs out to the side to avoid the rapidly turning pedals. Danny watched him out of sight, grinning; his cousin's legs were too long for the machine and he would have to put the seat up before the return journey. It was possible to freewheel most of the way from the farm to the village but coming back uphill Phil would have to use the pedals.

Danny turned back and began to walk towards the farm once more. This was his favourite part of the journey home from school. The leaves were beginning to fall and he could see through the towering hedge on his right-hand side; the meadow beyond sloped steeply down to a belt of trees and through them he could just glimpse the river where he and Phil had learned to swim when they were no more than four or five, and where now they fished for the brown trout which lived in the deep pools.

As he walked Danny spotted in the thinning hedge several nests, now abandoned, saw a busy hedgehog bustling its way along the bottom of the dry ditch, and further on caught a glimpse of the white scuts of rabbits making for the safety of their burrows, for the big buck rabbit on guard duty had thumped a warning as soon as he heard the sound of Danny's approach and saw movement through the autumn foliage.

When he reached the gate which led into the meadow, Danny stopped and leaned on it for a moment. Now he could see the river clearly, shallow here, as it followed the course of the valley. The water gleamed in the sunshine, and when he glanced to his left he could see the blue hills and the Ryland farmhouse, perched almost at the top of the rise. It was an idyllic scene and one of which Danny never tired, but he tore himself away and strode out, for he suddenly realised he was both hungry and thirsty; his school dinner seemed a lifetime away.

He rounded the last bend in the lane and there was Manor Farm, a long, low building, its black and white façade with the great wisteria to the right of the front door and the Virginia creeper to the left made glorious by the setting sun. The thatch of the roof was mossy with age but Danny's father said it was reed and not straw and should last another twenty years. The farmhouse itself was at least two hundred years old. On either side of the front door were two long flower beds, where the roses were still in bloom. Danny himself, however, never went in by the front door, nor even up the short gravel drive. Wriggling his satchel into a more comfortable position, he continued up the lane past the row of cottages, white-walled and red-tiled, in which his father's workers lived, until he was able to turn into the farmyard. He crossed it briskly, casting a quick glance at the farm buildings, but even a glance told him that these were empty. Everyone was apple picking, though his father would have told someone to fetch the dairy herd down from the high pasture for milking. The yard was cobbled right up to the back of the house, so nothing grew across it, though an ivy had rooted itself against the dairy and had already reached the ridgepole and was beginning to clamber down the other side. The windows of the kitchen overlooked the yard. Danny could see movement through them, and guessed that his mother would be providing a high tea for all the pickers, to be eaten as soon as dusk fell, and would have appealed to Auntie Daisy, and to the wives of the farmhands, to come and assist her.

As soon as he entered the kitchen, Danny saw that he was right. It was a very large room but even so it was crowded. Women were slicing and buttering, cooking over the Aga, washing up at the sink. Danny caught his mother's eye and grinned. 'I'm nipping up to change, Ma, then I'll go straight to the orchard; but when I come down would it be all right if I snitched a sandwich? Only I'm that hungry, I could eat a horse.'

'That'll be fine. Cheese and pickle do you? You won't want to waste time drinking hot tea but there's lemonade on the marble slab in the larder. Just help yourself; as you can see, we're pretty busy here.'

'Right you are,' Danny said, heading for the back stairs. He raced up them and turned into the bedroom which he had occupied for as long as he could remember. It was a nice room: the walls were whitewashed, the ceiling sloped as it did in all the bedrooms and the window was framed by the thatch. Small birds nested in the reeds, and at weekends during the summer Danny could hear them chirping and calling as he lay in his bed, watching the slow progression of sunshine across the ceiling. The window, which was long and low, overlooked the farmyard, and he could see the orchard beyond the cart shed roof. He could also see young Reg at the top of a long ladder, picking with amazing speed, yet putting each apple with infinite care into the bucket whose handle was looped over the top of the ladder.

It was the work of a moment to take off his school uniform, sling it on the bed, and scramble into a pair of worn corduroy trousers and a checked shirt. He kicked off his shoes without bothering to undo the laces, then padded across the room and back down the stairs. In the kitchen his mother handed him a large sandwich and jerked her head towards the larder. 'I've put a mug by the lemonade,' she said briefly. 'Did you see Phil as you came up the lane? He had to fetch something for his bike but he'll come and help with the picking when he gets back.'

'Yup; lent him my bike,' Danny said thickly, through a mouthful of bread and cheese. 'He's going to ask young Sophie to come up for the picking tomorrow; I said she could have her dinner and tea with us.'

'Right,' his mother said, not wasting words. 'Father says the weather is due to break so we'll probably pick straight through Sunday.' She gave him a small conspiratorial grin. 'Vicar won't like it, but he knows we'd not miss out on the service unless we had to. You off then? Tell your dad to send everyone in as soon as it's too dark to tell a russet from a Cox's orange.'

Danny nodded, then headed for the larder. It was a large cool room, not only a larder but also a storeroom. One entire wall was lined with shelves upon which stood a great quantity of bottled fruit, pickles and preserves. There was a long low window opposite the shelves, and beneath the window was a marble slab upon which stood butter, cheese and meat, guarded from the attentions of flies and mice by metal gauze covers. This was where his mother kept the lemonade. He splashed a quantity into the mug and drank it straight down, slaking his thirst eagerly. Then he turned and made his way through the workers to the back door, giving fat Mrs Ada Fuller a quick squeeze as he passed her. She was a rosy-cheeked, fair-haired woman, a good deal younger than her husband, and since they had no children of their own she had always spoiled Danny. She had made him gingerbread men when he was five or six, and had lined them up in the window of her cottage when they were baked and ready to eat, so that he could see them and pop in as he passed. Later, she provided him – and Phil – with more substantial snacks: wedges of apple cake, Cornish pasties, and a treat of which they were inordinately fond, hollow biscuits with a thick slice of her home-made cheese. She had once told him that hollow biscuits were unknown in Herefordshire, but she had been born and bred in Norfolk and had brought the recipe with her when she had come to the area as Fred's bride.

Now, Ada jumped and squealed, then turned and gave him a light tap on the head with a floury hand. 'You're a cheeky young bugger,' she told him, her voice pure Herefordshire, for she had lost her Norfolk accent within twelve months of marrying Fred. 'Get along wi' you now, for your pa says . . .'

'I know, I know. Just about every soul I've met has told me that Dad says the weather's going to break,' Danny said. 'See you later, Mrs Fuller.'

'Aye, and you'm very polite all of a sudden,' Ada said, for he had been using her first name ever since he started at the grammar school. 'You'll be glad to know there's a tray o' butter cakes in the oven what'll be cooked and cool in half an hour. Now off wi' you; I've got work to do even if you haven't.'

Danny chuckled, slid into his wellingtons and went out through the back door to hurry round to the orchard. His father saw him at once and advised him to start sorting the fruit which had already been picked into the large boxes which stood ready. 'Anything bruised or split, or with an insect hole, goes into the cider press, and for the rest the boxes are all labelled – your ma did that earlier – so it's not a difficult job,' he said. 'Tom says the press is half full already 'cos the kids have been picking up the windfalls after school for a couple of days now.'

Danny nodded and went over to the buckets full of apples waiting to be sorted. He would far rather have been doing the actual picking, for there was nothing he liked better than to be perched on a ladder, amongst the topmost branches of an old apple tree, picking the fruit with that quick twist of the wrist which took them off at the stem, and then placing each apple carefully in the bucket. But he could see that it was more important now to get the apples sorted, for his father would not want the unsorted fruit standing around in the buckets all night, a prey to passing birds or small mammals who might fancy a bite. Once the apples were sorted, they would be safe from such danger, for the boxes would be closed down and carried into the shed where John and Deborah would decide which fruit to carry up to the apple loft for their own use, and which to take to market.

So Danny began sorting, watched by Tandy, his father's border collie. Tandy was a typical working dog, soon bored with doing nothing, and now she heaved a sigh and looked hopefully at Danny, as though she would have liked to suggest that he throw an apple for her to retrieve, for there was nothing to else to occupy her.

He had been sorting for a good thirty minutes when his cousin strolled into the orchard, came over, and tweaked the cowlick of dark hair which habitually overhung Danny's brow. 'I gave your message to Sophie,' he remarked, squatting down and beginning to sort the bucket of apples nearest him. 'And I got my inner tube, so I'll be up early in the morning, putting it on. Thanks for the loan of your old crock, by the way, but isn't it time you got something a bit bigger? My knees were up by my lug'oles once I had to start pedalling.'

'I assumed you had sufficient sense to put the seat up; there are spanners and that in the bag behind the saddle,' Danny said mildly. 'But I suppose expecting intelligence from a yob like you . . .'

He got no further; in seconds the two of them were wrestling on the grass, giggling like maniacs and punching weakly whilst Nell and Tandy circled them, barking enthusiastically, and every now and then darting in to seize a boot or a shirt cuff. They were still at it, though half-heartedly, when John Brewster, looming enormous in the twilight, announced that there was no point in working any later and shooed everyone off towards the kitchen. 'But tomorrow I want every man jack of you here in the orchard at sparrow's fart,' he said jovially. 'And that means you girls 'n' all. We've done well today, and I reckon we'll do better tomorrow.'

'And better still on Sunday, 'cos everyone will be free to give a hand,' Reg remarked, as they began to trudge towards the house. 'My young lady works in Boots the Chemist, down the town, so she can't do no pickin' on a Sat'day, but she'll be here Sunday to make herself a bit of cash.'

'That's grand; many hands make light work,' Mr Brewster said. 'Eh, I'm that hungry, my stomach thinks my throat's been cut.' He began to usher everyone into the kitchen, then followed, closing the door behind him and looking hopefully across to where his wife was cutting into a large meat and potato pie. 'Save a bit of that for me, Deb,' he called to her. 'Remember, this'll be my first meal since breakfast!'

Sophie watched Danny out of sight, then wandered across the yard towards the back door of the cottage.

It had been nice to have Danny to herself, though it did happen quite often now, because whenever Mr Ryland needed his son's help in some way he kept him off school. This was a bonus for Sophie, who had hero-worshipped Danny since she was small, though she would never have dreamed of letting him know how much she liked him. The truth was, she had first spotted him when she had been very small indeed, not even a pupil at the village school. He had come down to the forge with one of the big carthorses, and when it had been shod he had called out to the farmhand who had been in charge and disappeared into Mrs Bailey's shop. He had emerged with a paper bag of humbugs, the stripy sort she particularly liked, and when he saw her watching he had held the bag out and insisted that she take two. 'One for each cheek,' he had said, grinning, and never dreaming, of course, that the gesture would make her regard him, in future, as a hero, someone who noticed small and scruffy girls.

Her friendship with Danny had only really come into being when she had been offered the scholarship to the girls' grammar school and had started using the same bus as the cousins. Danny had always chatted easily to her, saving her a place on the back seat if she was late, even giving her a hand with her homework. Phil on the other hand seldom took much notice of her and sometimes she was glad of it, for his teasing could be hurtful and he almost always contradicted any statement she might make on the grounds that there was no such thing as feminine logic.

But Danny was trustworthy. You could confide in him, knowing that it would go no further. Sophie was an only child, as were Danny and Phil, but the cousins had been brought up almost like brothers; indeed people often took them for brothers because they were seldom apart for long and frequently knew what the other was thinking. Physically, though, they were not at all alike: Danny was dark and Phil was fair. Sophie, however, knew them to be totally different in other ways as well. Danny was generous, patient and kind. Phil was impatient, quick-tempered, and only kind when it suited him to be so. When she was puzzled by schoolwork it was Danny who explained, whilst Phil called her dim or thick, and asked why they bothered to teach girls maths, or science, or Latin, since all girls wanted out of life was to be hairdressers and to marry money. She knew that Phil was only joking, of course, but his jokes had a sharp edge to them.

Sophie's hand was actually on the doorknob when the door opened, causing both Mrs Cantrip and her daughter to give a squeak of surprise. 'Dearie, how you startled me,' Sophie's mother said reproachfully. 'I was just going to ask Father if he fancied a cuppa. Be a good girl and see if he's finished with Dobson's pony.'

'Right,' Sophie said. She dropped her satchel on to the brick floor and then wriggled out of her coat. She had half turned back towards the forge when her father emerged and came towards her.

'I saw young Danny cycle past so I guessed Mother

would have a cup of tea on the go,' he said genially, pushing his greasy cap to the back of his thick grey hair. 'I hear they'm apple pickin' up at Manor Farm over the weekend. If you'm goin' to give them a hand we could do with a bag of them big Bramley cookers, isn't that so, Mother?'

'That's so,' admitted Mrs Cantrip as they entered the cottage kitchen. 'But Mrs Brewster knows we only grows eaters so I reckon she'll give you Bramleys without you havin' to ask. Now, come you along in and I'll butter a few scones.' She smiled fondly at her daughter. 'Our lass is always ready for a bite when she comes off the bus, eh, Sophie?'

On Saturday, the sun shone down out of a cloudless sky, and on Sunday morning the weather still seemed set fair, but other people knew the weather signs as well as John Brewster and by two o'clock a sense of urgency overcame them as clouds began to move, boiling up on the horizon, and the wind freshened. They were getting in the very last of the crop when Danny saw the rain begin, on the other side of the valley. It swept across like a grey curtain, scarcely giving him time to shout a warning before it was upon them, big heavy drops which hissed through the leaves, accompanied by hailstones which stung the skin and bounced off the branches. Danny, running with a full bucket in either hand and diving into the big cart shed, thought they had been extremely lucky to get the crop in before the hail could damage it, for the cider press had already been filled twice over. Cider usually went for home consumption so was not really profitable, though some was sold to townsfolk and those who did not have orchards of their own.

Once all the fruit had been carried under cover, Danny and Phil and the other young men charged out again to bring in the ladders. Then they settled down in the shed, for there was still fruit to be sorted. After the lids of the boxes had been hammered down, a sheet of paper was tacked to each box, naming the variety of apple within and the farm from which they came. Then the lads would be free to join the women, who had made straight for the kitchen as soon as the rain began.

Sophie had gone with the rest and some of the older farmhands had disappeared too, knowing that the younger ones could do the work which remained, and indeed, within ten minutes, Danny and Phil had nailed down and labelled the last box and were alone in the cart shed. They sat themselves down on a large crate, gazing out at the rain. 'Do you want to make a dash for it?' Danny asked presently. He had expected the downpour to ease after its first violence and indeed the hail had stopped, but the rain continued relentlessly. He raised an enquiring eyebrow at his cousin, but Phil shook his head.

'What'll we do in the kitchen?' he enquired. 'It's full of perishin' women trying to get the tea together. We'll give 'em twenty minutes, then go over. They'll have cut the sandwiches and made a big brew by then.'

'OK,' Danny said easily. He knew Phil was right; the kitchen would be a hive of activity and their presence would not be welcomed. Danny had seen his father, with a sack over his head, scooting for the stable, followed by most of the farmhands. He guessed they would be sitting in the tack room, smoking pipes or cigarettes and yarning about the old days. He and Phil would be tolerated there, not welcomed, so they might as well stay where they were.

He was about to ask Phil how they should occupy themselves until the meal was ready when his eye fell on the large label decorating the top of the nearest box. *Manor Farm Herefordshire Apples, Cox's Orange Pippins*, it said, and below that there was a large clear area of paper with no writing on it at all. Danny fished around in his trouser pocket and found a stub of pencil. Laboriously he wrote *Danny* and *Phil* on the paper, then grinned across at his cousin. 'I challenge you to a game of Hangman; my go first,' he said.

Rather more than twenty minutes later, Sophie shot into the cart shed, a borrowed raincoat over her head. She stared at the two boys, busily scribbling on the top of the apple box, then laughed. 'I might have guessed you'd have found something daft to occupy you,' she said. 'Your mother says it's teatime, Danny.' She glanced out at the still steadily falling rain. 'And I'm goin' to get soaked to the skin makin' my way home,' she added rather dolefully. 'What a fool I was; I didn't even bring my waterproof. But Mrs Brewster says I can borrow hers, and give it you back after school tomorrow, so she'll have it for Tuesday. Monday's washday so she won't be goin' far.'

The three of them scampered across the yard and burst into the kitchen, but when tea was over and the helpers were dispersing Mr Brewster caught Sophie's arm. 'Don't worry yourself, love,' he said. 'I'll not see you get half drowned when you've been good enough to come and apple pick for us. I'll get Bessie Bunter out of the shed and run you down to the village; 'twon't take more'n five minutes in the car.'

'Can I come too, Dad?' Danny said eagerly, but his father shook his head. 'No, old feller, I think you ought to give your mother a hand. I know Mrs Fuller and Mrs Coppack would willingly have helped out, but it's Sunday night and they'll have plenty to do in their own homes, so I told them that we could manage and packed them off home with the rest.'

'Tell you what, Mr Brewster, if you don't mind hanging around for a bit I'll give a hand with the clearing up,' Sophie said. She glanced across at Phil. 'Why don't you stay as well, Phil? I know you say women's work is beneath you but I reckon Mr Brewster would give you a lift as well if you'll stay and help out. Then Danny can come with us.'

Phil heaved an exaggerated sigh and lifted his hand as if to give Sophie a cuff, then pretended to recall his manners, slapped his own wrist and wagged his head in sorrowful self-reproach. 'I was forgettin' I'm a Ryland, and Rylands are gentlemen,' he said. 'It's one thing to cuff your cousin for being cheeky and quite another to cuff a young lady, even if she is a li'l brown mouse.'

'Stop it, Phil,' John Brewster said, but he was grinning, and though Sophie scowled at Phil, Danny could tell she did not mind his teasing. Mr Brewster glanced at his wife, busily stacking dirty crockery, cutlery and pans on the left-hand draining board. 'Are you going to wash them, my love? If so, then Sophie and myself will dry and the boys can put away, since they know where things go. C'mon now, let's get a move on, else it'll be pitch dark and the lane'll be like a river before you know it. And Bessie's headlights aren't too good; I reckon her battery's on the way out.'

Everyone began to work with a will, and despite the quantity of dirty crockery and cutlery it was washed, dried up and put away whilst there was still some light in the overcast sky. Mr Brewster and Danny donned macs and dashed for the shed because it took two to get Bessie going. She was an ancient bullnose Morris with a canvas hood and had to be started by cranking the engine whilst the driver delicately controlled the choke and revved the engine as soon as the spark caught. All went well and presently Danny jumped into the back seat and his father edged cautiously across the yard, stopping outside the back door and giving a long blast on the hooter. This was a mistake since the engine faltered and the lights dimmed for a moment, but it brought Sophie and Phil tumbling out of the back door to hurl themselves into Bessie Bunter's interior. 'All aboard!' Mr Brewster roared above the noise of the engine. 'Hang on tight; the lane's been dry for months so it won't take kindly to suddenly finding itself with three inches of water tumbling down it.' And with that he revved the engine again, swung the wheel, charged through the open gateway, and they were off.

It was a hair-raising ride. Sophie had somehow managed to bag the front seat and clung grimly on to the dashboard, glancing sideways at Mr Brewster every now and then. She could see he was enjoying himself hugely, bending forward over the wheel and swinging the car from side to side. His hair, dark like Danny's but streaked with grey at the temples, stood up with the wind of their going, for he always drove with his window down, using as an excuse the fact that the driver's door would not open from the inside. 'I don't mean to be trapped in my own car so I hangs one hand outside the door, ready to grab the handle and release myself if I see a collision coming,' he was fond of remarking. 'Though since I'm a careful driver, it's not likely to happen.'

Careful driver! Sophie thought she had seen more careful drivers on the Wall of Death at the Easter fair, but of course it would not do to say so. And besides, she admired Mr Brewster. She thought that when Danny grew up he might well look like his father, for they were already very similar. Mr Brewster was tall and heavily built, whereas Danny, Sophie thought, was still a bit on the weedy side, but they both had long bony faces, eyes which were golden brown beneath thick, straight brows, and a curious habit of smiling so that only their lower teeth showed. When they did this, a dimple appeared, in Danny's case on the left side of his mouth and in his father's on the right. Sophie supposed that Mr Brewster was not handsome, but thought his face was full of character. Mr Ryland was the more conventionally good-looking, with a square jaw and regular features, and Phil resembled him closely, yet to Sophie the Brewsters seemed to have much more lively and interesting faces. But of course I know them very much better than I know the Rylands, she was reminding herself as the car continued to bounce and sway down the narrow lane.

The rain was so heavy that it almost obscured the road ahead, but she supposed that both Danny and his father must have known the lane by heart, for even as Mr Brewster slammed his foot on the brake Danny seized her shoulders from behind, preventing her from catapulting through the windscreen as the car came to an abrupt halt. Mr Brewster slewed round in his seat to stare indignantly at his son. 'What did you do that for?' he asked in an aggrieved tone. 'Safe as houses she be. I never jerks the brakes; it's not good for poor old Bessie.'

Danny laughed a little breathlessly. 'Just a pre-caution, Dad,' he said soothingly, then lowered his voice to a whisper, his mouth only inches from Sophie's ear. 'Better safe than sorry,' he breathed.

'You aren't as accustomed to Dad's driving as me and Phil, but the worst of the ordeal is over. Dad knows he could meet other traffic once we're on the road . . .' He chuckled. 'He thinks all other drivers are madmen and acts accordingly.'

Sophie smiled to herself, recognising the indulgent affection in Danny's voice. She knew that when the weather was too bad for cycling Mr Brewster some-times ran Danny into the village in Bessie, to catch the bus; she had never before appreciated how brave her friend was. She turned her head to smile at him. 'I'm fine,' she said, keeping her voice low. 'No one would be coming up your lane at this time of night so your dad doesn't need to go slow, and I must say he's – he's an amazing driver.'

But now they were bowling along the tarmac road and Mr Brewster kept to his own side of the carriage-way, slowed for corners and generally behaved as a cautious driver should on such a night. Sophie felt Danny's hands leave her shoulders and settled comfortably back in her seat once more.

They reached the village and Mr Brewster indicated left by waving his right arm in a violent circular movement, as of one stirring Christmas puddings, and swung into the Cantrip yard, coming to a halt within a few feet of the back door. 'Here we are, safe and sound, close enough for you to keep dry if you run, lass,' he told Sophie. 'And thanks again for your help wi' the apples.'

'Thanks for the lift, Mr Brewster,' Sophie said sincerely as she climbed out of the car. It was easy to forgive him his mad career down the lane when one contemplated the alternative: the three-mile walk through the icy rain with mud splashing up to your knees with every step. She turned to the boys, grinning at her from the back seat. 'See you tomorrow morning, boys.'

'That's right; school tomorrow,' Danny said. 'Cheerio, Soph.'

'Thanks, Mr Brewster,' Sophie called again as the car was manoeuvred in a tight circle so that the open window came within a few feet of her. 'And thank Mrs Brewster for the lovely food,' she added. She was standing close against the back door but even so the rain was falling on her head and shoulders so she gave them a quick wave and then bolted into the house.

The back door led straight into the kitchen where her parents were sitting on either side of the open stove, her father reading a car manual and her mother knitting. The wireless was playing softly in the background and both parents looked up, smiling, as she entered.

'Phew, what a night! It's not just raining cats and dogs out there, it's blowing a hooligan, as Grandpa used to say. But I'm so skinny I can dodge between the raindrops . . . see, I'm hardly wet at all.'

Both parents chuckled and Bill Cantrip laid aside his reading matter, took off his spectacles and pinched the bridge of his nose between thumb and forefinger before remarking: 'You don't fool me for one moment . . . so skinny you can dodge between the raindrops indeed! I've ears and I'd know that engine anywhere.'

Mrs Cantrip laughed and put down her knitting. 'I guessed Mr Brewster had give you a lift, else you'd not be lookin' quite so cheerful, nor so dry,' her mother said. 'Fancy a hot drink, love? I'd offer you a sandwich only I know Mrs Brewster will have fed you all like fighting cocks.'

'Right on all counts,' Sophie said happily, shedding her coat and boots and padding over to pull the kettle across the flame. 'As soon as he saw the rain wasn't going to stop, Mr Brewster bundled us all into the car and drove down here. He is kind – I do like him.'

'Oh aye, he's a grand chap, though what he does to that old car I don't know, nor I shouldn't like to ask,' Mr Cantrip said, shaking his head at the unreliability of all drivers, save of course for himself. 'He brings her in here for a service and when she leaves my hands the engine is purring like a sewing machine. A week later, you can hear her coming a mile off, hiccuping and burping, and half the time not even running on all cylinders. He wouldn't treat a horse the way he treats poor old Bessie Bunter.'

'It's the lane,' Sophie said. 'It's awful rough, Dad. Danny told me a while back that after heavy rain the surface gets washed away, leaving quite big rocks sticking out. It can't have been too bad during the drought but it's plain awful in wintertime.'

At that point the kettle boiled and Sophie fetched cocoa and milk from the pantry and made herself a drink. She offered to do the same for her parents but they declined, saying it was too early for the cocoa they always took up to bed with them. 'But you go off, flower, you look worn out,' her mother said. 'You're back in school tomorrow and it's not often you spend a whole weekend apple picking. Oh, that reminds me. Have you done your homework?'

'Did it on Friday evening,' Sophie said, picking up the candle which stood ready, and lighting it from the lamp which illumined the kitchen. She headed for what looked like a cupboard in one corner of the kitchen which hid the rickety wooden stairs that led to the upper storey with its two large bedrooms and tiny boxroom beyond. 'I'll be down at seven to put the kettle on so we can all have a nice cuppa before we start our day.'

'You're a good girl; that first cup of tea sets me up for the whole day,' her mother said. Sophie began to climb the stairs, clutching her mug of cocoa in one hand and her candlestick in the other, and realised for the first time how very tired she was and how much she longed for her bed. It had indeed been a hard day.

Greatly to the boys' relief, Mr Brewster managed to coax the car back up the lane without once having to stop, so they did not have to get out in the rain. When they reached Hilltop Farm Phil thanked his uncle and bolted into the house while Danny climbed over from the back seat into the front as his father executed a U-turn then headed down the lane once more. They garaged the car and ran across the yard into the kitchen, slamming the back door gladly on the rain and wind without.

Half an hour later, Danny was tucked up in bed. He had hoped that the storm would ease but it seemed to him that, if anything, it was growing wilder. The wind shrieked round the old house and tugged unavailingly at the thick thatch; if we'd had tiles I reckon half of 'em would have been in the farmyard by now, Danny thought with satisfaction as the wind veered, sending the rain lashing against his windowpane. But thatch, if it was well laid, did not give an inch. He was so tired that he had expected to sleep at once, but though he dropped off at last, his sleep was disturbed. He dreamed of sailing ships floundering in terrible gales, the masts creaking and the wind and waves screaming, so that when at last he woke it was a relief. It was also seven o'clock.

Reluctantly, Danny knuckled his eyes and sat up, then got out of bed and went to the window. The rain appeared to have ceased but the wind still howled, tossing the branches of the great walnut tree which grew close to the house. Yesterday it, and the other trees around the farmyard, had been well foliaged still. Now they were showing gaunt branches, and Danny guessed that if the wind continued to blow they would be bare indeed before the day was out. Peering through his window, he could see one bit of damage which would have to be put right: the roof of the shed where his father garaged Bessie Bunter was showing a large gap in the tiles. Danny hoped that they had not fallen into the shed, but judging from what he could see of the cobbles most had been blown into the yard.

Sighing, he made for his washstand. Better get washed and dressed; with a bit of luck his father would be driving the tractor and trailer down to Edrich's auction yard in the town, so he might give his son a lift all the way to school. He would want to get the apples into the sale today, hoping for a good price, since he knew other farmers tended to wait until the whole crop was ripe before they started picking. Anyone whose apples had been on the trees when the storm started the previous evening would be offering most of their crop to one of the big cider-making factories, since they could not possibly sell hail-damaged fruit on the open market. Danny was not supposed to get a lift on the tractor but it was all right if he perched on the boxes in the trailer, and anything was better than walking down to the bus, which he would have to do otherwise because his mother would never let him take the bike in such a storm. She would say it was far too dangerous.

Danny scrambled into his clothes and was soon in the kitchen, where a disappointment awaited him. 'I am taking the apples to the auction, but I'll hang around for as long as possible before starting off because I fancy the rain will stop altogether in a couple of hours, and wet fruit in wet boxes don't sell as well as dry,' his father told him. 'I know your mother doesn't like you cycling when it's wild but I don't see no harm meself. But you'd best set off at once, lad, 'cos the lane might be bad.'

His mother was making breakfast, frying eggs and bacon in a big pan, and turned to shake her head indulgently at her husband. 'Let the poor lad get some grub inside him before you push him out into the storm,' she said reprovingly. 'I take it the wind has dropped some or you'd not have told him to use his bike.'

Danny's father was beginning to say that the wind had indeed dropped when Danny remembered the state of the garage roof; not that it really was a garage, but it had been used as such for as long as he could remember. He knew his parents' bedroom did not overlook the farmyard, but even as he began his tale his father nodded. 'Aye, there's a gap in the roof big enough for Bessie to jump out of, if she'd a mind,' he said. 'But she's not damaged; the tiles all slid down the roof and landed in the yard except for one, and that simply landed on her canvas hood.' He grinned at his son. 'Hope nothing of the sort happened up at Hilltop. It 'ud break Matt's heart if he so much as scratched that Bentley.'

Danny, in the act of sitting down at the table to eat the enormous bacon sandwich his mother had just handed him, nodded and returned the grin. His Uncle Matthew was not a good farmer, for his interest in his stock and crops was not strong. He did not come from a farming background. When he had married Aunt Daisy, he and his brother had owned a flourishing hardware store in the nearest town, and when Daisy's father had died and left the young couple Hilltop Farm Matthew had agreed to take a percentage of the profit from the store. But things had not gone well for Albert, Matthew's brother, so he had sold the business and moved away from the area to work for someone else. Matthew Ryland had remained in the old farmhouse, high on the hill, and had managed to scrape a living from his large flock of sheep and tiny dairy herd. He employed a couple of farmhands, rascally brothers who cheated him whenever the opportunity arose, and Deborah always said that her brother-in-law was his own worst enemy because he splashed out on any new invention when he had the cash, as though the profit from the farm was still just a little extra and his real money came from the hardware store.

Six months ago, Danny had been sitting quietly in a corner of the kitchen, doing his homework, when Aunt Daisy had rushed into the room, pink-faced and furious. 'You'll never guess what that gurt fool Matt has been and gone and done,' she had said breathlessly. 'We'm needing a new tractor chronical bad and he's sold all the young lambs for a decent profit, but does he buy a tractor? Does he hell! He's been and gone and bought a new car, one which will gobble up fuel and won't ever be any use on the farm. He's as proud as a peacock of the bloody thing, says he can afford it now he don't have to pay wages to those two idle fellers . . . I'm at my wits' end, Deb, and I feel so sorry for poor Phil, working all the hours God sends when he gets back from school for a fool of a father who's chucking away his inheritance every time he goes into town. And it's not as though the lad loves the land, because he doesn't. He'll want to leave as soon as he's full grown; he's crazy about engines . . . aeroplanes . . . stuff like that. He won't want Hilltop round his neck, not even if it were worth the work to put it right.'

Danny had never mentioned the outburst to anyone, certainly not to Phil, but it was always there in the back of his mind whenever he thought about Uncle Matthew and Hilltop Farm. Phil never complained about his father but Danny had seen him cast exasperated looks at the Ryland stable block. It contained, not horses, but a number of pointless buys, for Uncle Matthew was easily persuaded by any salesman with the gift of the gab. There was a mechanical hay turner, an automatic seed drill, and a muck spreader which might have been useful if one had twenty or thirty acres under plough, but could do very little on a farm that was mainly permanent pasture, a good deal of which was on steeply sloping ground.

Yet somehow Uncle Matthew never went completely broke, and the reckless buying of 'the very latest thing' had ground, or so it seemed to Danny, to a halt.

Danny finished his bacon sandwich and made for the back door, grabbing a round of buttered bread as he passed, and shoving it into his coat pocket. He galloped across the yard, glad that the rain had ceased, and mounted the bike before he remembered his bicycle clips, which hung on the handlebar. He stopped for a moment to pin his trousers firmly round his ankles. A quick glance at his wristwatch told him that haste was of the essence, though he had no particular objection to cycling all the way to school if he did miss the bus. He crossed the yard at speed and shot out into the lane, the right-hand side of which was running with so much water that it looked like a stream. Danny sighed, then pulled his school cap more firmly down over his eyes, for though the wind had eased it was still blowing pretty hard and he had no wish to find himself pursuing his cap over the surrounding countryside. Boys were forbidden to attend school without their caps so he could not simply abandon it if it did take wing.

As he turned the corner and entered the stretch of lane overhung by trees, he thought for a moment that the rain had started again, then realised it was just drops from the branches above. Nevertheless, it made it difficult to get a clear view of what was ahead, which was why, when he rounded the next bend, he was almost upon the fallen oak tree before he saw it. Desperately, he applied his brakes. The bicycle skidded wildly, then hit a projecting rock. Danny sailed over the handlebars and landed, cursing, half on the oak and half in the mud of the lane. He was shaken but not hurt, though the bicycle, poor thing, had a front wheel facing sideways and a split in the front tyre, and the bicycle lamp was in about a hundred pieces.

'Bugger, bugger, bugger,' Danny said with dismal

ferocity. 'Oh God Almighty, that's me dished.' He was beginning to heave the bicycle into an upright position when he heard what sounded like a badger's grunt. He looked around him and what he saw made his blood run cold. There was a car beneath the spreading branches of the oak, and when he looked more closely he recognised his uncle's Bentley. Hastily, he grabbed the nearest branch and tugged, but he might as well have tried to pull down the church tower. The oak was a mighty tree, probably a couple of hundred years old, and far beyond the strength of a puny fifteen-year-old to shift. Heedless of mud and his school trousers, Danny dropped to his knees and crawled as far as he could through the branches towards the trunk. He could see his Uncle Matthew slumped in the driver's seat. He looked awful. Blood-streaked, hatless, wild, but he lifted his head and grinned at Danny, though it was more of a grimace than a smile.

'Boy, am I glad to see you,' he said hoarsely. 'Rotten luck, wasn't it? I was on my way back from the village – I'd come down to buy some fags, so I'd dropped Phil at the bus stop – when I heard a very odd sound indeed, a sort of screaming, tearing noise. Like a fool, I stopped to investigate and that was the last I knew until I heard you ride straight into the tree and start cussing.'

'Are you hurt bad, Uncle Matt?' Danny asked anxiously. 'There's no way I can shift the tree, not even by an inch, but I might be able to heave you out.'

Matthew Ryland laughed rather feebly. 'I'm all

right, just a bit shook up, but I reckon my lovely car's a goner,' he said. 'Can you go back home, Danny, and tell John to fetch the tractor and all the men he can muster. Tell him I got a bang on my stupid head and a worse one on my shoulder, so I reckon it'll be hospital for me when they do get me out. And don't you go worrying Daisy; just say I've been held up.'

'Right,' Danny said briefly. He propped his bicycle against one of the larger branches, for it would only impede him now, and set off up the lane at a run. He thought that Uncle Matthew was probably anxious not to scare him as well as his wife, for how could he possibly have escaped serious injury from such an accident? So when he reached the farm, he tore across the yard and burst into the kitchen, shouting as he did so. 'Dad! Mum! The big oak's down, the one just after the first bend, and Uncle Matthew's underneath it. He says to bring the tractor and all the men . . .'

He stopped short. The men were here, sitting at the table, stolidly eating their way through the huge breakfast Deb cooked for them every morning. They did not stir, but their eyes rounded and their mouths stopped chewing. It was only John Brewster who jumped to his feet. 'I'll get the tractor. Reg, you come with me – we'll need the lifting gear. The rest of you make your way straight to the oak but don't do anything until I join you. If he's hurt bad, we could do more damage by an incautious move.' He turned to Danny. 'Is he still conscious? Could you see how badly he was hurt? A tree like that could crush the life out of a man.' As he spoke, he had reached down his coat from its peg and was beginning to open the back door.

'He's in the car, Dad; he reckons the Bentley took the force of the fall,' Danny said hastily. 'He said he'd had a bump on the head and another on the shoulder, said he'd have to go to hospital so I reckon it was hurting him. Shall I run up to Hilltop? Uncle Matthew said to say he'd been held up but I don't see the point myself. Aunt Daisy will want to know what's happened.'

The farmhands were finishing off their breakfasts at speed. 'What about Phil then?' Mr Fuller said through his mouthful.

'Uncle Matt had dropped him at the bus stop in the village – he'll be on the bus going to school by now,' Danny replied.

John Brewster had disappeared but his wife cut in. 'I'll nip up and tell Daisy. You, my boy, can get on your way to school,' she said firmly. 'Your father will manage very nicely without you and if you've missed the bus you've a long bike ride ahead of you . . .' She stopped speaking abruptly and stared at him as if seeing him properly for the first time since he had burst into the kitchen, her mouth at half cock. Danny was wondering why when she broke into speech once more. 'My God, boy, you look as if you'd been in a fight with Solly and lost!'

Danny grinned. Solly was his father's ram, an elderly, cross-grained beast who had been known to pursue – and vanquish – sheep-chasing dogs. 'It wasn't Solly, Mum,' he said. 'My bike tipped me off and now it's a wreck. I'd best get changed . . .'

'Get upstairs and put on your old things and bring everything else down,' his mother advised. 'I'll give you a jug of hot water – you can have a good wash while you're up there. You look as though you need it.'

Danny went upstairs and changed into an old grey sweater and corduroys, then accompanied the men down to the scene of the drama.

In the end it took the combined efforts of all the farm workers, a couple of tractors, and the big two-handled saw to free Matthew Ryland, and then to clear the remainder of the tree off the Bentley. Danny was sent down to the village to telephone for an ambulance to take his uncle to hospital, for though he declared himself to be pretty well unhurt his shoulder looked odd and it was obviously giving him considerable pain.

'Dislocated,' John Brewster said briefly, 'and a couple of ribs bust, and probably his collarbone.' He did not say this to Matthew, however, but to Danny. 'You had best go with him in the ambulance when it arrives. As soon as we've cleared the lane, I'll go and fetch Daisy and bring her to the hospital to find out what's what. Then you and I will go to the grammar school to get Phil and I'll take you both to Hilltop to do whatever's needed.'

By early December, Uncle Matthew was out of hospital, the huge gap in the hedge left by the oak had been fenced off and new hedging planted and Danny, who had been making his way straight to Hilltop every evening after school and spending all day there at weekends to help his cousin and aunt in any way he could, expected to return to his normal way of life. Phil had been granted leave from school for the rest of the term. Uncle Matthew's accident, however, had far-reaching consequences. His dislocated shoulder had been out of place too long to be simply manipulated back into its socket and had to be operated on. It was soon discovered that whenever he raised his right arm above shoulder height, or tried to carry anything heavier than a couple of pounds, the joint began to shift once more, causing him great pain. This meant that his wife and son had to do ninety per cent of the farm work, and it followed that they began to rely more and more on Danny's help. Rather to his own surprise, Danny coped pretty well. He and Sophie toiled over his homework on the bus coming home, finishing anything that still needed doing on the bus going to school next morning, and the chores that he normally took on at home were done by one of his parents, or the farmhands. Danny's marks actually improved, perhaps because he was having to give his whole concentration to the task in hand. Phil worked like a Trojan, of course, always seeming to be in two places at once, his fair hair standing on end and his blue eyes blazing as he endeavoured to do his father's work as well as his own. As soon as it became clear that Uncle Matthew was never going to be fully fit,

Phil volunteered to leave school, and his parents had little choice but to agree. Perhaps only Danny, who knew all about Phil's ambition to become a pilot, understood what it meant to his cousin to give up his studies, though Phil told him, confidentially, that he meant to continue with his maths and that the maths teacher at school, who thought he had great potential, had agreed to set him problems and to mark his work in his own time.

Aunt Daisy was a real brick, Danny thought. She was a slightly built, pretty woman, an excellent housewife and the sort of cook who could make a good meal out of almost nothing – she had to be, her sister Deborah had been heard to remark, since in the old days Uncle Matthew had thought nothing of spending her housekeeping money on some mad scheme to get rich quick. Then, she had somehow managed to feed her family from her store cupboards and from the vegetable garden she had always tended herself, but now she made sure she got her housekeeping money regularly. 'With so much work on the farm to do myself, I don't have time to make one week's money stretch to two,' she told her husband severely. 'You've often talked about having to pull our horns in so that you could save up for something you really wanted . . .'

'Something I really needed,' Uncle Matthew had said reproachfully, and Danny had been forced to smother a giggle, remembering the hay turner, the seed drill and the muck spreader, to say nothing of the gleaming Bentley, now in pieces and doubtless being broken up for any uncrushed parts. The family and himself had been sitting round the kitchen table having high tea when the subject of housekeeping money had been raised, and Danny knew that in the days before the crash his uncle would have pooh-poohed his wife's remarks; knew also that now he would not dream of doing so. With the loss of his beloved motor, Uncle Matthew seemed to have grown up in some peculiar way. He acknowledged now that he had been wrong to buy the Bentley in the first place, admitted that he could never afford to replace it and agreed with Phil that if they ever amassed sufficient money again, they would buy a new tractor and manage without a car. Danny thought cynically that his uncle's changed attitude probably had something to do with the fact that his shoulder prevented him from driving anything, even his old tractor, but held his peace: Danny was learning tact. As for saving up, this would be a slow business. Formerly, poor Aunt Daisy's money from the dairy and from the flock of hens which pecked and croodled around the farmyard had often been casually commandeered by Uncle Matthew, but Phil now insisted that she should keep every penny of it. Why should she not? She certainly earned it. At present, she and Phil carried her produce down to the Brewsters' on market day and piled it, along with the Brewsters' own goods, into Bessie Bunter. Then the two sisters drove into town and set up their stall. This was fine now, but Phil had reminded Danny that later in the year, when the hens were laying well

82

and there were fresh vegetables and fruit to be sold, poor Bessie would be swamped by the double load. 'I'm saving up for a pony and trap so we can be a bit more independent,' he told his cousin. 'Uncle John and Auntie Deb have been grand, and we'd never have managed without them, but we've got to stand on our own two feet. It'll be easier once Dad's hurts have completely healed, of course . . .'

Danny agreed but could not help wondering whether Uncle Matthew's shoulder would ever be right. If not, Phil would be tied to a poor farm, perhaps for many years, and be completely unable to get away to fulfil his own ambitions. As things stood, Danny knew his uncle and aunt relied heavily on his own assistance and could not help wondering what they would do if he went to university, which he knew was his parents' dearest wish. He voiced the thought one breakfast time, talking fast between mouthfuls, for somehow he was always in a rush first thing in the morning. His mother turned from the range and smiled at him. 'Dear boy, that's three years off! No need to worry yourself about it yet.'

'Yes there is, because if I'm not going to university then there's no need for me to matriculate; I can just get my School Cert.,' Danny pointed out. 'And if I'm going to work on the farm . . .'

His father had been eating solidly, a copy of yesterday's *Telegraph* spread out before him, but at Danny's words he cast the paper aside and fixed his son with a gimlet eye. 'You will go to university – Cambridge for preference – if I have to drag you every foot of the way,' he said. Though his voice was light, Danny could sense the steel behind the words. 'I missed my own chance of a university education because I was a young fool and wanted to start earning money and learning everything I could about farming. But I had a young cousin, Bev his name was, who went to Cambridge and got a first-class degree, what's more. He took over his father's farm, I admit, but not before he'd had ten years of well-paid jobs all over the world. He visited Australia, New Zealand, the Argentine . . . I'm telling you, Danny, I'd have given my eye teeth to see such places. So you'll bloody well matriculate even if I have to pay one of the farmhands to help that fool Matthew out.'

Deb made a clicking sound indicating disapproval, but Danny knew that she agreed with her husband's every word save for one, and that was calling Uncle Matthew a fool. So Danny sighed and capitulated, seeing the sense in his father's words. Farming was very different in the three countries he had mentioned and it had doubtless done Dad's cousin Bev a great deal of good to study abroad. No one could forget they were in the middle of the Depression, so few farmers could afford to send their sons overseas for long periods, but if you had a well-paid job in the country of your choice . . .

'Right, Dad, I'll give it a go. But there's no use denying I find Latin rare difficult,' Danny said. 'Mind, my maths is improving by leaps and bounds because I have to explain stuff to Sophie, even stuff

I'm not sure I understand, and somehow or other that seems to make it clear to me. I know you're right really, and I guess you know I'll do my damnedest to get at least some sort of degree.'

'Good lad,' John Brewster said, retiring behind his newspaper once more. 'You'll not regret it, I promise you.'

Chapter Three

December 1936

It was a freezing cold day and outside the windows of the café Tess could see that sleet was falling. It was growing late so she walked across to the two elderly women seated at the window table and smiled brightly at them both. 'Is there anything else I can get you?' she enquired in her sweetest tone. 'More hot water? Or a little more milk perhaps?'

What she would have liked to have said was, 'It's past closing time, me feet are killing me and I've messages to do before I can go up to the flat and relax,' but of course she had no intention of being so frank. The café, which Mr Mitchell had insisted on calling 'Restawhile', had been open for more than a year and was doing extraordinarily well. Tess knew Mr Mitchell was delighted and could not sufficiently praise her mother for the success she had made of it.

Tess herself hurried home every day after school, changed into a black dress with a frilly white apron and popped a little celluloid cap on her head, and took over as waitress from Mrs Bacon, who worked school hours only, since she had a growing family and liked to be home by the time they arrived back each afternoon.

Now, the women at the table smiled back at her

and asked for their bill, beginning to gather up their possessions, to shrug themselves into their coats and to fumble in capacious handbags for the money owing. Tess had a neat little pad and now she swiftly added up the cost of a pot of tea for two, an iced fairy cake and a buttered scone, tore off the page and placed it on the table. Her customers paid, added a tuppenny tip and trundled towards the door. Tess leaped ahead of them, holding the door wide and waiting patiently whilst they pulled on woolly gloves, turned up coat collars, erected large black umbrellas and finally left the shelter of the doorway to scuttle along the pavement, the larger woman almost decapitating a passing stranger with an incautiously held umbrella.

Tess loved her work in the café and appreciated the money she earned, for Mr Mitchell paid her half a crown a week and customers usually tipped her a few coppers. Sometimes, she took tips which should rightly have gone to Mrs Bacon, but the older woman always refused to take them, pointing out that the complication of sharing the odd penny or two would be more trouble than it was worth.

However, tonight Tess was anxious to get closed up and cleared away, for her mother needed cake ingredients and had given her a list. Quickly, she swung the 'Open' sign to read 'Closed' and began to clear the window table, then hurried back into the kitchen behind the café.

Her mother was cooking, rolling out a huge ball of pastry and lining half a dozen tins in which she would presently place various fillings. Tina was perched on a high stool, industriously making tiny figures out of leftover pastry, endowing them with currant eyes and brown sugar waistcoats. She looked up as her sister entered the room and beamed, slipping down from her stool. 'Shall I come in and help you clear, Tess?' she asked eagerly. 'Is they all gone? I see'd old Mrs Bellis eatin' a cake at table three, so I reckon I'd best bring a brush and dustpan. She always makes a mess if it's puff pastry, an' it was an apple turnover.' She looked, guilelessly, up at her mother. 'I love apple turnovers, so I does.'

'Mrs Bellis talks with her mouth full and sprays wharrever she's eatin' all over the show,' Tess grumbled. 'I pity whoever sits opposite her.'

'And whoever has to clean down the table when she leaves,' Laura pointed out, pressing pastry into a baking tin and trimming the edges with practised speed. 'Still, she's a regular customer and almost always has a cake with her cuppa.'

Tina, who had disappeared through the back door into the small yard beyond, reappeared with dustpan and brush and made for the café. 'I'll sweep up all through, and then I'll come wi' you to do the messages, Tess,' she said importantly. 'I aren't very big, but I'm strong, an' a bleedin' good carrier.'

'Well, I don't know; the weather's awful. When I came out of school it were just icy cold rain, but now there's snow in it as well. What do you think, Mam? I'd like Tina to come only she's bound to get wet even if we take the big brolly, and that makes carrying stuff so difficult.'

Laura looked up from her pastry for a moment. 'I think she had better go with you because she's right, there is an awful lot to carry,' she observed. 'Best put on your waterproofs, then you won't need the brolly. But although it's a fairly long list, everything's available locally so you shouldn't be out long.' She smiled at her two daughters and Tess felt instantly wary; she knew that smile. 'And there's a treat for our supper, girls! Mr Mitchell is going to buy fish and chips for everyone so we shan't have to cook. Can you call in at the shop on your way out to see if he wants anything?'

Tina beamed at her mother. 'Fish and chips! I like 'em almost best of everything,' she said enthusiastically. 'Will we have 'em here, Mam, in the café kitchen?' She turned to her sister, who was frowning. 'Wharrever's the matter, Tess? Isn't you pleased? Fish and chips is lovely and Mam always lets us open a bottle of Corona to go with 'em.' She cast a pleading look at her mother. 'And maybe there'll be something nice left over from the café what we can have for our afters.'

'Now why on earth should Mr Mitchell invite us to supper in anywhere but his own flat?' Laura said, lining the next tin. 'After all, he's got a grand big kitchen with room enough to feed a score of folk, I dare say.' She smiled down at Tina. 'And you're right, love, we should make some contribution to the meal so it might as well be a bottle of cherryade and the vanilla sponge cake; it's already a trifle stale, but I'll make a jug of custard to go with it. We've plenty of milk.'

Tess heaved a sigh and picked up the list. 'Do I have to go to the Mitchells', Mam?' she asked plaintively. 'You could tell Mr Mitchell that I'm having tea with a friend and won't be back till late.'

Laura shook her head reprovingly. 'I shall do no such thing. Why ever should I, queen?' she said. 'Don't you like Mr Mitchell? He's ever such a kind man, and a marvellous person to work for, yet lately you've been avoiding him whenever you can. Don't think I haven't noticed, because I'm not stupid, and I think you're being very silly as well as ungrateful. Now come on, Tess, just what has changed you?'

Tess stared at her mother for a long moment. Should she tell her why she had taken to avoiding the Mitchells? She supposed she would have to at some point. And you never knew, her mother might be able to ease the situation.

Tess was still hesitating, wondering how best to put into words how she felt, when Tina chimed in. 'Oh, Mammy, it's not Mr Mitchell, me and Tess like him ever so much, it's that bleedin' boy of his. He never takes no notice of me but he's always sneering at Tess an' calling her names. Yesterday, he were sortin' tomatoes in the shop and bawled something to Tess and when she took no notice he threw a rotten tomato at her and got her in the back. It squelched all over her coat.'

Laura stared from one girl to the other. 'Whatever

did he do that for?' she asked slowly. 'You must have said something to annoy him, queen. I mean, he's older than you and a great deal bigger and stronger. You *must* have said something!'

'I didn't,' Tess said truthfully. 'I don't know whether he's jealous because his pa is so nice to us, but ever since I started giving a hand with the greengrocery he's been horrible. Calling names, tripping me up if I walk past him, shouting after me in the street . . . honestly, Mam, I'd be far happier staying at home. I can have eggs on toast, or something.'

'He won't dare to be nasty to you whilst his father and I are around,' Laura said grimly. 'It might be better if he was, because I know Mr Mitchell wouldn't stand for it and would soon jump on young Mike and teach him some manners. In fact, I'll have a word with Mr . . .'

'Oh no, Mam, you'll only make it worse. He – he'd call me a tale-clat, and he'd be right,' Tess said, alarmed. 'Maybe he just hates girls, but honest to God I'd rather miss out on fish and chips than sit at the same table as that Mike Mitchell.'

Laura hesitated. 'Look, I know you'll think I'm being hard on you but I can't allow this to continue,' she said slowly. 'The café is our livelihood and it's owned by the Mitchells, to say nothing of the flat. We can't afford to fall out with them, queen. So either I talk to Mr Mitchell or you can have it out with Mike. Take your choice.'

'Oh, Mam,' Tess wailed. 'I'll try, but when someone

starts off a conversation by calling you Pig Face or Chinky Eyes, and says you must be a feller in a dress 'cos you're flat as a perishin' ironing board . . .'

'And then chucks rotten fruit at you,' Tina put in. 'Honest to God, Mam, he's a beastly boy, not a bit like lovely Mr Mitchell. Why can't *you* say something to Mike? He won't call you names, nor chuck rotten fruit at you.'

'Oh, Tina, because then he'll know I've told on him, can't you see that?' Tess said impatiently, glaring at her small sister. 'But if I tackle him . . .' She sighed, then went over to the back door, took down her waterproof and began putting it on. 'OK, Mam; he's making up orders in the stockroom right now. I'll have a word before I start on me messages.'

'Then I'm coming with you in case of flying tomatoes,' Tina said, struggling into her own waterproof and buttoning it up all wrong so that Tess had to do it again. 'I've gorra gang an' all; I'll tell bleedin' Mike Mitchell that if he's nasty to you I'll set *my* gang on him, and I will, too.'

Tess laughed but gave her little sister an impetuous hug. She knew all about Tina's gang. They were all six- and seven-year-olds who had played together all summer down on the recreation ground at the end of Mere Lane. Tina often boasted that though they were all quite small they were tough as old boots, and Tess could imagine that if they were to set on someone, he or she would soon bitterly regret it.

'Thank you, queen, but let's hope it won't come to

that,' she said, opening the back door and slipping out into the cold and sleet. 'Now we'll go straight to Mr Mitchell's stockroom and just tell horrible Mike that he'd best improve his manners, or else.'

In moments, the two girls had made their way along the jigger and into the Mitchells' back yard. As she pulled open the stockroom door, Tess felt her heart begin to bump uneasily against her ribs, but having made up her mind to tackle her enemy she had no intention of drawing back. As soon as they were inside and the door was closed, she looked across to where Mike, with an order in one hand and a brown bag full of fruit in the other, was making up boxes for delivery. Since this was her job on a Saturday, when she was not needed in the café, she guessed that Mike was nearing the end of his task, for they always packed the boxes in a predetermined order. Potatoes, carrots and swedes went in first, followed by cauliflowers, cabbages and sprouts, whilst tender luxury items were always placed on top. On a miserably rainy day like this, every box would be covered by a clean potato sack to keep off the worst of the weather. On a Saturday, Tess made up the boxes and Mike delivered them, but today, of course, he would be doing both jobs.

For a moment, Mike did not see the sisters, then Tina moved forward and he stared across at them, the enquiring look on his face gradually turning to the unpleasant belligerence that Tess knew well. She opened her mouth to speak but Mike was before her.

'What are you doing in here, Pig Face?' he said

nastily. 'If you're hopin' to nick some fruit then I'll be happy to help you. Here's a rotten apple . . .' As he spoke, he picked up an apple from the floor and drew back his arm. It was a bad one set aside, since Tess saw his fingers sink into it.

'Stop that!' and 'Don't you dare!' both sisters said at once, but it was too late. The apple sailed through the air and Tess only just dodged in time. Hot with fury, she ran forward, meaning to pick up some ammunition of her own, but Tina was before her. As Mike bent for another missile, Tina flew at him, thrust both hands deep into his curly red hair, and pulled as hard as she could.

'Hey, leggo, you little vulture!' Mike screamed and seized Tina's small wrists. Tess had never fought a boy in her life, but for one moment she truly believed that Mike was going to hurl her little sister to the floor. She shot forward, slapped Mike's face as hard as she could and then bit the long bony wrist protruding from the sleeve of his delivery overall.

Mike bellowed and fell over backwards, letting go of Tina as he did so. Tess drew back her foot, for the target of his bottom was a tempting one, but at that precise moment Mr Mitchell came through from the shop with another order in one hand. He stopped, obviously amazed. 'What on earth . . . ?' he began.

Mike started to struggle to his feet, saying as he did so: 'It ain't my fault, Pa. I were makin' up the orders like you said when . . .'

'. . . when he slipped on one of them rotten bananas and fell on his back,' Tina said glibly. 'I were helping him up, and so were Tess.' She turned to Mike. 'Ain't that so, Mike?'

Mike began to growl something beneath his breath, then he caught Tess's eye and, greatly to her astonishment, he suddenly started to chuckle.

Mr Mitchell stared uncomprehendingly from face to face, then down at the floor, a large area of which was now covered in squashed and rotten fruit. 'Well, I dare say it were all an accident but I don't like horseplay in my stockroom,' he said. 'Why, if Mike had fallen into one of the delivery boxes he's just made up, we could have been in trouble. Still an' all, there's no real damage done. Mike, start loading the boxes on to your bike. Tess, I know you aren't supposed to be working in here, but if you wouldn't mind clearing up the mess and giving the floor a mop . . .' He smiled at Tina, who was a great favourite of his, as Tess knew well. 'And you, princess, can come into the shop with me and I'll give you a couple of small bunches of grapes. I guess you're on your way to get your messages; your mother said she'd ask you to pop in and see if there's anything I need. Well, there is. I'm near on out of vinegar, and to my mind fish and chips without vinegar isn't fish and chips at all. So if you'll pick up a bottle of Sarson's on your travels, I'd be much obliged.' He dug into his apron pocket and produced a shilling. 'That'll cover it, I reckon; you can keep the change.'

Mr Mitchell turned and left the stockroom with Tina trotting at his heels. Mike and Tess looked at each other, then quickly away. 'I'll fetch the brush and dustpan,' Mike mumbled. He had hard greenish eyes which always made Tess think of gooseberries, curly reddish hair, pale eyebrows and lashes, and the freckled skin which goes with such colouring. It was odd that his face was round, because his body was long and bony, but Tess had once heard someone remark that boys' faces are childish until their voices change, when the bones begin to show, so she supposed that that was why Mike's face was rather fat. He was only just fifteen, she reminded herself, though he was so tall that folk thought him a couple of years older at least.

Now, Mike fetched the dustpan and brush whilst Tess got the mop bucket, half filled it with hot water, added soda crystals, and began to mop the floor. Neither said a word until the job was finished, and then Mike said, 'Ta,' rather grudgingly.

Tess pulled forward an empty apple box and sat down on it. 'It's all right,' she said gruffly. 'Look, I came in here to talk to you. Your dad has asked us to your place for fish and chips this evening. I didn't want to come because you don't like me and it's – it's awkward like. But your dad's been ever so good to us Collinses so I thought mebbe you could explain why you hate me so much. It can't be just because I'm a girl. I mean you don't chuck rotten tomatoes at every girl you meet in the street!'

Mike sneered, but it was pretty half-hearted compared to his usual efforts. 'I dunno what you mean,' he said loudly. 'Who said I don't like girls, anyhow?'

'Then if it's not that, what have I done to make you call me names and trip me up and give me a shove when you pass me on your bike?' Tess asked. 'You might as well tell me because otherwise I could feel obliged to describe how you looked sittin' on your bum in a sea of rotten fruit while my little sister tugged you backwards by the hair.'

Mike scowled but a tide of red crept up his neck and across his face and Tess guessed that he was imagining, all too clearly, how some of his pals would react if they heard of his downfall. Tess had always suspected that Mike had bought his way into their favour with gifts of fades from his father's shop and guessed that, if the other lads knew what had happened, he might become a victim of bullying instead of a bully, which was how she thought of him now. 'Well?' she asked belligerently, when he did not answer. 'Which is it to be?'

Mike heaved a sigh. 'I didn't want my pa to go opening that bleeding caff,' he said gruffly. 'And I didn't want a load of perishin' women livin' next door, either. Before you came there was old Mr Threadgold what owned the cobbler's shop, and his grandson, Billy. Billy were a couple of years older'n me but he were me best pal. We did all sorts together. I thought, when the old feller left the shop, that they'd move somewhere close, but they didn't. They've gone to St Helens.'

'I see,' Tess said slowly, but in fact she did not really. After all, it was scarcely her fault that the cobbler had moved away. She said as much, adding:

'I can understand you missing Billy Threadgold, but surely that's no reason for calling me names and chucking rotten fruit at me. I mean you can't think it would drive me away! I can't help being a girl, you know, any more than Tina can; well, you can't help being a boy for that matter. And come to think of it, you're never nasty to Tina.'

'She don't count. She's only a kid; she can't be more'n seven,' Mike muttered. 'And it ain't just that. When you first moved in, the fellers kept on about how lucky I were to have a gal like you next door. It made me mad 'cos it were as if they were sayin' you were better'n Billy.'

Tess stared. Then she pulled her long braid of black hair forward over her shoulder and began to nibble the end, as she always did when she was thinking deeply. 'They must have been having you on,' she said slowly. 'Or perhaps . . . look, I'm *trying* to understand. Can't you make it a bit easier for me?'

Mike stared back at her. Twice his mouth opened as if he were about to speak and twice he closed it again. Then, as though making up his mind at last, he burst into speech. 'Look, I can't explain because I ain't sure meself now why I – I took agin you. But I'll quit since it's the only way to shut your gob.'

'Good. Tell you what, we'll just have to take no notice of each other,' Tess said thankfully, deciding to ignore his choice of words. She had no desire to be friends with Mike since, in her experience, girls and boys simply did not mix; not once they reached their teens, anyway.

Mike was starting to speak once more when Tina erupted into the stockroom bearing two small bunches of grapes. She looked curiously from one face to the other, then handed Tess one of the bunches. Mike seemed to realise that this was the end of their talk for he began to load the big square carrier on the front of his bicycle with the boxes to be delivered. Tina, however, pulled a grape from her bunch and pushed it into Mike's hand. 'Are you and Tess friends now?' she asked. 'And me, of course? I hope so, or you'll be sorry; my gang's awful fierce, so they are.'

Tess half expected Mike to show some annoyance but instead he laughed, thanked Tina gravely for the grape, and finished loading up his bicycle. 'We're going to have an armed truce, if you know what that is,' he said. 'Now you two had best gerron with them messages, and don't forget the bleedin' vinegar or Dad'll have your guts for garters.'

Tess stood up, beginning to button her waterproof, and was about to follow Mike out of the stockroom when Tina gave a squeak and pointed dramatically to the empty apple box upon which Tess had been sitting. 'You and Mike are mean to me,' she said aggrievedly. 'You pretended you was cleaning up the floor but really you was playing Hangman on the top of that apple box.'

'We were not,' Tess began indignantly, then looked again at the label on top of the box. *Manor Farm Herefordshire Apples, Cox's Orange Pippins*, she read, and underneath it saw that Tina was right.

There was the usual stick man hanging from the gallows with all the dashes below filled in to form the word 'promise', and since the stick figure still lacked both legs the winner, presumably, had been called Phil. Danny, whoever he might be, had used the left-hand side of the label, and Phil had erected his gallows on the right-hand side. Intrigued, Tess wondered what word he had chosen, for the dashes beneath the gallows only had three letters filled in, though the stick man was almost complete. She stared down at the game and was pretty sure that the boys had been called away before it had been completed. Then Tina, leaning on her shoulder and breathing heavily, said querulously: 'If it weren't you and Mike what played Hangman, then who were it? Mr Mitchell's shop boys are called William and Wilf, ain't they? Who are Danny and Phil, Tess? Pals of Mike's?'

'I don't think so,' Tess said slowly. 'I reckon they were from wherever the apples came from. What does the label say?'

But Tina had lost interest and was buttoning herself into her waterproof and eating grapes as she did so. 'Manor Farm,' she said thickly. 'Come on, we'd best start them messages or the shops will be closed.'

The two girls made their way out into the steadily falling sleet and were soon going from shop to shop, buying the provisions their mother needed. But though she consulted her list, struck off items bought and jotted down prices, Tess's mind was not on her work. Finding the label on the apple box, she mused, was like finding a message in a bottle; you could not help wondering about the boys who had played Hangman all over the apple label. Of course, the game could have been played by almost anyone, for the apples had probably come a long way, though she had no idea where Herefordshire was. Come to think of it, she could look it up in her atlas when they got home, see where the apples had come from in relation to Liverpool. Had they come by train? She knew at least part of their journey would have been in the wholesaler's huge wagon, but before that they could easily have journeyed by train. She had seen orchards before, of course, when her mother had taken them into the country for a day out, and thought them beautiful and romantic places.

'Tess, will you stop dreaming, girl! Does we want some of them plain Marie biscuits, what the old ladies like, or is it them Lincoln Creams, the ones with bobbles on?'

Tess came abruptly back to the present. Probably the game had been played on some grimy station platform between a couple of ancient porters, with nicotine-stained moustaches and fingers bent with arthritis, for this was no romantic message in a bottle but a half-finished game scrawled on the bottom of a label. Hastily, Tess consulted her list, then smiled at Mr Arbuthnot, waiting patiently behind his grocery counter, pencil poised. 'Sorry, Mr A; I'll have two pounds of both, please,' she said, and forgot about the apple box for the rest of the day.

Mike pushed his heavily laden bicycle through the back yard and out into the jigger. The sleet was still falling and as he turned on to Heyworth Street the wind blew it straight into his face, but Mike was used to delivering whatever the weather and had already buttoned his waterproof to the throat and pulled his old sou'wester well down over his eyes. He waited until there was a gap in the traffic, then mounted his machine and began to pedal slowly up the hill, for the boxes were heavy. His first call was in Abbot Street, but mostly his customers lived further away. Still, the order was a large one and he would be glad to get rid of it. He was actually turning into Abbot Street, eyes half shut against the weather, when he suddenly remembered something and drew into the kerb with a curse. He had been so anxious to get away from those bleedin' girls whilst he still had some pride left that he had piled the boxes into his carrier in no particular order. Now he would have to sort them out. He looked wildly round for shelter but there was none. Sighing, shoulders hunched, he began to stand the boxes on the wet pavement. Damn, damn, damn. It was all that bloody girl's fault. If she hadn't come inter-fering into the stockroom, he would have made very certain that he had the boxes in the right order. As it happened, however, he was in luck; he only had to swap two boxes over and fortunately the bottom one, which had got wet standing on the pavement, was still the bottom one, so perhaps it would not be necessary to chuck a tomato at Tess next time he saw her.

Grinning to himself, Mike remounted his bicycle, reflecting that his secret was still safe . . . or secrets, rather. When Tess had first moved in next door, he had thought her a real looker with that long, pitch-black hair and very dark blue eyes. But she had ignored him, never appeared to look at him twice. At first his rudeness had merely been an attempt to get her to notice him, but it seemed he had gone too far and once he had started to insult her it proved impossible to stop. The second secret was a good deal more complex. He had been carelessly fond of his mother, though she had never seemed to have much time for him. It was his father who had organised the annual week's holiday in Rhyl and had played with the small Mike on the sands, paid for donkey rides and taken him to the funfair, whilst his mother lay in a deckchair.

She had stopped serving in the shop when Mike was seven and had taken a job behind the cash desk in the Electric Palace Cinema on Heyworth Street, explaining that this meant she would have her mornings free for housework and messages, but would work afternoons and evenings. Well, that had been what she had *said*, but Mike had soon realised that things were not right between his parents. Arthur Mitchell was doing well and he used to tell his wife frequently that there was no need for her to have a job outside the home. He went on saying it until the day a friend asked him where his wife worked now that she'd left the cinema. Arthur had gone out, leaving Mike in the charge of the woman who cleaned the shop after closing time. When his mother had come home that evening, there had been a row of colossal proportions. The young Mike had heard her go into the bedroom and begin slamming around; afterwards, he realised that she had been packing. He had watched her leave, half hidden by his bedroom door, had seen his father start to weep and had crept into his bed, retreating beneath the blankets and telling himself that it would be all right, that everyone quarrelled, that his mother would return next day, sorry for the cruel things she had said.

He had never seen her again but it had coloured his whole idea of marriage. A mother was someone who shouted and shrieked, who was never content, no matter how hard her menfolk tried to please her. After the first week of living alone with his father, Mike had known that this was infinitely preferable to the life he had lived whilst his mother was with them. For more than half a dozen happy years Mike and his father had enjoyed both work and play and a strong bond of affection had grown between them. In all that time, Mike had watched with a jealous eye, fearful that his father might consider remarriage, but had gradually realised that his dad never showed any interest in other women. He had, he thought now, been lulled into a false sense of security. Why should he not think that things would always continue as they had since his mother had left? Fat

Mrs Evans cleaned the flat and cooked their meals, appearing at nine each morning and disappearing by four in the afternoon. Father and son went to the football match on a Saturday afternoon, to the cinema when there was something suitable showing, to visit their relatives at Christmas and Easter. Mike's friends had envied him, and though he had felt an occasional jealous pang when a mother gave one of his pals a hug, his own mother had not been a demonstrative woman, so he was not aware of missing any physical closeness.

And then, out of the blue, his father had bought the cobbler's shop and turned it into the Restawhile Café and the three females had moved into the flat above. Mike had been instantly on the alert for he could not deny that Mrs Collins was a very pretty woman, and it soon dawned on him that he was not the only one who thought so. His father went out of his way to help the Collinses. It was true that he had not, so far, actually asked Mrs Collins to go out with him, but more and more frequently he had begun to pop next door to discuss some problem that had arisen and Mike thought that this fish supper they were to share might well be the thin end of the wedge and foretell the end of what he had come to believe was a perfect bachelor existence.

At this point in his musing, Mike reached his destination and stopped, propping his bicycle against the kerb. He took the top box off the carrier, stood it down and banged hard on the knocker. He was plainly expected for the door opened almost at once and a fat woman in a flowered apron took the box from him, pressed a penny into his hand and thanked him, calling him a good lad and sympathising with him over the dreadful weather. 'Glad it's yourself and not me what's gorra toil up and down Heyworth wi' other people's greens,' she said. 'See you next week!'

Mike grinned cheerfully and waved and was soon pedalling back down Abbot Street and heading for his next drop-off point. You're probably imagining that Pa's sweet on Mrs Collins, he told himself robustly. Why, anyone can invite a pal in for fish 'n' chips on a Friday night. It don't mean a perishin' thing. But there was still a shade of uneasiness in his mind as he continued with his deliveries.

An hour later, the Collins family made their way across to the Mitchells' front door. Tina stood on tiptoe and rang the bell and presently Mike came thundering down the stairs, opened up and ushered them ahead of him. 'You're in good time; I've just come back with the fish and chips,' he informed them, his voice almost friendly. 'Dad's puttin' them into the oven to keep warm so we'll be eatin' pretty soon.'

The two families had finished their meal and were ensconced in the sitting room when Mr Mitchell glanced at the clock on the mantelpiece and went across to switch on his wireless set. 'I believe the king is going to make a speech after the news; perhaps he'll tell us the date of his coronation,' he said. 'And after that's over, you youngsters will have to amuse yourselves, whilst Mrs Collins and meself discuss our plans for the coming year.'

The three sat impatiently through the news broadcast, but when King Edward began to speak, their attention was immediately seized by his emotional tones and the news which he had to impart:

At long last, I am able to say a few words of my own . . . I want you to understand that in making up my mind I did not forget the country or the Empire which as Prince of Wales, and lately as king, I have for twenty-five years tried to serve. But you must believe me when I tell you that I have found it impossible to carry the heavy burden of respon- sibility and to discharge my duties as king as I would wish to do without the help and support of the woman I love . . . God bless you all, God save the king.

As his voice faded into silence, Tina stared from her mother's face to Mr Mitchell's. 'What does it *mean*?' she said wildly. 'I don't understand. He *is* the king . . . he's Edward VIII, Mammy told me he was. So surely he shouldn't say God save the king, because he's really saying God save me.'

There was a moment's silence before Laura Collins answered her and Tess noticed that there were tears in her mother's eyes. 'Oh, Tina, love, it's awful complicated but what it means is that King

Edward VIII is going to stand down – that's what abdicate means – and let someone else be king of England; his brother, probably.'

'But why?' Tina squeaked. 'It must be grand to be the king, so why is he going to let someone else do it?'

Tess saw her mother fish a hanky out of her sleeve and dab at her wet eyes, then take a deep breath. 'The king is in love with a lady called Wallis Simpson. She's an American and has been divorced, so the government don't think she's a suitable person to be queen of England. Edward says he can only rule properly if he's allowed to choose his own queen.'

'But he's the *king*; he can do anything he wants,' Tina wailed. 'Why doesn't he just tell the government to mind their own beastly business and leave him alone?' Another thought occurred to her and she swung round to stare at the wireless for a moment before facing her mother once more. 'Oh, Mammy, you've gorrit all wrong. The king don't want to marry a feller!'

Tess giggled and decided it was time to put her oar in. 'She's a perishin' American, chuck, and the Americans have peculiar names,' she informed her small sister. 'Wallis Simpson is a woman all right – she spells it different from the way a feller would – though why the king wants to marry her is a mystery to me. It ain't even as if she's pretty, and she certainly ain't royal. She's what they call a commoner . . .'

Tina hissed in her breath dramatically. 'It's rude to call anyone common, and how do you know this Wallis woman ain't pretty?' she asked belligerently.

'You and me collect pictures of the princesses and the Duke and Duchess of York – oh, and we might have one or two pictures of the king – but I don't remember a picture of an American woman.' She looked enquiringly at Mike. 'I suppose she wears a ten-gallon hat and them tall riding boots, like in the Wild West? I've seen 'em on the fillums.'

Mike guffawed loudly. 'D'you think all Americans are cowboys, kiddo? I seen a picture of her once in a magazine and she looked just like all the other rich folk; you know, a long silky sort o' dress, pearls round her neck and a sparkly thing in her hair.'

Tina nodded. 'All right, I can sort of see why he can't be king; 'cos she's an American I 'spect he'll have to live there.' She whirled round on Tess. 'If *he* can't be king,' she said slowly, 'then it'll have to be his brother, Mammy said, and his brother is the Duke of York. That means our princesses will have a king and queen for their dad and mam. Have I got it right, Tess?'

Tess nodded. 'You have, and if *I've* got it right, then unless the Duchess of York has a son, the Princess Elizabeth will be queen one day.'

'Cor,' Tina said inelegantly. 'Has she got it right, Mammy? And wharrabout my princess what's the same age as me? Will she be queen one day?'

Laura got to her feet. 'No she won't,' she said firmly. 'And I think this conversation has gone on long enough. We're just ordinary people, and whoever is king it won't make any difference to us.' She turned to Mr Mitchell. 'I think it's time we took a look at my books; shall we go through to the shop?'

A week later, Tess, Tina and the whole nation knew what lay ahead. Prince Albert, Duke of York, would be king, but he would take the name George and would be the sixth monarch with that name. King Edward VIII, who would now be known as the Duke of Windsor, had agreed to live abroad and never to return to Britain, and the coronation of his brother would take place on 15 May.

'We'll have a holiday off school; bound to have,' Tess said exuberantly as she and Tina made their way home a week after King Edward's shock announcement. 'We'll have more than a day, I'm sure; think what happened when the old king and queen came to open the Mersey Tunnel.'

Tina hugged herself with delight. 'Will they come to Liverpool?' she breathed. 'If so, I'll be ever so, ever so good and old Loopy Knickers will let me go and watch 'em arrive 'cos they always let the goodest girls in the class do things like that.'

'How would you know? You've never been the goodest girl in the class, as you call it,' Tess observed, smiling at her sister.

'You don't have to be the goodest to know it's always teachers' pets what gets the treats,' Tina pointed out. 'Why are you so mean to me, Teresa Collins?'

'Because you're me little sister and if I'm not mean to you, you'll get cocky,' Tess said. Tina promptly began to kick out at Tess's woollen-stockinged legs and Tess held her off, laughing. 'Sorry, sorry, sorry! I were only teasin', you silly little sausage. As I was saying, the royal family won't come to Liverpool because coronations and that have to take place in London, and don't ask me why because I don't know the reason . . . yes I do, though, it's because London is the capital of Great Britain. But I heard two of the teachers talking the other day and I think they're hoping to take a group of children down to London, either to watch the coronation itself, or to go there afterwards to see the decorations. Of course, I don't know whether the infants will go, but I don't see why Mam shouldn't take us, for a special treat, like. There's cheap day returns from Lime Street, so she wouldn't have to splash out on an overnight stay. We'll suggest it when we get home.'

Tess had meant to warn Tina not to make the suggestion whilst her mother was hard at work in the café, but she was too late. Tina flew across the kitchen to where her mother was buttering a plate of scones and began gabbling at the top of her voice, so Tess was not surprised when her mother frowned and told Tina that May wasn't until the summer, and that was a long way off. 'A couple of weeks ago all you could talk about was Christmas and how you were going to write the longest list in the world so Santa Claus would have plenty of choice,' Laura said impatiently. 'I'm not making any plans until I know whether the entire country will shut down, or whether places like cafés and restaurants will stay

111

open. Now just nip up to the flat, Tina, there's a good girl, and bring down your Rainbow Reader. Tess will be waiting on until six and I don't want you alone in the flat until then.'

'I could play out,' Tina said eagerly. 'Me pals will be there doin' all sorts. Did I tell you, Mammy, that I'm champion skipper? Helen – she's a real big girl, she's almost nine – puts my name in the skippin' rhyme 'cos I'm so quick and neat, she says.' She struck an attitude: *'I like coffee, I like tea, I like Tina in with me.'*

She made as if to slip out through the back door, but her mother was having none of it. 'Come back, my lady, and do as you're told,' she said crossly. 'Take her upstairs wi' you, Tess; she can wait whilst you change into your frock and pinny, and then she can come downstairs and sit quietly in a corner practising her reading.'

Tess grabbed her protesting little sister and the two of them hurried up to the flat, where Tina snatched her book crossly out of the bookcase and slumped on to the couch, scowling dreadfully. 'I hate you, Tess; you never even tried to tell Mammy I'd be best off wi' me pals,' she said bitterly. 'You could have said a bit of fresh air would do me good, then she might have changed her mind.'

Tess, stripping off her school clothes and dragging the black dress over her head, smothered a giggle. 'For a start, it's perishin' well freezin' out there and I don't want a little sister what's turned into an icicle,' she pointed out. 'Besides, you know what our mam's like; you're a good reader so you'll get through your book quick as a wink and then Mam will let you make a little cake or something for your tea, or she'll get the coloured pencils out of the sideboard drawer so you can use 'em on a spare bit of paper. All I'll be doing is carting heavy trays into the café and agreeing with everything the customers say; there's not much fun in that, I'm telling you.'

'No, but you get paid,' Tina said. 'I know I get me Sat'day sixpence, but it don't go far these days. I wish Mam would let me wait on and earn some cash.'

'You're all right,' Tess said, pinning the white celluloid cap on to her hair and wincing as a kirby grip scratched her skin. 'And Mam always pays you when you get the messages, so you do quite well, one way and another. Have you got your reader? Right, then we'd best get downstairs before Mam finds herself waiting on as well as doing all the cooking.'

May 1937
Tess leaned back in her seat and looked out at the passing scene as the train began to pick up speed. Next to her, Tina was already asleep, her small head lolling against her sister's arm, and on Tina's other side their mother smiled dreamily into space, her lids already drooping. Tess thanked her stars that they had managed to get seats together, for the train was full to bursting. On the rack above their heads was a great deal of necessary paraphernalia, for, as Mr Mitchell had predicted, they had had to camp on the pavement last night. It had rained towards dawn, but

the exuberant cockneys stationed all around the Collinses had said this was a good sign. 'It always rains when there's something extra special goin' on, usually in the early hours,' a young woman had informed them. 'It'll be fine for the procession itself . . . jest you see if I ain't right.' She had been, too, Tess reflected, and now she had several hours in which she could think about her wonderful day. It had been beyond her wildest expectations.

Tess had asked Laura if she could possibly take them to London for the Coronation but their mother had been doubtful. 'It will mean being away from the Restawhile for at least two days,' she had said. 'You see, crowds will take their places overnight in order to be able to watch the procession, which means we would have to go down to London the day before. Even if I did a heap of baking before we left, I can't see the waitresses coping with everything for two whole days.'

Tess had been disappointed but not surprised, and had accepted her mother's decision with a good grace, but Tina had not been so philosophical. She had taken the matter to Mr Mitchell and he had said at once that he saw no reason why the Collinses should not have a day out. 'Coronation Day is going to be a national holiday, so both the shop and the café will be closed,' he had said. 'You can go up on a late train on the fourteenth – you'll need to do that so as to get a good place – and come back on the last train on the fifteenth. I dare say you'll all be very tired – you'll probably sleep in the train coming home – but it's not every day you have the chance to watch history being made. I'll have a word with your mam.'

Tess knew that her mother had not needed much persuading, and the three of them, heavily laden, had boarded a train in the early evening, along with a great many other people who were also intent upon watching the Coronation. They had chummed up with another Liverpool family and all of them had made their way to the spot Laura had privately earmarked on the route the newspapers had printed days before. And they had seen everything, Tess thought, hugging herself. Sleeping on the pavement with blankets round them and waterproofs over their heads had been a tremendous thrill, and when full daylight had arrived so did buskers and other entertainers, performing their routines to amuse the crowd and gathering up the coins which tinkled into the road as they passed. The procession itself had been dazzling . . . golden coaches, wonderful horses, men in rich robes and women in beautiful gowns . . . but what Tess knew she would remember best and think about most frequently was what had happened after the king, the queen and the princesses had left the abbey to return to Buckingham Palace. She had thought they themselves would return to Euston station, but the crowd had had other ideas and the Collinses had been carried along, to end up only a few yards from the railings outside the palace, watching the balcony upon which, the knowing cockneys told anyone who would listen, the royal party would presently appear.

And they had done so, accompanied by a roar from the crowd. The king still wore his crown and the ermine cape which covered the magnificence of his uniform, and the queen, also still wearing her crown, was clad in a wonderful ivory gown, richly embroidered. Tess could just glimpse the long purple train which hung from her shoulders. The little princesses both wore sparkling golden crowns and white dresses, and were waving and beaming at the crowd very much as Tina was waving and beaming at them.

For they had been fortunate, or rather Tina had. As the crowd jostled, stood on tiptoe and craned towards the balcony, a dark-haired boy of fifteen or sixteen looked down at Tina's curly head and then glanced towards Tess. 'All right if I put her on my shoulder for a couple of minutes?' he asked. 'She'm too little to see much, else.'

'It's awfully kind of you . . .' Tess was beginning uncertainly, but Tina had no such inhibitions.

'Oh, yes, yes, that 'ud be grand, so it would,' she squeaked, and was hoisted shoulder high at once. The dark boy was with a friend, a taller lad with light curly hair. He grinned at Tess as Tina began a running commentary on what she could see from her superior perch. 'Shall I give you a lift 'n' all?' he offered. 'You'm only a light little thing and I've twice the strength of my pal here.'

Tess giggled. 'Thanks very much, but I'm not that short,' she said. And it was true enough. The balcony was high, and except when people in front of her stood on tiptoe, or waved their arms about, she could see pretty well.

The royal party remained on the balcony for ten or fifteen minutes but then they filed back into the palace, and Tess looked round for her mother as the dark-haired boy lowered Tina to the ground. Laura was only a few feet away, but she had quite a struggle to reach them, and by the time she had done so the two boys had disappeared. 'Oh, Mam, those fellers have gone and I meant to thank them,' Tess said, dismayed. Tina had bounced joyfully up and down on the dark boy's shoulder to say nothing of shouting in his ear; it seemed both rude and ungrateful not to have thanked him.

'Yes, it was kind of the dark-haired one to give Tina a bunk up, because she wouldn't have seen much otherwise,' Laura admitted. 'I wanted to thank him myself. But isn't the queen the loveliest thing? And that dress . . .' She turned to give Tess's hand an impulsive squeeze. 'Oh, I'm so glad we came! I wouldn't have missed this for the world, but we'd best be making our way back to Euston now. We've all this stuff to cart so it'll take us a while to get there.'

Laura had begun to shepherd the children out of the crowd but had been stopped in her tracks by a motherly woman who caught at her arm. 'Don't be in too much of a hurry to leave. Jest you get them littl'uns close up agin the railings while the crowd's beginning to relax a bit,' she had advised in a hoarse whisper. 'The royals will be out again in twenty minutes or so and it ain't every day ordinary folk like us get to see the monarch in his robes.'

She had been right, but after the second appearance Laura had insisted that they leave. 'There'll be somewhere on Euston station, or nearby, where we can get something to eat,' she had said. 'Once we're on the train I want us to be able to rest, even if we can't sleep, and no one can rest when they're thinking about their empty stomachs.'

As Laura had hoped, they had found a barrow boy selling fruit and sandwiches and had bought a supply of both, though Tess had seen her mother's eyes widen a little at the price. Then they had climbed aboard the waiting train and had taken their seats. As the train had gradually filled with other folk, also bound for Liverpool, passengers had begun to exchange reminiscences about the day they had just enjoyed. Until she fell asleep, Tina had gabbled more incessantly than anyone: how they had spent a night on the pavement, how they had eaten the sandwiches they had brought and drunk tea from their flasks. How she had swapped a cheese and pickle sandwich for an egg and cress one, how a nice lady with purple hair had insisted that she accept a scrummy slice of fruitcake, how a boy had given her a shoulder ride so she could see over the heads of the crowd . . .

But once the train had begun to move, the rocking motion had proved too much and it was not only Tina who had slid into sleep. Indeed, by the time the train drew up and a porter had raucously announced they had reached their destination, Tess herself had been on the verge of sleep. She stumbled on to the platform and turned to help her mother, for Laura's arms were full of Tina, who slumbered still. Tess returned to the carriage for their baggage and was wondering how she could possibly carry it all when strong hands took her burden from her and a jovial voice said in her ear: 'You're all right, our Tess; me and Mike will carry this and you and your mam can wake young Tina up – unless you want to take turns to carry her, of course.' It was Mr Mitchell, beaming so widely that the ends of his moustache almost reached his eyes.

Tess smiled back at him. 'Oh, Mr Mitchell, am I glad to see you,' she said thankfully. 'I don't think Tina can possibly walk; it's been quite a day and she's only a kid.'

'We're only going as far as the taxi rank,' Mr Mitchell said firmly. 'I'm not having me manageress and me favourite waitress walkin' all the way back to Heyworth Street, no siree. We'll all ride in a taxi, like royalty does; even Mike here.'

Tess smiled rather uncertainly. The armed truce that she and Mike had agreed before Christmas was still in operation, but she sometimes thought that Mike liked her no better than he had done, and was simply putting up with her. So now she glanced quickly at him to see how he was taking his father's teasing. But he had tucked the bundle of waterproofs and the blankets under his arm and was striding ahead, apparently oblivious. Tess knew her mother had offered to take Mike to London with them if he would like to go, but he had said dismissively that royalty was for women, not men. Laura had pretended to be shocked, but she had told Tess afterwards that she understood. 'It would be different if his dad were coming along as well,' she had said. 'But Mr Mitchell has to be here to see to everything. Boys don't like to be the only feller in a group of girls, you know.'

At the time, Tess had agreed with her mother, but now, as Mike pulled open the door of the nearest taxi and began to usher them in, she remembered the boy who had put Tina up on his shoulder, and the other one – cheeky devil – who had offered to do the same for her. She had guessed from their accents that they were not Londoners, which meant that they had probably travelled quite a way to see the Coronation for themselves. For some boys, at any rate, royalty was not just for women.

Danny and Phil climbed aboard the last train for Hereford and, after a lengthy search, found their mothers sitting in a compartment towards the front of the train, their paraphernalia piled on the seats between them so that Danny and Phil would not have to stand. Both women looked tired but exhilarated and happy as Danny and Phil stacked the blankets and umbrellas up on the luggage rack and then collapsed into the seats which had been saved for them. They were only just in time, for as Danny turned to his mother to ask what had happened to them when the procession was over the train jolted, slid backwards for a couple of seconds, and then began to move forward.

'We're off,' Deborah said. 'Thank goodness for that; I can't wait to get home and into bed. We've had an unforgettable day, haven't we, Daisy? Believe it or not, we actually found quite a big café opening its doors, though it had been closed all day. By then we were both desperate for a drink and a sit down, and the woman in charge was ever so nice and let us use the WC because we were both bursting, and then we had a lovely pot of tea and two toasted teacakes. We did wonder whether to make our way to Buckingham Palace because folk kept telling us that the royals always appear on the balcony after a big event like a coronation, but to tell you the truth we were really very tired, so we came straight back to the station and stayed in the ladies' waiting room until the train drew in. In fact, I believe we both snoozed a little; I know I did.'

Aunt Daisy leaned forward. 'What did you lads do?' she enquired eagerly. 'Did you get near enough to Buckingham Palace to see what was going on? You're a good deal younger than us and you weren't lugging blankets and umbrellas and that.'

'Oh, Ma, I am sorry,' Phil said remorsefully. 'We meant to come back and share the carrying of our stuff, but in a crowd like that there's small chance of going the way you want. You just get carried along. It's fighting against the tide if you try to turn back, and by the time we realised you weren't following, you'd disappeared.'

'It's all right; we understand. But did you reach the palace and see the royals on the balcony?' Daisy persisted. 'Those glass coaches are all very fine, but you don't see much detail, and those sailors, or whatever they were, who were lined up to stop the crowd from surging into the road got in the way something dreadful.'

'Yes, we got to the palace and saw them on the balcony,' Phil said. 'And Danny here rescued a maiden in distress. He hefted her on to his shoulder, because she was only six or seven years old and couldn't see anything of what was going on.' He grinned at his mother. 'I offered to give the bigger one a shoulder ride too, but she turned me down. Nice kids, I thought; I reckon they were sisters even though they weren't much alike. The littl'un on Danny's shoulder had light brown curls and the big 'un had a long black plait.'

'I don't care if they were both bald,' Daisy squeaked, exasperated. 'I want to know whether you got a good view of the king and queen, and the little princesses. What were they wearing? I know the queen was in white with a long purple cloak thing, but we couldn't see any detail from where we were standing.'

'Aunt Daisy, Phil and I don't know anything about clothes,' Danny protested, seeing his cousin's baffled expression. 'But they had beautiful golden crowns on, even the little girls.'

Daisy leaned back in her seat with a sigh. 'Oh well, at least we've done more than most people. Only I just know that the first question every woman in the village will ask is: "What were the dresses like?" and I shan't be able to tell 'em.'

Deborah smiled at her sister. 'Of course you will. You'll say that the queen wore a wonderful gown of priceless silk, richly embroidered with dazzling gems, and the little girls wore white, similar to their mother's, only not quite so rich.'

Several people in the carriage smiled at this and a motherly woman leaned over and patted Daisy's hand. 'I mean to get up early and buy me a newspaper, 'cos there's certain to be a whole issue all about the Coronation,' she said. 'You do the same, my dearie, an' everyone will think you got near enough to shake their hands. You know what folk are.'

After this, the conversation in the carriage became general. But as the train continued on its way, more and more people closed their eyes, and presently Danny followed suit. By the time they reached Oxford, where they had to change, a porter had to rouse practically everyone on board and they stumbled on to the platform looking thoroughly bewildered. Danny and Phil had to return to the carriage to get their things off the rack and Daisy had to be almost carried aboard when their connection arrived, but nobody minded; a day such as they had enjoyed was worth a little trouble.

Chapter Four

Spring 1938

Tess looked through the window of the Restawhile
Café and groaned, though not aloud, because
customers were already beginning to trickle in and
one did not show customers anything but a friendly
and smiling face. It was a truly beautiful day. The
spring sunshine made Heyworth Street look very
attractive, but though her mother had promised she
should have an hour off once the lunchtime rush was
over, today there would be small chance of enjoying
the sunshine for long. The staff were taking it in turns
to go for gas-mask fittings, so Tess's precious hour of
freedom would be spent queuing up in the dusty
church hall in order to have the ugly snout-like
contraption fitted over her head. Tina had been given
her mask in February though she had sworn that she
would rather be gassed than wear the horrible thing.
'I looks like a perishin' pig,' she had wailed tearfully.
'And that rubber band thing at the back pulls your
hair out at the roots, honest to God it does. Besides,
there ain't no war. The teachers at school keep saying
there ain't going to be a war and you've said the
same, Mam, you know you have. So why have I got
to have a gas mask? Tell me that if you can.'

She had been addressing her mother at the time

but it was Tess who had answered. 'Because bloody Hitler won't keep his word,' she had said bluntly. 'Don't you listen to the news on the wireless, you silly little girl? Them perishin' Nazis marched into Austria last month; what's to say they won't sneak across the Channel and start gassing us all in our beds?'

'That's quite enough of that, young lady,' Laura had said sharply. 'You're old enough to know better than to try to scare your little sister. And you know I don't like to hear you use bad language.' She had turned to Tina and given her a cuddle. 'It's all right, queen. The gas masks are what you might call a precaution. In other words, if a war does come – and I'm sure it won't – then everyone will be able to withstand a gas attack. See?'

Tina had leaned against her mother, glaring at Tess as she did so. 'Ye-es, I do see that, but what I don't understand is how they're goin' to do it. I mean they can't sneak into each house and puff gas into all the rooms.' She stared defiantly up at Tess. 'Go on, 'splain that away!'

Tess had smothered a giggle, thinking, not for the first time, that young Tina was sharp as a needle. 'It's had me wonderin' an' all,' she had admitted. 'But they did it in the last war, so I s'pose if they could do it then, they'll be able to do it now.' She had turned to her mother. 'What do you think, Mam?'

'I don't have time for idle conjecture, I just do as I'm told,' Laura had said briskly, smoothing a hand over Tina's shaggy curls as she spoke. 'And this little person thinks a good deal too much, so since we don't want nightmares we'll change the subject, if you please.'

Tess had bitten back an urge to say that Tina had started it and had begun to discuss their latest venture, which was a lunchtime special. They had always gone in for snacks but had not attempted a hot meal until Mr Mitchell had walked into the kitchen one day to announce that he had just ordered the very latest in catering equipment. It was a wonderful gas cooker, with two ovens and eight burners as well as an enormous grill, and it had been Tess's suggestion that they should offer their customers either a roast, complete with all the trimmings, or a steak and kidney pie, or perhaps chops, at lunchtime each day. Laura had been doubtful because it would mean employing an extra member of staff but Mr Mitchell, clearly dying to see his wonderful new acquisition begin to earn money for them, had been enthusiastic and very soon the lunchtime special was the most popular item on the menu. Despite the fact that they only served it between twelve and two, they had been forced to employ not only a second cook but also another waitress, and had bought a bain-marie in order to keep the vegetables hot. Even so, profits soared.

Now, however, Tess glanced around the café, then began to clear the tables nearest her. Today's special had been an egg and bacon flan, and since it was five past two her mother and the other two waitresses could probably manage without her. Tess returned to the big kitchen with her loaded tray and took it over to the sink. 'Gone two o'clock, so no more specials,' she called. 'Have we got much left over, Mam? If so, I'll have it for my dinner. It smells really good.'

Brenda, a married woman who was happy to come and waitress for three hours a day when her children were in school, and farmed them out at holiday times to a neighbour living a few doors away, wagged an admonitory finger at her. 'No you don't, young Tess. I were first in the queue, and there's only one slice of that flan left. But you can have some lovely mashed potato if you like . . . or beans on toast or a poached egg.'

Tess pulled a face but knew better than to argue. 'I'll have poached eggs, please, Mam. Two would be nice, with a bit of bacon on the side if there's any left.'

'Coming up,' Laura said cheerfully. 'And as soon as you've finished, you'd best go round to the church hall to get measured. Everyone else went early this morning and no one was kept waiting for longer than half an hour, so maybe you'll have some time to spend in the fresh air afterwards.' She smiled affectionately at her daughter. 'I know you hate being cooped up on a day like this. Early afternoons are always quiet, so I can do without you until half past three, say, if you want to do a bit of shopping or visit that pal of yours who works in Bunney's.'

'Thanks, Mam,' Tess said gratefully. I am lucky to work for someone like Mam, who understands her staff and tries to do what is best for them, she thought, running up the stairs and going into her bedroom to change, for she could scarcely turn up at the church hall in her uniform, with the celluloid cap pinned to her hair. Since she was now working full time and considered herself grown up, she wore her long plait in a coronet on top of her head when she went out, though for work the long black braid was simply looped up, because the coronet style got in the way of her cap. Having changed into an old jumper and skirt, Tess considered herself in the mirror. Her mother did not approve of make-up for young girls but Tess had a small lipstick hidden away in the back of her underwear drawer which she sometimes used on her day off. She was cautious in her use of it and Tina had remarked that by the time she had blotted off all the excess she looked exactly the same as she had done before applying it, but Tess thought this was just a sisterly comment aimed at putting her in her place. Anyway, the mere fact that she was wearing lipstick made her feel grown-up and sophisticated. She began to fish in her underwear drawer, but even as her fingers closed on the small cartridge she changed her mind. It was ridiculous to go and queue in the church hall looking one's best, particularly as she had worn her skirt and jumper to school and both were old and faded, so she pushed the lipstick back into its hiding place, hurried out of the bedroom, and thundered down the stairs.

Once outside Tess loitered along the pavement, glancing into shop windows as she passed and wondering what it was like to work behind a counter for someone who was not one's mother. She guessed it would be less tiring but suspected it would also be less fun, because being a waitress one grew to know one's customers, to share a joke with them and to learn a surprising amount about their lives. Tess had her favourites and knew that they, in turn, came to prefer one waitress or another. The 'special' customers were more exciting than the coffee-and-cake ones because they came from the shops and offices where they worked, were usually younger than the coffee-and-cakes, and were often male. She had seen the four young men from Alecto, the engineering company, breaking into a sprint in order to beat a group from Regal Assurance to the café and knew that this was because the table they all wanted was one of hers. It was gratifying to be popular but Tess realised that the office workers liked her because she was quick, and willing to exchange banter with them after she had delivered their orders. Some of them, she knew, thought she put a little extra on the plates of her regular customers, but this was not so, though if there were half a dozen laden plates waiting to be carried out from the kitchen she always chose the biggest portions for her own tables and supposed other waitresses did the same. Brenda, however, who had arthritic hands, preferred the lighter plates and always beamed when her 'special' customers chose the vegetarian alternative, which was usually cheese or hard-boiled eggs with a green salad.

Tess reached the church hall and was not too pleased to find that folk were queuing simply to get inside. Undecided, she watched for a moment, wondering whether to continue into the city centre and look round the shops, in the hope that the queue would lessen as the day wore on. Then she noticed that they were moving quite quickly and joined the line. Once the office workers were free to come and be measured, she realised, there would be twice as many people waiting; it was obviously better to get it over now rather than later.

The people directly in front of Tess were chatting amongst themselves, and she was just wishing that she had thought to arrange to come with her friend Liz when someone caught hold of the loop of her plait, pretended to knock on her back with it and said jovially: 'Hello 'ello 'ello, fancy seeing you! Why didn't you come down this morning to get measured, when your mam did?'

Tess whisked round and smiled at Mike Mitchell. He was no longer his father's delivery boy; for at least a year now he had been employed in an engineering works as an apprentice, and the Collinses scarcely saw him, for his new workplace was out at Aintree. Tess had passed his factory a month earlier when she and several of her friends had decided to walk the Aintree course before the Grand National was run. She had been impressed by the size of the works and had looked for Mike on the racetrack, but it would have been difficult to pick out one person amongst the crowds, mainly of men, who were also walking the course.

Tess had never been to the actual race but Mr

Mitchell had announced that he meant to go, and to take Laura along. 'You can manage just for the one day, can't you?' he had asked Tess. 'You can have Brenda in, and Zoë. That should cover the lunchtime specials.'

Tess had assured him that she would be fine, and, having studied the list of runners, had laid five shillings from the tip money she was saving towards a bicycle on a horse called Battleship. 'Since everyone's talking about the war I'll see if I can make myself a bob or two,' she had said. Mr Mitchell had pocketed her money, saying as he did so: 'Five bob each way?' which had surprised Tess more than a little; did this mean that the horses ran the race clockwise first, and anti-clockwise second? But she did not mean to show her ignorance, so merely said loftily: 'I don't mind, Mr Mitchell; you choose.'

Mr Mitchell had chuckled but said that she might do better to put it on the nose, which had mystified poor Tess as much as his comment about betting each way. However, she kept her puzzlement to herself and was glad she had done so later that day when Mr Mitchell had handed over her winnings. It had seemed a small fortune at the time and Tess had celebrated by spending two shillings on a box of chocolates and a trip to the cinema for herself and Liz.

But Mike was waiting for an answer to his question. 'Mam and I don't usually leave the café at the same time,' Tess explained now. 'But how come you know when my mam was measured? Come to that, why are you here and not up in Aintree?'

'Questions, questions,' Mike said, pulling a face at her. 'I know when your mam came down to be measured because my dad came at the same time.' He grinned down at Tess. 'When I were young I didn't much like my dad being so friendly with your mam, but after all this time – lordy, it must be three years – I've decided that Dad really meant it when he said they were just pals like. I know they go about a lot together, but why not? They gerron ever so well, and your mam looked real pretty in that sort of smoky blue dress she wore when they went to the New Year's Eve dance at the Grafton together. And no one goes to a dance by their selves, do they?'

'True,' Tess said thoughtfully. She had known, naturally, that her mother had gone out on New Year's Eve, but since she and Tina had gone over to Aunt Millie's to see the New Year in with their cousins she had not worried much over her mother's whereabouts, had not even asked Laura where she had been when they met at breakfast next morning. Now she looked up at Mike. 'To be honest, I never knew they had been dancing together. I'd have thought they were too old.'

Mike snorted derisively. 'My dad's forty-one and your mam's in her mid-thirties, isn't she? That ain't old, not really. Folk get married at that age, sometimes.'

Tess felt herself beginning to bristle. She liked Mr Mitchell all right – he was a kind and generous employer – but that did not mean she wanted him for a stepfather. Nor did she much fancy having a stepbrother thrust upon her. However, now she thought about it, she realised that Mr Mitchell's friendship with her mother had made Tess's own life a lot easier. She could go to the cinema or the theatre with a pal without feeling guilty because she had not invited her mother to accompany them. Shopping trips with girlfriends were perfectly acceptable because if Mam wanted to shop, then she would go either with her old friend Ena or with Mr Mitchell. Tess could remember when she, too, had resented Mr Mitchell's obvious pleasure in her mother's company because she feared it might lead to something warmer, but it had not happened and now, for the first time, Tess wondered why. If they had gone to a dance together, it must mean, surely, that there was more than casual friendship between them. Yet there had never been, to her knowledge, any question of marriage.

The queue shuffled forward another few feet and Tess decided to satisfy her curiosity. 'If your dad really does like my mam, enough to take her dancing, then I wonder why he's never asked her to marry him?' she said bluntly. 'Or has he? Do you know, Mike?'

'Oh, I know all right, and I should have thought you'd have guessed,' Mike said offhandedly. 'My dad's still married and someone once told me you can't get a divorce unless you can find the other party. My mam went off wi' a sailor, as I guess you know, and the pair of 'em have simply disappeared. They could be dead for all we know . . . but I can't say

I'm bothered one way or t'other. I'm not jealous of your mam any more like I was when I were a nipper. In fact I'm grateful to her, because before you Collinses moved in next door my dad were often miserable and bad-tempered. When I gorrin from school I used to pop into the shop before I even went up to the flat, to see where his moustache was, and if it were . . .'

Tess gave a crow of laughter. 'You mean if it were on his face or lyin' on the counter?' she asked, still chuckling. 'Where his moustache was, indeed! You ain't just got a screw loose, you're tenpence in the shilling!'

Mike grinned. 'Yes, all right, I asked for that one,' he said. 'But haven't you ever noticed? When Dad is happy his moustache springs up, the ends almost touchin' his eyes, but when he's cross or miserable the ends droop down towards his chin. I'm tellin' you, that moustache used to be like a bad-weather warning. Thanks to your ma, it's almost always on the up and up now, and has been for ages.'

At this point, the queue carried them inside the church hall and Tess remembered her second question. 'You've not said why you're here and not in Aintree,' she reminded him. 'Don't say you've left your lovely job! I heard your dad telling my mam that one of these days, when your apprenticeship is over and you've passed all your exams, you'll do awfully well.'

Mike punched her lightly on the shoulder. 'Haven't you ever heard of a day off?' he asked derisively. 'And anyway, you're supposed to go to the centre nearest where you live, so I'm down for this one.' He bowed mockingly and Tess realised, with some surprise, that he was not a bad-looking fellow at all. In fact, she could imagine that some girls might find him attractive, though she did not think that she was one of them. He was tall and broad-shouldered, but the main change was in his face. The roundness had disappeared, showing high cheek-bones and a jutting, determined chin, whilst the eyes she had once likened to gooseberries were lively and full of humour. His mouth was firm, though, like his father's moustache, it curved upwards most of the time.

The queue shuffled forward once more and very soon they reached the head of it. Tess found the experience quite as horrid as her sister had said it would be. The inside of the mask reeked of rubber and made her remember the one that had been put over her face when she had had a tooth pulled out as a small child. And the rubber strap that went round the back of her head tugged at her hair just as Tina had warned her it would. She was glad when the fitting was over and she and Mike were free to leave, gas-mask cases over their shoulders. As they left the hall Mike pushed a hand up through his reddish curls and let out his breath in a long whistle. 'Phew! Well, now that's over, how about you an' me going to the flicks? There's a good film on at the Lecky Palace. Or are you due back in work any minute?'

Tess was so astonished that she could only stare.

Could this count as being asked for a date? No, it could not possibly be any such thing; after all, she was only just fifteen and she and Mike were not even what you might call friends. He was not looking at her, which made it easier to reply, casually: 'I've got to be back in the café no later than half past three. Mam said she could manage till then but fair's fair and she let me leave at two o'clock, so I will have had half an hour longer than usual. Sorry, but it's not possible.'

'It don't matter,' Mike said. 'But I hate going to the flicks by meself, particularly in the afternoons when the place is half empty. Come to that, I hate going by meself in the evenings an' all. You finish at six, don't you? We could go this evening, if you want.'

Tess hesitated, astonished at the suggestion, but before she could say a word Mike had flushed to the roots of his hair and begun to explain.

'Look, if you've got other plans, you've only got to say,' he said gruffly. 'It's no big deal, it's just that it's me day off and all me pals seem to be in work, and if I hang about at the shop Dad'll have me counting oranges or polishin' apples. If you want, we could take Tina as well; it's the sort of film she'd enjoy.'

'Take Tina?' Tess squeaked. 'Have you ever been in the cinema with Tina, Mike? She wriggles, she talks in a loud voice, she wants to go the ladies' every other minute and she bobs up and down so the people behind always complain. I'm telling you, I'm downright glad I don't even have to take her to the Saturday rush any more. She goes with a heap of horrible little pals – her gang – and they like to sit in the balcony so's they can spit through the projection light and see it come up on the screen. Believe me, if you had a little sister of your own you wouldn't even suggest it.'

Mike laughed. 'Oh, all right. I'll sort oranges for me dad instead,' he said, grinning. He glanced at the clock above the chemist's shop as they passed. 'I dursn't offer to mug you to a cup of tea and a bun in your own café 'cos I reckon the moment we walk in the door your mam will send you upstairs to change into your uniform.' They were within a few yards of the café and now Mike drew her to a halt. 'So we'd best go our separate ways. Ta-ra, queen.'

Tess opened her mouth to say cheerio and found, to her own astonishment, that her mouth had other ideas. 'Hang on a sec, Mike,' she said urgently. 'I never said I wouldn't go to the pictures this evening, I just said I didn't want to take Tina. What's the film?'

Mike turned back towards her, a slow grin dawning. 'It's *A Day at the Races* with the Marx Brothers,' he said. 'D'you remember me old pal Jacky, him what works as a porter on Lime Street station? Well, he's been to see it three times 'cos he says it's a real laugh. Wharrabout it then, queen? D'you fancy six penn'orth o' dark?'

'No I don't,' Tess said quickly, beginning to bristle. 'Not if that means the back seats of the stalls and a lot of old nonsense.'

Mike struck his head three times with the back of his hand, though Tess saw he was still grinning.

'Sorry, sorry, sorry,' he said. 'I shouldn't have said that . . . didn't mean it. It's just what the fellers at work say. What time shall I pick you up?'

'Tell you what, come into the café at six, when we close,' Tess said. 'Mam will give us our tea; she's awful good like that.'

Mike's grin widened. 'That'll be grand,' he said joyfully. 'See you at six!'

Tess spent the rest of the afternoon wondering whether she had gone temporarily insane. She had agreed to go to the pictures with a boy almost two years older than herself; a boy, furthermore, whom she had regarded as an enemy for years. She would have to tell her mother, of course, but since she had been mad enough to invite him to join her in the café for tea, she could not expect to keep her madness a secret from anyone. Tina would tease her unmercifully, pretending to believe that Mike was her boyfriend, telling everyone that her sister had a feller at last. Tess groaned to herself and was grateful to her mother for the matter-of-fact way she accepted the news that Mike was going to pop in for tea before they went on to the Electric Palace to see a film.

To her pleasure, Laura Collins merely said that it would do her good to get out and that, since his father owned the café, Mike had a perfect right to pop in for a meal whenever he wished. Tina immediately began to caper and jeer, making kissing noises and remarking, in swooning accents: 'Oh, Mike, you're me first sweetheart. I shall kiss you all over, even your horrid red hair . . .'

Tess rushed at her sister but Laura was before her. 'You're being extremely silly, Tina,' she said coldly. 'Tess and I don't say stupid things when you go off to the Saturday rush with Harry and Ron, and I don't want folk thinking that Tess has a boyfriend, because she's only fifteen. You've both known Mike for years so it's perfectly natural for him and Tess to go to the cinema together and I won't have you making trouble; understand?'

She had seized Tina and held her still, staring down into her daughter's small face until Tina nodded sulkily. 'All right, all right, I won't say nothin',' she promised. 'I won't even tell nobody, if that's what you want.'

'It is,' Laura said, releasing her small prisoner. 'Now off you go, young lady, and play with your pals, but mind you're back here before closing time.'

Tina danced out of the café and Tess picked up a tray and went out to clear tables. She half expected to see her sister hanging about outside in order to pull faces at her through the large plate glass window, but there was no sign of her, and very soon the teatime rush started and Tess became too busy to worry about her sister's reaction to her news.

Tess had expected that she and Mike would have their tea in the flat, but her mother must have spoken to Mr Mitchell at some time during the afternoon, for while Tess was closing up she said airily: 'Don't lock the door yet, chuck, because not only is Mike having tea with us, but Mr Mitchell's coming along as well. It seemed foolish for him to make a solitary meal up

139

in his flat when his son was down here, eating with us. So he'll be round as soon as he's finished cashing up for the day, and I told him the front would be unlocked since that was the way Mike would be coming.'

So it was a real family party which gathered round the staff table at the back of the café. Far from offering everyone tea and a sandwich, Laura had cooked a plateful of sausage rolls and another of individual meat pies. Tess asked her whether such largesse was to be accompanied by bread and butter but Laura, smiling, shook her head. 'No, because Mr Mitchell is going to buy a big paper of chips and bring them with him,' she said gaily. 'To tell you the truth we're doing all this to butter you up, young Tess, because Mr Mitchell and meself want to go to the cinema tomorrow evening. Which means, my love, that we're going to have to ask you to stay in with Tina.'

'Oh, Mammy, if it's a funny film why can't I go as well?' Tina wailed. 'If it's really funny then it's probably a U certificate. Oh, you might take me as well. I'd be ever so good, honest to God I would.'

'You go to the cinema every week on a Saturday morning,' Laura said repressively. 'And the last time I took you to the pictures you dragged me to the lav half a dozen times so that I lost track of the plot. And you kept whining that you were bored and didn't understand why everyone else was laughing. No, Tina, your company at the cinema is something I can well do without.'

Tina giggled. 'You should see us on a Saturday; we

have a grand time, so we does. The fillums is always good, cowboys or comedies, but we're often so busy we don't see the half.'

Laura sighed. 'I shan't ask you what you're busy doing,' she said resignedly. 'I shall simply thank my lucky stars that you won't be with us tomorrow night.'

Before Tina could answer, the café door opened and Mr Mitchell and Mike came in, Mr Mitchell carrying a large newspaper-wrapped parcel. Tess and her mother immediately rushed into the kitchen to fetch the warmed plates and the dishes of sausage rolls and meat pies, and very soon they were all tucking in. When Tess and Mike left for the cinema, they were comfortably full and felt at ease in one another's company, having shared both the meal and a great many laughs.

Just before they had set off, Tess realised, rather belatedly, that though Mike had asked her to go to the cinema with him, he had not actually offered to pay the admittance charge, so she had taken the tips from her apron and shoved them into her coat pocket, thinking, rather apprehensively, that she would look a great fool paying for her ticket in pennies and ha'pennies. But she was spared the humiliation. Mike paid for two one and ninepennies, and when he slid into the seat beside her informed her that he had bought a quarter of Everton mints and a quarter of sherbet lemons since he had once heard her expressing a preference for those sweets.

For some reason, Tess found this infinitely

comforting. It was such a very unloverlike thing to say. She had heard older girls talking about their dates and the hand holding and squeezing of knees which had followed, but such carryings-on had been preceded by boxes of chocolates, not bags of sticky sweets, so it seemed to her that, though Mike might be almost seventeen, he still regarded her as being too young for such shenanigans. And indeed, nothing could have been less amorous than his behaviour in the cinema. He did not once take her hand, far less slip an arm about her shoulders, and when he bought choc ices in the interval he spotted one of his workmates and introduced Tess to him as 'me next-door neighbour'. In fact by the time they left the cinema, Tess thought she could not have asked for a pleasanter companion. He had laughed uproariously at the Marx Brothers' antics, as had she, but had remained quiet and intent during the B feature, which Tess really appreciated.

When they left the cinema it was already dark, and when they came to cross the busy road Mike took her arm and steered her to the opposite pavement. Tess thought his behaviour had been so exemplary that he deserved a little treat, so she tucked her hand into the crook of his arm and, when he took her down the jigger and into the café's back yard, would actually have accepted a kiss on the cheek as being a fair return for a truly delightful evening. But Mike watched her unlock the back door, gave her a quick pat on the shoulder and bade her goodnight, turning away and crossing the yard again at a lope. Tess felt a slight stab of chagrin, then rebuked herself. He had said he simply wanted company, he had promised that there would be no funny stuff, and now he was ending the evening as any friend would. Hastily, she ran back across the yard. 'Thanks for a grand evening, Mike,' she called softly.

'Any time,' Mike called back. 'See you, Tess.'

'Mike, I like you right well, you know I do – I reckon we've come a long way since last April – but if you keep talking about the war as though it were going to start tomorrow, you and me will fall out. Didn't you *hear* Mr Chamberlain's speech on the wireless? And there were all those pictures in the newspapers of the old feller waving the peace agreement and shaking hands with Hitler. Peace in our time, he said, and I reckon he knows a lot more'n you do.'

It was a bright October day and Mike and Tess had taken the ferry over to Woodside, determined to enjoy the fine weather while it lasted. Then they had caught a bus, alighting from it deep in the country-side, for Mike was a great walker and Tess enjoyed the exercise, though since she was on her feet all day in the café she also enjoyed having a prolonged lunch or tea in one of the several farmhouses which catered for walkers.

Now, however, she and Mike were perched on a stile overlooking a bridle path through a broad, sloping meadow. The path led down to where a stream meandered slowly along, overhung by trees whose leaves were already beginning to curl crisply as autumn advanced. And they were arguing because Mike was certain that war was coming and Tess could not bear to talk about it. All through the Civil War in Spain she had tried to avoid the reports in the newspapers which told such horrific tales of the mass bombings and killings which had taken place in that war-torn country, and the thought that something similar might occur in Britain if war with Germany actually happened terrified her. But the Spanish Civil War was over, thank God, she reminded herself, and the British volunteers were to be allowed home, though at first General Franco had been reluctant to let them go.

But now Mike was staring at her with incredulity. 'After all you've read in the papers and heard on the wireless, you're still like a perishin' ostrich, burying your head in the sand,' he said reproachfully. 'Don't think I want war, Tess, but it's plain daft to pretend it ain't comin'. The bleedin' Nazis marched into Austria months ago and the RAF were recruiting soon after that. Then the government bought a thousand Spitfire fighters. What do you think they wanted them for? To make pretty patterns in the sky?'

Tess gave a reluctant laugh. 'I'm not burying my head, not really,' she said. 'And I suppose I do know that war is coming, but oh, Mike, it scares me most horribly. And I know you're interested in the air force because your dad told me when they had that recruiting campaign you went straight round and got all the information leaflets and things. I bet if you'd been old enough you'd have signed on and they

144

would have sent you away, abroad maybe.' She picked up Mike's hand and squeezed his fingers gently. 'I feel we've only just got to know each other, really, and I don't want you to be bundled off to some other part of the world. I mean, look what happened in Spain! And one of my customers was saying that if war does come, the Huns will bomb the ports, and that means us.'

Mike squeezed her hand hard, then let go of it and slung his arm round her shoulders. 'All the more reason to be prepared,' he said. 'Now let's gerron with this walk else we shan't reach Mrs Mimms's farmhouse in time to bag the biggest slice of steak and kidney pud. An' I promise I won't talk about the war any more today. Will that satisfy you?'

'Yes, of course it will,' Tess said, jumping off the stile and beginning to walk along the dusty lane. 'Thanks, Mike. You are kind to me.'

Mike chuckled and took her hand, pretending to bite it. 'It's all an act to lull you into a false sense of security, but later, when it's dark, I'll turn into a vampire and gobble you all up,' he said. 'Oh, Tess, I don't want to fight the Germans, honest to God I don't, and I don't want to leave you either, not now we're gettin' on so well.'

'You promised you wouldn't talk about war,' Tess said, and punched him in the stomach. Mike declared that he had not mentioned the word war, and pulled her pigtail. Tess retaliated and the two of them continued to laugh and squabble until they reached the farmhouse.

'Steak and kidney pud; I thought as much,' Mike said contentedly as they took their seats. 'And treacle tart for afters! It makes walking worthwhile, don't it, Tess?'

Spring 1939

Laura was doing a big bake in the café kitchen, for now that the place was so busy she often spent Sunday simply filling up the cake tins and preparing meat pies, sausage rolls and fruit flans for the week ahead. Tess was always very good and offered to help, but now that spring had arrived at last Laura thought it only fair that her daughter should have a proper day off, which she could spend either with Mike or with her friend Liz. Tina had a great many little friends and in fine weather they all played in the yard or the jigger, or went down to the recreation ground at the end of Mere Lane. During the winter, Laura had allowed them to play in the living room of the flat provided they did no damage and behaved themselves.

Today being a fine one, Tina and her pals could be heard laughing and shouting in the yard, and Laura, glancing at the clock, knew that any minute now her daughter would come in to ask, plaintively, if they might have some buns and lemonade for their elevenses. Perhaps this would be the best moment, Laura reflected, to break the news she wished to impart to her younger daughter, for Tina had gone off with her pals immediately after breakfast. Laura had told Tess, of course, and guessed that Mr

Mitchell would have told Mike; no doubt the two of them would talk of little else, for it had been Mike's intention to take Tess to visit a small fair which had set up on a field not far from the city.

For Mr Mitchell had finally obtained a divorce despite not being able to trace his wife. He had done everything his solicitor had advised, advertising widely for news of her, and when this had proved fruitless had applied for a decree on the grounds that she was missing, presumed dead.

Laura was smiling as she swung open the door of the first oven and drew out the pies, cooked to a delicate golden brown. Arthur was a good man and did not deserve the treatment he had received from his wife, or rather his ex-wife now that the divorce had been made absolute. And the very first thing Arthur had done when his solicitor had told him he was free to do so had been to ask Laura to marry him.

Laura lined up the cooked pies to cool on the big wire racks and replaced them in the oven with the next batch for baking. It would be foolish to pretend that she had not expected his proposal, for they had talked of the possibility of marrying for almost two years, but nevertheless, she thought now, Arthur had made it a moving and tender moment, perhaps all the more tender because in the past they had had to pretend complete indifference to one another. The solicitor had told him that if it was suspected that Arthur himself was in a relationship, then the authorities could deny him a divorce.

Laura knew that the news of her impending

marriage had not come as any sort of shock to Tess, for she told her mother that she had been expecting it for ages. 'And I couldn't be more pleased, Mam, because me and Mike reckon you and his dad were made for each other,' she had said. 'But I hope you don't want me to be a bridesmaid; I think that would be going a bit too far, don't you?'

'Yes, I agree with you, especially since both Arthur and myself have been married before, so can't have a church wedding,' Laura had said. 'In fact we shall be married very quietly in a register office. We shan't have a honeymoon, not with everything so – so uncertain, but I shall ask the waitresses to close the café at two in the afternoon on our wedding day, and stay behind so that we can all enjoy a wedding breakfast.'

'That'll be grand,' Tess had said, and Laura had gone on to explain other arrangements, all of which had thrilled Tess, though she did say, rather apprehensively, that she hoped no one would expect her to think of Mike as a brother. 'He's me first boyfriend. I know you think I'm too young to be serious, but I can't imagine ever liking anyone else as much as I like Mike,' she had said. 'I reckon he don't think of me like a sister, what's more.'

Laura had smiled to herself, for though she believed Tess to be truly fond of Mike she remembered all too clearly how her daughter had once regarded him – and all other boys for that matter – as someone to be treated with caution, as though he were of a different species. She had been the same until she had met and married her darling Alf. She still had a photograph of him in the little gold heart-shaped locket that she wore for best, still had a mental picture of him on their wedding day. He had been laughing down at her, a wing of black hair falling across his brow, his blue eyes tender with love. Tess had inherited his looks and colouring, but Laura told herself that her daughter was much healthier than Alf had ever been, for her husband had been delicate from a child. He had begun to suffer from chest infections even before Tess was born.

Outside in the yard, Laura heard Tina's shrill little voice shout: 'C'mon, Harry, Ron . . . I reckon it must be elevenses time,' and then the back door shot open and the three youngsters tumbled into the room. Harry was twelve, a sturdy dark-haired boy with rosy cheeks, and Ron was small and fair, with a mischievous grin. Laura liked them both – though she knew Tess referred to them as right little hell-raisers – but at this moment what she most wanted was Tina's attention, so she plied the boys with cakes and mugs of lemonade and then shooed them out into the yard. 'I want a word with my daughter, fellers,' she told them. 'It won't take but a minute, and then I'll send her out to you and you can go on with your game.'

'What have I done wrong this time?' Tina wailed, eyeing the back door as though it opened on to the Promised Land. 'What's up now, Mam? It weren't me wharrever anyone says! Nor it weren't Harry or

Ron.' Her face grew pink with passion. 'We've been in the yard since breakfast, playing quiet as you like. It couldn't have been us.'

Laura opened her mouth to contradict this blatant falsehood, for the three children had cleared off almost as soon as breakfast was finished and had only just returned to the yard, but decided not to allow herself to be distracted.

'Do be quiet, Tina,' she said crossly. 'I don't know what you've been up to and I don't want to know. I've – I've got something to tell you, some rather nice news. If you'd not rushed out so quickly after breakfast, I'd have told you and Tess at the same time, but as it is, you can just sit down and listen for once.'

'Oh, so you told Tess; Tess always knows everything first. It ain't fair,' Tina said, her eyes beginning to sparkle. 'Just because she's the eldest . . .'

'Will you be quiet for a moment,' Laura shouted. Really, the child was impossible. 'If you must have the word without the bark, Mr Mitchell and me's getting married.'

'Oh! But I thought Mr Mitchell *was* married,' Tina said. 'Can you be married twice, Mam?'

Laura sighed deeply. 'Mr Mitchell has got a divorce from his wife because no one can find her, so it's possible that she's dead,' she said, separating each word clearly from the last. 'That means Mr Mitchell will be your stepfather, but you won't mind that, I dare say.'

'No, I shan't mind; he's nice is Mr Mitchell,' Tina said. 'Mam, if he's to be my stepfather shall we be able to use his bathroom? I've always wanted to have a go in a real bath with taps and that. It 'ud be much more fun than trying to wash properly in that little old tin thing you stand in front of the kitchen stove on a Friday night.'

Laura could not help smiling to herself. The way to a man's heart was said to be through his stomach; clearly, the way to Tina's was via mod cons such as the joys of a bathroom. 'They've got an indoor lavatory as well; that's the little room right next door to the bathroom. You'll be able to use that during the night if you're caught short, instead of your old jerry. And it'll mean you and Tess having a room each instead of having to share with me,' she added, for she knew how the two girls squabbled over having to share not only a room but also a bed, to say nothing of the rather small wardrobe.

Tina stared at her, eyes positively popping. 'D'you mean to say the Mitchells has four bedrooms in their flat?' she asked incredulously. 'Well, I never knew that!'

'No, no, they've only the two bedrooms,' Laura said hastily. 'The way we've planned it is that you will have our present bedroom for your very own, and Tess will have our present living room as her bedroom. What do you think of that?'

Tina pulled a face. 'It's a bleedin' long way to go for a piddle. It 'ud be quicker to use the lavvy in the yard rather'n walk all the way round to Mr Mitchell's front door. And then we'd probably wake you thunderin' up the stairs.'

Laura giggled; she couldn't help it. Tess had raised none of these objections but it was typical of Tina to look at the advantages and disadvantages from her own point of view. 'I'm sorry, darling, I haven't explained very well,' she said. 'We're going to knock a hole in the wall between our flat and Mr Mitchell's, and put a door in it so you and Tess can come through to use the bathroom and the lav whenever you want. How does that appeal to you?'

Tina considered for a moment, then she gave her mother a broad grin. 'It's grand, really grand,' she said joyfully. 'We'll be able to use their kitchen so we shan't have to cart our meals upstairs any more. And I bet Mr Mitchell will let us have all the fruit we want. Of course, Mike's got a proper job now, but when he were my age he got a whole bob for pocket money. I 'spect Mr Mitchell will want to give me pocket money, 'specially when I tell 'im you only give me sixpence and you make me pay for me own seat at the Sat'day rush.'

'I don't think we ought to start discussing pocket money . . .' Laura began, but she was interrupted.

'What'll we call him, Mam? Not Daddy! Norreven Dad, 'cos he ain't our father. Oh, I know I never called our dad anything, but I'd feel right daft saying Daddy to Mr Mitchell! And what'll Mike call you?'

'We've agreed that you shall call him Uncle Arthur and Mike's going to call me Auntie Laura,' her mother said. 'Is that all right by you? And you've not asked me when we're getting married, or where for that matter.'

'Oh, I never thought,' Tina said. 'But I bet it'll be soon. Mammy, will you have to *kiss* Mr Mitchell?' She frowned darkly at her mother. 'I hope no one's expectin' me to kiss that moustache 'cos I won't do it. Nor I won't kiss 'orrible Mike neither.'

'Tina, you like Mike, and you like Mr Mitchell,' Laura said reproachfully. 'As for kissing, I'm sure neither Uncle Arthur nor Mike will expect it. And for your information, we're getting married in a month's time in the register office. Do you want to be a bridesmaid? Only I'm not getting married in white so I thought I'd just buy you and Tess something really pretty, but not bother with bouquets or satin slippers, or anything of that nature. And now, if you've no more questions, you might as well join Harry and Ron because I've still got quite a lot of cooking to do.'

Tina hurtled to the back door but stopped with her hand on the knob. 'No I *don't* want to be a bridesmaid; bridesmaids is soppy,' she said scornfully. 'Is it all right for me to tell the fellers, Mam? Only I'm going to have to practise saying Uncle Arthur, and if I don't tell 'em they'll think I've gone mad.'

Laura was far too relieved at Tina's acceptance of the situation to object to her daughter's telling everyone within hearing that her mother was about to become Mrs Mitchell. 'Yes, you might as well tell your pals; it'll save us putting an announcement in the paper,' she said rather sarcastically, for she had often told Tina that her voice was loud enough to qualify her as a town crier. 'And I'm doing lunch early today so Tess and Mike can have the afternoon to themselves. You and I will go window-shopping to see if we can find something suitable for you to wear . . .' But her last words were lost in the slamming of the door as her youngest flew off to join her playmates.

Alone in the kitchen once more, Laura checked the oven, decided that the pies could do with another ten minutes, and began to make the pastry for the sausage rolls. She was just rolling it out when the back door opened once more. She looked up impatiently, thinking that it must be Tina, but it was Arthur, beaming all over his face and tiptoeing into the room as though he suspected that hasty movements might ruin pastry. Laura dusted off her hands and went quickly towards him, reflecting that it was bliss not to have to hide their feelings for each other any longer. She began to tell him that she had now broken their news to both girls, but had scarcely begun to speak before he had taken her in his arms and started to kiss her. Laura felt the warmth rise in her cheeks and rejoiced in the embrace, thinking how very lucky she was. No one could be kinder or more understanding than my fiancé, she thought, as they drew apart and the morning sunlight glinted off the three small diamonds on the third finger of her left hand. She and Alf had never dreamed of spending hard-earned money on an engagement ring, but it was different for Arthur. He had no need to scrimp and save, and had insisted that she should have an engagement ring. They had gone together to Beaverbrooks on Church Street and after some quiet conversation between Arthur and the shop assistant a tray of rings had been produced – not a price in sight, to Laura's secret relief – and she had been bidden to choose anything she liked. After trying on practically every ring – that had been a treat in itself – she had decided to go for the diamond hoop. It still felt a little strange on her finger and she knew she ought to take it off when making pastry, but at the moment she loved it too much to remove it even for half an hour.

'Well, sweetheart? I gather you've told the girls. How did they take it?' Arthur said; he looked a little anxious and Laura hastened to reassure him.

'They were fine. I think Tess had guessed that we meant to get married as soon as we could legally do so and she was really pleased for us. Tina was pleased too, I think.' She chuckled. 'Especially since she'll be able to use your bathroom . . . and the smallest room in the house, of course. Oh, and I'd better warn you that she intends to see if she can wangle an extra bob a week pocket money out of you. She says it's what you gave Mike when he was her age. I meant to tell her what a help Mike has always been to you but she shot off before I could say a word, to share the news with her horrid little pals. I know you're rather fond of her, Arthur, but I do think she should work for any pocket money she gets, over and above her Saturday sixpence, so mind you stand firm.'

Arthur looked rueful but said he would try, then added: 'I told Mike this morning, just before he went off to meet Tess. I think he was really pleased, but fellers of his age don't show their feelings much and of course he'll be leaving home one of these days, so what we do won't affect him for long.'

'That's true; Tess must realise that she won't be living with us for ever, too,' Laura said. 'Are your ears burning, Arthur my love? Because I reckon Mike and Tess will be talking of nothing but our wedding and the changes it will make in their lives.'

Mike had bought two return tickets on the Overhead Railway, telling Tess as they climbed aboard that it should be an interesting ride since, according to his pal, the docks were crowded with shipping. 'We'll get out the other end and have a bit of a walk along the shore, because I've something to tell you,' Mike said, as they found themselves seats and settled down. Normally, the carriage would have been crowded, but because today was Sunday there were only a few people dotted here and there, mainly folk like themselves, enjoying an outing and a good look at the various craft which seemed to fill every dock.

Tess stared at her companion. 'You've something to tell me? You don't imagine that my mam hasn't already told me that she and your dad are getting married, do you?' she asked incredulously. 'Because if so, you couldn't be more wrong. She could scarce wait for us to finish breakfast before she began to gabble. And she were bubbling over with excitement. I don't think she was even worrying over whether I'd be pleased or not. Poor Mam, she and your dad –

only Mam says I'm to call him Uncle Arthur – have waited a long time for this moment. I reckon they'll be happy as sandboys, don't you?'

'Yeah, I reckon so,' Mike said. He looked rather surprised, as though their happiness was something he had taken for granted. 'It's about time something went right for me dad. I've never said much about me mam but I'm telling you, she led him the devil of a dance. I were only a kid when she left but I already knew she went out with fellers what Dad knew nothing about. And she were always snitching money out of the till, though God knows me dad's never been mean and shelled out whenever she asked.'

Tess nodded wisely. 'My mam and your dad have never mentioned your mother or what happened, but of course you can't stop the neighbours from gossiping, and I've heard all sorts since I've been working in the café. But that's past and best forgotten. Mam says they'll be married in a register office and thank heaven they don't expect me and Tina to be bridesmaids.' She grinned at her companion, her eyes twinkling with mischief. 'So it looks like you won't have to be a pageboy either,' she finished.

Mike grinned back. 'There, wharra disappointment. I can just see meself in a little blue satin costume, with long white stockings and pompoms on me shoes,' he said. 'But of course I knew your mam would have told you all about the wedding. This is quite different news. The fact is, queen, I've been and gone and put me name down for the Royal Air Force. I reckon if I join up early, I'll have a better chance of getting an interesting trade. Why, I might even get took on as aircrew. Me sight is twenty-twenty, you know – that means just about the best – and I'm pretty fit. They told me when I applied that it might be a good few months before I'm took on, but I wanted you to know how things stood.' He put out a hand and took Tess's, interlacing their fingers and rocking her hand to and fro whilst looking anxiously into her face. 'I know you hate the thought of war, queen, but it seemed the right thing to do. What d'you think?'

Tess took a deep, steadying breath and tried to smile, though she guessed from the look in Mike's eyes that it was a pretty feeble effort. Ever since the Nazis had marched into Prague, she had been expecting something of the sort to happen and had known, what was more, that she must accept the inevitable. Everyone seemed to acknowledge that war was coming, and at sixteen years old she was no longer a child and should support Mike in every way possible. So she returned his hand squeeze and said with as much fortitude as she could muster: 'You've done the right thing, Mike, I know you have, even though I'm going to miss you.'

'What'll you do when war comes? Not that it'll concern girls, I don't suppose – though women fought in Spain during the Civil War.'

'I don't know,' Tess said vaguely. 'I used to think I'd join the women's air force but I'm not qualified for any of the things they need. I've never worked in an office in my life and I'd be useless as a driver because I've never even been in a car as a passenger. But anyway, by the time I'm old enough, the war could easily be over.'

Mike snorted. 'That's what they said about the last lot, and it went on for years,' he pointed out. 'Tell you what, love, you join the air force and perhaps we'll get posted together.' He grinned at her, his face full of mischief. 'When I'm doing my Red Baron act and shooting down the Huns, then you can be me right-hand woman and service my Spitfire's engine whenever it's not in use, 'cos I've always fancied being a fighter pilot.'

He laughed, and Tess laughed with him. Teasing each other, talking about the war as though it were a great adventure, made it seem less terrible somehow. She opened her mouth to cap his joke with one of her own, but at that moment the train drew to a halt and Mike pulled her to her feet. 'Now for a walk along the shore,' he said breezily. 'And when we get back to the Pier Head, I'll treat you to char and a wad; that's what they call tea and a bun in the air force. No one can't say I'm mean; generous to a fault, that's me.'

Chapter Five

Herefordshire, spring 1939

Danny was sitting alone on the bus today, contemplating the passing scene and wishing that Sophie was beside him so that he could tell her what he had been doing these past two days. He had told his parents that he had to go to London for a couple of days to see an engineering exhibition which was being held at the Science Museum, but in actual fact he had gone to Adastral House, the headquarters of the Royal Air Force, for an interview and a medical examination. He had applied to join the air force a good twelve weeks ago, but had guessed they had been inundated with applicants, ever since the Nazis had marched into Austria. There was no more talk of '*if* there's a war' because everyone, or everyone that Danny knew, had accepted the fact that Hitler simply had to be stopped before he completely overran Europe.

Danny had been pretty honest and had told his parents that he meant to join the air force but they had wanted him to finish his matriculation examinations first. His father had actually said that farming would be doubly important when war came because it would put a stop to the cheap foreign imports which had been strangling British farming for the best part of the decade. He had said he thought farmers would be exempt from conscription because they would be needed on the land, but when Danny had explained that he felt he must volunteer, both John and Deborah had understood. The only reason that he had not told them about the medical was because he feared he might not pass it well enough to be trained as aircrew. Danny knew that once, when he was very small, he had suffered from something described by his mother as 'sticky ear'. He did not know precisely what it was but feared it might mean he had a perforated eardrum, and he knew from friends that such a condition would prevent him from flying. If he was not pronounced A1, then he would rather nurse his disappointment in private before sharing the bad news with his parents and relatives.

But it was all right! The Board had passed him on all counts, so whatever had been the matter with him as a small child must have righted itself. He had caught the home-going train at Paddington, positively bursting with delight, for though the officer who had collected the papers he had had to fill in had been unable to promise him aircrew training, he had been very optimistic. 'You're a fit young fellow, just the sort of bod we need,' he had said encouragingly, 'and you applied well before conscription kicked in, which looks like being next month, and that shows you're keen. So I don't think you need worry.'

The maddening thing was that there had been no one on the train in whom Danny could confide.

When he reached Hereford, he had humped his overnight bag out to the bus stop, for it was time for the school bus and he had hoped to find Sophie aboard. There were several grammar-school pupils already seated but no one at all from the Fifth or the Sixth, and Danny remembered, crossly, that it was an examination day.

The annoying thing was that he would have loved to pop into the blacksmith's and share his news with Sophie but his conscience would not allow it. It would have been different had she been on the bus, but as it was, his parents must be the first to know and would be hurt if they thought he had considered the Cantrips more important than themselves. Besides, he had no excuse for visiting the forge since he had not ridden his bicycle into the village the previous occasion. His father had run him to the station in the car but because he had had no idea at what time he would arrive back he had decided to make his own way home.

The bus rounded a corner and drew up with a screech of brakes alongside Mrs Bailey's little shop. Danny got down and looked around him, half hoping that his father might be in the village for some purpose and therefore able to give him a lift home. There was no sign of the battered old car, however, and Danny was making up his mind to a solitary three-mile walk when he heard a shout, and turning to look over his shoulder saw his cousin Phil emerging from the blacksmith's.

'Have you got your motorbike?' Danny asked

hopefully as his cousin approached. 'If you have, we could wedge my suitcase between us and you could give me a lift on the pillion. Not that it'll hurt me to walk,' he added hastily, as Phil shook his head, 'because I've been sitting down for what feels like hours, so a bit of exercise won't harm me.'

'Good thing, since we're both doomed to Shanks's pony,' Phil observed, falling into step beside Danny. 'Old Cantrip keeps telling me it's time I bought myself a new bike but I reckon there's a few years left in the old girl yet.' He grinned down at his cousin and Danny grinned back. He tried not to envy Phil his superior height and knew that, whereas once they had been evenly matched, Phil now outstripped him on almost all counts. Because he was now working full-time on the farm, Phil was taller, broader and stronger than Danny, though John Brewster had told his son that this might be partly due to heredity. Uncle Matthew had once been a great oak of a man, but ever since his accident his health had grown steadily worse. He was now a victim of chronic arthritis, scarcely able to do anything for himself without pain, and no help at all with the physical work of the farm. Phil, however, had proved himself to be more than capable of running Hilltop. Until he needed their wages to pay for the Bentley, Uncle Matthew had employed the Baggott brothers, who had been idle and dishonest, and he had let them get away with murder, but his son was a far harder taskmaster, possibly because he was still longing to escape from Hilltop and knew that the only way to do so with a clear conscience was to make the farm profitable so that he could arrange, somehow, to pay a manager of some description to take his place, to tell everyone what to do and when to do it, and to stop his father from ruining it all. So Phil employed two cousins from a neighbouring village and worked them as hard as he worked himself. When he had taken them on, he had told his mother, brusquely, that she must feed their new workers twice a day, and feed them well, because he had noticed how willing his uncle's farmhands were to work hard after the excellent meals which Aunt Deborah put before them. 'We'll pay the set rate per hour, same as Uncle John does,' he had told his parents. 'But we'll see our fellers get little extras, as well. I'm going to put down a good half of Baxter's Piece to vegetables and a few goosegogs, currants and the like. If you give the workers their share, they'll come in on time and won't leave early. Oh, I know it's easier for Uncle John because he's got his cottages for his farmhands and that's something which we can't provide, but I'm telling you, Dad, a contented worker has a head start on someone like they Baggott brothers, who had a chip on their shoulders and a grumble on their lips from the moment they arrived late until they slipped off home as soon as your back was turned.'

Danny remembered that Uncle Matt had harrumphed a good deal over providing meals, but his son had been firm and he had soon been proved right. When seasonal workers were wanted – in the case of the Rylands this was usually at haymaking and sheep dipping, as well as when they picked the small orchard – folk from the village and the surrounding countryside queued up to work for young Phil Ryland.

John, who was very down-to-earth, had once said that the girls from the village wanted to work for a golden-haired young giant and didn't give a hoot for meals or perks from the Ryland market garden, but Danny thought the local girls were far too hard-headed not to look carefully at every job on offer, regardless of the sex appeal of the offerer.

However, Baxter's Piece was proving to be a useful addition to Hilltop Farm, because what had once been a small vegetable patch now encompassed most of the isolated meadow, the only level piece of land that the Rylands possessed. At first, Phil and his mother had done all the work on it, but now they employed old Mr Sampson, who truly loved the soil and had green fingers into the bargain. Mr Sampson was the father-in-law of one of John Brewster's workers and lived with the Cotter family in their small cottage. He had once been head gardener on a big estate and had hated retirement, living with his daughter and her husband and having nothing to do all day but fret over his enforced inactivity. Now he left home when his son-in-law did to work on Baxter's Piece, trundled up the lane to take his share of the ample breakfast served by Mrs Ryland each morning in the farmhouse kitchen, and then returned to Baxter's Piece. He was paid the same hourly rate as a farm worker but Phil acknowledged that he was worth very much more and always made sure that the old man took home enough fruit and vegetables to fill his daughter's needs.

'Well, young Danny? How was the Science Museum?'

Danny's thoughts had been far away, seeing Baxter's Piece as he had seen it last, with the young seedlings beginning to show and the cloches still in position against the thick hedge, sheltering the salad crops which Mr Sampson would harvest later in the season. Before he could stop himself, his head had jerked round and words rose, unbidden, to his lips. 'Science Museum? What on earth . . . ? Oh!'

Phil laughed. 'If you think I'm that easily fooled, you great lummock, you're much mistaken,' he said. 'I knew you were up to something when Auntie Deb ran on to my mum about how there were some exhibition on in London which you felt you couldn't afford to miss. What sort of exhibition is so perishin' interestin' that a farmer's boy has to go all the way to London so as not to miss it? My mum's a trusting soul but even she looked somewhat surprised. Good thing Dad weren't there or he'd have asked awkward questions, knowing Dad. What was it, then? Don't say my good little cousin was having a dirty weekend in the big bad city!'

Danny laughed, tacitly acknowledging the truth of what Phil had just said, though the epithet 'young Danny', coming from Phil who was a mere twelve weeks older than himself, was rather a cheek. Still, he and Phil had shared all their secrets for most of their lives, and indeed he would have told Phil all about it had the letter commanding his presence in London not been held up somewhere and only arrived a couple of days before his interview was due, so that he had had no opportunity to tell anyone. He would never have kept the knowledge of his true where-abouts from Phil and was grateful, now, that his cousin had not shared his suspicions regarding the apocryphal Science Museum exhibition with his mother and his aunt. He said as much, then added: 'But as for a dirty weekend, I was away Wednesday and Thursday, and somehow a dirty midweek lacks a certain something. As for why I went, can't you guess?' He saw a guarded look come over Phil's normally transparent face and spoke hastily. 'It was the interview with the RAF and a medical. I passed A1, so now it's just a matter of waiting for papers to arrive, then I'll be off. I'm hoping for aircrew, of course, but I'll have to wait and see.' He glanced at his cousin as he spoke and surprised a quick flash of anger in the other's face. For a moment, Phil did not speak, but as they turned into the lane Danny slowed, stood his suitcase down, and pulled Phil to a halt beside him. 'What's up, old chap?' he said quietly. 'I know full well I can't pull the wool over your eyes, but it's the same in reverse, you know; you're an open book to me.'

Phil stared at Danny, the expression in his eyes so antagonistic that Danny almost flinched. Then Phil said, clearly keeping his voice low and level with a considerable effort: 'You've bloody well got it all, haven't you? Right from the moment we were tiny kids, you've had everything. A farm which has made money from the start, a healthy father who knew what he was doing, a brand-new tricycle when I had to make do with your old one with the pedals attached to the front wheel, not a proper tricycle at all, a grammar-school education . . . why, Auntie Deb told my mum they're going to give you a bloody car for your eighteenth birthday. Imagine that! There's my dad, crippled with arthritis, ignorant of the simplest things about running a farm, dipping his hand into any profit I might make as though he thought I had the Midas touch . . . and now the air force have accepted you and by the time I'm cutting the hay in Coppice Meadow you'll be up there in the blue somewhere, piloting a Spitfire, with every girl in the neighbourhood chasing after you, and Auntie Deb sending you food parcels in case the air force don't feed her boy right. Why, you swine, you know very well that I've always meant to fly, ever since I was knee-high to a grasshopper. You know it, yet you, who don't care for anything but the bloody land, are the one who will be up there, whilst I . . . oh, God, what's the bloody use of talking? I'm trapped like a rabbit in a snare!'

To Danny, it seemed incredible that his big, handsome cousin could be jealous of him, let alone that his ownership of a brand-new tricycle, at the age of three or so, still rankled. But Phil was continuing, actually grinding his teeth: a feat Danny had thought was only achieved by villains in storybooks. 'It's so bloody unfair! I've always longed to join the air force; even when I was quite young I talked about learning to fly . . . remember? But then Dad had his accident and I had to leave school early . . . I'm not saying I was as clever as you, though I was – still am – damned good at all types of maths, but I was no slouch, you've got to admit it. And now, though I've worked like a slave and pulled the farm round a fair bit, there isn't the money yet for a farm manager and I still dare not leave . . . I'm stuck here, I tell you, very likely for the duration, so there's small chance of me following your bloody lead! I'll be trapped here, staring at those bloody hills, stifled by 'em, whilst you've got right away.'

'Oh, come on, Phil, it can't be that bad,' Danny said rather feebly. He was reeling from the shock of his cousin's words. He realised that he had always seen the blue encircling hills as the palm of a loving hand, cupped to protect their farms. Now he knew that Phil saw them as an impenetrable barrier, fencing him in. 'I was sure you'd probably already sent in your own papers . . . why, when I told you I'd been into Hereford with Sophie and gone into the recruiting office, you said you'd go along in a couple of days . . . you said . . .'

'Oh, I said, I said; I say all sorts of bloody stupid things,' Phil said savagely. 'What chance do I truly have of getting away? Answer me that! What the devil do you think would happen to Hilltop if I buggered off and left Dad in charge? I'm telling you, he'd ruin us in a month. He doesn't *care* for the land,

Danny, and never has, and he doesn't know a damned thing about farming. I once heard Mum and Auntie Deb talking about it and Mum said when her pa left them the farm he did my dad the worst turn he could. I s'pose Grandpa thought that Dad would take to farming like a duck to water – probably thought any fool could farm. And in those days, Dad had the income from the hardware store so he could afford to act like a gentleman farmer. But once the shop was sold . . . oh, what's the good of talking? You've always been the lucky one, right from the start. I'll never get away, never.'

Danny stared up at Phil, almost unable to believe his ears. In his own mind, the boot had always been on the other foot. Phil, his senior by three months, was so confident, so efficient and over six foot tall, with golden hair and bright blue eyes. Danny, short, square and dark, had taken his cousin's superiority for granted. Now, he was hurt and amazed to recognise the resentment which must always have existed in Phil's mind. He began to stammer an apology, not for the Ryland farm, or for his parents' financial security – that was impossible, would only make things worse – but for not telling Phil that he was off to London. He was even apologising for his crass stupidity in boasting of his success when Phil suddenly gave him a great buffet on the shoulder, snatched up his suitcase and began to stride up the lane again, walking so fast that Danny had to run to keep up.

'You fool. Can't you take a joke?' Phil said, as

Danny fell into step beside him. 'I was only kidding. Good God, Danny boy, if I wanted to quit the farm and join the air force, then I'd do it with my parents' blessing, even though things would be hard for them.' He glanced down at his cousin, his eyes soft now, reflecting the friendship they had always shared. 'I thought you said you could read me like a book? I'm sorry, old feller, I shouldn't tease you, not over something as important as your joining the air force. Do I take it your parents really believe you went to the Science Museum, and if so, in God's name why? You know they'll be behind you, every foot of the way.'

If there was a trace of bitterness in the last sentence, Danny decided to ignore it, to pretend to accept Phil's explanation, even though in his heart he knew it was false. 'I didn't tell them – didn't tell anyone – because I've always been afraid I'd fail the medical,' he admitted. 'Remember I had that ear trouble just before we started school?'

'We both had it,' Phil said, nodding. 'They called it "sticky ear", or some such name. I've always believed it affected my hearing, because if I lie on my left side, with my left ear buried in the pillow, I don't always hear the alarm too clearly, and I reckon you're the same.'

'That's right,' Danny said untruthfully. He knew he had no hearing loss in either ear, but he had known also that, had his eardrum been perforated, he would not have passed the medical A1. 'I shall feel a bit of a fool admitting to Mum and Dad that I lied

171

to them – now that I know it's all right, it seems a stupid, petty thing to have done – but I reckon they'll understand when I explain.' He looked up at his cousin's fair face, at the expression there, unruffled and placid once more, and wondered how long it would take him to forget Phil's outburst. Forgiving would be easy, because, now that he thought about it, he realised every word Phil had said had been true. In everything but looks and physique, Danny had had all the luck. But his cousin was doing his best to make up the deficit.

They were level with the cottages now and further up the lane was the field which his cousin's efforts had turned into a market garden. Danny knew that it made money constantly, knew that Phil was proving himself an intelligent and foresighted farmer, knew also that Phil was right. If his cousin left, it would not be long before Uncle Matthew began to interfere with the running of Baxter's Piece, not bothering to manure or to rotate the crops, probably deciding he had a better use for the money he paid old Mr Sampson, announcing breezily that the farmhands could do the work, in their spare time!

Danny slowed as they reached the gateway to Manor Farm. 'Want to come in? It's too early for supper but you know my mum; her cake tins are always full and it doesn't take a moment to put the kettle on the hob.'

He did not expect Phil to accept and was not surprised when his cousin shook his head. 'No, I'd best be getting back. We'll be milking in half an hour or so and the cows have to be brought down from the high pasture, but thanks all the same,' he said breezily. He handed Danny his suitcase, giving him a quick embarrassed glance as he did so. 'God, Danny, I don't know what came over me! You passed on your little trike to me the best part of fifteen years ago and I drag it up as if it were yesterday. You will forget it, won't you?' He gave Danny a rueful grin. 'I had no idea I felt like that. I swear it was as much a surprise to me as it must have been to you when my gob opened and all that rubbish spilled out. Can you forget it?'

'Yes, of course I can,' Danny said. 'You've got it off your chest, that's the main thing, and thinking about it you spoke no more than the truth, except for one thing, old fellow. If I remember rightly, and I'm bloody sure I do, I got given the brand-new tricycle all right but I scarcely ever had a chance to ride it because you were bigger than me and used to take it over as soon as we left the farmyard.'

Phil gave a bark of laughter and nodded his head. 'You're right. I remember your little legs whizzing round as you tried to keep up on that miserable little trike,' he said cheerfully. 'And when you got your Raleigh and I got the old boneshaker from Mr Cantrip, the only thing that stopped me making you swap was because my legs were too long for your machine.'

'Aye; but until your legs got too long you rode the Raleigh pretty often,' Danny reminded him. 'And what about Dusky? Now I come to think of it, you were always quite happy to ride Gulliver, even though he wasn't anywhere near as good a point-to-pointer as Dusky.'

'As if you didn't know!' Phil said scoffingly. 'You're a much better rider than me, old fellow, so I've always been quite content to amble along in your wake on Gulliver. He's like me and prefers to go round an obstacle rather than soar over it. But if Dusky had been a motorbike, it would have been a different story.' He grinned again, rather shame-facedly this time. 'I'd have pinched a Harley-Davidson off you in no time, though I wouldn't have grudged you my old Triumph in return.'

'Oh, thanks very much! Personally, I think my pushbike is safer and more reliable than your old banger,' Danny said sarcastically. 'And if I ever save up enough to buy myself a Harley-Davidson, then I'd chop your hands off at the wrist if you so much as swung your leg over it.'

Both boys laughed and Danny realised, with pleasure, that the tension between them had eased. As he let himself into the house, he found himself wondering just what would happen to Phil. Everyone knew that conscription was coming, but it would not affect his cousin, who as a producer of food would be considered an essential worker. There was still time for Phil to decide which was the greater sacrifice: to abandon the farm into his father's careless hands, or to abandon his hopes of a career in the Royal Air Force.

As he entered the kitchen, he saw his mother

heaving the heavy kettle off the stove and greeted her cheerfully. 'I'm back, Mum. Any chance of a cup of tea and a slice of fruit cake? I've had to walk from the village so I'm starving hungry.'

Deborah looked across at him and beamed. 'Oh, Danny, if only we'd been on the telephone, Dad could have picked you up. Your father put our name down for one ages ago, and it will be installed some time next week – just too late for you to benefit! But I was just about to make a pot of tea, so take your coat off and settle yourself down while I cut the cake.' As she spoke, she was pouring water into the big brown teapot, and presently she and Danny settled down at the table with a cup of tea and a slice of cake before them. Deborah leaned her elbows on the table and looked across at her son. 'How was the exhibition? Was there anything useful for farmers?'

Danny took a deep breath. 'Ma, I'm afraid I told you and Dad an enormous whopper,' he said apologetically. 'I really went to London for an interview and a medical with the Royal Air Force.'

Phil had continued his walk up the lane after he and Danny had parted, still feeling sick at having given himself away. Once, envying Danny had been the last thing on his mind, but ever since his father's accident two and a half years ago it had become more and more apparent that Danny was the luckier of the two. He had money, security and loving parents who never quarrelled. Since the accident, Daisy and Matthew often bickered, contradicted one another, took opposing views simply to be difficult and increasingly of late appealed to Phil to take one or other side in an argument.

Then there was Sophie. He had not taken much notice of her when they had travelled to and from school together in the bus, had realised she was Dan's friend rather than his own and had not minded in the least. She had been small, skinny and plain, just a village girl who happened to be brighter than most. When he went out with a girl he went for looks and, he supposed wryly, some sort of social standing. Rich farmers' daughters or the offspring of successful professional men were his own personal choice. He had long ago decided to marry money so that he could buy an easier farm to run than Hilltop. Of course, he would have to love the girl – that went without saying – but he was sensible and he would steer well clear of the pretty and penniless. The blonde and bubbly Lizzy Pinfold from the village was a case in point; nice to play with but not to marry.

Lately, however, he had run into Sophie when visiting the blacksmith and had noted, with some surprise, that she was growing pretty. Her hair had always been straight as rain, but now she was doing something with the ends so that they curled under in a gleaming pageboy, and her brown eyes shone with humour and intelligence. Her mouth – he had to admit it – was downright kissable, whilst her figure . . . well, it was as good as Lizzy Pinfold's any day, though a deal more slender. However, she was still just a village girl and he knew she and Danny, despite their youth, had some sort of understanding. And isn't that just bloody typical, he found himself thinking savagely, that Danny had picked a girl of whom the Brewsters would thoroughly approve; a nice girl, a girl who fitted in with the Brewster family.

But what a fool I'm being, Phil told himself. It isn't as if I want Sophie, though I dare say I'll keep an eye on her for Danny, once he's joined the air force. He smiled to himself as he strode up the lane, glancing appreciatively into Baxter's Piece as he passed the stout wooden gate. It was about the only gate on the farm which was brand new and sported barbed wire festooned along its top bar, and a large padlock through its latch. He could not imagine anyone trudging all the way up the lane in order to steal his crops, but old Mr Sampson had insisted that this might happen, particularly if war came. 'I remember some buggers diggin' up every onion on my dad's allotment,' he had said bitterly. 'Then they went for his carrots. In the end, the fellers what owned the allotments had to keep a twenty-four-hour watch, armed with an old shotgun.' He had chuckled grimly. 'A nice bit of shot winging past their ears soon put a stop to their thievish ways.'

As he continued to climb the hill, Phil began to justify to himself what he had said to Danny, and by the time he was crossing the farmyard he was sure that all would be well. Danny was a good sort, generous and easy-going, like his father. Phil remembered when Uncle John had paid for the whole family to have a holiday in Aberystwyth, where an enterprising young man had been offering flights round the bay in an elderly biplane. Both Daisy and Deborah had been appalled at the idea, but Phil remembered how his father and Uncle John had overridden all objections and had taken their sons for their very first flight; eyes gleaming with anticipation, clearly not grudging the expense but revelling in the excitement.

From that moment on, Phil had been determined that one day he would learn to fly an aeroplane, swooping dizzily through the sky, seeing the houses as matchboxes and the folk on the beach as ants. Danny had agreed cautiously that it would be fun, but Phil had always known that Danny's feet were firmly anchored on his own acres. Oh, he might learn to fly, do a thousand and one other things, but at the end of the day he would return to Manor Farm and be content to stay there for the rest of his days.

And now Danny was going to do just what his cousin had always longed to do – for Phil had little doubt that Danny would be accepted for pilot training. And he, Phil, who would be so much better at it, he was sure, would remain on the farm.

Phil sighed, then fixed a pleasant expression on his face, opened the back door and walked into the kitchen. His mother was ironing, three flats standing in the hearth ready to be used as her present implement cooled down. His father was sitting on an upright chair, a large cushion wedged behind his back, reading a copy of yesterday's *Telegraph*. They both looked up as he entered the room. 'What did Cantrip say?' Daisy asked, finishing off the garment she was ironing and adding it to the pile by her side. 'Can he put it right?'

'Yes, but he needs to get a new part,' Phil said, dropping into the chair opposite his father's. 'He'll have to send away for it, so it may be a day or two . . .'

'More like a week or two,' Matthew said cynically, peering at his son over the top of the paper. 'And if a war comes – I mean when a war comes – then that old bike will be like gold dust and new parts will be scarcer than hens' teeth.' He turned irritably on his wife. 'For God's sake, woman, what are you thinking of? The boy's been working hard all day, then he had to push that old wreck of his all the way into the village and come back up the hill again, and you don't even pull the kettle over the fire, or offer him one of those scones you baked earlier.'

'By which, I take it, you mean you're gasping for a cup of tea, but are too lazy to get up and put the kettle on, let alone fetch the cake tin through from the scullery,' his wife said bitingly. She turned to her son. 'You aren't helpless, Phil; make us all a cup of tea, there's a good lad. I want to get all this stuff ironed before I start cooking supper.'

War was declared on a Sunday, by which time Danny had learned that he had matriculated and had been accepted for aircrew training. He was already in London at Air Crew Reception Centre (mockingly called Arsy Tarsy by the cadets) doing his basic training. For four long weeks they were kitted out, marched up and down and given lectures on every conceivable subject, including how to avoid contracting venereal disease. 'Chance would be a fine thing,' the cadets said to one another, for their days were crammed from the moment they woke until they fell into bed at night. Outside the centre London hummed and buzzed, but they had no opportunity to sample the daylife, never mind what went on at night. When the news that Britain was at war was announced over the tannoy there was jubilation, even cheering, and Danny, though he understood and indeed shared the feelings of his fellows, could not help wondering how the news had been greeted by the civilian population. He guessed that his mother would have wept and his father, who had fought in the trenches in the last lot, would have looked grim, but he supposed that others would be relieved that a decision had been taken. There were few things worse than waiting.

Danny made a number of friends at Arsy Tarsy, most of whom had been in the ATC, as Danny had. They were all eager to learn to fly and one man, a little older than the rest, had become Danny's particular friend. Ray Westwood had fought in the Spanish Civil War, and because of his experiences in that country had decided to join the air force around the same time as Danny had made his own decision. The two had liked one another from the first moment they had met, which had been in the queue for uniforms on their arrival at Arsy Tarsy. Danny had been deeply interested in the Spanish Civil War and the use Franco made of aircraft, and had decided that fascism must be stamped out. The Nazis were fascists, therefore they must be defeated, and the best way of doing so, for him at any rate, was from the air.

Ray had been halfway through a university course in maths and science when the war in Spain had broken out, and along with a good many of his fellows he had abandoned his college to join the International Brigade. The two men had a good deal in common, therefore, including a similar sense of humour and a vested interest in the land, for Ray's father farmed sheep in North Wales.

'Sheep farming never made anyone a fortune, but we get by,' he had told Danny. 'And the country's grand. I started climbing with my dad when I was eight or nine and as soon as I was old enough I got into the mountains whenever I could. When someone is reported missing, experienced climbers go out to search, and when the war's over I'd like to try to organise something official along those lines. I began to take people climbing in the long vac and really enjoyed it, but one of my students was a young Spanish woman . . . you can guess the rest.'

Danny could, particularly when Ray told him what had happened to the girl upon her return to Spain. She had joined the Women's Militia and had been killed in the siege of Madrid. She was twenty-two years old.

Waiting, it seemed to Danny, was the name of the game. When their month in London was over, they were dispatched to Scarborough for their Initial Training Weeks. Danny and Ray were billeted in the Astoria Hotel where once more they were subjected to countless lectures, examinations and tests of fitness. They both emerged successful at the end of three months and had a week's leave before being sent off to the Flying Training School at Scone, in Scotland. There, feeling justifiably pleased with themselves, they would learn to fly in Tiger Moths, going solo after seven or eight hours, and, if they performed satisfactorily, be deemed ready to continue their training somewhere other than Great Britain. At last, Danny thought, the real adventure was about to begin.

Chapter Six

When Tina had heard the announcement on the radio that Britain and France were at war with Germany, she had wanted to rush round to her friends Harry and Ron to see how they were taking the news. Laura, however, had insisted that she remain in the flat, for there was a great deal to do.

'You know very well that you'll be packing a suitcase and going along to the station first thing in the morning, with all your pals from school,' she said. 'They've already started evacuating children from London, so you won't be the first to leave home and I don't suppose you'll be the last. I'm making you a packed lunch. The letter from school said that at some stage you would be fed and watered, but with so much going on, you might be forgotten.'

'Going away? But I'm not going anywhere,' Tina said wildly. 'Oh, I know they talked about it in school but Harry says they can't make you go and I bleedin' well won't! I'm stayin' here with you, Mam, and Uncle Arthur, and with Tess; if it's safe for you it must be safe for me.'

'That's not the point, Tina. Just think for once instead of getting in a rage over what can't be helped,' her mother said. 'It isn't just the children who are being evacuated, it's the teachers as well, so there'll be nobody in school to give lessons.'

The whole family had been sitting round the table having their elevenses, with the Sunday roast beef in the oven, and a bowl of batter standing on the side, ready to be made into Yorkshire pudding. Laura had placed a plate of biscuits and some slices of Battenburg cake in the middle of the table, and now Tess leaned across and helped herself, giving her mother a broad smile as she did so. 'That were the wrong thing to say, Mam; I saw our Tina's eyes light up with glee at the thought of no teachers to take classes,' she observed. She turned to her small sister. 'Kids are a nuisance in wartime because mams will have to take full-time work as well as dads. Honestly, Tina, you'll be far better off in the country; you'll have a lovely time. Besides, whatever Harry may have said, I bet his mam and dad have put him down for evacuation, and Ron, too.'

'I don't want to go, and I won't go,' Tina said, though without much conviction. She turned to her mother. 'Wharrif Harry and Ron ain't goin', Mam? Can I come home then?'

'No you can't,' Laura said firmly. 'All your cousins are going – the younger ones, that is. Look, queen, there's a plain postcard packed in your little suitcase so that you can send me your new address when you arrive. But there's a bit of money as well, so if, after a week, you're truly unhappy, you can go down to the local post office, buy some writing paper and a stamp and tell me what's happening. Understand?'

'I shan't bother wi' writin'. If I'm unhappy I'll bleedin' well run away,' Tina muttered. She turned to Arthur, who had been sitting at the table beside her mother, studiously avoiding so much as glancing towards the combatants. 'Uncle Arthur, *you* don't want me to go, do you? I'm a rare help to you in the shop, ain't I? Why, I could be your delivery boy, 'cos Wilf's bound to be called up sooner or later and I can ride his bike; I've been practisin'.'

Arthur looked hunted, and for the first time since the announcement had been made Tina smiled to herself. She knew her stepfather tried never to interfere and always left decisions such as the one under discussion to his wife. But Tina knew herself to be Uncle Arthur's favourite and decided it was time she had someone on her side. 'Well, Uncle Arthur, ain't I a great help to you?' she said, in her most wheedling tone. 'Be honest now; how would you manage without me to go through the grapes, pickin' off the rotten ones when they're startin' to turn? And it's me what goes through the apple boxes, settin' aside fruit with only one little hole in, 'cos that means a maggot's got in and ain't got out again. And – and Christmas is comin'; think what a help I was last year! Sortin' the nuts into pound bags, makin' sure none of the oranges had gone mildewy . . .'

'Eatin' everything you could lay your hands on,' Tess interrupted. 'Nickin' sprays of holly to tie on the saddle of Wilf's bicycle, selling fades – which weren't fades at all, really – to your little pals so you could buy a whoopee cushion for your teacher's chair. If I were you, young Tina, I'd keep me gob shut, because I reckon for every hour you're helpful and good, there's three you're bad as can be.'

Tina began to ruffle up. 'I didn't ask you, you nasty, spiteful girl,' she said vengefully. 'I asked Uncle Arthur, 'cos he's the one I help the most.' She turned to her stepfather, wiping the fury from her face and replacing it, she hoped, with a look of angelic long-suffering. 'Tess is always horrible to me because she's older, but I weren't askin' her in any case.' She jumped to her feet and ran round the table, casting herself on to Arthur's lap and throwing her arms round his neck. 'You love me, Uncle Arthur, even if Mam and Tess don't. You tell Tess she's wrong! Tell her I'm a real help and you can't do without me.' She smiled, beguilingly, up into his embarrassed face. 'Go on, you tell her.'

'Well, there's been times . . .' Arthur began uncomfortably, but was quickly cut short.

'Tina, love, you're not being sent away because you're a nuisance or because we don't love you,' Laura said. 'All the children from the big cities which are liable to get bombed are being evacuated into the country where they'll be safe. Grown-ups – that's Uncle Arthur, meself and Tess – have to stay behind in the cities to man the factories, shops and offices which will be the targets for the bombers. So you see, we're sending you away because we love you, not because we don't.'

'But what about *you*?' Tina wailed, suddenly recognising the seriousness of the situation. 'If you and Uncle Arthur and Tess get bombed, then what will happen to me? I'd rather get bombed as well than be all alone in the world.'

'Oh, Tina, really! This house has a grand deep cellar and we've already ordered a Morrison shelter. And there'll be really safe deep public shelters all over the city; some have already been built,' Laura said reassuringly. 'Look, chuck, you're ten years old and a lot of the kids being sent away are even younger, so just you be sensible and don't give me any more trouble. And now Tess will take you to your room and help you to check your bag, all right?'

Tina slid off her chair with a resigned sigh. 'I suppose it's all right. And when we've done that, can I go round to Harry and Ron's? Only I want to make certain sure that they really are going, same as me, and to the same place. It won't be so bad if we're all together.'

The children left on the Monday and the expected postcard arrived on the Thursday. It contained little beside Tina's new address, but there was an ill-spelt and ill-written line along the bottom of the card: *It's allrite hear. School mornins only. Tina.*

The family had been sitting in the kitchen having their breakfast when the postman delivered the card, and Tess leaned across the table and picked it up when her mother had finished reading it aloud. She looked at it thoughtfully, then turned to Arthur who was munching toast. 'Manor Farm, near Hereford,' she said. 'We get apples from them, don't we, Uncle

Arthur? When I was waiting for Mike I used to sit on the apple boxes, and I'm pretty sure some came from a Manor Farm.'

'I dare say there's more than one Manor Farm in Herefordshire,' Laura said. 'But I expect when Tina's letter comes it will tell us a lot more than the card can. I just hope she's with really nice people.'

'If it is an apple farm, then I suppose they'll be picking any time now,' Tess said. 'Our Tina will like that, even if she eats so many she gives herself a belly-ache.' She looked across the table at her mother, hesitated, then plunged in. 'Mam, they're advertising for girls to make wireless parts for the aeroplanes. They need people who are neat and nimble-fingered, and they're prepared to take on school leavers, so I'd be all right. The money's awfully good and I'd really like to apply, only I don't want you to feel I've left you in the lurch.' She looked eagerly across at her mother as Laura raised her head and their eyes met. 'It's not as though waitressing needs any special sort of training; in fact I've often heard you say that older women are better at it than young ones, as well as being more reliable, and I would like to feel I was helping with the war effort.'

Laura glanced at Arthur. Of course the café was still owned by Tess's stepfather, but her mother usually took most decisions about its running, knowing that Arthur trusted her completely. Why was this different, then? But before she could put the thought into words, her mother spoke. 'You're right, of course, darling, and it'll be better for you because you'll be working with other young people just like yourself. Since Ellie left to join the ATS, you're the only person under forty working in the café. When are they interviewing? Would you like to go as soon as breakfast is over?'

'Oh, Mam, you're wonderful,' Tess said sincerely. 'But I'm the only one on this morning, so I'll leave it till two or three this afternoon, after Mrs Bagshot gets in. The work in the factory will only be a stopgap, mind, because as soon as I'm old enough, I mean to join one of the services.'

Her stepfather put down the piece of toast he was about to pop into his mouth. 'I don't want to put a spoke in your wheel, queen,' he said slowly, 'but if you're serious about joining the services, you'd do best to give the factory the go-by. One of me customers told me that her daughter, what's in munitions, applied to join the WRNS and was turned down since she was already doing essential war work. If you stick to the café for another, what, six months, then you'll be free to join anything you've a mind to.'

This eminently sensible point of view struck both mother and daughter and Tess was telling her step-father how grateful she was for his timely interjection when her mother broke in. 'Tess, would you do me a favour? I more or less promised Tina, when I said goodbye to her on Lime Street station, that I'd take time off from work and go to visit her just as soon as I can. But with so much going on, and the café full to bursting, especially on a Saturday, I don't think I can be spared just yet. This Manor Farm is a good way off, but if I give you your train fare and enough money for while you're there, would you go and visit your little sister? I'll get Liza Slim to cover for you so it won't affect business.'

'Oh, Mam, I'd love to!' Tess said. Her outings with Mike had given her a deep, if romantic, love of the country and she could imagine no greater pleasure than actually spending time on a farm. 'Why, I could help with the apple picking, or whatever it is they're doing at the moment. I'd love it, Mam. You'd be doing me a favour by letting me go.'

'That's grand then,' Laura said, looking relieved. 'But you don't want to go too soon or Tina will probably try to come back with you. We'll let her get well and truly settled in before your visit.'

Danny had looked forward to his leave because he realised that he might not be back in England for some considerable while. The cadets had all been warned, when they had first gone to Scarborough, that there were far too many young men wanting pilot training. They had been advised that the wait for such training might be lengthy, and of course the training itself would take some while; training as a navigator or bomb aimer would be shorter. Danny and Ray had agonised over this but decided to stick to their guns.

Danny was glad they had done so when he got back to the farm, for Phil bombarded him with questions, assuring him that as soon as he had 'sorted the farm out' he, too, would join up and train as aircrew. 'If you can do it and get through all the exams and that, so can I,' Phil assured his cousin. 'And I'll go for pilot training, too, you can be sure of that.'

Naturally enough, Danny had met up with Sophie as soon as he possibly could, for the two of them had been exchanging letters and even the odd phone call ever since Danny had joined up. Now, they visited the cinema in order to cuddle in the back row, and went to a couple of village hops, and of course spent time together as they had always done.

The pair of them were sitting beside the river in the wintry sunshine one afternoon, watching the brown trout flickering through the dappled water, their minds far from the rural scene around them. Danny squeezed Sophie's hand, suddenly aware that such times would be rare once his training started. 'Will you keep writing to me?' he asked, keeping his eyes fixed on a brown trout gliding serenely past amongst the rushes. 'I mean . . . if you've got time, of course.'

Sophie turned and smiled at him. 'If you want me to, of course I will,' she said, and Danny watched the soft pink flush warm her face. She chuckled softly. 'It's a good thing I enjoy writing letters though, because I suppose there will be an awful lot of them to write once all our other friends join up.'

'Just so long as you keep writing to me, that will do,' Danny said contentedly. It was, he realised long afterwards, the closest he came to making any sort of commitment to the girl he liked so much.

Despite everyone's good intentions, it was December before Tess was able to go down to Manor Farm. Tina had written enthusiastically about her new life, but with war preparations and rationing Tess was needed at home. Tina had said that she had helped to pick hops, though she had not enjoyed this task nearly as much as the picking of apples the following month. She had watched a calf being born and described the event in graphic detail, and had helped to round up the sheep when Mr Brewster wanted some yearlings taken to market. She regularly searched for eggs in barns, hedges and of course the nesting boxes inside the chicken house. She had boasted, triumphantly, that she could now tell a broody hen from one which was just cross, and had taken to calling Mr and Mrs Brewster Uncle John and Auntie Deb, since they had suggested it.

School had got scant mention, though she had talked quite a lot about Joy, Megan and Eth, her fellow evacuees, and when Tess had announced her desire to come and stay for a few nights she had been pleased, but not ecstatic.

Auntie Deb says you're very welcom and can sleep in her son's room. He's in the air force, like Mike [she had written]. *There will be land girls after Christmas because the farmands have been con-scripted (Auntie Deb told me that were the right word and how to spell it). That means us kids will have to share one room, but we think it will be good fun like in* The Naughtiest Girl in the School, *you know, dormitries and all that. Then the land girls will have the other three bedrooms between them, so it's a good job you'll arrive before they does. Auntie Deb says the winter's always quiet on the farm but of course the animals still need looking after. Auntie Deb says she's going to teach us to write and spell proper over the winter months, when she'll have more time. I don't mind, she's real nice. See you soon.*

Love, Tina.

The letter arrived, as all Tina's letters did, by the first post, whilst Laura, Arthur and Tess were having their breakfast. Usually, the letters were addressed to Mr and Mrs Mitchell, but this one had been sent especially to Tess because it was she who would presently be arriving at the farm. Tess read the letter, chuckling over the spelling, then handed it to Laura, saying as she did so: 'She's having the time of her life, Mam, not like some of them other kids. Mrs Madison came into the café yesterday – you know, she's the fat, untidy one, with five daughters. She says they're billeted with a real mean couple who grudge them so much as an extra slice of bread, and now that the government wants Mrs Madison to pay six shillings for every evacuated child she's decided she'll have to bring them home. And she said, "Why not?" because nowhere's been bombed yet, and she doesn't think it'll ever happen.'

'Aye; they're calling it the phoney war, but

because no one's been bombed yet it don't mean to say no one ever will be,' Arthur said, taking the letter as Laura finished reading it. 'And where's that poor woman to get thirty bob a week, eh? As I recall, her husband's a merchant seaman, norra perishin' banker.' He read Tina's letter, then turned to his wife. 'How d'you feel about having young Tina home for Christmas, my love? Oh, I don't mean for good, I mean just for a couple of weeks. Tess could bring her back with her, and then take her back to the farm so's she'd be there when school starts again.'

'Goodness, look at the time!' Laura said. 'Tess, be a dear and clear away for me. I've got some baking to do and poor Liza will be knocking on the door and thinking I've overslept. We'll discuss all this later.'

As soon as his wife had left the room, Arthur got up and headed for the kitchen door, clearly intending to go and open the shop, but with his hand actually on the doorknob he stopped and glanced at Tess. 'When you get the chance to have a word with your mam, tell her Arthur says to spill the beans. Only don't do it when all the staff's around you,' he said. 'OK?'

Much mystified, Tess agreed to do as he said, then whipped through the rest of her work at top speed and hurried down to the café. It had occurred to her that Tina might well not want to come back to the city for Christmas. To be sure, theatres and cinemas and other such places, which had been closed when war was first declared, had now reopened, but because of the blackout the city seemed a dismal place to be, and despite there having been no bombs there was a good deal of misery amongst ordinary people, particularly mothers of young children. Many of them had been evacuated along with their little ones, but a good number had returned to the city only to find that their husbands had been conscripted, and living on the government allowance was next to impossible. Young women who had shopped regularly at Mitchell's and had popped into the Restawhile afterwards for coffee and a bun no longer did so. And though trade continued brisk, Laura had told Tess that she did not know how they would manage when rationing started in early January.

As luck would have it, Tess found her mother alone in the kitchen. She was cooking bread rolls because they now sold filled rolls to customers who wanted to take them back to their shops and offices. She looked up enquiringly as her daughter entered the room. 'All shipshape and Bristol fashion up there? You are a good girl. I can always leave things to you, knowing you'll do just as you ought.'

Tess smiled somewhat perfunctorily then burst into speech. 'Mam, Uncle Arthur said to tell you to spill the beans. Wharrever did he mean?'

Laura was already flushed from bending over the oven, but now her face went slowly scarlet, the colour even blotching her neck. She looked all round as though expecting a spy to be hiding behind every kitchen unit, then leaned closer to Tess. 'Yes, I know he did. In fact we've just been discussing it. I'm . . . we're . . . what I want to say is . . . would you –

would you like a – oh, Tess, I'm going to have a baby.'

Tess was flabbergasted. She had had very little time to wonder what beans her mother was about to spill, but knew that if she had been given a month to guess it would never have occurred to her that Laura was in the family way. Before she could stop herself, she blurted out: 'You can't be, Mam! You're too old. Oh, it's awful. What'll I tell me pals? Well, don't ask me to push it round in a pram 'cos everyone will think it's mine. Oh, Mam, how could you?'

The bright colour had fled from Laura's face, leaving it white and strained. She said, uncertainly: 'There's nothing wrong with having a baby, chuck. And think on before you say cruel things. Aunt Millie is years older'n me; she had Basil eighteen months ago when she was around forty-six, forty-seven, but you didn't think that was awful.'

Tess flung her arms round her mother and kissed her pale cheek. 'I didn't mean it. It were the shock, and – and what I know me friends will say,' she gabbled. 'And I know you aren't old really, and nor's Uncle Arthur of course, but Mam, how on earth will you manage? You can't run the café and look after a little baby at the same time. And then there's the danger. Suppose Uncle Arthur wants to send the baby into the country . . . you'll have to go as well. Oh, Mam, don't cry, I'm telling you it was the shock speakin', not your own Tess. When's the baby coming? You don't show at all.'

Laura gave her daughter a watery smile, then

fished a handkerchief out of her sleeve, mopped her streaming eyes and blew her nose resoundingly. 'It's due in May,' she said, obviously trying to speak normally though her voice was husky with tears. 'As for leaving the city, I wouldn't dream of it. Arthur's going to need me more and more as young men and women are called up or sent to work in munitions factories and the like. Oh, Tess, I'm sorry to have given you such a shock, but to tell you the truth, Arthur's so thrilled at the thought of being a father again that he's like a dog with two tails, and I was afraid he'd forget himself and say something in front of you before I'd had a chance to tell you myself. He wanted me to tell you as soon as the doctor confirmed that I was expecting, but I felt it was too soon. However, we realised that it wouldn't be fair to tell Tina the news in a letter, which was why we agreed that you should go down to Hereford. Then Arthur thought it would be even better if we told you both together, which meant bringing her home, of course, because you know how cross she gets if she feels she's been left out.' As she spoke, she was sliding the cooked bread rolls on to a wire cooling tray and now she smiled up at her daughter. 'But I'm glad you know now, queen! I was dreading telling you but I was sure you'd forgive me for not being frank earlier and would persuade Tina that a little brother or sister is a good thing. So what do you think we should do? Bring her home for Christmas, or let her stay where she is and simply tell her the news and promise her I'll go down to the farm myself when spring arrives?'

'I'll go down as we planned next week,' Tess said firmly, 'and I'll ask her if she wants to come home with me for Christmas. If she does, that's fine, and I won't say anything, but if she doesn't – and honestly, Mam, I don't think she will – then I'll tell her myself that we're going to have a baby brother or sister, and promise you'll visit, yourself, in the spring. How's that?'

'It's fine, but what makes you think she'd rather stay on the farm than come home for a couple of weeks?' Laura asked doubtfully. 'Think of the fuss she made when she knew she was being sent away. Oh, I know we'll send her presents in good time if she decides to stay in Hereford, but it won't be the same.'

Tess smiled. 'Remember how busy we are in the run-up to Christmas,' she reminded Laura. 'We don't have proper meals or any time to ourselves at all, really. Shopping has to be fitted into any odd moment we can spare and poor Uncle Arthur's run off his feet seeing that customers get what they want. And of course all Tina's best pals will be away so she won't have anyone to play with. In fact, she'll get roped in to help – she was last year, remember? – and she won't like that!'

Laura sighed, picked up the next tray of rolls waiting to be cooked and slid them into the oven, then shut the door and turned back to her daughter. 'We'll do it your way,' she said. 'And thanks, Tess.'

Tess had written to the Brewsters telling them which train she would catch and the time she hoped to arrive, but the journey turned out to be far more complicated than she had imagined. She missed her connection in Shrewsbury so had to catch a small local train which stopped at every minor halt, the driver frequently alighting from his cab and going round to the guard's van to help take out a crate of hens or a couple of milk churns.

Arriving at her destination almost two hours later than planned, Tess had no expectation of being met and so was doubly delighted when, as she dragged her bag across the platform, a small figure came hurtling out of the darkness and grabbed her round the waist, almost knocking her over. 'Tess, oh, Tess, it's grand to see you, so it is. Mr Brewster got the stationmaster to ring through to Shrewsbury to find out what had happened when you weren't on the earlier train and they said you'd missed the con- nection and would be catching the local. They was ever so good, even telling Mr Brewster what time you would arrive – all being well of course – so he drove back home to do the milking and I stayed here so's there would be someone to tell you what were happening. But it's all right, the car came back ten minutes ago and it's parked right outside, by the ticket office, so we'll be home in no time.' As she spoke, she was leading her sister out of the station and across to where several cars were parked. Because of the blackout Tess could not tell one car from another and she hung back, guessing that several of them were taxis, but Tina had no such qualms. She threw open the back door of an elderly car just as the driver climbed out and extended a hand. 'How do you do? I'm John Brewster and you'll be young Tina's sister, Tess. Nice to meet you, my dear, though I'm sorry you've had such a tedious journey.'

Tess could see very little besides his big silhouette against the starry sky, but his hand was large and warm, and his voice welcoming. 'How do you do, Mr Brewster? Thank you ever so much for meeting me. I must admit I'm pretty tired.'

'Aye, and I reckon you're well overdue for a bite of supper,' Mr Brewster said comfortably. He took her arm and led her round to the passenger door, saying as he did so: 'You come and sit beside me, Miss Tess, whilst Miss Jabberwocky there sits behind us, otherwise neither you nor I will get a word in edgeways.' He had taken her bag and now put it in the back beside Tina, before returning to the driver's seat and starting the engine. 'It's a shame it's dark because I always think it's a pretty drive from here to Manor Farm, but you'll be able to explore for yourself tomorrow. Miss Jabberwocky will be able to show you round since it's a Sunday; nice that you've arrived on a weekend, when life's a little more leisurely. Now, I hope you're as fond of a nice steak pie and mashed potato as your sister says you are, because Mrs Brewster cooked one 'specially, guessing you'd likely be late and might need something that can be popped into the Aga so it's ready for eating in two shakes of a lamb's tail.'

A voice from the back chirruped up the moment he

stopped speaking. 'Steak pie and mash is your favourite, ain't it, Tess? Auntie Deb's a prime cook, as good as our mam. She says I'll eat meself square, but of course she don't know wharra good cook our mam is. I mean if I were going to eat meself square I'd have done it at home. But the farmer at Hilltop – he's Auntie Deb's brother-in-law – says I've got hollow legs, and their son, he's rude, you won't like him, says I've got a great huge worm inside me what gobbles up everything what passes me lips, and that's why I'm always hungry.'

Sitting beside her, driving the car cautiously along a winding road and leaning forward a little, the better to see what was ahead through the miserable amount of light which was all drivers were allowed to show, Mr Brewster chuckled. 'Phil's all right,' he remarked. 'Only he doesn't know much about children and sometimes his teasing gets a bit rough.' His window was half wound down, and despite the fact that they appeared to be the only vehicle on the road Mr Brewster stuck his arm out to indicate that he was turning right and hit the horn a couple of times with the heel of his hand. 'This 'un's our lane; Manor Farm is about a mile off now and Hilltop, my brother-in-law's place, a further half mile after that. And don't you listen to young Jabberwocky there, because my nephew's a hard worker and doesn't always get the support he needs.' He turned to her and even in the dark she could see the flash of his teeth as he grinned. 'You'll like him all right; all the girls do.'

Tess opened her mouth to reply but Tina was

before her. 'We're here, we're home!' she shouted. 'Give a toot on your horn, Uncle John.' Swinging into the farmyard, Mr Brewster honked the horn, and immediately the back door shot open and three small girls tumbled out and raced across the yard, rushing over to peer, curiously, at Tess as she began to get out of the car. As she did so, Tina seized her bag, and Tess found herself being hustled towards the doorway through which golden light gleamed.

'Hey you, showin' a light! Don't you know there's a war on?' Tess said jokingly, blinking in the sudden brightness and warmth. 'Or is it all right in the country?'

'No it is not,' a motherly woman, removing a pie from the oven, said at once. 'These girls have heads like sieves. Pull that curtain across, Ethel, or I shall make you pay the fine when the government discovers which farm has forgotten the blackout.' A tiny girl, who could be no more than six or seven, clapped a hand to her mouth, then shot across the kitchen and pulled what looked like a thick black blanket across the doorway. 'Sorry, Auntie Deb,' she squeaked. 'I forgetted. But Uncle John ain't in yet.'

Mrs Brewster, for it was clearly she, smiled at Tess and held out a hand. 'You poor little thing, you must be worn out,' she said kindly. 'I'm Mrs Brewster, as you'll have guessed, but you must call me Auntie Deb and I shall call you Tess. Now take your coat and hat off and rinse your hands under the tap whilst I dish up your supper.'

*

Tess awoke on the Sunday morning to find pale sunshine streaming through her window and got up eagerly, for Tina had promised to take her round the farm provided it was not raining, and she was looking forward to the day ahead.

Naturally, however, as soon as she and Tina were alone she put forward the suggestion that her sister might like to come back with her when she returned to Liverpool the following Tuesday. 'Mam thought you might like to come home for Christmas and be back here in time for school starting,' she said. 'What do you think, queen?'

The sisters were in the big hay barn searching for eggs which had been laid astray and Tina, rooting around in the back of a manger, turned to stare incredulously at Tess. 'Go home for Christmas? Oh, but I couldn't, Tess. Didn't I tell you? I'm the inn-keeper's wife in the nativity play and I'm singin' a solo in the carol concert. And none of the others are goin' home and Auntie Deb says if we go up to Ridley's Wood and cut holly she'll take it in to market next time she goes and it'll give us some extra pocket money for Christmas presents. And what'd I do in Liverpool? All me pals are here now.'

Since Tess had expected this response, she nodded understandingly, then said: 'In that case, chuck, I've got a bit of news for you. Mam and Uncle Arthur wanted to tell you themselves, which is why they suggested you might come home, but they said I might break the news if you meant to stay at Manor Farm over the holiday.'

Tina looked at her expectantly. 'Well, go on then, tell me,' she said. 'Are they going to come and see me, both of them? Mam always says the café's dead during January and I reckon the shop's not much better. Is it that?'

Tess shook her head. 'No, it's not that, though Mam did say she'd come and spend some time with you in the spring. The fact is, Tina, we're going to have a little brother or sister.'

'Oh,' Tina said, looking disappointed. 'Who is it? One of Aunt Millie's kids? Only they've been evacuated too, haven't they?'

'No, that isn't what I meant. I meant our mam is going to have a baby,' Tess said baldly. 'It will be born in May and she and Uncle Arthur are thrilled to bits, and I'm pleased too, of course.'

'Well, I never did,' Tina said, but she sounded neither surprised nor indignant, not even particularly interested. She's so wrapped up in the life of the farm that nothing which happens in Liverpool seems quite real to her, Tess realised. Well, it's probably for the best, and at least when I get home I can tell Mam that Tina took the news in her stride.

'By the way,' Tess said, remembering a question she had been meaning to ask. 'There's a photograph on the living-room mantelpiece of their sons, when they were about ten. They look nice little boys, though very different. One's fair and the other's dark; I suppose you've met them?'

Tina snorted. 'Oh, that photograph. I know the one you mean. But only the dark boy is Mrs Brewster's son. The other one's his cousin, the one I told you about. And they don't look like that any more because they're grown-ups now.'

'I see. And is the dark boy Mrs Brewster's only child?' Tess asked.

Tina nodded vigorously. 'Yes. Ain't it a pity, Tess, that people aren't like dogs and cats and pigs? 'Cos Mrs Brewster likes kids ever so much, and she'd have loved a big family.'

Tess laughed. 'Well, she's got a big family now,' she observed. 'Her boy may have gone off to the war, but she's got four little terrors in his place, and very soon three land girls will be arriving. Now that really *is* a big family!'

After that, Tina conducted her proudly all over the farm, not excluding fields, meadows and copses, though there was little enough to see in a ploughed field in December. Later that day, Mr Brewster helped Tess to climb aboard the pony which pulled his wife's trap when Mrs Brewster went to market. Tess had fed lumps of sugar or withered apples to milkmen's horses and the mighty shires which pulled the brewery drays, but she had never before sat astride a pony and discovered that Cloud was very different from the donkey she had once ridden on the Rhyl sands. She felt a long way from the ground, and when the pony broke into a trot slipped helplessly sideways, and was only rescued from an ignominious tumble by Mr Brewster, who grabbed the pony's bridle just in time and helped Tess to dismount.

On Monday afternoon, Mrs Brewster asked her, apologetically, if she could ride a bicycle and when she replied that she could suggested that she might pop down to Mrs Bailey's shop in the village and purchase a bag of ground almonds. 'I bake my Christmas cakes a couple of months in advance, but I leave making the marzipan until the last moment,' she explained.

So Tess climbed aboard the bicycle – it belonged to the Brewsters' son so had a crossbar – and cycled cautiously down the lane, avoiding the potholes and splashing through puddles. She emerged on to the road with some relief and decided that on the return journey she would push the bicycle rather than ride it, since it was all uphill.

In the main street, she looked round her with considerable curiosity, knowing that several of Tina's friends were billeted here, but perhaps because it was drizzling with rain now and extremely cold the village street was deserted. Also, Tina had told her that at first the school had been used by the evacuees in the mornings and the village children in the afternoons, but now the teachers had taken over the village hall and all the children were working a proper school day.

Tess realised it would be easier to have a look round before doing the shopping so she cycled slowly along the street, pausing on an ancient stone bridge to gaze down at the river below, then going on to take a look at the village green and the pond, where half a dozen ducks paddled about the margins, investigating the thick growth of reeds and quacking companionably to one another. The school overlooked the green, and presently the strains of a familiar carol drifted to Tess on the breeze. Almost magically, it seemed, the drizzling rain stopped and a ray of sunshine lit up the scene just as a child's clear treble voice began to sing the third verse of 'O Little Town of Bethlehem'. Tess recognised the voice at once as her sister's and stood, spellbound. How lucky Tina was! To have even a tiny share in this peace and beauty was more than most city children ever had. But then a bell rang and immediately the singing ceased, to be replaced by a cacophony of noisy young voices all shouting at once. Hastily, Tess remounted the bicycle and returned to the main street. She did the shopping and went back to the farm, reaching it shortly before the children came home. Tess helped Mrs Brewster to get their tea whilst the little girls searched for eggs, and were generally as useful as they could be. Tess found herself envying them. Helping on a farm would be far more fun than typing letters or driving a lorry on an air force station. For the first time, she began to consider joining the Land Army, and decided it would be grand to help the war effort and enjoy herself at the same time.

I'll do it, she told herself, buttering bread. How strange it would be if I got posted here, to this very farm! Yes, I'll apply to the WLA just as soon as I can.

*

On the Tuesday morning Tess got up very early, for she was catching the first train in the hope of getting home before it grew dark. Mr and Mrs Brewster were both up, Mrs Brewster making breakfast for the three of them and cutting a generous supply of sandwiches for Tess's journey, whilst Mr Brewster was already seated at the table, drinking a cup of tea. 'Good girl,' he said approvingly, as Tess entered the room. 'If you sit down right now and eat your breakfast, we'll be at the station with time to spare.'

Tess complied and was very surprised when Tina presently appeared, for the sisters had said goodbye the previous evening and Tess had not anticipated seeing Tina again before she left. She said as much and Tina shrugged and looked shifty. 'I wanted a word wi' you, before you go,' she said. 'Are you takin' the rest of that Christmas cake we made you, Tess? The surprise one what me and the other girls cooked our own selves, I mean.'

'Of course,' Tess said. 'Why, Auntie Deb was telling me that you actually bought the ingredients with your own money so I needn't feel guilty about taking it away with me.'

Tina nodded and hung around, staring very hard at Tess, and when Mr Brewster went out to start the car and Mrs Brewster had carried the porridge dishes through into the scullery to soak in the sink, she addressed her sister in a hissing whisper. 'Tess, I'm real worried. Last night we were talking about babies and that and little Eth said her mam died when her baby brother were born. Then Megan said her Auntie

208

Maud were real ill when she were havin' a baby and oh, Tess, I love me mam so much! I'm scared as scared that she might die like Eth's mam did.'

Tess gave her sister a hug. 'It's too late to change your mind now and come back with me,' she observed. 'But I'll tell you what, chuck, I'll get our mam to come and visit you at the farm as soon as the Christmas rush is over. She'll put your mind at rest and I dare say you'll feel better if she tells you herself that she had no trouble birthing you and me, so she won't have no trouble with the new one either.'

The anxiety cleared from Tina's face and she beamed at her sister. 'That 'ud be grand, just grand,' she said joyfully. 'I never thought that it might make Mam miserable when she heard I wanted to stay here over the holiday and didn't want to go back to Liverpool, even though it meant being without me real family. But if she comes here . . . that would be even better because Auntie Deb would make a real fuss of her. It 'ud be a holiday for Mam and mams don't get many holidays, does they, Tess?'

Tess was agreeing with these wise words just as Auntie Deb came bustling back into the kitchen, telling Tess to wind her scarf round her mouth and to turn her coat collar up because there was a heavy frost and the car was always cold and draughty. 'Do you want to go down and see your sister off, Tina?' she asked, rather doubtfully. 'You can, of course, but it might make you late for school because Uncle John means to go on to the feed merchant's once he's seen your sister on to her train.'

To Tess's secret relief, however, Tina shook her head. 'No, it's all right, I'll give you a hand with the breakfast for the other girls 'cos we promised Miss Williams we'd get to school early today so's to help her decorate the hall for the carol concert,' she said. 'Bye bye, Tess. Have a safe journey!'

Chapter Seven

January 1940

Tina thundered down the stairs and burst into the kitchen, closely followed by Eth, Joy and Megan. The four girls skidded to a halt by the big kitchen table and Tina addressed John Brewster, who was sitting at the table eating bacon and eggs. 'Is the weather better? Can we get into the village? Only we're that fed up of being shut in the house, and when Phil popped in yesterday he said all the kids what are billeted in the village were going sledging today. And we're desperate to go, ain't we, girls?'

John Brewster grinned at them. 'If you could get into the village, you could go to school,' he observed. 'How does that appeal, eh? But there's no question of your even getting down the lane; there's snowdrifts above my shoulders for over a mile. Why, poor Sophie came up to help the Rylands with the morning milking three days ago – Phil fought his way down to the blacksmith's forge and fairly begged her to go back with him – and she's been stuck at Hilltop Farm ever since. She's worried that her parents may run out of food – it's happening in small rural communities all over England, they say – but for all his promises, Phil hasn't managed to get her back to the village yet.' John Brewster chuckled. 'Not that

Phil's that keen to see Sophie go home, because with Hilltop so cut off he needs all the help he can get and Sophie's a grand little worker. But he's a good lad; when he does take her home you can be sure he'll give the Cantrips all the eggs and butter and cheese they need, as well as a share of the bacon from the pig they killed in the autumn.'

Auntie Deb bent and peered through the low kitchen window, half obscured already by the heavily falling snow. 'I doubt anyone will be going anywhere today,' she observed. 'Never mind, there's books and games and all sorts in the cupboard in our Danny's room, and the minute the snow stops Uncle John will dig his way across the yard and you can follow him out and have a bit of a snow frolic.'

The children cheered and Tina began gobbling her food as fast as she could. 'I'm the best milker of the lot of us, ain't I, Uncle John?' she said through a mouthful of bacon and egg. 'If you dig your way to the cowshed, then I'll be close behind you. Bags I start on Violet; she's me favourite of all the cows.'

At first, Sophie had not been ill-pleased to find herself stranded at Hilltop Farm because she knew herself to be of real use there. She slogged around the farm in the enormous waterproofs which she had inherited from Mr Ryland, who rarely left the warmth of the kitchen, save when Mrs Ryland or Phil wheeled him through into what had once been a study. Now it was Mr Ryland's bedroom, since he could no longer manage the stairs. For twelve months now, Mr Ryland had been confined to a wheelchair and though in fine weather he did a number of small jobs about the farm such as bagging up and preparing fruit and vegetables for market, washing the eggs and grading them, and even feeding motherless lambs with bottles of warmed milk, he was totally housebound by the snow and had to content himself with keeping the farm books up to date and working his way through the mass of papers with which the Ministry bombarded all farmers.

Naturally enough, this made Sophie's help all the more valuable and the fact that she enjoyed it was an added bonus. She did not really worry that her parents might run out of food, for they were right in the village with shops within a few yards of the forge, and besides, having her up at Hilltop meant there was one less mouth to feed. What was beginning to worry her by the third day of her incarceration was Phil's attitude towards her. At first, he had joked with her and teased her about the letters she constantly wrote to Danny, even though she could not post them – or receive replies – until the snow cleared. Then the teasing became, in some strange way, less amusing and more – more physical. He had always acknowledged she was Danny's girl and had sometimes been quite insulting, wondering aloud what Danny saw in such a little brown mouse of a thing, and then abruptly changing tack to wonder what she saw in stocky, dark-haired Danny when she was apparently content to ignore the charms of the beautiful blond beast, as Danny had sometimes nicknamed him.

At first Sophie had laughed at this, told him he was a conceited pig and added that Danny was worth three of him, but this made his eyes sparkle dangerously and he would grab hold of her, give her a hard hug or kiss the back of her neck and tell her she didn't know a real man from a boy.

'It's his money you're after,' he had said, teasingly. 'I've always said Danny had it all, but you don't want to be fooled by that. Once this bloody war is over I'll be way ahead, just you see.'

Sophie had made some joking reply, uneasily aware that beneath the banter which Phil handed out so regularly ran a deep vein of bitterness, of envy even. She would have to be careful because Danny and Phil had always enjoyed a warm, close relationship and some instinct told her that she must take care not to encourage Phil to believe that her feeling for Danny, and his for her, was some sort of trophy which Phil could snatch from them just to prove he was the better man.

On the fourth night of her stay, when they had finished the milking, she climbed up as usual to the hayloft above the stalls. It was her task to throw the bales down to Phil, who opened them up and distributed the contents amongst the herd, but on this occasion, when the last bale had gone down through the trap, Phil came bounding up the ladder, told her she had done a good job, as usual, and that her reward was on its way. Expecting an apple, or a piece of the chocolate bar which Phil had teased her with earlier, she was astonished and mortified when he pushed her into a pile of soft hay and started kissing her in a hungry and somehow desperate fashion, quite different from the casual embraces she had tried so hard to avoid on previous occasions.

'Get off, Phil!' she squeaked as soon as her mouth was free from his. 'Don't be such a fool . . . you're hurting.'

He laughed in a breathless, silly sort of way, and before she knew what was happening his hands were creeping under the thick jersey she wore and she felt his fingers, strangely hot, on her skin.

Sophie found what followed both frightening and humiliating, for though she fought with all her strength she was no match for Phil, and when she shouted, desperate for help, desperate for anything which would bring Phil to his senses, he put a large hand over her mouth and nose, almost suffocating her, and would not let her go, whilst he whispered that she was enjoying it really, that she would find it much more fun than anything she had done with Danny. To poor Sophie, those words were totally meaningless. She and Danny had kissed and cuddled, held each other close, talked of the future when they would be truly grown up and could afford to marry, but there had been none of the painful, horrible, embarrassing attentions which Phil was forcing on her. Danny had never so much as touched her breasts, let alone yanked her jersey up and pulled other things down, making her feel stupid, scared, and extremely vulnerable.

Frantically she tried to escape, to argue, but whether by design or accident he rolled her sideways at some point, clouting her head against a low beam so that for a moment her wits were addled and she almost lost consciousness. She was still muzzy when, at last, he finally rolled his considerable weight off her and began to do up his clothing, actually leaning over her as she lay in the hay, too crushed and broken to move. 'There! It wasn't too bad, was it?' he said, buttoning up. 'It's better after the first time, but I reckon you'll realise how I feel about you now, how keen on you I am.'

For a moment he stood looking down at her and even through the tears in her eyes she could see the uncertainty in his face, though he was trying to grin. 'Don't look so upset. I thought you and Danny . . . I didn't realise it was your first time or I'd have . . . oh, dammit, Soph, it has to happen, you know. I thought Danny would have seen to you before he left.' He reached down and took her hands, pulling her to her feet, and when she would have fallen, for her legs seemed to have turned to jelly, he said with a sort of rough kindness: 'Oh, God, Soph, what I'm trying to say is that I didn't realise you were . . . you know . . . I thought you and Danny were lovers.'

For some reason, the words dispelled Sophie's weakness, gave her strength. She pushed Phil away with all her might and began to pull her clothing into respectability, though she was still shivering with cold and shock. When she could speak, she said, scornfully: 'Keen on me – you? That's a laugh! And what's more you're a bloody liar, Phil Ryland, because you knew Danny would never do anything so disgusting. I was sixteen when he left and he was only a couple of years older. We – we were just getting to know one another, but you were even jealous of that, weren't you? What a fool I've been! Fond of me indeed – that's a joke! Why, you did what you did because you're eaten up with jealousy of Danny, and I thought you were such good friends! Well, don't think I'll tell him what you did, because it would only hurt him, but I shall hate you for the rest of my life, and I'm going back to the village tonight if I have to dig my way through a mile and a half of twenty-foot snowdrifts. And now get out and leave me alone, d'you hear?'

Phil sat on his makeshift bed in the living room and cursed himself for a fool. He should never have treated Sophie the way he had and explaining it away was going to be next to impossible, but explain it away he must, for his plans for the future included Sophie and the thought of her returning to her parents and never speaking to him again, let alone joining the WAAF and perhaps being posted to the other side of England, was a prospect too unbearable to contemplate.

The trouble was, he told himself, he had got carried away, for he had not expected any sort of fight or argument once they got past the initial stages of lovemaking. Other girls, he thought resentfully, had said no and meant yes; how was he to know that Sophie was different?

But he had known, of course; if not immediately, then quite soon after he had begun to wrench at her clothing. Only then some devil in him had made it seem like a contest which he was bound to win and of course he had told himself that she would enjoy the experience once she stopped struggling and let things take their course.

But he had been horribly wrong, he acknowledged that now. He had hurt and humiliated her and had made things worse by insulting Danny, insinuating that the other man would have taken her virginity before joining the forces. What a complete and utter fool he'd been! She was in love with Danny, and though his cousin might be neither as strong nor as good-looking as himself, he had qualities which Phil now acknowledged that he himself lacked. Danny was self-controlled, sweet-tempered and extremely loyal. He had never looked at any other girl than Sophie and probably never would. Knowing how much the two of them had been together, Phil had pretended to be astonished to discover that Sophie was a virgin, but his surprise had been faked, and Sophie had known it. Phil had had affairs with various girls, teasing or cajoling them into compliance, but, thinking about it now, he realised how right Sophie was. Danny was very different from himself, and he had kept his feelings under control.

Phil thumped his fists on his knees and cursed

himself for his sheer, undiluted stupidity. The trouble was, from the moment that Sophie had said she did not intend to join the Land Army he had been in black despair. He needed to be able to leave the farm in her hands if he was to join the RAF. She was capable and efficient and could deal with his father now that Matthew was so disabled. He had even meant to suggest marriage, but some chance there was of Sophie's accepting him now. She was determined to become a Waaf. He had tried talking her round with absolutely no success.

'I've already told you I don't want to spend the whole war milking cows and cropping potatoes. I want to do something truly useful,' she had said. 'When I join the WAAF I could be one of those girls who guide the pilots down after a raid. Or I could be a plotter – a friend of mine from school does that, and she says it's really exciting. But whatever I am it'll be something different.'

He had begun to bluster, to tell her that there was nothing glamorous about office work, but she had shaken her head at him. 'You're talking through your hat, Phil Ryland,' she had said reprovingly and had turned away, ending the conversation.

He had seen the justice of it, and that, somehow, had made him angrier, more determined. If he did not act quickly it would be too late. So he had followed her up into the hayloft . . . and ruined everything. Or perhaps not. Despite her boast that she would return to the village even if it meant digging her way through twenty-foot snowdrifts, she had not done so, since they had emerged into the yard to find themselves in the middle of a raging snowstorm. They had entered the kitchen and Sophie had gone straight up to her room, but this was nothing unusual since she always changed out of her working clothes and cleaned up before the evening meal, as indeed he did himself. The four of them had later sat down to boiled beef, carrots and potatoes and no one had commented on the fact that the meal was taken almost in silence and that Sophie, who usually tucked into her food with an excellent appetite, had pushed it round and round her plate and started the washing-up before Mrs Ryland had produced the apple pie and custard which was to be their dessert.

To be sure, Mrs Ryland, knowing of Sophie's fondness for apple pie, had asked if Sophie wanted her to save a piece for later, but Sophie had simply said that she was not hungry, that in fact she had a headache and meant to go to bed early. 'I wanted to make my way back to the village after milking but the snow is still falling too heavily,' she had said. 'However, if it eases off tomorrow, I really must go home.'

Phil had looked at her white and furious face and had known that she meant it. Tomorrow, when it was light, she would go and of course his parents would insist that she must do as she wished, and all his plans would be in ruins.

Finally, he decided on a course of action that might go some way towards mending a situation which, he now acknowledged, had been entirely of his own making. He was still fully dressed but in his stockinged feet, so he padded softly upstairs and crossed the landing to his own bedroom, now occupied by Sophie, and opened the door very, very softly. He entered the room and knew at once she was awake by her startled intake of breath. He spoke quickly, urgently, before she could scream. 'Sophie, it's all right. I won't come in any further, but we must talk, you know we must. I did a terrible, unforgivable thing and I want to tell you I'm sorry from the bottom of my heart. The honest truth is I've always fancied you, always envied Danny, and this evening I think I went a little mad. Can you . . . can you ever forgive me?'

Sophie sat up in bed. She had pulled back the blackout curtains and in the faint light from the window he saw her face white and set, her mouth tightly closed but her eyes blazing. He had expected her to be frightened, perhaps even weeping, for he still thought of her as the little brown mouse of a girl his cousin Danny had taken under his wing. But now he saw that she was not afraid, only absolutely furious.

'Forgive you?' Sophie's voice was laden with scorn. 'I said at the time that I couldn't, so what d'you think has happened to change my mind? Of course I can't, Philip Ryland, because what you did *was* unforgivable. I had come up to the farm to help you and your family in any way I could and when I got trapped by the snow I simply thought I could be of even more use to you, being on the spot. I was a guest in your house, Phil; a guest, can you understand that? If you like, I was a paying guest because I'd paid for my bed and board by working as hard as I could at any job you gave me. Since ancient times, a guest in one's house has been treated with special care and attention. You violated all the laws there are by raping me in a cruel, greedy and painful way . . .'

'Not rape,' Phil muttered, glad that the moonlight could not reveal his scarlet cheeks. 'It – it might have been seduction, but not rape, never rape!'

Sophie stared at him incredulously. 'Not rape?' she said and Phil heard her voice rise to a squeak with some apprehension; his mother was growing deaf and his father slept downstairs, but even so, he wanted no audience for the conversation that was taking place. 'You're not trying to pretend I was willing?'

'No, no . . . Do keep your voice down. We don't want my mother coming in,' Phil mumbled. 'I – I came to apologise, to tell you how desperately sorry I am and – and to ask you to marry me. I couldn't think of any other way to put things right.'

'Don't be absurd,' Sophie said tartly. 'Marry *you* when Danny means so much to me? And even if he gets killed in this damned war, I wouldn't marry you after what you did.'

'But suppose there were – consequences?' Phil said rather hopelessly. He found he could not put into words what he really meant, but Sophie had no such inhibitions.

'A baby, you mean?' she asked. 'There won't be a

baby; one of the village girls – I think it was Lizzy Pinfold – said you can't get a baby the first time, and she should know. And now go away, Phil, because I've nothing more to say to you. I'm leaving in the morning, regardless of the weather, and if you try to prevent me I'll have to tell your mother what you did.'

Phil waited for a moment, staring down at the small straight-backed figure. He had never admired her more. Then he spoke as humbly as his nature allowed. 'I'm truly, truly sorry for what I did and I'll get you back down to the village tomorrow if I have to carry you every foot of the way. Please, Sophie, even if you can't forgive me now, say you'll try to forgive me one day, say you won't hold what I did against me for ever.'

Sophie shot down the bed and pulled the covers up over her shoulders. 'Bugger off,' she said uncompromisingly, 'and shut the door behind you.'

Tina thundered down the stairs and took her place at the breakfast table, closely followed by her fellow evacuees. 'It ain't fair,' she wailed. 'My mam should have been here a fortnight ago. Why, there hasn't even been any post 'cos Mr Currie can't get up the lane. I didn't know weather in the country was so much terribler than in towns. And if I have to make another snowman in the yard, I'll go stark staring mad, honest to God I will.'

Auntie Deb, frying bacon and eggs, shook her head reprovingly at Tina's cross face. 'Don't you go

223

blaming the country for the snow, because it's just as bad in towns and cities,' she said. 'This is the worst winter within living memory and I'll be bound it'll be as bad in Liverpool as it is here. Why it said so the other evening, on the news, and you heard it, young lady! That there river of yours has frozen over and even the docks have iced up. What's more, there isn't an airfield open in the whole of Britain, so let's hope the Luftwaffe is grounded as well as our boys. And I'll tell you another thing – the wireless is beginning to talk about remote communities running out of food. At least we're not facing that . . . not yet at any rate.'

'And it isn't as bad today as it has been, 'cos the snow ain't actually falling,' Tina remarked. She had gone over to the window and cleared herself a porthole on the steamy pane. 'Hey up, there's someone in the lane, I can see movement! Oh, suppose it's Mr Currie with the post! He might be bringin' a letter from me mam or Tess!'

Mrs Brewster joined her at the window, then turned to speak to her husband, half hidden behind an old farming magazine since he had been denied his daily paper for many days. 'It really must be better, John, and you may yet get your *Telegraph* and some post as well,' she observed. 'If I'm not mistaken, it's Phil and young Sophie, making their way down to the village. Phil's a thoughtful lad; I'm sure he'll pick up the mail and the papers for us as well as Hilltop after he's delivered Sophie.' She turned to the children. 'It looks like you'll get outside for an hour or two this morning; why, if no more snow falls you could be back in school tomorrow!'

Joy nudged Megan. 'That would be grand, Auntie Deb, ain't that so, Megan?' she said. "Cept for one thing; even if we could get into the village, we couldn't go to school. Pretty well all the schools is closed . . . so that's something else which we've got to thank the weather for.'

'And we are lucky,' Megan pointed out; at eleven, she was the oldest evacuee and a sensible child with two short fair plaits and a pair of wire-rimmed spectacles which were always slipping down her blunt little nose, so that half the time she viewed the world over the top of them. 'Auntie Deb lets us go out to do all sorts of jobs. We feed the hens, collect the eggs and get hay from the barn for the horses. And there's that smashing slide that we made, right down one side of the yard. We can have goes on that whenever it isn't actually snowing.'

John Brewster looked up from his farming magazine and stared accusingly at the four small girls. 'Tom found that slide when he was on his way to do the milking,' he said reprovingly. 'I never saw a man go further faster. I dunno where he might not have ended up if he hadn't crashed into that enormous snowman. And it weren't a soft landing either, 'cos the thing's been there long enough to turn to solid ice.'

Eth, Joy and Megan looked conscience-stricken and began to murmur apologies, but Tina was made of sterner stuff. 'I wish I'd seen him,' she said wistfully. 'But I don't see what he were doin' walkin' over that side of the farmyard, 'cos it don't lead anywhere. We wouldn't have made a slide where we thought anyone might get hurt,' she finished virtuously.

Auntie Deb, clattering plates down in front of the children, snorted. 'I can tell you why Tom walked on that side of the yard and why he went such a purler,' she said. 'He was carrying a couple of mangel-wurzels which he meant to stick on the snowman's front. He told me what he was going to do and I absolutely forbade it, but of course he took no notice; you know Tom, obstinate as a mule. So when he crawled into the kitchen with a damn great bruise on his forehead and the palms of his hands raw from skidding over the ice, I told him it was a judgement.'

'I don't gerrit. What's wrong with mangels?' Tina asked, genuinely puzzled. Megan and Eth looked mystified too, but Joy gave a knowing smirk. 'He meant to give the snowman busts, like ladies have, I suppose,' she informed her cronies in a whisper. 'We've never made a lady snowman; shall we do that today?'

By halfway through May, Tess had done as she had intended and joined the Land Army. Naturally enough, when she had gone along to the Women's Land Army Headquarters in Liverpool, she had mentioned that she had a sister who had been evacuated to Herefordshire and said she would like to be posted to a farm in that area. She had not been

226

particularly surprised, however, to find when her posting came through that she was to make her way to the small village of Ludham in Norfolk. In fact, when she had looked it up in her old school atlas and realised it was close to a number of airfields, she had felt downright pleased. She knew that Mike Mitchell was already piloting fighters, so there was a good chance that she might be within spitting distance of him.

She received her railway pass and her posting by letter, but later the same morning a large box arrived. Tess and Laura opened it with some excitement, and it proved to contain Tess's uniform, for she could not travel on her rail pass in civilian gear. Giggling, she and Laura examined the clothing and the heavy leather brogues, and laid everything out on the bed. Then she dressed herself in one of the Aertex shirts, the green jumper, the brown corduroy breeches – much hilarity since Laura could have fitted comfortably inside them with Tess, despite her condition – and a pair of long fawn socks. Then she pulled on the heavy lace-up shoes, knotted the tie round her neck, and regarded herself somewhat doubtfully in her dressing table mirror. She had to anchor the breeches in place with the heavy leather belt but she thought, secretly, that the breeches were the only really ugly part of the uniform. The rest was trim and attractive and when she plonked the cowboy-style hat on her head Laura clapped and Tess, though she scoffed, knew she would feel quite proud to be seen in the streets in her new garb.

The rail pass was made out for the following Monday, which gave Tess almost a week to make her arrangements. Since she was living at home and working in her stepfather's café she did not have to give notice or to pack any belongings other than those she thought she might require in her new life, so she was able to take time to buy herself a pair of stout rubber boots and a couple of pairs of tough gloves. The information sheet which had accompanied the uniform announced that rubber boots were in short supply as were working gloves and asked that, where possible, land girls should provide their own.

This amused Tess and Laura since waitresses were not in the habit of wearing rubber boots and Tess had never possessed such things, but she managed to buy a pair and took the advice of the shop assistant, a round-faced, bespectacled girl, who had volunteered some information as soon as Tess told her why she wanted the boots. 'I've a cousin what works on a farm just outside Neston,' she told her customer. 'She joined the Land Army as soon as war were declared and she told me that rubber boots is the coldest thing in the world, 'specially when 'tis snowy under-foot. She axed me to buy her a pair – she called them gumboots only that's the same thing – a couple of sizes too large, so she could wear extra socks.' She looked, calculatingly, at Tess. 'And that ain't all. She sent me money to buy some men's thick socks 'cos she said the Land Army gave her three pairs and that ain't much when you're wearin' 'em two at a time, if you understand me.'

So when Monday morning arrived, Tess began what proved to be a long and arduous journey, clad in her new uniform and carrying a couple of stout canvas bags containing the few personal possessions she had finally decided upon. It was difficult to imagine ever being cold, for it was a warm and sunny May morning and she found, when she changed trains at Rugby, that she was far too hot. She shed her green jersey thankfully and was tempted to remove her tie and open the neck of her shirt, but she had heard from girls in the services that there were severe penalties for misuse of uniform so she merely loosened her tie a little.

She had left Liverpool Lime Street very early but soon realised she would still arrive at her final destination very late. She had hoped, and expected, to find other land girls catching the same trains but it was not until she embarked on the last leg of her journey that she saw a girl, cowboy hat tipped to the back of her head, jumper tied round her waist by its sleeves, climbing aboard the train for which she herself was heading. Tess had been feeling lonely and apprehensive, but at the sight of the other girl her heart bounded with relief. Anything was bearable, she felt, if it was shared. She had been about to climb into a carriage opposite where she stood, but this was not a corridor train so she sprinted along the platform, her canvas bags banging against her legs and impeding her progress more than a little, and managed to climb into the same compartment as the other girl just as the guard came along the platform, slamming doors shut and warning bystanders to keep clear for the train was about to depart.

Tess collapsed into a seat, not bothering to put her bags on the overhead rack since she and the other land girl were alone in the compartment. Instead, she dumped them on the seat beside her and turned to her companion. 'Phew, am I glad to see you! I expected that there would be dozens of us, all heading for Norfolk, because when I registered I was told that the big arable farms simply devour land girls and need them desperately, particularly at this time of year.' She beamed at the other girl and held out a hand. 'How do you do? I'm Tess Collins from Liverpool, and I'm bound for a village called Ludham. I don't know whether I'm to be living at the farm or in digs, but I'm to report to a Mrs Yallop at Lavender Cottage. Then tomorrow morning I'm to make my way to Grange Farm.'

The other girl shook hands, her smile open and friendly. 'Oh, thank God for someone in the same perishing position,' she said. 'I'm Sue Pritchard and like you I'm bound for Grange Farm via Lavender Cottage. But I've only come from Norwich, lucky old me.'

Tess stared at her, taking in for the first time the fact that her companion was startlingly beautiful, with rich, dark hair curling to her shoulders and beautifully winged eyebrows above large dark eyes, which seemed to have a smile in them even when her mouth was serious. She also had what Tess thought of as a posh voice, unmarred by any regional accent.

In different circumstances, this might have made Tess feel uneasy, but the other girl's friendliness and the fact that they both wore the same uniform made the differences between them seem of no account.

Tess, who had stood up to shake hands, plonked herself down again as the train began to pick up speed. 'I say, what fantastic luck!' she exclaimed. 'I was dreading having to find Lavender Cottage in the blackout, and then having to rouse Mrs Yallop from her warm bed, but at least if there are two of us we'll have some moral support.' She glanced curiously at her companion. 'But why are you on this train? I mean, I set off at six o'clock this morning because cross-country journeys are pretty difficult, even in peacetime. But your journey should have been quite straightforward, shouldn't it?'

Sue Pritchard nodded ruefully. 'Yes, it should have been, but though my home is in Norwich I've been working in London for the past couple of years. The theatre doesn't open on a Sunday but the cast held a farewell party for me – and one or two others – on Saturday night after the show. I'm afraid it went on rather late, or perhaps I should say rather early, since I seem to remember staggering back to my flat share around three in the morning. Then of course I crashed out and practically slept the clock round.' She gave Tess a wicked, rueful glance. 'I meant to get up early this morning because my mother had telephoned me to say that my luggage had arrived in Cringleford, only somehow I managed to oversleep and didn't get to Liverpool Street until halfway through the afternoon. I had to telephone Daddy from Thorpe Station to come and pick me up and when I got home I had to wash off the grime of the journey from London, unpack my uniform, change into it and repack my bag . . . I expect you can guess the rest.'

'Yes . . . but are you an actress?' Tess breathed, much impressed. 'And on the London stage, too! But whatever made you want to join the Land Army? I remember someone telling me that there was a special unit of actors who would entertain the troops. I can't remember what it was called . . .'

'ENSA,' her new friend supplied, nodding. She laughed and Tess saw a dimple appear beside her mouth. 'I'm not in that class; you've got to be really well known to entertain the troops, honey! But I was on the stage, all right, as a member of the dear old chorus.'

Tess gazed at her, awed. 'A dancer?' she squeaked. 'Oh, Sue, what show were you in? And why on earth did you join the Land Army?'

'I was in a review called *Carry On, Sailor!* and I joined the WLA because I'm a farmer's daughter, and one day I'll be a farmer's wife,' Sue said seriously. 'I have a fiancé in the Royal Air Force but I didn't fancy putting myself in uniform and sitting behind a typewriter for the duration of the war. Besides, I like farm work, really I do. I know it's hard, I know I'll freeze in winter and scorch in summer, but I also know how desperately important food production is going to be in the next few years. Farming was in a poor way in 'thirty-eight because we had begun importing cheap food from the United States and Europe and British farmers couldn't compete. But the war has changed all that, of course; foreign countries have their work cut out to feed themselves and our merchant shipping is under constant attack from the Jerries. A number of our farms have been allowed to fall fallow – that means they're not being worked – so now we're going to need all the help we can get to make the land productive again.'

'Gosh!' Tess said. 'What a lot you know, Sue! And what a piece of luck us meeting up like this! Though I don't suppose you feel anywhere near as strange and lost as I do.'

'Well, I don't now I've met you, but I felt pretty horrible before. I was beginning to think I might have made an awful mistake,' Sue admitted. She ferreted in an old knapsack which she had slung on the seat beside her, then held out a crumpled packet of Players No. 1. 'Here, have a fag . . . I've got some matches somewhere.'

Tess, who had never smoked a cigarette in her life, extracted one gingerly, watched Sue apply a match to the end of her own, and then tried to emulate her, drawing in such a huge breath that she nearly choked herself, and coughed so violently that tears poured down her cheeks. Sue, laughing, took the cigarette from her and extinguished it. 'Sorry. You're a lot younger than me – I'm twenty-two – but I expect you'll learn to smoke once you've found your feet. Very steadying for the nerves, smoking. Now, where was I?'

'You were saying you thought you might have made a mistake in joining the WLA,' Tess said eagerly. 'That's how I've been feeling, but I don't see why you should.'

'Oh, because I put in to work for my father but most of his farmhands are too old to be called up and he got a couple of land girls at the very start of the war, so they said it was out of the question and posted me to Ludham,' Sue explained. 'Fortunately, I'm not the shy type, so I expect I'll fit in. On Daddy's farm, which is mainly dairy, all the workers have known me since I was knee-high to a grasshopper, but I don't know Ludham at all, let alone Grange Farm.' She hesitated, giving Tess a curiously shy and uncertain look for one so self-assured. 'There are some people who think you're stuck up if you went to a decent school and don't have a local accent. There are others who think actresses, or perhaps I should say chorus girls, are high-class prostitutes. So you see working for Daddy was one thing, but working for a stranger is quite another.'

'Well, I'm sure no one would think you were anything but a lady,' Tess said warmly. 'As for believing chorus girls are prossies – that's what we call them in Liverpool – they're no such thing, and anyone who says so is just bleedin' jealous. Why, there are all sorts in the services; my boyfriend is a fighter pilot now, but before the war he worked in a big engineering factory, so you see there's bound to be a mix of all different sorts of people, whether you're in the Land Army or one of the forces.'

Sue was beginning to answer when the train juddered to a halt and they flew to the window to peer out. All place names, including those on stations, had been removed in order to confuse an invading army, so Tess had no idea where they were, but fortunately the dim figure of a porter came along the platform, opening doors and announcing, in an accent so broad that Tess would never have understood him left to herself, that they had arrived at Wroxham.

She and her companion gathered up their belongings and jumped down on to the platform, then looked rather helplessly about them. Tess saw a sign which said 'Way Out', and headed for it. 'I wonder if there's a taxi?' she said anxiously as they passed the ticket office. 'My letter said we'd be met but I guess we're later than we should have been so probably whoever was meeting us gave up hours ago.'

However, this did not prove to be the case. As they left the station they saw a pony trap pulled up by the side of the road, and even as they hesitated, looking round them for a taxi, they found themselves addressed by a figure standing at the pony's head. 'Would you be heading for Ludham, young ladies?' a woman's voice asked. It was what Tess would have described as a posh voice. 'I can see you're WLA and I've been told to meet two land girls who'll be working at Grange Farm and to take them to Mrs Yallop, in Ludham.'

'Yes, that's us,' Sue said eagerly. She held out a hand. 'I'm Sue Pritchard and this is Tess Collins and we're most grateful to be met at all because we're awfully late.' She slung her bags into the trap, then gestured for Tess to do the same. 'How did you know what train to meet, Mrs . . . er . . .'

'Mrs Randolph. I'm chairwoman of the local WI. I had a phone call from Norwich telling me there had been delays and asking me to turn up at the station around ten o'clock.' She smiled at them and helped Tess to climb into the trap, for though Sue had hopped in blithely, Tess was not used to such conveyances and missed the step at her first attempt. As soon as they were settled, Mrs Randolph climbed aboard and clicked to the horse and they set off. The motion was soothing and Tess, who was very tired, soon began to nod, though Sue and Mrs Randolph had a sprightly conversation as they wended their way along a winding but pleasant road, tree-lined in places and apparently unfrequented by much traffic, for they met no other vehicles in the course of the five-mile journey. Mrs Randolph said, in heartening tones, that though the girls started work on Grange Farm at seven in the morning, they themselves would not be expected to do so the next day since they had arrived so late. 'Mrs Yallop's a friendly soul but I'll give her the word to let you lie in tomorrow,' she said. 'Grange Farm is several miles from the village so you will be provided with bicycles; I take it you can both cycle?'

Tess and Sue both said that they could do so, though Tess said dreamily: 'I used to ride me boy-friend's delivery bicycle, a great heavy old thing with a huge basket on the front, so I reckon riding a proper bicycle will be a piece o' cake.'

Mrs Randolph turned and grinned; Tess could see the flash of white teeth in her round and cheerful face. 'Most of the Land Army bicycles belonged to telegram boys or postmen at some stage in their careers,' she observed. 'They're pretty old and battered, not exactly sports models, but they'll get you to and from your digs a good deal quicker than Shanks' pony. Mind, I'm not saying you'll be with Mrs Yallop for long, because billeting in a rural area isn't always easy and you may find you're moved around a bit. But you'll be there for a few weeks, I dare say.'

'I always imagined we'd be actually living on the farm itself,' Tess said. 'It 'ud be a lot easier for everyone, wouldn't it?'

'Well, it would certainly be easier for the land girls,' Mrs Randolph admitted. 'But several of the farms took in evacuees at the start of hostilities and although some of the children went back home during what they now call the phoney war a good many stayed, so the farms don't have a great deal of spare room.'

As she spoke, she had been glancing to right and left, and now she nodded approvingly. 'We're just entering the village and I'm happy to see that there isn't a single light showing. Folk in rural areas don't always realise how important it is never to show a light. Now let me see . . . Lavender Cottage . . . here it is!' She drew the pony to a halt, then inhaled deeply and turned to her passengers. 'Can you smell that lilac? Isn't it just the most glorious scent? I once asked Mrs Yallop why her cottage wasn't named after the lilac trees which grow on either side of the gate, but she had no idea. All she said was that it had always been Lavender Cottage and always would be, even if she never grew so much as a sprig of the stuff.'

Chuckling, Mrs Randolph dismounted from her perch and went to the horse's head to loop the reins round the gatepost. 'Sheila – that's the pony – won't dream of moving off until she's told so I'll just pop in with you, introduce you to Mrs Yallop, and then be on my way,' she said. 'It's most awfully late but she won't have gone to bed, though I dare say she'll be in dressing gown and slippers. Got all your belongings? Good; I'll hold the gate open for you.'

Chapter Eight

July 1940

Mike sat in the mess clutching a handful of envelopes, for today's post had been a rich one: three letters from Tess, one from Laura, one from his father and one from Tina. He loved getting letters – everyone in the forces did – but he had been starved of correspondence whilst he was in France covering the retreat. Not that he had remained in France for long; the air force had realised that the heavy losses which would have resulted had they not withdrawn their air power would have left England unprotected in the event of an invasion. So they had clawed back the squadrons and closed down the airfields in France very soon after they began evacuating the troops from the beaches and the result was that Britain still had planes and pilots to defend her land. Of course the plan had had its detractors, and you could scarcely blame them; Mike had heard a great many soldiers saying bitterly that they had not so much as glimpsed 'the Brylcreem Boys' whilst they crouched in the dunes and queued up to their necks in water to board the craft which would, they hoped, carry them to safety. Mike and his fellow fliers knew that the air force's actions had been sensible, for the Luftwaffe was better equipped and had many more aircraft than did Britain, but it was difficult to explain these facts to men whose friends had been strafed and killed by Messerschmitts on the long, pale beaches whilst they looked in vain for the small planes with the roundels on their wings to come to their rescue.

But right now, even the most sceptical were beginning to realise that Dunkirk, as it was being called, had indeed been a strategic withdrawal and not the ignominious defeat which some people had made out. The air force was preparing to attack the troops and vehicles which had been gathering at the Channel ports ever since France had fallen, the army was retraining and re-equipping the many thousands of men who had managed to get back to Britain, and the Navy was doing its best to guard the merchant ships as they tried to transport vital supplies across the Atlantic. The Americans still held aloof from the conflict, but they were selling the Allies weapons of war as well as desperately needed supplies.

And then there was his darling Tess, hoeing carrots, cutting hay and cycling miles on a dreadful, creaking old bicycle to get to work every day at some ungodly hour. She had sent him a photograph of herself in her uniform – it stood beside his bed in a cheap Bakelite frame, one of his most precious possessions. When she had written to tell him she had been posted to Norfolk it had meant little to him – he had been in France – but now he thought there was a good chance that he, too, might end up in that part of the country. Every airfield needed fighters to protect it at present because it was assumed that Hitler meant to bomb them out of existence so that there would be no air power when the invasion began. But we're not as green as we were, Mike told himself with satisfaction; the Luftwaffe may have a lot going for it in sheer weight of numbers, but our pilots and our Spitfires and Hurricanes are more than a match for the bloody Hun, no matter what they may think.

But now he must open his letters and he decided to start with the one from Laura. He was fond of her, thought her an excellent and hard-working wife for his father, but ever since the birth of his young half-brother David her letters had contained little else but what Mike thought of as 'baby news', like tales of a desperate search for muslin nappies because David's little bottom had thrown out a nappy rash and the towelling ones made it worse. He was a good baby, for though he was still only seven weeks old he slept from ten at night until six in the morning and rarely cried. Laura was not yet working full time in the café but they were very busy so she gave a hand whenever she could and still did most of the cooking, though of course cafés were rationed, not only in what they might buy, but also by what they could find, for some things were in short supply and made cooking what was needed even more difficult.

So, since Mike always opened his letters in turn, saving the best till last, he read quickly through Laura's description of the baby's hair – as ginger as his own – to his smile, which was warm and delightful and produced every time he saw his parents' faces. There were a few little snippets about customers he would remember and a lively account of a meeting with one of his old classmates after a rare trip to the cinema, then she signed off as she always did: *From your loving stepmama, Laura.*

Mike wavered between Tina's letter and that of his father, finally deciding to read his father's first since Arthur was a poor correspondent, relying on his wife for a livelier account than he could manage himself. The letter was brief, as Mike had expected, though it said they were all well and that his new delivery boy was an eleven-year-old girl called Biddy: *. . . not that she'll be with us for long, since the shop's half empty and folk, except for the very old, are glad enough to carry home whatever they can buy themselves,* he had written. *Those bastards sink a good few of the ships loaded with oranges, bananas and such, but as Tess wrote when I complained of the shortages, she and her mates are doing their best by growing acres of carrots and swedes, and will turn their attention to oranges and bananas just as soon as they have the time.*

It made Mike laugh and Tina's epistle made him laugh more, partly because her spelling was somewhat hit and miss, and partly because she wrote as she spoke, diving into whatever subject or grievance was uppermost in her mind, recounting everything that happened to her as though he knew intimately all the people of whom she spoke.

Today's letter was no exception. A few weeks ago she, and she alone, had been searching for eggs in the hedge which bordered the lane and had seen Mr Cantrip, Sophie's father. Who the devil is Sophie, Mike wondered, another evacuee? A friend from the village? But Tina did not bother over such trifles and ploughed on. Apparently, she had been much surprised by the appearance of the blacksmith since it seemed he never strayed from the village. But all soon became clear.

> *He must have been coming up to see the Rylands about the wedding* [she wrote excitedly]. *None of us had any idea that there was going to be a wedding cos Sophie wanted it quiet like, but they're married now and Sophie's moved up to Hilltop. Mrs Ryland wanted to have a little party after the rejister ofice, which is where they got married, but Sophie and Phil said no, not in wartime (Sophie's Mrs Ryland as well now, don't that seem strange)? Mr Brewster said, 'It's a damn shame, the poor kid was set against it but of course the Cantrips are old-fashioned . . .' and then he saw me and Megan scrubbing spuds in the skullery and shut up. We all think it were a shame, not to have a party, but war makes a difference I suppose.*

Mike read the rest of the letter with a smile curling his mouth. He did not know either of the two people concerned but he realised from Tina's description that it had been a shotgun wedding and one, furthermore, not wanted by either participant. Still, even in this enlightened age, fellers had to pay for their pleasures and no doubt both parties would settle down to married life happily enough now that the knot had been tied.

He put Tina's letter down and reached out for Tess's, seeing with approval that she had numbered them on the back of the envelope, as she always did, so that he could take them in order. He began to read.

The post always arrived at Lavender Cottage long after Tess and Sue had cycled off to work, for they had to leave by about twenty past six to reach Grange Farm in time for the muster, when all the girls – and those farmhands too elderly to be called up – congregated in the big modern farmyard. When it rained they met in one of the barns, but today was fine so they would be out of doors, waiting to hear what jobs they were to do and whereabouts on the farm they should go.

Sue and Tess always worked together if possible, usually with Jenny and Bet, another couple of land girls who were billeted in the farm cottage belonging to their foreman, Tosher. Tess had never learned his real name but liked the little man, with most of his face burned reddish brown by being constantly out of doors and his brow, protected by a greasy flat cap, white as driven snow. At first, Tess had suspected that he kept his cap on at all times to hide the fact that he was bald, but the day he fell off the hayrick she saw that he had a thick crop of bushy, greying hair, so presumably he wore the cap because he liked to do so. It protected him from the weather, of course, but there was very little weather in the farm kitchen where they took their midday meal and Tosher's cap remained firmly on his head even there. Jenny and Bet, when questioned, said that Tosher did not doff his cap when he entered his own cottage, and the girls speculated whether he wore it all night or whether, perhaps, he replaced it with a scarlet nightcap pulled well down over his two-tone brow.

Today, however, Tess and Sue cycled off without even their headscarves, enjoying the July sunshine, and as they began to cross the marshes the salt breeze which blew to them from the sea made Tess think, nostalgically, of trips to New Brighton – a rare treat – and of a long-ago excursion to Seaforth Sands before Tina had even been born. It had been lovely getting the undivided attention of both parents as they vied to dig the biggest castle in the world, with the deepest moat.

But now Seaforth Sands was too close to the constant flow of shipping coming in and out of the docks. Her friend, Nell, had written to Tess telling of how she had taken her boyfriend down to the sands and been disgusted by the piles of oily waste and puddles of the beastly black stuff. *It's ruined, so it is,* she had written sadly. *I hope they'll clean it up after the war because poor kids relied on Seaforth for the sand and that in the old days; not everyone could afford to take the ferry to New Brighton.*

'I say, Tess, why don't we go down to the shore the next time we have a day off? We could, you know – it's not very far away. Why, we cycle ten miles, and often more, each day and it would be such fun to mess about on the beach like a couple of kids.'

Tess stared at Sue. 'But don't you remember what young Beasley told us? He and his lady friend went down to Sea Palling and they couldn't get on to the beach at all. There were notices warning folk to keep off, barbed-wire entanglements, the lot.'

Sam Beasley was one of the many airmen from nearby Coltishall who enjoyed a drink at the local pubs and had become friendly with the land girls. He was a pleasant youth and enjoyed lending a hand at Grange Farm when he was not actually on duty.

'Of course, I remember now. It's because of the bloody invasion that everyone is so sure will come,' Sue said gloomily. She brightened. 'But I do remember somebody saying that they couldn't mine or barbed-wire entangle every bit of the beach, because they had to leave room for the lifeboat to get in and out. I wonder, is there a lifeboat at Sea Palling? Or Walcott? Or Happisburgh? If so, it wouldn't be that much further to cycle and oh, I do long to bathe in the sea again.'

'It's all very well for you, Sue. I can't swim. Girls can't usually, where I come from. But I could splash about a bit and play in the rock pools,' Tess said, thinking nostalgically of New Brighton beach once more. 'Come to think of it, I might easily learn to swim in the sea. Boys in Liverpool usually learn in the Scaldy – that's what we call the part of the canal where Tate's pump out their unwanted hot water – but it's easier in seawater. I remember my stepfather saying that one day he would take us all on a seaside holiday so's he could teach me and Tina to swim.'

'I don't know about your canal but I do know there aren't any rock pools on Norfolk beaches, because there aren't any rocks,' Sue said. 'But there are low-waters . . . still, no point in discussing it since we'll have to find the safe part of the beach where there's a slipway for the lifeboat before we can so much as paddle. Ah, we're in good time; there's old Tosher ambling out of his cottage and he's always early.'

'Let's get a move on and beat him to it,' Tess said, standing up on her pedals. 'What a fantastic day! Even harvesting acres and acres of perishin' carrots will be fun today.'

'It might not be carrots,' Sue said breathlessly, as they whizzed past Tosher and turned into the farmyard. 'The plums will be ripe quite soon. And old Tosher said something about a second crop of hay; I really enjoyed haymaking.'

The girls dismounted from their bicycles and wheeled them into the big shed where already Jenny and Bet were parking their own machines. They, too, had been billeted at Lavender Cottage until Tess and Sue arrived, and had been allowed to keep their bicycles. Without them their social life would have been very restricted, for the farm was some way from the nearest village.

'Why have you come in on your bikes?' Sue asked. She tutted. 'You young things get lazier and lazier; I don't know what modern girls are coming to.'

Jenny turned and grinned at them. She was a

small, square girl with a cap of shining dark hair, very light blue eyes and an engaging grin. 'There's a dance in the village hall at Hoveton. It starts at eight o'clock – well, the doors open then, anyway – so we got permish from Mrs Turnbull to bring our civvies up to the farmhouse. She's going to let us change in one of the bedrooms, and have a wash and so on, and then we'll cycle straight off to Hoveton. Why don't you two come?'

'Oh, damn, why didn't anyone tell us?' Sue said mournfully. 'But we can't. By knocking-off time tonight we'll be filthy and no matter how quickly we manage to get back to Lavender Cottage it'll take ages to clean ourselves up and get into civvies. Besides, Mrs Yallop will have made our supper and she'd be really upset if we missed that.' She shook a reproving finger at the other girl. 'Just remember, in future, that it's your duty to let Tess and me know whenever there's a dance, or a party or anything, so we have time to make arrangements. And now, give us a nice surprise; tell us we're not lifting carrots all day. The ground's too wet. It would be like – like pulling teeth.'

The two girls giggled and Bet, the youngest of the four at barely seventeen, whose light brown hair started each day in a neat bun on the back of her head and ended up each evening hanging down to her shoulders, pulled a face. 'It's carrots. Prue is driving the tractor and the rest of us will follow. But Tosh said if we work hard and the weather stays fine, we should finish with the carrots by this evening. So that's a mercy because I don't think I've got a single nail left whole on either of my hands.'

Prue Turnbull was the farmer's eldest daughter. She was waiting to join the WAAF, and everyone knew that when she did so Sue and Tess would vie for the job as tractor driver, though probably Sue, who had been driving her father's cars for years, would get the job. Still, one can't help hoping, Tess told herself as she and the other girls reached the enormous carrot field and Prue on the tractor lowered the ploughshare and began to turn up the carrots. The girls followed in her wake, each provided with a large sack into which they piled the produce, having first knocked off as much earth as they could. Later, they would return with their booty to the farm where they would pull off the tops and remove any loose earth remaining.

It was backbreaking work especially as it had rained in the night, making the soil gluey and the carrots difficult to get out, and they were all glad of a break when half past twelve arrived. Everyone was filthy and sick to death of carrots, but they produced sandwiches and bottles of cold tea, or lemonade if they were lucky – Prue had lemonade – and began to eat and chat. No one lingered over their food, however, since they were all keen to finish off the field and get back to the farm in good time. Tess worked grimly on, her back feeling as though it must presently break, but she knew from experience that the pain would reduce to a dull ache as time passed. At first she had expected that backache would keep her awake, but she was always so tired by the time she got to bed that she slept deeply and at once, though when she awoke in the mornings she was often stiff from remaining in the same position for hours at a time.

She and Sue often discussed their fear that they would end up with muscles a man might have envied, but after only a couple of months they realised that muscles or no, land girls tended to be a lot fitter than those in other occupations. Jenny had once told them how, pre-war, she had spent most winters – and often spring and autumn too – suffering from colds, tonsillitis and other such ills, but since joining the WLA, and despite the awful severity of the previous winter, she had not had so much as a sniffle. 'Though we all had dreadful chilblains, but I reckon they're a hazard of the job,' she had told them.

By a quarter to seven they had finished the field and were making their way back to the farm in a tired but cheerful group. They were perched on the trailer upon which they had piled the full sacks of carrots and were dreamily contemplating the evening ahead. 'I suppose if we really hurried, we might make the dance at the village hall by half time,' Sue said lazily. 'Only the thought of biking all that way and then having to quickstep or foxtrot with some horny-handed farm worker does rather make my blood run cold. I mean, Tosh says he'll put us on blackcurrants for the next few days, which is easier work than harvesting carrots, but I bet we'll find there are snags even in picking blackcurrants, so maybe it'll be best if we go home and collapse into bed, as we usually do.'

Jenny, sitting between Sue and Bet and ruminatively chewing a fat grass stalk, smiled at the older girl. 'Audrey and Netta have been in the WLA for over a year and they go to everything, even making their way into Norwich if there's a flick they want to see,' she observed. 'They say you get used to the work and find you can go out in the evenings and enjoy yourself without affecting how you get on next day. But you've only been at it for a couple of months – not even as long as Bet and me – so of course you're finding it hard.'

'That's true,' Tess said, nodding. She admired the lively manner in which the other land girls behaved, going off at a moment's notice to any sort of entertainment on offer, yet managing to arrive on time the following morning and doing their share of any work without a word of complaint. 'Well, at least we started on the land at a good time of year. Imagine being posted here last winter when the whole country was at a standstill because of the snow! And that reminds me.' She turned to Sue, so often a mine of information on various topics. 'I know we're only meant to have one day off a week, but a day isn't long enough for me to get all the way to Liverpool and back. As you know, I've got a new little baby brother that I've not so much as set eyes on and I really would love to see him, and my mam of course. I was wondering whether I might save up a couple of extra days by working when I was supposed to be off? If I

251

could, then I'd rush home for a crafty weekend with my folks. What do you think?'

'I'd ask Mr Turnbull,' Sue said, after some thought. 'I don't see why they should object because, damn it all, we're always having it impressed on us that we're non-combatants, not members of the armed forces. We don't get half the privileges they do, yet whoever saw ATS with tommy guns, or Waafs working as tail gunners? You ask Mr Turnbull, honey; I'm sure he'll agree.'

Laura poked her head round the kitchen door and glanced towards the bedroom. She did not want to shout to Arthur in case she woke the baby, but she had managed to acquire two magnificent sausages, now cooked to a turn and bursting out of their skins, and the thought of Arthur arriving late to find two blackened objects on his plate was too awful to be contemplated. Sausages were a rare treat, though Mr Sandon, with whom they were registered, always did his best to see that good customers got any off-rationed treats such as sausages or offal when they were available. Sizzling in the pan beside the sausages was a large tomato, as well as a slice of fried bread; Arthur was not a greedy man but he adored fried tomatoes and was a great believer in a cooked breakfast, though he was happy enough to skip lunch if the shop was busy. So Laura returned to the kitchen, pulled the pan off the flame and was on her way back towards the bedroom door when it opened and Arthur emerged. He was sniffing the air ecstatically and gave her a smacking kiss on the cheek before slipping an arm round her waist and propelling her back to the kitchen. 'I swear I can smell sausages, you little miracle worker, you,' he said, giving her a squeeze. 'You're the most wonderful woman in the world, and I'm the luckiest feller in Liverpool.' They entered the kitchen and he glanced hopefully towards the cooker. 'Ooh, tomatoes! Wharra grand woman you are, queen.'

'Cupboard love,' Laura said teasingly, beginning to dish up. 'Only another day and Tess will be here! I wish Mike could have made it at the same time but no such luck. I reckon all the armed forces are on standby, waiting for an invasion, but it'll be grand to see Tess and grander for her to see David. I just wish Tina could have come back for the weekend, but at least she has seen the baby. She was very sweet about him but disappointed that he couldn't *do* anything yet.' Laura had undertaken the trek down to Herefordshire a month earlier and though Tina had said, dutifully, that her little brother was lovely, she had been disappointed when he took no interest in the new lambs or the little pigs in the sty and had made it clear to her mother that she thought farm babies much more interesting than human ones.

Laura had only been at Manor Farm for a couple of days but she and Mrs Brewster had enjoyed one another's company. 'Your little girl and the other evacuees are a great help around the farm and they're growing used to us and our ways,' Mrs Brewster had said. 'I know you must miss her horribly but you'd not want her to go back into danger, not with the threat of invasion very much with us.'

It had not really been a question but Laura had answered it anyway. 'No, much though I miss her, I wouldn't take her back whilst things are so uncertain,' she agreed. 'We've been lucky so far, but the Luftwaffe have dropped bombs in Wales, and of course they're always attacking the convoys and Liverpool, as you know, is a very important port. No, Tina's best where she is.' She had smiled at Mrs Brewster. 'And by the time the war's over and Tina's at home again David will be old enough to be interesting, though of course the age gap means they're unlikely to be pals,' she had ended regretfully.

Now she sat down opposite her husband, smiling with pleasure because she could tell how the sight of a cooked breakfast pleased him. Without waiting to be asked, she pushed the bottle of Flag sauce nearer him. He cut into the first sausage, then hesitated with it halfway to his mouth. 'Where's yours?' he demanded. 'You need a cooked breakfast even more than I do, because of the little chap. And don't try to kid me that you ate earlier because the smell only reached me ten minutes ago.' He put down his knife and fork and pushed back his chair, getting to his feet and reaching down a plate from its place on the Welsh dresser. 'We'll have half each and fill up with toast and margarine. No arguments; I'm the master in this house and what the master says goes.'

Laura protested, reminding him that she had

never been fond of sausages, but she might as well have saved her breath. The breakfast was divided scrupulously and presently the pair of them began to eat, Laura thinking, lovingly, that no other man of her acquaintance could match Arthur when it came to generosity, let alone affection. He says he's lucky but I reckon I'm luckier, she told herself as they finished their meal. It sounds ridiculous to say we've never had a cross word, but we never have. And what other man would do his share of getting up in the night to see to the baby? I thought Alf was a wonderful husband but he wouldn't even push the pram in public in case folk thought him a sissy. My Arthur will change a dirty nappy and do all the cleaning-up business so that David ends up as comfortable as though I'd done the job myself. Arthur's a *real* man because he's never afraid of what people think.

'That were a grand breakfast, love. I shan't need any dinner . . .' Arthur was beginning when they both heard the clatter and thump as the post shot through the letter box. Laura immediately hurried out of the room, hoping for a letter from Tina, and was not disappointed. She returned to the kitchen clutching the mail, and gave the one in Mike's familiar handwriting to her husband.

'It's nice for you to have Mike back in the country,' she said contentedly, as Arthur began to open the envelope. 'We were out of touch for ages while he was doing his pilot training in Rhodesia, and then he was in France covering the retreat, with no time to write so much as a line. I don't believe he ever got half our letters either . . . still, things are easier now. I just wish he could get some leave.'

'I'm sure he'll come home, if only for a forty-eight, once the threat of invasion is over,' Arthur said comfortably. 'Though whether he'll come here I'm not so sure. He's nearer Norfolk, you know, and he's mortal fond of your Tess. I know he's not seen David yet, but babies don't mean much to young fellers and it's months since he and Tess met. Oh aye, I reckon he'll go and see her as soon as he gets the chance. And now you read your letters and I'll read mine, then I'll get the shop opened up and you'd best clear up here or Mrs Tasker will be coming up for her orders before you're ready.'

Mrs Tasker was a skinny, energetic woman in her late forties, who had brought up a family of five boys without any sort of help since her husband had died of TB when her youngest child was only two. The boys were grown up now, of course. Three had gone to the States where they had married and were raising families of their own. One was in Australia and the other had married an Irish girl and lived in Connemara, seldom contacting his mother. When the boys were small she had cleaned public houses, taken in washing, sold her own baking from door to door, and done anything else which would bring in a few shillings. As soon as the children were old enough to be left, she had started regular work in Scott's bakery on Knowsley Road, slaving in the hot bakehouse from three in the morning until three in the afternoon, or sometimes later. Once her children were grown and off her hands she had looked about her for pleasant and easier work and had first come to Restawhile as assistant cook, but had speedily risen to the position of manageress, sharing the job with Laura at first, but taking over – with an increased salary – now that the baby took up so much of her employer's time.

Laura glanced at the clock above the mantelpiece. Mrs Tasker was always on time; she would arrive at half past eight, not a moment earlier or later, and it was only a quarter past now. 'Right you are; I'll read my letters and still have time to wash the breakfast things before Mrs T arrives,' Laura said, and settled herself at the table. 'There's nothing from Tess, of course, but Liza has written.'

'Who's Liza?' Arthur asked absently. 'Mike's on standby again, but he managed to get into Lincoln on the liberty truck . . . what on earth's that? . . . He says it's a fine city.'

'Oh, Arthur, you can't have forgotten Liza Slim! She was the first waitress to leave when the war started: a pretty girl with curly brown hair . . .'

'Oh, yes, I remember,' Arthur said. He pushed his letter towards Laura and stood up. 'I'd best get off now, but you might as well read this one whilst you're waiting for Mrs T.' He leaned across the table and kissed the tip of her nose. 'See you later, sweetheart. Love you.'

Laura watched him go, thinking again how unashamedly affectionate he was. She wondered if

257

Mike would take after his father; if so, Tess was a lucky girl. She sat at the table for a moment, thinking about her daughters and the fact that they both seemed far happier living in the country than they had been in the city. Would Tess really want to marry Mike and settle down in Heyworth Street? But she knew she was being foolish. The war would change everything, which meant that Mike would almost certainly change too. He might have no sort of urge for city life when peace came. The pair of them might buy – or rent – a smallholding, and spend the rest of their lives rearing pigs and poultry. You simply never knew.

Smiling to herself, Laura returned to her letters.

Sophie sat at the table in the Hilltop Farm kitchen. Phil had been lecturing her on what instructions she should give the land girls, but now he had gone off on some ploy of his own, leaving her to finish her breakfast before beginning work for the day. It was August and she was hot, cross and, she felt sure, the size and shape of an elephant. The baby was not due for another couple of months but she was convinced that she looked as if she were about to give birth immediately; certainly, she felt so uncomfortable that this might indeed have been the case. And instead of understanding this and encouraging her to rest, Phil drove her as though he truly expected her to manage the farm and to learn all the complexities the Ministry demanded.

Left to herself, Sophie had had a plan all ready to

put into operation as soon as she realised that Lizzy Pinfold had been mistaken. She had meant to pretend she was about to enter the services, whilst really she would have gone away, given birth to the child, had it adopted and then joined the WAAF. But she had been foiled by Phil himself. He must have guessed, from the thickening of her waist, that she was pregnant and had gone down to the forge when she had been shopping in Hereford. He had told her father that he had got Sophie into trouble and had offered to marry her, had insisted that he do so, telling her parents that he had always loved her, always envied Danny. He had managed to insinuate that she loved him too, but had been ashamed of her change of face, which was why she had stopped visiting Hilltop Farm.

She had returned from Hereford to find that, between them, Phil and her parents had got everything arranged. The young couple were to marry as soon as possible; Mr Cantrip was to go up to Hilltop Farm next day to arrange details with the Rylands and as soon as the ceremony had been performed she was to move up to the farm. To her astonishment, they had not been angry; indeed, they had seemed rather pleased. They liked Phil, admired his parents, thought she had done well for herself even though it was a shame that she and Phil, as her father put it, had 'jumped the gun'. Anger had only surfaced when she had said, firmly, that they had got it all wrong. She did not want to marry Phil, she wanted to join the WAAF. Her father had stared at her in round-eyed disbelief. 'If you didn't want to marry the fellow then why did you let him put you in the family way?' he had asked. 'And don't say you were missing Danny because that's no excuse for what you did.'

Sophie had tried to explain without actually revealing what had happened in the hayloft, for Mr Cantrip, though normally placid, had a terrible temper when roused. She could imagine, all too clearly, her father storming up to Hilltop Farm, armed with his twelve-bore. And if he had killed Phil, she knew she would never have forgiven herself. Of course Phil had been a brute but she supposed that he must really be as fond of her as he said, for he had offered marriage and had sworn that he would take care of her and be true to her for as long as they both lived.

In the end, she and Phil had discussed the whole matter seriously, without emotion, and had decided on the course of action they must take. He had promised – had sworn on the Bible – that it should be a marriage in name only and so far he had lived up to it. They slept in single beds and respected each other's privacy. He did not force his attentions upon her, or expect anything from her apart from companionship and a great deal of help in the running of the farm. Sophie told herself that her shape must have made abstinence a great deal easier, for what virile young man would want to make love to an elephant? But when he was not driving her to learn all sorts of things about growing turnips and the like, he was thoughtful and considerate, even letting her vent her ill-humour upon him on the rare occasions when the miseries of her situation got the better of her.

It had taken her a while to accept the fact that she must tell Danny of her new circumstances, partly because she knew it would hurt him deeply and partly because he had been sent abroad on the last leg of his pilot training and would let her know where to write as soon as he had a proper address.

Danny and Ray looked round the empty hut. They were off at last, accepted as aircrew, having flown solo to the satisfaction of the air force, and passed a mass of tests and examinations, medical and dental checks. In fact Danny felt that he himself had been accepted, quite literally, by the skin of his teeth. He had always hated visiting the dentist and once he was old enough to go by himself had consistently missed appointments and failed to make more. Why should he? He had strong white teeth which had never given him a moment's trouble. When the air force dentist had examined his mouth, however, Danny had been shattered to be told that he needed half a dozen fillings and would not be allowed to continue his training until he had had them done.

He had been mortified, for his flight had just been told that they could have a week's leave – embarkation leave, they called it – before boarding the *Louis Pasteur*, the troop ship which was to transport them, and a great many others, to the unknown destination where they would become pilots at last.

He had toyed with the idea of going home, of having his teeth seen to in Hereford, but realised in the end that it was just not practicable. Instead, he installed himself at a boarding house in the nearest town, asked at the local RAF recruiting office for the name of the best dentist they knew, and booked sufficient appointments to ensure that his mouth would pass muster. It was not the ideal way to spend one's embarkation leave but at least it would ensure that he sailed with all his friends and would not be dismissed ignominiously to sink back into the ground crew. For the air force could afford to be extremely choosy, since virtually everyone wanted to be aircrew. Already Danny had seen men who had failed tests in just one subject dismissed from the training. Indeed, a good friend of his had landed untidily once, after a solo flight, and had been told that he had flunked the course. So though it was sad to have missed his leave, it was worth the sacrifice to have passed his last dental examination with flying colours, and to know that his place on the course was safe.

'Got everything? I wonder what the *Louis Pasteur* is like? Someone said it used to be a cruise ship so maybe we'll have a comfortable billet for the next few weeks.'

Ray Westwood's words brought Danny back to the present with a jolt. He bent to peer under his bed, then straightened, hefted his kitbag on to his shoulder and set off towards the open doorway and the truck which would carry them down to the docks. 'Yes, I've got everything,' he confirmed. 'But as for a comfortable billet, I rather doubt that. Oh, I know it was a cruise ship once, but it was a French cruise ship, and you know what the Frogs are like. Besides, it's been a troop carrier for a while, so even if us flyers treated it with respect, you can't believe the brown jobs would do the same!'

Ray laughed. They had come into contact with a couple of Frenchmen also keen to become aircrew, and though one had been a pleasant enough fellow, the other had been slovenly and lazy, never washing unless his hut companions forced him to do so, and sneering at all things British. 'You're somewhat prejudiced, aren't you?' Ray asked, as they clamb-ered aboard the truck already more than half full of other men bound for the docks. 'Still, we shan't have long to wait, and even if the old *Pasteur* isn't exactly the lap of luxury, it's the first step towards flying.'

The men had heard stories about the over-crowding on troop ships and now they experienced it for themselves. They were provided with hammocks and told to sling them in any space they could find. No one had been told their destination, but since everyone had been issued with tropical gear they were able to deduce that they were not heading for anywhere cold. Rather to Danny's relief, the *Louis Pasteur* was sailing alone and not in convoy, though she zigzagged continually in order to avoid any U-boats which might be lurking beneath the waves. Had she been in convoy, other ships would have held her up for, heavily laden as she was, she was still a fast craft.

The voyage was a long one, and most of the air force personnel soon realised that they were bound for somewhere on the African continent. 'I've heard both South Africa and Rhodesia are beautiful countries, full of young ladies anxious to befriend their allies,' Ray said hopefully. 'Oh, God, it's nearly dinnertime; we'd best get below. I wonder what ghastly dish the cooks have invented this time? I thought they couldn't sink lower than goat sausages and boiled parsnips, but I dare say they'll surpass themselves yet.'

Danny chuckled. The food was absolutely appalling and had not even been particularly plentiful, but now, though they were still a hundred miles from the coast, they were encountering what the seamen told them were called the Cape rollers. These mighty waves caused the *Louis Pasteur* to take on a dreadful, wallowing, bucking motion and at least half the aircrew aboard suffered from appalling seasickness. In fact, so few people were now going down to the mess for meals that the cook had been able to offer second helpings. Previously, most of the men had got used to the fact that the *Louis Pasteur* zigzagged her way along as soon as they met the open sea but now, with the Cape rollers to contend with as well, this only added to the misery of those with delicate stomachs. Danny and Ray were lucky and did their best to keep fit by joining any exercise class going, and walking miles round the decks a couple of times each day.

But it was still a relief to disembark when they reached Cape Town, for there had only been one other shore stop where Danny had been able to send off the letters he had penned over the past few weeks. It was a brilliant day and the town and surrounding countryside were so tempting after weeks at sea that Danny and Ray longed for a chance to explore. And it seemed that their wish would be granted. They were billeted in a pleasant reception area and speedily learned that they would be here for three weeks, since the men whose places they were to take at the training centre were still working their way through the course.

Danny and Ray loved Cape Town, with its wide streets, its welcoming people and the wonderful countryside, full of flowers and trees, which surrounded it. And there were pretty girls in plenty, all anxious to befriend these young men from what they still considered to be the 'mother country'.

The usual procedure was to meet at the statue of Van Riebeeck and then to decide how they should spend the evening. Danny and Ray soon chummed up with a couple of very pretty girls, Louisa and Amanda. They took them to the cinema, known locally as the bioscope, which was very different from cinemas back in Britain. The film was shown in the open air for a start, and halfway through there was a long interval during which coffee, biscuits and delicious little cakes were served. Ray said the interval was in order that the management might change the reels, but Danny thought that the locals used it as a time to socialise. One wandered around chatting to friends, introducing and being introduced and admiring the women's dresses, for the girls looked bright as flowerbeds when compared with the dark greys, navies and blacks so prevalent at home.

The alternative to the bioscope was the Hotel Del Monico in Adderley Street, where most of the aircrew ended up. It was a fascinating place with a huge high ceiling, upon which appeared all the constellations of the South African sky, giving one the impression that the room was roofed only by the heavens. Even more wonderful to Danny's unsophisticated eyes was that the constellations were not painted upon the ceiling for, as the evening progressed, the stars moved in their courses, and though Danny and Ray often tried to work out how it was done, they never managed to do so.

Danny had done his best to write interesting letters home, particularly to Sophie, and Cape Town was an absolute gift for any letter writer. There was so much that was strange and wonderful and he wrote at length of the beauties of the town, promising to send a large parcel home before he left for the training centre. He and Ray had walked down Adderley Street to the junction with Trafalgar Place, bowled over by the beauty of the flowers being sold there. He knew both his mother and Sophie would have loved just one of the exotic blooms, but he could hardly send them home and so had to content himself with a description. When they visited the central market, however, they had scarcely been able to believe their eyes. Each stall was separated from the next by a wall, twelve to eighteen inches high, made up entirely of glorious golden pineapples, and these exotic fruits could be bought for as little as tuppence for the smaller ones and fourpence for the giants. Danny, prowling amongst the stalls, decided to send his mother a large quantity of dried fruit and nuts, several yards of really pretty cotton material which she could make up into a skirt or a dress and a good sized tin of tea, since he understood that the ration for this precious commodity was very small.

For his dear little Sophie, he chose some filmy white material embroidered with silver thread, which would make a beautiful dance dress, and a pretty suede jacket. To his shame, he sometimes found it difficult to visualise Sophie's small heart-shaped face, for Amanda who usually partnered him was a vivid and exotic creature, whose straight blonde hair hung in a curtain à la Veronica Lake, so that her large pale blue eyes peeped provocatively from behind it. She was great fun and totally without inhibitions; Danny was pretty sure that she would have slept with him had he suggested it, but unfortunately his own inhibitions were still very much with him. He told himself that a man should be experienced; it was women who prized innocence.

But he might have done nothing about it had not a letter from Sophie arrived on the breakfast table when they had been in Cape Town a fortnight. He had opened it without the least premonition of the bombshell it contained, and begun to read. And as he had done so, he had felt an awful coldness creep over him so that the hand holding the letter shook and he felt sure the blood drained from his face. She was married! She and Phil had tied the knot whilst he was still bucketing across the seas on the *Louis Pasteur*. In her small neat writing, she had told him the truth, as she had always done. She was expecting Phil's child and had moved into Hilltop Farm.

Everyone is being very kind to me. Daisy and Matthew are glad of my help and, as you know, I've always loved farm work. I expect this will be a shock to you but everyone says such things happen in wartime. You and I have always been good friends and I hope we will continue to be so. Please write and tell me you're not angry.

She had begun to sign off, as she always did, with the phrase *Your loving Sophie*, but had crossed out the first two words so firmly that nothing of them remained.

Danny had put the letter down on the table and stared dumbly at the two unopened letters still sitting beside his plate. He had felt sure that the men around him must realise that he was reeling from a body blow, but they had continued to eat and chat, and read their own letters, clearly having noticed nothing. Danny had hastily picked up his knife and fork and begun to eat. Presently, he had opened his other two letters. One was from Phil and must have been written before Sophie's, since he had merely said that he and Sophie, having jumped the gun so to speak, were getting married in a week. *I know she and you were great pals*, he had written. *But there was nothing else between you, was there? She's a nice kid and works like a Trojan on the farm. I know you'll wish us happy because the three of us are such old friends. All the best, Phil.*

His mother's letter had only mentioned the wedding in passing; her talk had been of farming matters, old friends and relatives revisited, the price of butter, the health of Tandy, their old dog.

Danny had spent the next couple of days, in between subjecting Amanda to a whirlwind courtship, trying to rationalise the news that Phil and Sophie were now man and wife. He had no right to feel aggrieved, he knew that. He had never suggested marriage to Sophie, had not even asked her to wait for him. Had he done so, he might have had a right to feel indignation, but as it was, he must accept the fait accompli and get on with his own life.

He had done this with vigour and enthusiasm and actually had a photograph taken of himself and Amanda, tightly clasping each other and gazing, laughing, at the camera. He had ordered two copies and sent one to his mother, hoping she would show Sophie and Phil, and had kept the second for himself. He had made extravagant promises to Amanda, knowing full well as he boarded the train which would take him up to the training camp that as soon as he was out of sight she would find a replacement. Well, what did it matter? He was beginning a new life, he was thousands of miles away from Herefordshire, and he was a man of experience, thanks to her. But he sat in his corner seat in the train and gazed out at the countryside whizzing past, and forbade himself to think of Sophie, forbade also the shedding of a tear for what he had lost. He had written a brief note congratulating Sophie and Phil but did not intend to write to Sophie again. She was a married woman and should not expect letters from other men, not even from such an old friend as himself.

By the time they had been at the airfield for six weeks, Danny and Ray had fallen into a regular routine. Today, the two men had completed their work and had done as they did every evening, going to the cookhouse for a meal and then jogging twice round the perimeter track, for at this stage in their training they spent a great deal of time attending lectures and sitting down to answer test questions. Then they had made their way back to their hut, had had a shower, for the weather was hot, and were now contemplating the evening ahead of them. Back in England, there had been a good deal of talk about the marvellous social life which one could enjoy whilst pilot training in South Africa, but this promise had proved to be fairy gold for the airfield was in the middle of nowhere, so one's social life was confined to the NAAFI. There were a few Waafs on the station, but they were so outnumbered by the men that such entertainment as dancing was out of the question, and besides, the courses were so intensive, and the heat so enervating, that the men had little energy left with which to pursue social activities.

Sitting on his bed in shorts and plimsolls, a towel draped round his neck, Ray looked hopefully across at his friend. 'What'll we do? Not that there's a great deal of choice, but we don't have a test tomorrow because we're flying, so no need to study.'

'I could do with a cold beer,' Danny said yearningly. 'And suppose there's some post; you never know? All the boats carry mail and there's always fellers finishing their course and going back to Blighty and a new draft coming in.' Everyone was talking about the air battle taking place, mostly over south-eastern England. There were several wireless sets on the station so they knew that Hitler's efforts to destroy all British airfields, and their aircraft, had failed, but of course it was impossible not to worry that your own particular friends – families even – might have been victims of the conflict. Bombs aimed at runways could end up on private houses, on railway stations, on churches even. Until you had a letter written fairly recently, assuring you that everyone was safe, you would continue to worry.

Ray's girlfriend was called Jean; she worked in a factory just outside London, making parts for Spitfires, and this factory would, naturally, be a target if the Luftwaffe identified it. Both sides had spies, that was all too obvious, so one could only hope and pray and listen to the crackly broadcasts which were relayed to them from local wireless stations.

'You're not the only one who fancies a cold beer,' Ray acknowledged now. 'And I like to check the letter board every day, just in case. So we might as well go along to the NAAFI for half an hour.' He stood up and reached for a shirt. 'I wonder why they don't have some sort of refrigerator to keep the beer cold? Or perhaps they think we like warm beer.'

'Well, it's better than no beer,' Danny pointed out as the two of them ambled across to the NAAFI.

Chapter Nine

Sophie felt the first uneasy stirrings of pain in her lower back some time in the early hours. She sat up on one elbow and stared towards Phil's alarm clock, which had luminous numbers. Unfortunately, it was on the little bedside table on the far side of his bed, and though she was almost sure that the minute hand pointed towards half past something, the hour hand was hidden by the empty mug of cocoa which Phil had carried up to bed with him, hoping that it would help to send him to sleep.

The discomfort in her back – she could scarcely call it pain – gradually ebbed and Sophie lay down again. It was probably just indigestion, though by her calculations the baby should have been born a week ago. She had said as much to her mother-in-law, but Daisy had just smiled and said that pregnancy always seems to last a hundred years, which at least means that the expectant mother is glad when the pains start.

Five minutes later the pain – and it was definitely a pain now – jabbed at Sophie again. It was undoubtedly the beginning of labour, but the mid-wife who was now calling weekly had said that there was no need to panic until the pains were both violent and close. Sophie, who had risen on her elbow once more, decided she would try to go back to sleep and cuddled into her pillow. No point in rousing the household from their slumbers; better to join them so that the time would pass more quickly.

An hour later, however, the pains were hot, strong and getting closer. She swung her legs out of bed and jabbed Phil spitefully in what she imagined were his ribs. This baby was as much his as hers, even if she hated to admit it, so he might at least wake up and share her anxiety, if not her pain. From her present position she could see the clock properly. It was almost four. She jabbed Phil again and he groaned and rolled over. 'Whazzat?' he said, his voice muzzy with sleep. 'Wha'z happening? Am I on early milking? Did I miss the alarm?'

'No you didn't, but the baby's started and the pains are pretty close,' Sophie said brusquely. She had passed on to him very little of what the midwife had told her and now she saw that his eyes were wide with what appeared to be horror. 'Get up, Phil! Nurse Denham's telephone number is on the pad in the hall. You can either go down to the public box, or wake Uncle John and use their phone. Only hurry, will you!'

The last remark was unnecessary since Phil was already dragging his clothes on over his pyjamas. 'I won't have to wake Uncle John,' he told her, crossing over to the window, pulling down the blackout blind and producing a box of matches with which he lit their bedroom candles. 'He lent me a back-door key weeks ago 'cos he said babies are like calves and usually put in an appearance in the middle of the night.' He headed for the bedroom door, opened it, then paused in the doorway to look back. 'Anything you want before I go? A drink? A hot-water bottle? Shall I wake Mum? She'll come up and rub your back.'

'No, don't wake anyone, I'm best left to myself,' Sophie said. She meant to sound cold and in command, but despite herself her voice wobbled a little. 'Just go as fast as you can. Nurse is an essential user so she'll probably bring the car, which means she could be here in half an hour or so and I can cope for half an hour. Do *hurry*, Phil.'

She sounded both cross and impatient and was not unduly surprised when Phil said reproachfully: 'Of course I'll hurry. And I'll come straight back.'

He left the room and Sophie realised for the first time that the wind was getting up. Now and again, rain pattered against the windowpane and she told herself that with a bit of luck Phil would get a good soaking. Then, when he came home, he would want to get into dry things and make himself a hot cup of tea, and by the time he had done that perhaps the baby would be born. She certainly hoped so. She had told Phil, in no uncertain terms, that she did not want him around once she was in labour. He had looked at her with honest astonishment. 'Don't worry, Soph,' he had said fervently. 'I'll keep well clear. Cows and pigs are one thing, but I've never seen a baby born and I don't intend to start now.'

'I've never seen a baby born either, but women can't get out of it the way men can,' Sophie had said stiffly. Then, for some reason, she had felt sorry for him. Oh, he had treated her badly, but he had done what he thought to be the decent thing in marrying her and she had been punishing him with barbed remarks and snubbings ever since. So she had turned to him and given him a small grin. 'Just keep boiling the water and tearing my petticoat into strips,' she said, quoting from an old Western film he had taken her to see the previous week. He had suggested it to take her mind off the imminent birth of their child, not realising that though it was billed as a cowboy film, a good half of the action took place in a remote and run-down ranch house where the rancher's young wife was discovered by the hero, alone and terrified and about to give birth.

She sat up in bed once more, glancing across at the clock. It was twenty to five. The midwife should have been here ten minutes ago! Once more, Sophie swung her legs out of bed and stood up. She would go downstairs, riddle the Aga and pull the kettle over the flame. Then she would make herself a nice cup of tea and lie on the sofa in the living room until Nurse Denham arrived.

Halfway across the room, she hesitated. She felt as though her insides were about to descend on to the floor; a truly horrible feeling. Did this mean that the birth really was imminent? She wished she had paid more attention to the midwife's recent lectures, and regretted that the book on childbirth which Phil had bought for her had been shoved deep into the heart of the fire, unread, so that he might know how totally she despised any effort of his to help her.

Yet when the child within her had first moved, beginning to kick, squirm and wriggle, she had felt the strangest tenderness towards it. Poor little creature, it should not be blamed for the manner of its conception. Left to herself, she would have had it adopted, but now Aunt Daisy had made it plain that she would take over. Sophie might have to feed the child for a while, but she need do nothing else. Phil's mum had wanted a large family and was absolutely delighted at the thought of becoming a grandmother and having a baby, actually living in the house, on whom she could lavish all her love. Phil was a grown man and furthermore an independent one, not given to shows of affection, even though Sophie knew he loved both his parents dearly. In the old days, when Matthew had been fit, or at least more capable, Phil had resented first the way he ran the farm and then, as Phil himself gradually took over, his attempts to interfere. But now he treated Matthew with great gentleness, seeming to understand the terrible frustration of being totally dependent upon others. Daisy, too, had softened towards Matthew, and had even moved out of Phil's old room, where she had been sleeping since Sophie's arrival at the farm, to share his bedroom downstairs.

But I don't mean to waken anyone because all I want is a cup of tea, Sophie told herself now, gingerly making her way down the stairs. It really wouldn't be fair to disturb either of them at this hour. No, I won't . . .

Suddenly, the feeling that her innards were about to descend became, at least partially, a fact. There was a moment of great heaviness, and then a tremendous feeling of relief as water – or was it blood? – gushed forth, soaking her nightdress, drenching her legs and feet and puddling the stairs. Sophie was carrying her candle and was relieved to see that it really *was* water. She remembered vaguely reading somewhere that this was a sign of the baby's imminent arrival and hesitated. Should she go back to the bedroom or continue to descend the stairs? She took a tentative step forward and the decision was taken for her. Her foot slipped and she careered down the rest of the flight on her bottom, ending up in the hall feeling considerably shaken.

Of course her fall had not been silent for the shock had made her squeak and gasp, so it was no surprise when Daisy emerged into the hall. She was clad in a long white nightgown and her hair bristled with curl papers but she took in the situation at a glance and hurried across to where Sophie, giggling weakly, was trying to get to her feet.

'Are you all right, chick?' Daisy asked anxiously. 'Has it started? I thought I heard someone coming downstairs a while back but no one knocked at the door, or tried to rouse me.'

Sophie, now on her feet but clutching her mother-in-law's arm firmly, felt the pain begin again and began to head for the kitchen. 'Yes, it's started; Phil's gone for the nurse,' she said. 'I was desperate for a cup of tea though, only I slipped on the stairs . . .'

By now they were in the kitchen. Sophie slumped into a chair with a sigh of relief whilst her mother-in-law bustled about pulling the kettle over the heat and remarking that Phil, on his way to get the nurse, had very sensibly riddled the ash and made up the fire, which was why the kitchen was already comfortably warm and the kettle full. 'You'll have your cuppa in five minutes, but I shan't try to get you back to bed until Phil's here to give a hand,' she said. 'And whilst the kettle boils, I'll just get the mop and clear up the water on the stairs. I expect you realise that your waters have broken, which means . . .'

'I know. That's why I slipped,' Sophie explained. 'I just hope Nurse Denham gets a move on, that's all!'

The baby was born before the nurse arrived and Sophie, holding the small, solid body to her breast and looking down into the little red face with its puffy, tightly closed eyes and pouting mouth, knew such an overwhelming rush of love that it left her breathless. He was perfect! She knew then that she could never have had him adopted, never have handed him over to another woman, and she was doubly grateful to Daisy for her generous insistence that she would do everything possible for the child.

Phil ushered the nurse into the kitchen to find Sophie lying on the couch and his mother holding what, for one startled moment, he took to be a baby pig. Nurse Denham rushed forward to take the child and before

Phil could make any comment his mother had pushed him out of the kitchen, advising him to go to his father and wait until he was called. 'You've got a dear little son. He's well and healthy, and so is Sophie, but he was born only minutes before you and Nurse Denham arrived; I've not tied off the cord or anything, nor cleaned Sophie up,' she hissed. 'Tell your father it's a boy and as soon as we've finished in here I'll call you through.'

'Right, right,' Phil said. He made his way to his parents' room where he found his father sitting up in bed, looking pale and anxious. 'What's happened?' Matthew asked gruffly. 'Is Sophie all right? She fell down the stairs, you know; we both heard her go, only then she started giggling so I thought she couldn't have hurt herself.'

'It's a boy!' Phil said, suddenly aware of a glow of pleasure. He had never thought much about the sex of the baby, hadn't thought it mattered, really, yet now that the child had been born he realised that having a son was an achievement. In normal circumstances, both he and Sophie would have been delighted and proud, but he had acknowledged long ago that the circumstances were not normal. Sophie had not wanted to marry him, but marriage had been part of his plan, which was why he had told her parents that she was pregnant before she had had a chance to do so herself.

Now, he grinned at his father. 'I've been turned out while they do all the things women do after a baby's born,' he said cheerfully. 'Mum's going to come and fetch me presently, and then she'll bring the baby in here so you can see your first grandson.'

'What'll you call him?' Matthew asked eagerly. He was grinning from ear to ear, looking younger and happier than he had looked for a long while. 'How about a family name?' He cast his son a shy glance. 'There have been Matthews and Philips in the Ryland family for generations . . . but I s'pose that might be confusing. Another family name – my middle name actually – is Luke. What about Luke?'

'We'll talk about it . . .' Phil was beginning when the door opened and his mother's head appeared.

'Everything's fine, though Sophie's pretty tired, of course. You can come through now, Phil.' She turned to her husband. 'I'll bring the lad in to see you in a moment . . . he's got a name already. He's called Christopher Matthew, but of course he'll get called Chris. Nice, isn't it?'

Phil had not expected to feel anything in particular for his son, and was astonished by the strength of emotion which overcame him whenever he so much as looked at the baby, let alone took him in his arms. He felt a deep affinity for the tiny mite, and never lost an opportunity to hold him. He sang him lullabies, took his turn at bathing the small, strong little body, and never let him cry for more than a few minutes when he knew the baby would be pacified at once if plucked from his cot and cuddled. It made his plans for the years ahead even harder, but it was too late to try to change things now, so when Christopher was a week old, and Sophie up and about once more, Phil took her out for a meal, saying that it was about time they talked. Sophie had stared at him. 'We talk all the time, or at any rate you do,' she had said rather nastily. 'Why can't we talk at home? What's the point of trekking miles just to stare at each other across a white linen cloth instead of the kitchen table and eat food which cost ten times as much as it does at home?'

'At home someone's always around,' Phil had said reasonably. 'We've got to talk properly, about the baby and the future.'

Sophie had shrugged but consented and now the two of them were sitting in a quiet restaurant which specialised in seafood. They had started the meal with a prawn cocktail and were awaiting their main course, which was to be sole served in a black butter sauce.

Phil had talked about the farm, about how Sophie would manage with the baby, even about hiring an extra land girl, but he was finding it increasingly difficult to broach the subject uppermost in his mind. He guessed Sophie must suspect something was wrong, though she could not possibly know what he planned to do, and when their main course arrived he took a deep breath, helped himself to vegetables from the dish which the waiter had set down in the middle of the table, and began to speak.

'Sophie, when we first got married I promised you that it would be as though we were just friends, not husband and wife. I've done my best to make up for the way I behaved but you've always made it pretty obvious that you'd be happier with my absence than with my presence. So I've signed on for the Royal Air Force.'

Sophie had been staring down at the food on her plate but now she raised startled dark eyes to his face. 'You've – you've signed on for the Royal Air Force?' she said, her voice rising to a squeak. 'But how the devil am I to manage? Oh, I know you've been teaching me how to run the farm and I know you've kept saying that I'm as capable as you are yourself, but I've got Christopher now and I'm not as strong as you – physically I mean. If you think you can just walk away, leaving me to cope with everything, then you're even more of a rat than I thought you!'

Phil grinned, but only to himself. He had always known Sophie had spirit and he thought now that this would carry her through, but knew it would be mad to say so. Instead, he leaned across the table and took her hand. 'Sophie, listen to me! Do you remember Nigel Brown? He joined the army back in 'thirty-eight and was one of the troops evacuated from Dunkirk. He was badly shot up, poor fellow; he's lost a leg, but he's agreed to come and help you manage Hilltop. Once I'm gone, you can move into my old room, the one Mum used before she moved downstairs to be with Dad again, and Nigel and his wife – oh, did I say he was married? – can move into our bedroom. Does that sound reasonable?'

Sophie stared at him. 'Have you told your parents about this? It's pretty damn clear you must have been planning it for months without giving me so much as a hint, but surely you must have treated your parents a little more fairly? I mean, their house is going to be invaded by two strangers, and what use will this Nigel be with a leg missing? I take it he's the fellow who used to be Grimshaw's cowman? You and he were always thick as thieves.'

'That's right, he worked for Grimshaw's,' Phil acknowledged. 'He was a damned good worker, too; he serviced all the Grimshaws' farm machinery and even now, with only a peg leg, he can do just about everything he did before. Only of course Grimshaw replaced him when he joined the army, so now Nigel's looking round for work. We met in the village a month or so back, and I sounded him out about a job then. He was working in a factory in Hereford, which he hated, so it all fitted in rather nicely.'

'Have you told your parents?' Sophie insisted, and Phil saw the pink deepening in her cheeks. 'Don't avoid the question, Phil. I want the truth.'

'No, but I shall do so when we get home this evening. They'll be unhappy, but once Nigel is installed I'd be called up anyway, I wouldn't have any choice. The only reason I haven't already been conscripted is because the authorities acknowledge that Dad's condition makes him incapable of running the farm. Any more questions?'

'How about a statement instead,' Sophie said, her voice dangerously steady. 'I've always longed to join the WAAF; you know I have. Well, I'm bloody well going to do it; see how you like that!'

Phil laughed and tried to take her hand but she jerked crossly out of his reach, stabbed a potato and pushed a generous forkful into her mouth. 'You won't leave our little boy,' he said, matter-of-factly. 'I saw you looking down at him when you were breast-feeding and the expression on your face was so beautiful that it made me want to cry. Oh, I know Mum adores him and would do her best, but you're not leaving, no matter how much you'd like to see me chained to a farm, and a life I hate. Besides, I refuse to have to tell Christopher, one day, that I was about the only able-bodied man in Herefordshire who didn't join the forces during the war. I've got to do my bit, Sophie; can't you see that?'

Sophie stared at him, her eyes hard and aggressive, and then they softened. For a moment Phil thought she was beginning to see his point of view, but her next words dispelled the hope. 'If it weren't for the baby, I'd light out this very night and leave you holding the fort,' she said. 'But none of this is Chris's fault and the farm will be his one day. I'd be ashamed to hand over Hilltop in the sort of run-down state it was in when your father had his accident. And you were right about one thing. Chris and I will be a good deal happier and better off once you've gone.'

Despite Phil's hopes, it was mid-November before he packed up and left Hilltop Farm, and by then Nigel and his wife Patsy had moved in. Patsy was a great asset, capable and willing, and she cooed over Chris and loudly envied Sophie and Phil. 'We've been married seven year and no sign of me bein' in the family way,' she said regretfully. 'But you never know. My ma was forty-two when I were born and I'm the eldest of three.'

Phil devoutly hoped that she would not suddenly start producing young, for the situation at the farm was now just as he had planned it. Sophie, Patsy and the two land girls who lived in the village all got on well and worked extremely hard, and to Phil's great relief Sophie was perfectly willing to obey Nigel's instructions when he knew more about a job than she. As Phil had said, Nigel was a wizard with machinery of all sorts, as well as being an excellent cowman, and he and Sophie soon became good friends, as well as colleagues. Nigel acknowledged that she was the boss, and never tried to make her feel inferior because she was a woman and not as experienced as he.

Now, Phil was making his way down to the village, for Mr Cantrip had offered to take him to the station in the old pony trap. Phil respected his father-in-law and liked his mother-in-law but, apart from having Sunday tea with them every other week, he saw little of the elderly Cantrips. However, they adored Chris, Mrs Cantrip even undertaking the long walk up to Hilltop in order to watch the baby having his bath. Afterwards, Sophie would lie Chris naked on a rug before the kitchen fire, so that he might kick and squirm to his heart's content. 'You can almost see the little lad a-growing,' Mrs Cantrip always remarked. 'He'll be demandin' egg and bacon for his breakfast before you know where you are. Good thing, he'm a farmer's son.'

When he and Sophie had first married, Phil had dreaded the institution of Sunday tea, despite his admiration for the Cantrips. His parents-in-law were a silent couple, not given to chatting, and their reticence had made for long and awkward pauses whilst Phil racked his brains for some suitable remark and glared at Sophie because she would not do her share. The Cantrips insisted that Phil call them Mother and Father – which was what they called one another – and Phil was quite glad of it when he learned that Mrs Cantrip's Christian name was Hermione and Mr Cantrip's Jeremiah. Dreadful names, he thought, and when Christopher was born he was thankful that Sophie, having decided to call their son after both his grandfathers, had chosen Mr Cantrip's middle name. 'A lot of folk call the po under their beds the jeremiah,' she had told Phil, and had actually given him a tight little grin. 'I didn't want to saddle him with that, but Christopher's rather nice, don't you think?' Phil, who would have preferred something shorter – James or John – had said that it was a very nice name.

Now he was setting off on his new life, and as he passed amidst the familiar fields and brushed across a verge which crackled with frost, for it was a cold day, he suddenly felt a rush of excitement: after years and years of bondage, he was free at last. Soon he would be soaring beyond the blue hills which surrounded Herefordshire, learning the skills which his instructors would impart. He had always seen himself as a pilot and had envied Danny wildly when his cousin had written from South Africa, telling him how grand it was to climb into the air on a grey day, and then to burst through the clouds into brilliant sunshine and see the blue sky arcing above and cotton-wool clouds below.

He reached the village and crossed to the Cantrips' yard. His father-in-law was leading the pony and trap into the road and greeted him almost jovially. 'Mornin', lad; so you're off at last, eh? We'll miss you, there's no doubt o' that. How's little Chris this morning? Oh, and the gal, o' course.'

Phil laughed and slung his belongings into the trap, then climbed aboard himself. His father-in-law's enquiry about Sophie had been very much an afterthought. However, it would never do to say so. 'Everyone's fine, thanks,' he said, settling himself into the cracked leather seat. 'Sophie was just getting the baby up for his six o'clock feed when I left.'

Mr Cantrip climbed into the trap and clicked the pony into motion, only to rein in at the sound of a shout from the cottage behind him. 'Wait on, Father,' Mrs Cantrip hollered. 'I've put up a few sandwiches and a bottle of cold tea for young Phil. You know what train journeys are like in wartime; it could be tomorrer before he gets a proper meal inside him.'

Phil hopped down and ran back to collect the rather untidy parcel jammed into a string bag which his mother-in-law was waving at him. He thanked her effusively and hoped Mr Cantrip would not notice the canvas bag stacked with fruit, sandwiches, cakes and lemonade which his mother had already pressed upon him as he left Hilltop.

And presently, they reached the station and shook hands, and then Mr Cantrip turned the trap briskly back the way it had come. Phil was lucky. His train chuffed in a mere twenty minutes late and he climbed aboard and found a seat, then settled down to stare out of the window and dream of the excitements ahead.

It was April 1941 before Danny and Ray returned to England as fully fledged sergeant pilots. 'I trust this old tub isn't as crowded as the *Louis Pasteur* was,' Danny said hopefully, as they carried their kitbags up the gangway. 'But I don't hold out much hope. Oh, God, they're handing out those bloody hammocks! That means they're going to cram us in like sardines in a tin and I never really got the knack of sleeping in a string bag last time.'

'Well, I'd have been out a dozen times a night if we'd not been packed in so tightly,' Ray said. 'Will we get leave when we get home do you suppose, or will they send us straight to our new stations? I heard on the news that Liverpool took quite a pasting over Christmas, and I've got relatives there. My family are all right but I'd like to check up on pals and so on.'

'Now you mention it, I remember Mum saying something in her last letter about the evacuees,' Danny said. 'They come from Liverpool and a couple of 'em went home for Christmas. Mum said they were full of horror stories when they got back to the farm. Poor little devils, but at least they had somewhere to run to. Imagine what it must be like for folk who have to stay in cities because of work and that, and face the bombing night after night.'

'I can imagine all right, only I'd rather not,' Ray said grimly. 'But what about leave? What are our chances, do you suppose?'

'I imagine we'll get at least a week,' Danny said. 'After all, we weren't given any leave on the course and I reckon there will be a fair amount of sorting out to be done before we can be sent to a station. Yes, I'm pretty sure we'll get leave.'

It was May, and the blitz on Liverpool was in full swing. Laura sat in the underground shelter with the baby asleep in her arms and smiled ruefully at her daughter, sitting on the bench beside her. Arthur, who had volunteered as an ARP warden, was on duty somewhere above them. 'Tess, me love, I feel so guilty! Bringing you back here just in time for the worst bombing we've ever had. But tomorrow you really must go back to your farm. God knows, I wish I could go with you because I'm just about worn out, but I can't possibly desert Arthur. There's so little available to sell in the shop that he's taken to closing around lunchtime so he can give a hand in the café. But there's no way he could manage without me, nor me without him of course. You will go back to Norfolk tomorrow, won't you?'

Tess was beginning to laugh and shake her head when a tremendous thundering *crump* sounded and the whole shelter shook. Several people screamed as the curtain which guarded the doorway blew inwards, letting in a cloud of dust. Tess coughed and waved her hand in front of her face. 'That was a close one,' she remarked. 'As for you apologising because I came home for my week's leave, that's daft! You can't pretend you invited the Luftwaffe to have a go at Liverpool almost as soon as I arrived back, and as for deserting you and going off back to Norfolk, I'll do no such thing! At least while I'm here I can give a hand, both in the shop and in the café, so you and Uncle Arthur can have a few hours' sleep during the day. And I'm getting to know my little brother.' She looked round the crowded dusty shelter, then glanced down at the basket lodged beneath the bench upon which she and her mother sat. 'How about opening that flask of tea and having a sandwich? My throat's dry as a bone and all this dust hasn't helped. We've been here over two hours; surely the all clear will go soon? Only we'd look daft carrying a full basket back to the flat, don't you think?'

'Yes, you're right. Isn't it a good job Davy's still asleep? That last bomb would normally have woken him up with a jump, but I reckon he's so tired that it just didn't penetrate,' Laura said, gazing fondly down at her sleeping son. 'Can you hold him for a moment, queen, whilst I pour us both a drink and get the food out?'

Tess took the baby eagerly. David stirred but did

not waken and presently the two women took it in turns to drink from the cap of the flask and ate a jam sandwich each. Laura had to speak quite loudly, for whenever there was a lull in the noise from outside the folk in the shelter took advantage of the temporary quiet to talk amongst themselves. Neighbours and customers who knew Tess wanted to discover what life was like for the land girls and asked a great many questions. Tess answered as best she could, guessing that folk were eager to discuss something other than the bombs raining down on the city. She did not want to disillusion anyone, but she thought it only fair to admit that the work was extremely hard and that sometimes girls were billeted in homes where their presence was resented. As for being better fed than ordinary folk, she pointed out that this varied with your hostess. True, land girls were allowed an extra eight ounces of cheese per week, but that was the only concession made to them, and quite often the farms upon which they worked were too closely scrutinised by the authorities to part with little extras. Tess felt guilty saying this because she and Sue were two of the lucky ones. The Turnbulls were extremely generous and were forever sending a few eggs, some pats of butter or a covered pail full of still warm milk down to Lavender Cottage, where Mrs Yallop saw to it that the girls got a fair share of everything that was going. However, as the posters stuck up all over the place proclaimed, 'Walls have ears', and there might be someone standing right next to you who would inform the authorities that

Grange Farm was a place to be watched. The posters of course referred to a listener who might be spying for the enemy, but so far as most farmers were concerned the authorities were the enemy, so Tess was careful to keep certain facts to herself.

'My goodness, I needed that!' Laura said, screwing the cap back on the Thermos flask. She cocked her head, listening. 'It's still quiet; I wonder if I dare sneak out and take Arthur the rest of the tea? He won't be far off, and if I wait until the marshal's back is turned I can slip out just for a moment.'

Tess looked doubtful. Shelter marshals were there for a purpose – to make certain that no one mistook a lull for the end of a raid, amongst other things. To be sure, she did not think she could any longer hear the drone of aircraft overhead, but after four nights in the city as the worst blitz she had ever imagined rained down upon them she knew that this meant nothing. A lone bomber could have fallen behind for some reason; you could never tell. It was not safe, or sensible, to leave the shelter until the all clear was sounded. Tess began to remind her mother of this just as the shelter marshal got ponderously up from his place and set off towards a woman with a couple of young children, who was beckoning him. In a moment, Laura was on her feet. She gave Tess's cheek a quick pat, bent and kissed the baby softly, and was through the curtain at the end of the shelter before her daughter had more than opened her mouth. Tess sighed and settled Davy more comfortably in her arm.

Despite her brave words, she could not help wishing that she had not taken her leave at this particular time. She had only done so, in fact, because Mike had written that he expected to get leave soon and thought he ought to return to Liverpool, since he believed his flight would be posted abroad when he got back. Mike and Tess had enjoyed a few halcyon days together earlier in the year and she had been anxious to repeat the experience, though she realised, now, that her presence was making things much easier for both her mother and her stepfather. She just wished she could persuade them to move into the country, but every time she had suggested such a move she had met with opposition from them both. 'Hitler's bombers have done their worst so far as Liverpool's concerned, and as soon as they think they've put the docks out of action they'll move on and start on some other poor bloody city,' Arthur had said reassuringly. 'So your mam and meself don't mean to do what the old bugger wants – Hitler, I mean – which is to cut and run. We've got two active businesses and believe me, when the war ends folk will remember we stuck by 'em.' He had turned anxiously to his wife. 'But if you'd go, and take our little lad, I'd be happier. Don't think I'd let the Restawhile founder, because I wouldn't dream of it. I'd put someone in to help Mrs Tasker.'

'I'm not going anywhere unless you do, wack,' Laura had said firmly. She had grinned at her daughter. 'He just wants rid of me so's he can employ some fluffy blonde, like that Jane in the *Daily Mirror*!'

They had all laughed, for the strip cartoon she mentioned was the main reason most people – particularly men – bought the paper, and Tess knew that she herself, having absorbed the war news, always turned next to the cartoons to see what predicament the lovely but unfortunate Jane had fallen into this time.

Now, however, little David had suddenly opened his eyes and was struggling to sit up. He was not talking yet, though he babbled endlessly in his own language, but Tess saw his tongue flicker out to wet dry lips and guessed that he wanted a drink. Holding him carefully in one arm, she reached into the basket and drew out the bottle of milk which Laura had stowed away earlier. 'Want a drink, me darling?' she enquired.

The baby reached eagerly for the bottle and seconds later was sucking enthusiastically. Tess saw the level of milk rapidly falling and wondered what she should do if he wanted more once it had all gone. She kept glancing anxiously towards the curtain which hid the steps leading up to the surface, but Laura had still not reappeared when the baby fell asleep once more, and presently Tess followed suit.

Laura ran lightly up the steps, emerging into a street that was scarcely recognisable as the one she and Tess had traversed some hours earlier. The bomb which had filled the shelter with dust really had been close, for the crater was no more than twenty yards away and was at least ten yards across. Laura felt her heart jump into her mouth and stared round wildly. This was Arthur's beat; suppose he had been patrolling this part of the street when the bomb had fallen? She had meant to nip out of the shelter to see whether he was nearby, hand him the Thermos if he was and then return to Tess and Davy, but now she realised she would simply have to search for him. Suppose he was lying somewhere, badly injured? She thanked God that Tess had been with her in the shelter and was thus able to take care of Davy whilst she herself looked for her husband.

She picked her way carefully across the ruined street. She could see no living soul but that meant little. She knew the docks were supposed to be the Luftwaffe's target but it was pretty clear that tonight they had decided to wreak havoc on the city centre – or possibly their bomb aimers were not as accurate as they boasted. Having crossed the road, she glanced to her right and then to her left and saw, with some relief, a figure coming towards her. The moonlight was almost as bright as day and she recognised the ARP uniform. Please God let it be Arthur, she prayed, beginning to run towards the figure. But she had only gone a few feet when she heard the drone of an aircraft overhead. Glancing round wildly, she saw a deep shop doorway which might offer some sort of shelter. She dived into it, heart hammering, as the drone of the plane's engines grew louder.

Arthur saw the woman and felt his annoyance rise. What the devil was she doing out on the street when the raiders might return at any moment? He had heard that on at least one occasion the bombers had droned over Liverpool and continued on to bomb Barrow-in-Furness before returning to drop the rest of their cargo on Liverpool. Judging by the ferocity of the earlier attack, this had not been one of those occasions, but, even so, the streets were dangerous.

He was walking briskly but then he heard the drone of engines overhead and began to run. The woman heard them too. She dodged into a doorway and in that moment Arthur recognised her. It was Laura! And that building was just a façade, a shell! As soon as they were able, he and the other wardens were to fence it off, put up warning notices. But such a thing was impossible at the height of a raid.

Shouting, breaking into a positive gallop, he hurtled along the street, not bothering to watch where he trod, so that he slipped on a long shard of windowpane and landed painfully hard on the broken and glass-scattered paving. He was scrambling to his feet, screaming a warning, when he saw the building in which his wife had taken shelter begin to tip and tilt. He no longer felt the pain of his recent fall, but simply ran like a mad thing; was within three feet of his wife's white and frightened face when the world fell on him and he plunged into darkness.

Tess, numb with shock, had moved in with her Aunt Millie, though neither the café nor the shop had been bombed. However, Arthur would be in hospital for some time and Tess could not face the thought of going back to Heyworth Street alone.

'It's a terrible, terrible thing that your mam should have been killed and her wi' young Davy not yet a year old,' her aunt had said. 'But you must thank God, queen, that we aren't plannin' a double funeral. Your dad were real lucky to escape wi' nothin' worse'n a few broken bones and a con – con – wharrever they call it. It's going to be rare hard on Davy, but I reckon you and me between us will manage somehow.'

'Concussion, you mean,' Tess had said automatically. At the time, she had accepted her aunt's assumption dully, not having thought things through, but now she realised that Aunt Millie, generous though she was, did not understand Tess's own commitment to the WLA. She could not possibly become a surrogate mother to her small brother. She had important work to do, and though she would willingly have taken Davy back to Grange Farm with her, she knew that Arthur was clinging to the boy and would not for one moment consider parting from him.

When the funeral was over, therefore, she went to the hospital to talk things over with her stepfather. She did not take David, for children were not allowed to visit, and though she could have pleaded that seeing the baby would do her stepfather nothing but good she was fearful of being turned away, thus losing her last opportunity for a quiet discussion with Arthur. She had been ordered back to Norfolk next day.

The shop was still closed but Mrs Tasker was doing her best to keep the café open, though without Laura's help she did not unlock the doors until noon and closed up again at three o'clock. When Tess had talked to her, she had said she needed someone to come in and cook and someone else to wait on. 'Though when your pa's fit and well he's a real help: chats to the customers, sees to the baby when your ma's busy – sorry, love, I didn't think – and, of course, does the paperwork. I'd kind o' hoped you'd leave that there farm and come home to take your mam's place, but I dare say that ain't on?'

Tess had assured her that it really was not. 'They'd gobble me up for a munitions factory or some other sort of war work, because runnin' a café can be done – is being done – by women of sixty or more. No, Mrs T, I can't possibly come back to the Restawhile until the war's over.'

Mrs Tasker had acknowledged the force of Tess's argument and now Tess was visiting her stepfather partly to discuss her small brother's future and partly to get his agreement to Mrs Tasker's employing more staff.

Quietly, she entered the long ward and approached Arthur's bed. He was asleep, so she had a chance to study his pale face and to be moved by the change in him. Her mother had been dead ten days and whilst she herself wept for Laura every time she thought about her, she knew it must be worse for Arthur, who had not even been able to attend the funeral. A solemn little Tina had come up from the country, accompanied by Miss Jones, one of the school-teachers, who also hailed from Liverpool. Tina had worn a skimpy black skirt, an over-large black coat, and a headsquare which Mrs Brewster had dyed black when she could not find a hat to fit her charge. Tess and Tina had held hands all through the service and the committal, and Tina had followed Tess's example and picked up a handful of earth to drop on to the lid of the coffin. Then she had given a stifled sob and had turned to bury her face against her sister's dark grey jacket.

At the time, Tess had thought it cruelly hard that Tina, who had looked forward to her mother's next visit to Manor Farm, should have had to undertake the long journey only to be forced to acknowledge that her mother was lost to her. The child and her teacher had travelled back to Herefordshire the next day leaving Tess to manage alone. But now, looking at Arthur's pale face, unnaturally shadowed and thinner than she had ever seen it, she thought that perhaps it had been better for Tina to have said goodbye to her mother and sobbed out her grief in the churchyard. Before the funeral, Tess had found herself looking for Laura in all the old familiar places where she and her mother had spent their lives. After the funeral, she realised she no longer did so. It might not be complete acceptance, but it was acceptance of a sort.

Quietly, Tess pulled out the bench from under the bed and sat herself down upon it. Arthur's right leg was in traction, and he had broken some ribs. One arm was in plaster from his elbow to his knuckles, and though the cuts and contusions on his face were beginning to fade, Tess guessed that he would bear the scars to the end of his life.

Perhaps it was the intensity of her stare, but even as she prepared for a wait Arthur's eyes opened. He could not sit up but he said: 'Tess!' and sounded pleased. 'Oh, I'm that glad to see you, queen. I had an awful nightmare last night. I dreamed you'd gone back to that farm of yours – Grange Farm, ain't it? – and left the baby with your Aunt Millie. So of course I went round there and she said you'd took the baby wi' you and if I wanted to see him I'd have to learn to fly an aeroplane because Hitler had bombed all the railway lines, and the only way to get to Norfolk was to learn to fly or to go on foot. Dear God, it were an awful dream; I woke up sweatin' like a stoker an' trembling like a kid of five.'

'Oh, poor Uncle Arthur!' Tess said, leaning forward and clasping his good hand. She was thankful that he did not know she had actually considered such a move, but at least she had had sufficient sensitivity to realise that parting David from his father was not an option. 'Aunt Millie is a grand woman but, as you know, she's managed to get herself war work so we've been discussing what to do with David until you come out of hospital. He's such a darling and ever so good, but much though I'd like to I can't stay here and look after him for you, and of course Aunt Millie can't give up her factory work. However, the factory has what they are calling a crèche where working mums can leave their small children and Aunt Millie thinks they'll accept David there whilst you're in hospital and unable to take care of him yourself. The plan is that she will take him to work with her each morning at eight o'clock, leave him in the crèche and pick him up again at six in the evening. I've explained that you'll want him back in Heyworth Street as soon as you're there yourself, but I had a talk to Sister and she thinks it will be a couple of months, perhaps even three, before your leg's out of traction and you're able to go home. What do you think, Uncle Arthur?'

To her dismay, Tess saw that her stepfather's eyes had filled with tears, which were now flowing copiously down his thin cheeks. He sniffed and began to search under his pillow for a handkerchief, but Tess produced one of her own and offered it to him, turning tactfully aside and looking out of the window as he began mopping-up operations by blowing his nose heartily.

'Sorry for making a fool of myself, but I'm afraid I do it all the time now – cry, I mean,' Arthur said. 'I'm that grateful, queen, both to you and to good old Millie, but the thought of being away from David for three months . . .' The tears welled up again and this time he made no attempt to apologise. 'However, Sister's a good sport. If you explain, I'm sure she'll let my little lad be brought on to the ward three or four times a week, else he won't recognise me when we go back to Heyworth Street, and that's a complication I can well do without. Poor little fellow, wharra future:

'no mammy and a daddy he won't know from Adam.'

'I'm sure we can arrange something,' Tess said soothingly, though in fact she believed it would be an uphill struggle for, charming though Sister was, she had told Tess that rules were rules and could not simply be broken for one patient without, as she put it, 'giving everyone ideas'. But Tess knew that her stepfather could be both charming and persuasive and trusted that Sister would give in gracefully when she realised how important it was for her patient to see his baby son.

But right now, Tess had another burning question, and since she had no idea when she would next be able to visit Liverpool she felt she had to sort it out now. 'But that isn't the only thing, Uncle Arthur,' she said gently. 'How will you manage when you're back in the shop?'

'I'll cope, queen,' her stepfather said robustly. 'Don't you worry your head about us, because we'll manage just fine. There's women what'll come in and give a hand. Now, I take it that the reason you've called today to try to sort everything out is because you've had your recall. When's it to be?'

'Tomorrow,' Tess said regretfully. 'But you won't miss me, Uncle Arthur, because Mike's got a forty-eight. I'm meeting him at Lime Street at four o'clock this afternoon.' She beamed at her stepfather. 'I know you've seen him several times since he left home, but this will only be the second time he and I have met.'

'And you go first thing tomorrow, I suppose?' her

stepfather said thoughtfully. 'But you'll come here with Mike for the evening visiting?'

'Well, I expect Mike will want to see David before he goes back, so I thought I'd visit the hospital and then have an early night, because I'm catching the first available train in the morning.'

Her stepfather nodded understandingly, and Tess wondered whether he thought she meant to spend the night with Mike. If so, he was too tactful to remark on it. As for herself, Tess had made no decisions. It would be a good deal easier if she could spend the night in Heyworth Street – she and Mike each had a bedroom there after all – but she had decided to play it by ear.

Mike had always been a good-looking young man, but since joining the air force he had matured, becoming even more attractive. His ginger hair had darkened until it was almost coppery, his shoulders had broadened and he seemed both older and more serious. Tess supposed that when he had joined up he had been a boy, and now he was a man. Such things happened in peacetime, of course, but war seemed to accelerate everything, including the ageing process. Tess knew that young men in the services matured quickly, and she also knew that, wherever they went, eager young women pursued them. She herself had gone to the cinema and to dances with a number of the young air-force chaps from the Norwich airfields, and she guessed that Mike too would have taken girls out from time to time. So far as she was concerned, however, Mike was special, and she hoped, during the course of their time together, to discover whether he still felt the same about her.

She said none of this to Arthur, though, only reminding him that trains were often late these days and promising to come straight to the hospital as soon as Mike arrived. Then she said she must hurry back to Blenheim Court to make sure that all was well with David, kissed her stepfather, and left the ward.

As Tess had anticipated, Mike's train was late, so after hospital visiting and popping into Aunt Millie's to see David the two of them went straight to Heyworth Street. They were both starving hungry, since they had not had time for a meal, and Tess guessed that there would be food in the café, even if it was only tea and buns. She said as much to Mike, but a disappointment awaited them. They both had keys to the flat, but the door which led down into the Restawhile was firmly locked, so they had to make do with a cup of tea and beans on toast, the toast made from very stale bread. Tess ferreted around and produced a tin of pre-war peaches, but Mike shook his head. 'You open them if you're still hungry, queen, but I'm so tired that all I want to do is sleep,' he said frankly. He got up from the table and walked across to Tess, wrapping his arms about her and resting his chin on the top of her head. 'I love you, Tess, you're the sweetest thing, but I reckon you'll be no keener to start something we can't finish than I am. In a week or two I'm definitely being posted abroad and anything could happen. What time are you leaving in the morning?'

'Somewhere around five o'clock, I suppose,' Tess said. Her heart was beating very fast and she could feel hot colour creeping up her neck. 'I – I know what you mean, Mike, but if you want to – to – oh, you know, then I would understand.'

By this time she knew her face must be scarlet, knew too that her voice was shaking and pitched higher than usual, but Mike seemed oblivious of both facts.

'Darling Tess, I'm so glad you understand me,' he said softly. 'I'd love to be with you until you leave, but it wouldn't be fair to either of us. Take care, sweetheart, and wake me in the morning – bang on my door – so we can say goodbye properly.' He gave her a bright smile but avoided her gaze. 'Off to bed with you now; sweet dreams.'

'Good night, Mike,' Tess said numbly. She felt as though she had been doused in ice-cold water. She thanked God he had cut in before she had actually said what had been on her mind – that she wanted to sleep with him – but his firm rejection hurt horribly. He had tried to make it appear that he was turning her down for her own sake as much as his, but surely, if he truly loved her, he would have wished them to become one? That was what the girls back on the farm said, at any rate, though most of them had the strength of will to refuse such overtures. Some got married, of course, but this was considered risky indeed by men who took their life in their hands night after night and grew superstitious over their chances of survival. Getting oneself a wife would change things, and men who placed faith in such small obsessions as always putting their left foot into its flying boot first would not willingly give a hostage to fortune.

Because she felt rejected Tess not unnaturally began to suspect that Mike probably had a girlfriend back in Lincolnshire. A knowing girl, who was able to sleep with him regularly. Tess imagined a bosomy blonde, or a dashing redhead, and cried herself to sleep. She had put her little travelling alarm clock within a couple of inches of her head, but woke seconds before it went off, so was able to prevent it from ringing and waking Mike. She tiptoed around the room getting dressed, then made for the kitchen, stealing past Mike's door since she had no intention of waking him. Being rejected once was quite bad enough; she did not intend to let it happen a second time. She went into the kitchen, put the kettle on the stove, cut another slice from the stale loaf and spread it thinly from a jar of marmalade which she found in the cupboard. She made herself a cup of tea and was munching and sipping at the kitchen table when the door opened and Mike came in. He was fully dressed and came over to the table, leaning across it to kiss Tess's forehead before pouring himself a cup of tea and sitting down opposite her.

'I won't ask you why you didn't wake me,' he said, and his eyes were so full of understanding that Tess forgave him for the previous night. 'Oh, Tess, this war's got a long way to go and God knows what will happen to you and me in the course of it. We used to know each other so well that it seemed as if nothing could ever part us, but we've already changed and we'll change more. I believe what I feel for you is real love, the sort that nothing can alter, but you were me first girl and I'm not sure of anything any more. If we'd shared a bed last night and something had gone wrong, you could have found yourself with a kid on your hands. I wanted you desperately, of course I did, but in my book it would have been a wrong thing to do. Understand?'

Tess nodded, though tears formed in her eyes and ran down her cheeks. 'Yes, you were right,' she whispered. 'But – but is there – is there anyone else, Mike? We're only human, both of us. I've been out with other fellers, dancing and to the flicks, and I reckon you've been out with other girls. So is there anyone else? If so, I'll understand and back off.'

She saw a look of total astonishment cross Mike's face before he jumped up and came round the table, taking hold of her beneath her arms and pulling her to her feet. He half carried her across to where a small square of mirror hung on the wall, then he rested his chin on her head and made her look at their reflections. 'Have I got someone else?' he said incredulously. 'Look at yourself, Tess Collins! You're beautiful, and I'm a ginger-haired, green-eyed lanky bugger who never dreamed I'd be lucky enough to get any girl, let alone a real little smasher like you.'

Tess giggled, but a fiery blush burned up in the face in the mirror. 'It's what's behind those two faces that counts though; character and so on,' she reminded him. 'Oh, Mike, I'm so glad we've had this talk. And you aren't any of those rude things you called yourself – you're gorgeous and I can't ever imagine loving anyone else the way I love you.'

She turned in his arms and for a moment they stood completely still, kissing hungrily. Then the kitchen clock chimed the half hour and Tess struggled free. 'Go back to bed, Mike darling, and get what sleep you can,' she instructed him. 'I've simply got to go. I dare not risk missing my train!'

Chapter Ten

Summer 1943

Tess was at the top of the tallest plum tree in the orchard, picking furiously. She had a canvas bucket slung across her chest and she was competing with several wasps who thought their right to the fruit was every bit as good as hers. The plums in the orchard, it seemed to the girls, had been hard one day and ripe the next, though of course Tess knew that this was not so. It was just because there had been a late raspberry crop which had kept the girls too busy to think about plums, and when Mr Turnbull had announced that the fruit was ripe and needed picking, it had seemed only yesterday that they had been spraying the trees and cursing windy days because then the spray in the guns was apt to blow back into their faces, coating them with an unpleasant sticky substance and leaving the aphids as healthy as before.

Tess and Sue usually worked together, but today Tosher had pointed out that they must clear the orchard as quickly as they could. They usually had volunteers from the nearby RAF stations, who would pick fruit quite happily in exchange for one of Mrs Turnbull's excellent teas and the company of a number of pretty girls. The men came when they could, but the land girls started as soon as it was light and would continue to pick until it was dark, for not only were the wasps eager for the plums, but the birds enjoyed them too: blackbirds, thrushes and other fruit lovers were welcome to the overripe and wasp-bitten fruit which fell to the ground, but they seemed to prefer to perch on the branches where they would take a few beakfuls from each ripe fruit before moving on to the next.

So, at an unearthly hour that morning, the girls had marched into the orchard and begun picking. They had stripped the lower branches first and then climbed the wooden ladders to reach the rest of the fruit, which was difficult because one had not only to push through leaves and twigs but also to beware of the wasps. Tess had already been stung twice, once on the wrist and once on the tip of her right fore-finger, and both stings throbbed unpleasantly, though Mrs Turnbull had produced a blue bag and a piece of gauze bandage, so that at least Tess would not be stung in the same place twice. The blue bag was supposed to ease the pain but Tess, reaching for a plum well above her head and popping it into her bucket, did not think it was particularly effective. She knew from experience, though, that by the next day she would scarcely notice the stings at all.

Right now, however, a wasp was buzzing her, hovering in front of her face as though selecting a target. Tess called it an evil name and leaned sideways. Just above her head and to the right there was a branch positively laden with plums, juicy and ripe, and so far as she could see as yet untouched by bird or insect. She leaned precariously over and began to pick the fruit with great care, then glanced hopefully down at the ground. Her bucket was full; someone should be hovering close at hand ready to take the filled buckets and hand up empty ones to those girls still perched in the upper branches of their chosen trees. Tess peered through the leaves. She could just make out two figures in air force blue, one tall and fair, the other shorter and dark. She saw that they were in shirtsleeve order which must mean that they were here to help; good! 'I say, fellers, I'm at the top of the plum tree almost directly in front of you,' she called, 'and my bucket's full to the brim. Could one of you take it and hand me up an empty one? Only I've so many branches sticking into me that if I try to get down I'll bring half the tree with me.'

The two young men came over until they stood directly beneath the tree. They were grinning and Tess guessed that the sight of her hot red face, hair full of twigs and cotton overalls covered in plum stains and dirt must be enough to make a cat laugh. She began to struggle out of the strap which held the bucket, then leaned to the left so that she might pass it down, edging her hand along the branch as she did so in order to keep her balance.

Beneath her, the taller airman bent and picked up an empty bucket, then reached towards her to take the full one dangling from her hand. 'That's right, sweetie. Pass me your bucket and I'll . . .'

Tess was about to comply when she felt a sharp

pain in the palm of the hand which gripped the branch. Another bloody wasp! She gasped and shrieked, tried desperately to save herself and then fell, crashing through the lower branches and landing, with a thump, right on top of the fair-haired airman. He grabbed her, though she felt the air whoosh out of his lungs as her weight hit him, and she found that she was giggling, almost sobbing with the pain of the sting, and trying to thank him all in one breath.

He stood her down on the ground, but retained a hold on her upper arms whilst Tess, still feeling shaky from her fall, tried to thank him all over again. He interrupted her, however. 'Hey, sweetie, why didn't you tell me you meant to jump?' he said aggrievedly. 'I damn nearly dropped you and the ground's really hard after so many days of sunshine. It's lucky for you that I'm so fit; not everyone could field a land girl the way I did.' He looked her over appraisingly. 'And you aren't exactly skinny, either. It's clear Mr Turnbull feeds his land girls well.'

Tess was beginning to reply indignantly that she had fallen because a wasp had stung her when the dark-haired man interrupted. He had been picking up the fallen plums and replacing them carefully in the canvas bucket, and now he turned to grin at her. 'Don't take any notice of Phil. He's always insulting people without realising it,' he said cheerfully. 'I don't suppose anyone has ever called you fat before, but you can trust old Phil to open his mouth and put his foot in it.'

The fair-haired one stared, round-eyed, at his friend, his expression that of injured astonishment. 'Me? Insulting people? You're just jealous, Danny, because she fell on me and not on you.' He was still holding Tess, but he was looking at his companion, which gave Tess the chance to study his face. He was extraordinarily handsome, fair-haired and blue-eyed, and when he grinned, which he was doing now, a long crease appeared in one cheek. Tess frowned. He reminded her of someone; a customer at the Restawhile, perhaps? No, it wasn't that, but then she remembered she had attended several dances at local airfields and had met dozens of air force personnel. Yes, that would be it. She knew she had never danced with him, nor the dark-haired one either, but now that she came to really look at them she was pretty sure that she had seen them before somewhere.

At this point, however, her thoughts were interrupted. 'Didn't you say you'd been stung? It wasn't a bee, was it? Bee stings can be quite unpleasant, though of course the poor bee dies. Let's have a look.' It was the dark-haired one. Tess held out her hand, palm uppermost. The sting was swelling and turning scarlet, and it really did hurt, but she knew very well that it had been a wasp and not a bee and thought, bitterly, that wasp stings were every bit as unpleasant as bee stings.

'It was a wasp all right and I'm happy to say I felt it crunch as my hand slipped on the branch,' she informed the dark-haired airman. 'And it's bloody unpleasant, I can tell you!'

The dark-haired one grinned. 'I can't offer to go up the tree in your stead because if I get covered in green stains I'll be put on a charge,' he said cheerfully. 'But my pal Phil here – he's my cousin actually – is taller than me, so he can continue picking whilst I take you up to the farmhouse to get some blue bag on that sting.'

'Hey, Danny, don't you try stealing a march on me,' Phil said indignantly. 'Why should I stay and do all the work while you whisk away the prettiest girl I've met for months? It's not good enough . . . I saw her first! Dammit, I saved her from crashing to the ground and doing herself all sorts of mischief. You stay here and get on with the picking whilst I . . .'

But the young man called Danny simply blew a raspberry at his pal and then took Tess's uninjured hand and led her at a brisk pace through the orchard and back to the farmhouse. They entered the kitchen, which was deserted, but the blue bag, a bowl of water and a tin with a large red cross on the lid lay on the kitchen table. Tess grinned, indicating the collection to her companion. 'This is my third sting today and it's pretty clear that others have suffered as well,' she said cheerfully. 'I thought the one on my forefinger was pretty bad – the pain, I mean – but this one's worse. I can't see myself picking any more today. Still, I reckon I've done my share. We were picking at six . . .' She glanced at the clock on the mantel. '. . . Gracious, we've been at it for eight hours already, so I don't think the Turnbulls will blame me if I have a go at the sorting and packing, and leave the picking to the uninjured.'

Danny nodded abstractedly. He had taken her hand and was holding it over the bowl of water whilst he applied the sodden blue bag to the sting. Tess would have given up after a minute, but when she tried to take her hand away he shook his head chidingly. 'Impatience won't help,' he told her. 'My mother always reckons to apply the blue bag for five solid minutes by the kitchen clock, so just you hold still while Dr Danny gets on with his cure. Oh, by the way, we haven't introduced ourselves. I'm Danny Brewster and my companion who's still in the orchard is Phil Ryland.'

'I'm Tess Collins.' She glanced at him curiously. 'I don't think I've seen you here before, at Grange Farm I mean, but I'm sure I've seen you somewhere. Which airfield are you at?'

'Rudham, though we haven't been there long,' Danny said. 'We've just swapped from Wimpeys – they're Wellingtons, as I expect you know – to Lancasters.' He grinned at her, then removed the blue bag from her palm, patted her hand dry on the towel which Mrs Turnbull had laid across the back of a chair, and indicated the kettle steaming on the hob. 'Shall I make you a cup of tea? For shock, you know.'

'Good idea,' Tess said, sinking into a chair. What with her sudden descent from the tree and the throbbing pain in her right hand she was beginning to feel quite light-headed, and she realised with a slight shock that, apart from a quantity of plums and a cheese sandwich, she had not eaten since the previous day. Mrs Turnbull would normally have provided a proper lunch since they had started so early, but because of the urgency she had simply made an enormous number of cheese sandwiches, put them on an old card table in the middle of the orchard, and told the girls to help themselves. Tess had managed to grab one sandwich but then she had ascended the tallest tree in the orchard – the one from which she had fallen – and had not bothered to eat again.

Now, Tess looked curiously up at her companion. 'But you said what's-his-name – Phil – was your cousin. How come you managed to get together? Or is it simply a coincidence – that you're both at Rudham, I mean?'

'We've been together for a year and a half,' Danny said. The teapot and tea caddy were conveniently to hand, so he spooned tea into the pot, then began to pour boiling water on to the leaves. 'Phil's my flight engineer and acts as second pilot when necessary. He's a grand chap for all his jokey talk; knows his job and is always reliable. In fact I'm one of the lucky ones with an excellent crew to back me up. We all liked the old Wimpey but we're agreed that the Lanc is even better.'

'Oh, I see,' Tess said. 'But you're a flight lieutenant, because you've got two stripes and your cousin hasn't.'

'True,' Danny said, carefully pouring tea into two tin mugs. 'I don't suppose you take sugar, 'cos nobody does these days, but how about a saccharin tablet? And rank doesn't matter, you know, not once you're in the air.'

'No, no sweetener, but I do like milk,' Tess said, getting up from her chair and fetching a jug of milk from the slate slab in the big walk-in larder. She returned to the kitchen. 'I'm still intrigued by the fact that you two are cousins; you aren't a bit alike, as I'm sure you know. And where do you come from? You're obviously not from Norfolk because the Norfolk accent is unmistakable.'

Danny grinned at her. 'I'm from Herefordshire. And you're from somewhere up north . . .'

'Liverpool, though I seem to have lost most of my accent since moving to Norfolk,' Tess said, nodding. 'I've a younger sister who was evacuated to your part of the world at the start of the war, but she's back home now. We've a younger brother, Davy, and my stepfather paid a nice young girl to take care of him whilst Uncle Arthur – that's what we call my stepfather – was at work. Only one day he went upstairs early and found Davy playing with all sorts of unsuitable things in the kitchen, and the girl and her boyfriend carrying on in Uncle Arthur's bed. He dismissed her at once, of course, and begged Tina to come home to look after Davy, because he knew he could trust her. And there was our Tina beginning to talk about getting a job down Hereford way. Only of course she wouldn't have dreamed of letting Uncle Arthur down and agreed to go home to Liverpool just as soon as it could be arranged. You see, there's a great deal of war work available in Liverpool now, and it's extremely well paid. I believe my stepfather did start interviewing girls but he found he dared not trust any of them; he kept remembering that Davy had been alone in the kitchen with the front of the stove open and a kettle boiling on the hob. Apparently, he'd got all the cleaning materials out of the cupboard under the sink – Vim, Brasso, shoe polish and a big bottle of bleach – and a selection of big knives out of the drawer. He got the knives because he couldn't unscrew the bleach and planned to chop its head off, he said.'

'Gosh,' Danny said inadequately. 'I can understand how your stepfather felt. It was good of your sister to agree to return to Liverpool, though, if she was happy in the country.'

'Oh, sure, but Tina's a really good girl. Poor little Davy wasn't even a year old when our mam was killed in the May blitz of 'forty-one, but I'm sure he'll be fine with Tina; she's young enough to sympathise with him but old enough to control him. At least I hope so. And now my stepfather's mind is at rest and he can concentrate on his business whilst he and Tina between them make a good home for Davy.'

'That's a nice story with a happy ending,' Danny said contentedly. 'We had evacuees at Manor Farm, though I think most of them have gone home now. My mum writes pretty regularly but now it's mostly about how difficult farming has become and how marvellous the land girls are. They've got four or five, and I bet my mum spoils them like anything. Why, she's been known to . . .'

'Manor Farm?' Tess said, her voice rising to a squeak. 'And didn't you say your name was Brewster?' She began to laugh. 'Well, and I said it was a coincidence you and your cousin flying in the same aircraft! My sister, Tina, was evacuated to a Manor Farm in Herefordshire and I'm pretty sure the folk who took her in were a Mr and Mrs Brewster, though she always called them Auntie Deb and Uncle John. Are they your parents, Danny? If so, I've actually met them, which makes the world a much smaller place than I ever thought!'

For three days after their visit to Grange Farm, Danny struggled with his conscience. Truth to tell, he was amazed at himself. Why had he not said a word to Phil about the strange coincidence which he and Tess had discussed whilst they were alone in the kitchen? It was not as if he and Phil had not talked about the occasion, for they had done so several times, both saying that they meant to revisit the farm and help out whenever the opportunity occurred. 'And that Tess is the prettiest popsie we've come across yet. I mean to get to know her better,' Phil had said. 'We could make up a foursome; someone said she and Sue were billeted together. Sue's the glamorous one who used to be on the stage.'

Danny had grinned at his cousin. 'How the devil did you find out so much in such a short time?' he had asked. 'But don't forget, old chap, that you aren't free to start getting serious.'

Phil had pulled a face. 'We've discussed all this before, young Danny, and you agreed to keep your trap shut. I told you that I had no intention of misbehaving with anyone, but I also told you that I meant to have some fun and you agreed that that was fair enough, you know you did.'

'Yes, because I did see your point. Fellers who've been married for a while and talk a lot about their wives do tend to get left out of things. Plain girls may be happy enough to go out with them, but the pretty ones steer clear,' Danny had admitted grudgingly. 'But you promised you wouldn't go breaking hearts and I must say you've been pretty good so far, so I'll keep my trap shut, as you elegantly put it, so long as you don't go overstepping the mark.'

Danny had agreed not to mention Phil's marriage, partly because he trusted Phil's promise of good behaviour, but possibly more because of Phil's crushing disappointment that he had failed to complete his pilot training and had had to become a flight engineer instead. Danny had not liked to ask just what part of the training his cousin had failed and Phil had never volunteered the information, but he had done enough of the course to be able to fly the Lanc when Danny had 'urgent business' towards the rear of the fuselage, or simply needed a spell away from the controls.

Phil always acted as though he was a pilot when talking to girls, however, and Danny, who loved his cousin, simply went along with it. After all, it hurt no one and Phil was always careful to choose girlfriends who were neither Waafs nor knew too much about the air force. In fact, he usually picked 'good-time girls', sometimes actually saying to Danny that a good few of his temporary partners were married themselves, and made no secret of it.

So now, waking in the early hours with the grey light of dawn creeping in through the window of his billet, Danny wondered for the umpteenth time why he had not told Phil that Tess Collins had actually visited Manor Farm, had been on friendly terms with his parents, might even have visited Hilltop for all he knew. Indeed, she had told him how interested she had been in a photograph on the living-room mantelpiece, the photograph of himself and Phil as ten-year-old boys on the beach at Aberystwyth. There could be no harm in telling Phil, not if his cousin really meant to behave himself, but Danny had been struck by the way Phil's eyes had followed Tess as she moved around the farm kitchen helping her employer to get the tea. It was a far softer, gentler look than that which Phil usually turned on girls who interested him and Danny was worried by it. Already, he himself liked Tess very much and intended to see more of her. Why not? *He* wasn't married, did not even have a girlfriend any more. Was that why he did not mean to let Phil know that Tess had visited his home and knew his parents? He supposed it must be and felt a little ashamed.

Having satisfied himself on that score, Danny

heaved the covers up over his shoulders and tried to go back to sleep, but just as he was on the verge of dropping off, he remembered that Grange Farm would be cutting the corn any time now and decided that he would go over and give a hand, if he wasn't flying that night, of course. It was mucky work but it would give him a chance to meet Tess and he knew Phil intended to get the liberty truck into Norwich where he meant to try to buy a record of a Vera Lynn song which all the chaps were whistling. Yes, he would tell Phil he'd changed his mind at the last minute and did not mean to accompany him, though even as he drifted off to sleep he told himself that his plan was doomed. Phil would never go off without questioning him as to his intentions and Danny had never lied to his cousin, nor did he mean to do so now. Still, you never knew.

Presently, he slept.

Tess woke early and glanced towards the window because today they were harvesting corn and it was important that they should have fine weather. The summer had been a poor one but September had come with bright sunshine and today was no exception, for as soon as she sat up she saw golden light and blue sky. Joyfully, she hopped out of bed and ran to the window. She and Sue were still billeted in Lavender Cottage and Mrs Yallop took such good care of them and fed them so well that when an opportunity had come to move in with old Mr and Mrs Saunders they had refused the offer politely but firmly. Mr and Mrs Saunders had a farm cottage within a hundred yards of the Turnbulls' and their daughter had joined the ATS, thus freeing her room for other occupants. The Saunders were a very old couple indeed, both in their eighties, and the land girl who had been billeted with them in the early days had once found a large bluebottle cooked to a turn in her portion of mashed potato, and frequently complained that there was more meat in the sprouts on her plate than there was on the tiny chop she was occasionally served. So Tess and Sue had agreed that a five-mile bike ride was a piece of cake compared with bluebottle stew, and had continued to live in Ludham village itself, despite the fact that in winter they could not always cycle but sometimes had to trudge through snow, ice, flood and mud in order to reach their workplace.

This morning, however, Tess thought, gazing gleefully out at a perfect September day, they were in luck. She was to drive the tractor today, whilst Sue operated the binder it would pull. When the corn was bound into large sheaves, the other land girls, and any helpers, would gather these up and stand them into stooks so that the grain could finish drying off. When it was dry, the sheaves would be made into stacks to await the thresher, a mighty machine worked by no fewer than four land girls, with a male foreman. Since they threshed all the grain on all the farms in the area, it might be midwinter or even spring before they got round to Mr Turnbull's place.

Tess had watched the girls on the thresher with

real admiration, but was tremendously grateful not to be one of them. She and Sue moaned about broken fingernails, work-roughened skin, and the muscles which had appeared all over them, ruining, Sue said, their otherwise perfect figures. They suffered from chilblains in winter and sunburn in summer, but none of it compared with the awfulness of working the thresher. Those poor girls were perpetually filthy and the dust from the machine got into everything, including their sandwiches, so they always enjoyed working at Grange Farm because Mrs Turnbull invariably insisted that they come into the kitchen and share the family's midday meal.

The window of the small bedroom which Tess and Sue shared was open wide and Tess was in the act of thrusting her head and shoulders out into the freshness of the morning when a sleepy voice spoke from behind her. 'What's up, Tess? I didn't hear the alarm.'

Tess turned back into the room. Sue was sitting up in bed, curl papers on end, vigorously rubbing her eyes. 'The alarm hasn't gone off yet but the sunshine woke me,' Tess said. 'Mr Turnbull said we'd start cutting the corn today if the weather was OK, and it is!'

Sue digested this whilst leaning over to slap the button on the alarm clock since they no longer needed it to ring. 'That's good,' she said at last. 'Though I hate it when the rabbits come out of the last stand. Now, were Danny and Phil flying last night? If so, they'll be sleeping today and won't want to come corn cutting. On the other hand, if they're flying tonight, they won't be coming over either. Damn this perishing war. We simply can't guess, can we?'

Tess, pouring water from the jug into the china bowl, giggled. 'I must remember to tell the air force that they should manage their war better,' she observed. 'Because night flying ruins Sue Pritchard's social life. But you know Danny and Phil; if they can possibly get over they'll do so.'

'I've never worked out whether they come over for Mrs Turnbull's grub or for the pleasure of our company,' Sue said, rolling out of bed. 'Hurry up and wash, woman, and hand me that hairbrush. I might as well unroll my curlers whilst I wait.'

'I don't see why you say that,' Tess said, reaching blindly for the towel which hung by the washstand, for she had just lathered and rinsed her face, and her eyes were screwed shut. 'I've been to the flicks three times with Danny and we've been to the dances at the base four times, and surprise surprise, Mrs Turnbull wasn't catering for any of those events.' She scrubbed vigorously at her face with the rough towel, then turned to eye Sue, who was brushing her thick dark hair in front of the small square of mirror propped up on the washstand. 'But of course you may have seen Mrs T lurking in the cinema, I suppose, and handing out cakes and sandwiches,' she added with a grin.

Sue sighed, gathered her mass of curls into a rubber band, emptied Tess's washing water into the slop bucket, and poured out some for herself. 'I don't see how you can make that remark considering Danny and Phil act like a couple of perishing Siamese twins,' she said bitterly. 'I get an invitation from Phil to see *Casablanca* and the following day Danny asks you if you'd like to see *In Which We Serve*, and uh-oh, when we meet them off the gharry, and they realise we're bound for two different destinations, there's a hurried confab between the two of them and we all end up going to see the gorgeous Humphrey Bogart. Next time there's a decent flick on at the Regal, Phil asks you if you'd like to see it and then Danny asks me. Then we all go together again! It's almost as if they've decided to share us!'

She sounded so indignant that Tess giggled again. 'Now you come to mention it, it's pretty much the same when they take us dancing. We swap partners until I feel quite dizzy. But there's always that lovely moment when we say goodnight . . . I usually get Danny at the end of the evening and you usually get Phil.'

'True, and Phil is by far the better-looking,' Sue said, fumbling for the towel. 'But I always feel he's somewhat lightweight. Not that I mind.' She dried her face and then turned to look, almost shyly, at her friend. 'As you know, Malcolm and I had a thing going last year, but after he was killed . . . well, I decided that any sort of serious relationship only laid one open to pain. I really loved Malcolm, even though he wasn't anywhere near as handsome as Phil, so I told myself after that that I should take a leaf out of your book. You've got that fellow who's flying fighters abroad somewhere – Mike, isn't it? – yet you have lots of friends who take you about without trying to get heavy. That's what I mean to do, so I shouldn't grumble when Danny and Phil do the same.'

'That's a foul lie – that I go out with lots of fellers,' Tess said indignantly, pulling on her working dungarees. 'OK, if someone asks me to dance I do, because it would be very rude as well as unkind to refuse. But until Danny and Phil came on the scene I didn't accept invitations to go to the flicks because I didn't fancy fighting off an octopus in the back row. And you can't tell just by looking at a chap what type he'll turn out to be.'

Sue, now scrambling into her own dungarees, had to agree that this was so. 'But sooner or later, I mean to sort Danny and Phil out,' she said with determination. 'And now let's get down to breakfast before the porridge goes cold.'

The weather continued brilliant for the entire wheat harvest as well, and to the girls' pleasure Danny and Phil came over several times. They were hard workers and because they both came from farming backgrounds, Tess supposed, seemed to know by instinct where they were most needed. Tess and Sue did not see as much of the two young men as they would have liked, but they all sat together in the long grass at the edge of the cornfield, eating Mrs Turnbull's delicious harvest pie with rounds of bread and butter and a good deal of what she called her harvest fruit cake. Both young men talked knowledgeably to Mr Turnbull about the rigours of farming in wartime, the stupidity of the Ministry rules and regulations, and the astonishing way that city girls had become as expert as any farm worker.

'That there little Jenny, I reckon she's as strong as a man and a good deal more willing than most. Old Tosher taught her how to thatch a stack, which is dirty prickly work, and I heard Tosh say the other day that she's as quick as he is. And I tell you straight, she's even neater,' Mr Turnbull told Danny and Phil. 'In fact all the land girls are grand workers – just as good as the men they replaced. Look at Tess – she's a real city girl what never so much as picked an apple until she joined the WLA. Now she can plough as straight a furrow as any man I've ever employed, and I'd trust her to help at a difficult calving sooner than some of the fellers, 'cos she's got more patience and a gentle touch. Oh aye, when we were first told we'd got to employ women my heart sank into my boots, but the girls have proved me wrong. Especially city girls, like young Tess here.'

Overhearing, Tess blushed rosily, more delighted with this tribute than with any compliment she had previously received. Sue, also listening, poked her in the ribs. 'That's the reason Danny and Phil are so keen on the two of us,' she whispered. 'Mark my words, when the war ends they'll propose marriage – it doesn't matter which one of them asks which one of us – and get themselves first-rate farm workers for free.' She looked consideringly at the two young men devouring harvest cake and talking of farming matters through full mouths. 'Yes, that will be the reason that they shower us with attention.'

Tess pretended to agree but in her heart she thought there was a far simpler explanation. They had known Danny and Phil for only a couple of months, but in that time Tess had noticed the subtle change in them the day after a raid on Germany. Their faces were drawn and tense and they scarcely ever referred to the raid except in jokey, dismissive terms. They take us out and talk about farming to forget the strain of their regular job, she told herself. I'm sure they like us but they aren't going to commit themselves any more than we are because they must be well aware that any sort of planning for the future is dangerous. Today they're alive; tomorrow they might not be. She said none of this to Sue, however, though she had told her about the strange coincidence of her sister's being evacuated to Danny's farm. Sue had said that no doubt that was the reason why Danny seemed more interested in Tess than in her beautiful self, but Tess had only laughed and shaken her head. 'I don't think it's important; it would be different if Tina was still there, perhaps, because I'd probably visit her, but as it is my connection with Manor Farm no longer exists. And now let's talk about something else.'

'Come you along, my woman! If we get a move on we'll finish this here field afore the light goes.'

Tess jumped guiltily to her feet and smiled at old Tosher, who had spoken. 'Sorry, Tosh, I was dreaming,' she said apologetically. 'To tell you the truth, I've eaten too much harvest cake; I was nearly asleep just then.'

Danny and Phil grinned at her. 'It'll be a good thing if we do finish the field this evening, since I doubt we'll be here tomorrow or the day after,' Danny said. He flung a casual arm round Tess's shoulders and gave her a squeeze. 'But we'll be free by the end of the week. Someone said there's a hop at the village hall on Saturday night. It might be fun to go . . . unless we're on standby, of course.'

Tess turned to look at him and for a moment saw the unguarded fear in his eyes. Not a fear that they might be on standby on Saturday but the fear that they might not return from whatever bombing raids they would be carrying out over the next few days. Impulsively, she put out a hand and took one of his, giving it a gentle squeeze. 'Yes, there is a hop; entrance two shillings, scones and orange squash to be provided by the WI,' she said gaily. 'And I'd love to go with you, Danny, unless Mr Turnbull works us so hard that we drop in our tracks before then.'

She tried to sound light and amusing but realised that Danny must have read the warmth and sympathy in her glance, for he squeezed her hand very hard for a moment before saying in a lowered tone: 'Oh, Tess, you're a lovely girl! I just wish . . . but you *do* understand, I've always thought you did. How about if you ring the station on Friday, late afternoon? Of course I won't be able to say much over the

331

phone but if I say "no hopping" then you'll know what I mean, won't you?'

'Of course,' Tess said, aware that this was the closest they had come to admitting that there could be more between them than just friendship. One did not ask a casual friend to ring the officers' mess. She liked Danny but had been careful to keep their relationship on a friendly footing because of her feelings for Mike.

By now, however, they had reached the tractor and Tess swung herself into the driving seat whilst Danny walked round to crank up the engine. They smiled at one another and Tess thought they were probably both aware of a subtle change in their relationship. She sighed to herself as the engine caught and began to roar. Mike hadn't written for weeks, or at least she had not received a letter, and she realised guiltily that she dared no longer take it for granted that the pair of them would marry one day. War changes all of us and I'm really fond of Mike, but in this war it truly can be 'here today and gone tomorrow', so I mustn't let myself get too involved with anyone.

Work began once more.

Danny and Phil said little as they scrambled aboard the gharry, sat down on the uncomfortable metal bench, and eyed each other cautiously. How much had Phil heard? Danny wondered. In fact, it was not in words that he and Tess had suddenly grown closer, but in a glance that Danny thought had brought understanding to them both, but it was words which had alerted Phil's suspicions. He turned to stare at Danny, his eyes hard and bright. 'You told Tess to phone the station, to find out whether we'd be able to go to the hop in the village hall,' he said accusingly.

'Yes, that's right,' Danny said mildly. 'Why not? Have you any objection?'

There was a longish pause, then Phil spoke slowly and deliberately. 'Yes, I have. I've played around with a lot of girls since I joined but I've never been serious about anyone. Now I am serious about Tess and you have to come horning in. Why do you have to start getting heavy over the only girl I've ever truly fallen for?'

For a moment Danny simply stared at his cousin, scarcely believing what Phil had just said. He wondered, wildly, if Phil could be joking, but saw from his face that he was deadly serious. So his own answer must be serious as well. 'Phil, you're a married man. I know I promised to keep it a secret but that doesn't change the fact. You're a married man with a son; remember? And though I've never reproached you, way back before the war if Sophie was anyone's girl she was mine. I'm not blaming you over that; she was only a kid when I left to join the air force and it's pretty clear you swept her off her feet. Why not? You're a damned good-looking bloke and, perhaps most important of all, you were there when she needed you. But you can't have it all ways, old chap. Not even you can imagine that you can have Sophie and Tess!'

Abruptly, Phil dropped his head into his hands. 'I've never told you this – never told anyone – but I never was in love with Sophie,' he said drearily. 'She's very sweet and when I realised she was pregnant I knew I'd got to do the decent thing and marry her.' He raised a haggard face to stare across at Danny. 'The fact is, old fellow, I've never been in love, didn't know what love was. But I know now. The feeling I have for Tess isn't at all the way I felt over Sophie. It's – it's a much quieter, more peaceful emotion somehow. I'm happy when I'm with her and I'm unhappy when I'm not. Can you understand that?'

'No, I can't,' Danny said bluntly. 'All I can think of is the little boy who wanted my trike, then my bike, then my new sledge. You told me once how hard done by you'd been as a lad, but even then I couldn't really see it. What you hadn't got by right you took and I'm telling you, Phil, you aren't going to take Tess. God, man, if I let you, what sort of person would that make me? You'd be breaking Sophie's heart, to say nothing of Chris's. Uncle Matt and Aunt Daisy would have to choose between their daughter-in-law, who's been a proper little brick running Hilltop and seeing to everything whilst you've been away, and their son, who doesn't even pretend to like the farm or to care what happens to it. And then there's Tess. Quite apart from the fact that I'm beginning to get fond of her, there's your attitude to take into account. How many girls have you had since you joined the air force? How many have you dumped? Your way with girls is a byword. Love 'em and leave 'em is your whole philosophy. You say you love Tess, but then you said you told Sophie you loved her; you must have done or she'd never have slept with you. So even if I didn't like Tess, I'd warn her to steer clear of you, Phil, because I couldn't bear to see her hurt.'

The gharry began to slow down and the cousins could hear the sound of voices coming from the men waiting for the vehicle to pick them up. Phil spoke quickly. 'But you gave your word, Dan old feller . . . you gave your word that you wouldn't tell anyone I was married. If you go back on it, I swear to God I'll kill you.'

Danny gave a bark of laughter. 'Don't worry, I shall keep my word. But that doesn't mean I'll step aside and let you walk in, as you've done before. This time, I'll bloody well fight back.'

For a moment the two glared at each other, then Phil gave a small complacent grin. 'Tell you what, when I've got Tess, you can have Sophie. Not the kid – I adore that little boy and he thinks the sun shines out of his daddy – but I agree with you, no man can have two women, so . . .'

Danny had always thought himself even-tempered, but before he knew what he was doing he had bunched the fingers of his right hand into a fist and hit Phil on the point of the chin so hard that he actually lifted him off the metal bench. Fortunately, at that very moment, the gharry jerked to a halt and Danny was able to pick his cousin off the floor and pretend that Phil had fallen off the seat as the lorry stopped, hitting his chin on the seat opposite and knocking himself cold. The men climbing into the gharry were highly amused and Phil recovered consciousness quickly, appearing to accept Danny's explanation of how he had come to be knocked out.

He was very quiet for the remainder of the journey and Danny began to wonder, uneasily, if Phil had actually forgotten what had happened, but as they made their way into their billet Danny said casually: 'Are you coming to the ablutions? I could do with a shower before bed,' and for the first time in his life received from his cousin a look of unadulterated hatred – and no reply.

So he really is serious about Tess. Dammit, I should have kept my big mouth shut. The truth is you've only got to look at Tess to see that she's not really interested in Phil. What a fool I was! If I'd pretended my own interest was simply casual, we could have stayed on friendly terms, because Phil believes he only has to crook his little finger and any girl will come running. Still, the cat's out of the bag now, Danny thought wearily, undressing and stepping into the shower cubicle. I suppose I'll have to put things right before our next op because dissension in a crew is the quickest way to get ourselves shot down. But this time I simply won't give in.

Danny and the rest of his crew were heading for Germany. They always kept conversation to a minimum because once you got over Europe you never knew who might be listening in, but even had Danny not insisted on silence, he knew there would have been no word from his flight engineer.

Phil was not speaking to him, had barely spoken since their row over Tess, which had been several weeks ago. Of course he spoke when he had to, when there was a real need to communicate, and in the heat of action he might shout a warning to someone else, but he did not address Danny directly. Fortunately, no other member of the crew had so much as noticed. Once they had laid their eggs they would make for home with all possible speed, and very tired, but still hyped up, they would chat casually once they had crossed the coast. Because conversation was general, no one noticed that Phil, usually the most loquacious of men, never addressed the skipper. Then, at the debriefing, everyone told his own story, and after that they made for the cookhouse, where they had a pretty uninspiring meal in the silence of exhaustion before going to their billets.

Since the row with Phil, Danny had spent a good deal of time at Grange Farm, had returned to Lavender Cottage twice for high tea, and had taken Tess to the cinema in Norwich, to hops at the local airfields and once to a dance at the Samson and Hercules ballroom in the city. The last had not been the wonderful evening he had planned since the ballroom was crammed with American soldiers and airmen, one of whom had had the cheek to try to get off with Tess. Tess, however, had made it perfectly plain that she was with Danny and the GI had backed off, saying apologetically that he had no intention of spoiling sport; it was just that Tess reminded him of his 'l'il sweetheart back home in good old New York'. Tess had laughed, rather unbelievingly, but later Danny had been glad of the interruption since it enabled him to suggest that they left the dance early, and this meant they had more time for a kiss and a cuddle before making their way to Castle Meadow to catch the liberty truck.

Phil still came to the farm whenever he could, but since it was no longer possible for the cousins to go out in a foursome he gradually stopped seeing Sue. Danny did not think that Sue cared at all, for there were always young men anxious to take her about, and he was delighted when Tess told him, guilelessly, that twosomes were more fun than foursomes. The two of them had taken to hiring a rowboat on Hickling Broad and spent many a peaceful sunny afternoon sculling gently around the reed beds. Sometimes Danny fished, sometimes they birdwatched, enormously thrilled to actually see a bittern trying to disguise itself as a clump of reeds, its only movement that of its little yellow eyes as it searched the water for small fish. There were butterflies too, great yellow and black swallowtails, red admirals and peacocks. There were dragonflies, some small and electric blue, darting hither and thither with such speed that predators had small chance of catching them. Several times they saw water voles diving into their holes in the bank, and once they disturbed a dog fox eating a fish which some angler had failed to return to the water.

These trips were especially delightful because Phil was not involved, and because they could only go out in the boat when Tess's day off coincided with Danny's not being on standby they were even more precious. However, as autumn advanced, work on the farm increased to fever pitch and Danny, knowing the importance of harvesting every crop before winter was upon them, spent all his spare time working alongside Tess and the other girls at Grange Farm. Inevitably, his relationship with Tess strengthened, perhaps all the more because he and Phil still avoided one another and scarcely spoke. The invisible cord which had bound them for so long had all but snapped and Danny knew that he himself regretted its passing but could do nothing about it. He had tried, but Phil had not responded, so the coolness between them continued.

Evenings out started late, which meant that the girls were often extremely tired on the day following a dance or a visit to the cinema. Yet somehow they could still work, though Tess once remarked to Sue that for the first time in her life she would not be sorry when winter came.

'You will then,' Sue said positively. 'Remember last winter? Sprout picking when the damn things were covered in frost so the skin between our fingers cracked open and bled? Opening up the mangel clamps and chopping the wretched things into bite-size pieces and half the time almost chopping off our fingers because we couldn't grip the cleaver properly? And fetching spuds in from the potato clamp, and the stench off the ones that had got frosted and gone all liquid? I won't deny we get to bed earlier and sleep in a bit later, but otherwise winter is sheer hell.'

Tess groaned. 'Why did I ever join the WLA?' she said plaintively. 'Oh for a nice warm office, or the control tower on an airfield, or almost anything where I wouldn't have to ever see another sprout, or chuck away another rotten spud!'

'Well, we needn't think about winter yet,' Jenny said. The girls were in the big barn, eating their sandwiches and drinking the tea Mrs Turnbull always provided, whilst outside golden sunshine illumined the yard. 'Someone said this is what they call an Indian summer and it'll likely last a while longer, so we might as well enjoy it.'

'Aye, I reckon this'll go on till the autumn gales start in early November, if we'm lucky,' Tosher said, through a mouthful of bread and cheese. 'And look on the bright side, my woman; there's apples and pears to be sorted and graded, and that's done in the sheds, out of the weather, so that isn't a bad job.' He stood up and took a last swig at his mug of tea. 'C'mon then, let's be havin' you. I want to get the twelve-acre ploughed afore the end of the week.'

Chapter Eleven

'You all set, gal? Nervous, are you? Not that you've any need to be, I'm sure, since you passed the interview and you're a bright kid. What's more, it'll do you good to gerrout of this flat and be wi' young people your own age. Now, don't you bother wi' washing up the breakfast things, 'cos your dad and meself have come to an understanding. I'm coming up every morning to see you're all fed and watered afore you goes off to work and I'll clear up, put everything away and do what I can towards your supper. Your dad will have his dinner in the café, same as usual. Now go get yourself and the kid ready, 'cos the rain's blowin' horizontal out there. No use takin' a brolly. Just you wrap up as warm as you can. There's a tram in ten minutes, so if you hurry you'll scarce have time to get wet.'

Tina, who had been piling the crocks in the sink, turned to smile gratefully at Mrs Tasker as the older woman entered the room. She rubbed her hands dry on the tea towel and hurried across to take Davy's waterproof off the hook on the door. As she did so, the little boy came in. He was an attractive child, rosy-cheeked and bright-eyed, with reddish blond hair that curled all over his small round head, and a pair of enormous grey-green eyes. He looked like

a perfect cherub but, as Tina already knew, he was a
real little devil, up to every form of naughtiness. He
was three and a half but often seemed older, for being
what amounted to an only child he had been
dreadfully spoiled by Arthur. Davy thought – knew
– that he could get his own way in almost everything,
and when Tina had returned to the fold some time
earlier he had resented her deeply and had refused to
do as she told him. But Tina was wise beyond her
years and realised that she would have to cajole
rather than order. In fact, for the first three or four
weeks she had ruled with a series of treats, so that if,
say, she wanted to go shopping, the trip would end
with a visit to the swings and the park or the
purchase of a small toy from a market stall. She was
careful to try to obtain food which her little brother
most enjoyed, and when she made pastry – which
was not often for Tina was no cook – there was
always a small piece left over so that Davy might
manufacture dreadful little grey pastry cases into
which she would empty half a teaspoonful of their
precious jam.

Now, Davy ran across the room towards her, a big
smile upon his face. 'Is we ready, our Tina?' he asked
eagerly, then turned to Mrs Tasker. 'Us is goin' to
work makin' kecks and guns, and maybe even
swords an' bullets; did you know that, Auntie
Tasker?'

Mrs Tasker, busy at the sink, said comfortably:
'Aye, that's right, chuck,' but Tina corrected him at
once.

'We're going to make uniforms; not guns, and not bullets,' she said firmly. 'And we shan't be muckin' around with swords, either. And you, young feller-me-lad, you'll be goin' into the nursery which the factory runs for workers' children who ain't old enough for school yet.' She saw Davy's face fall and added hastily: 'But you'll have a grand time, so you will. They've got sand trays, building blocks, and all sorts of toys, and you'll get a drink of milk and a biscuit for your elevenses. And on fine days there's swings in the play area and a slide . . . a little roundabout . . . oh, all sorts.'

She began to help Davy into his waterproofs, buttoned him up and slapped the sou'wester on to his curly head. 'There you are; you look just like a lifeboat man. Now, if you go over to the counter by the pantry, you'll find your little satchel. It's got your sandwiches inside and a real treat, only you shouldn't look now, you should wait until we get to our factory.' The child's satchel contained a round of egg sandwiches, a nice rosy apple and a packet of Smith's crisps. Tina knew the crisps to be a great favourite with her little brother and had searched most of Heyworth Street before finally running a packet to earth.

Now, she picked up her own sandwiches, donned her waterproof, grabbed Davy's hand and set off, shouting goodbye to Mrs Tasker as they began to descend the stairs. Mrs Tasker now had to do all the cooking in the café as well as a good deal of waiting on, so there was no question of her looking after

Davy, but the fact that she was coming in early five days a week in order to clear breakfast and start preparations for supper was a tremendous help. It would mean that Tina and Davy came home at around half past six to find potatoes peeled, vegetables washed and meat – if they had happened to obtain some – ready for cooking. Shopping in these days of shortages was a long and exhausting job and, to Arthur's great surprise, an aunt of his who lived further up Heyworth Street with her even older husband had offered to take on getting their messages. She was a spry old lady in her late seventies and had said she would regard Arthur's marketing as doing her bit for the war effort. Tina thought, secretly, that Great-aunt Jemima had not wanted to be asked to look after Davy, who could be such a little devil, and had seized on getting their messages as the lesser of two evils. Even so, it would be a tremendous help, and both Tina and her stepfather were grateful to be spared at least one task. Because of Davy, Tina had been employed as a day-shift worker only but this meant she would be in work five days a week until six o'clock in the evening. Most of the shops, and even the market stalls, now closed at six, and had Aunt Jemima not volunteered Tina supposed that she would have had to spend all day Saturday combing the shops. She was suitably grateful, and hoped that the old lady would continue to do their messages at least until young Davy was in proper school. Then she supposed that she herself would work shifts, which would at least mean she would have some time to herself during the day.

The two young people emerged on to Heyworth Street. As Mrs Tasker had said, the rain was blowing sideways and it was very cold. Despite the fact that Christmas was only a couple of weeks off, the faces of the folk hurrying along the street were pale and grim; hateful weather, hateful shortages, hateful war! But Davy, who had known nothing else, gave a shout of glee and broke into a run, towing Tina along behind him. 'That tram goes where we's goin'!' he squeaked joyfully. 'C'mon, Tina, I know you're old but you've simply gorra run else we'll miss it.'

'We shan't. There's a queue a mile long,' Tina pointed out breathlessly, but she ran all the same, splashing in and out of the puddles and realising with some dismay that her left boot had a hole in the toe and was letting in a great deal of icy cold water. 'Anyway, how do you know it's our tram? You can't read.'

'I can in a way 'cos I know me numbers and that there tram's the one we want,' Davy panted. 'Let's go to the front of the queue; they'll let us on 'cos we's kids.'

Tina, however, took him firmly to the back of the queue and the conductor pushed the last remaining passengers aboard, shouting, 'Move further down the car, please,' as he did so. She and Davy were hauled off the step and into the body of the tram by folk who were soaked and should have been cross and uncooperative, but were not. Tina remembered how shocked she had been on returning to the city after so long away. The extent of the bombing had horrified her, naturally, but she had been prepared for that. What had truly upset her were the grey, tired faces which surrounded her. In Herefordshire, and particularly on Manor Farm, everyone was sun-tanned and rosy-cheeked. Food was far easier to obtain in the country, where one grew quantities of fruit and vegetables, killed a pig every autumn and had as many eggs as the hens decided to provide. It was in the big cities that the shortages were felt most acutely. No one had gardens, so they could not grow vegetables, and those who had had the foresight to rent allotments soon discovered that they would never taste the fruits of their labours unless they organised themselves into a rota of people to keep watch day and night.

Tina had never lived through the sort of raid to which the citizens of Liverpool and other big cities had become accustomed, though Liverpool had not suffered a serious attack for almost two years and its citizens were once more enjoying unbroken nights, though like everyone else they suffered times when the electricity and gas were switched off and taps mysteriously refused to deliver water. Now, chatting gaily to Davy and exchanging quips with other passengers, Tina realised again how lucky she had been: easy-going schoolteachers who released their pupils without question whenever they were needed on the farm, ample food always on the table and eight hours' sleep every night. She had not even worried particularly over Uncle Arthur and Davy, having no idea how hard things were in cities, or of the sort of life they were living, but already, in the time she had been back in Heyworth Street, she had realised that whilst it was mainly the south-east of England against whom the Luftwaffe operated, the difficulties of feeding a family were as bad in Liverpool as in any other city. But we're better off than most, she thought now, as the tram began to slow for her stop. Uncle Arthur gets his fruit from the shop, Mrs Tasker usually manages to save us some food from the Restawhile, and Tess has sent us some lovely parcels. Why, even Mike, who's miles and miles away in Tunisia, has sent us dates and dried fruit and some sweets from the bazaar. Oh aye, we do better than most.

But right now they were scrambling off the tram and heading for what was a big adventure for them both. On their arrival, Tina took Davy into the cloak-room, showed him how to hang up his waterproofs and to change his wellington boots for the soft little slippers which she had brought from home in the pocket of her own waterproof, and accompanied him to the crèche. Davy clung to her hand and Tina was secretly nervous that he would not let her leave him, but by a great piece of good fortune the first person he saw there was a tiny boy with a huge army lorry clasped in his arms. Davy marched straight across to him and laid a hand on the lorry. 'Why don't us fill it full of sand – it's a tip-up, ain't it? – then we could drive it round to where them red bricks are piled up in the corner, and tip it out just like real builders do,' he said. 'Oh . . . bye, Tina. See you later.'

Tina watched for a moment, hovering in the doorway, but soon realised that the two small boys had forgotten all about her. They had taken the lorry to the nearest sand table, where Davy had shouldered his way to the front with scant regard for anyone in his way and begun to heap sand into the lorry with a prodigal hand, ably assisted by his new friend. Tina winced at the thought of what the nursery teacher would say when she found her sand table bare and its contents heaped all over the red building bricks, but she told herself that it was no longer her concern and hurried through the rain to the factory foyer, where a great many women and girls were patiently queuing to clock on.

Tina had been told to make her way to Room 49 where the supervisor, Mrs McKay, would take charge of her. She was relieved to see, just ahead of her, Mary Williams, a girl who had been in her class at school. She was instantly recognisable with her bush of light fair hair, though Tina had not set eyes on her for several years. Now, Mary's hair was tied back with a rubber band, so Tina leaned forward and tugged at a lock of it. Mary swung round and grinned delightedly when she recognised Tina, dropping back so that they might talk more easily. 'Well I never did!' she exclaimed. 'Fancy seeing you after all these years, Tina. But wasn't you in the country? My mam brung me back that first Christmas – I were in Hereford, same as you – but when the bombing started me and my sister Ivy went to North Wales. In fact I only come home a couple of months ago and that were because once I were fourteen, Mam thought I could help out, earn some money.'

'Oh, that's a bit like me,' Tina said. 'My mam were killed in the May blitz but my stepfather let me stay on in the country until a few months ago. He wanted someone he could trust to look after me little brother, so back I had to come. I did all sorts at first, but of course I couldn't earn much 'cos of having to give an eye to Davy. Then I saw the factory job advertised, saying they had nursery facilities, so I applied and gorrit. Wharrabout you, Mary? D'you like factory work? What room are you in? Is anyone else from our class working here?'

'I dunno; it's me first day, same as you,' Mary said. 'I were told to go to see a Mrs McKay in Room 49, but I dunno if I'll be working there or if this McKay woman will send me on somewhere else. But there's several of us girls workin' here. I heard about the job from Bessie Longbottom and she said Nellie Bunn – remember her, fat girl with a squint? – and Lucy Hinde are here 'n' all. Apparently, they puts the youngest girls on to mekkin' kecks and the older ones on battledresses. Bessie says they like it all right, 'specially the money which is a deal more'n you could earn in a shop or an office.'

An hour later, Tina was sitting at a long workbench with a commercial sewing machine in front of her. Bessie Longbottom was on her left and Mary on her right. 'We're allowed to talk so long as we keep our voices down and don't never stop working,' Bessie had explained. 'We have to be in our places by eight o'clock, then we have a ten-minute break at half ten when the tea trolley comes round. We can't drink tea at our benches in case we spill something on the material so we drink it standing, then go straight back to work as soon as Mrs McKay blows her whistle. We have thirty minutes from half past twelve for us dinners, then another tea break at four – ten minutes again – an' we goes home prompt at six, though they expect you to finish the piece of work you're doing and remove it from the machine before you leave, ready for the night shift to take over.'

It seemed fair enough to Tina, and though she found the work difficult at first she did not let this worry her. Both she and Mary found it hard to go fast and produce straight seams, but watching Bessie from time to time she saw how confidently the other girl zipped the material in and out of her machine, her seams straight as a ruler, and guessed that in time she and Mary and all the other new girls would reach a similar state of expertise.

She was relieved when the six o'clock whistle sounded, but conscientiously finished her seam before hurrying over to the nursery, where a bright-eyed Davy awaited her. To her question as to how he had enjoyed his day, he told her it had been pretty good, and elaborated as they waited for their tram. 'Me and Jacky played at builders until elevenses time,' he said importantly. 'Us had lickle bottles of milk and two bickies. Then the rain stopped and Miss Taylor took us for a walk. Then we come back and had us sarnies. I were the only one wi' crisps, thanks ever so, Tina. So I give Jacky some in his hand an' he give me a tiny bit of his sticky bun. Then Miss Taylor gave us a pillow each and a tiddly bit of blanket, and told us to lie down on the floor and close our eyes. I did what she said and, Tina, I were *'stonished* 'cos I never thought I'd go to sleep in the day, norra big boy like me, but we *all* did, even Billy, and Jacky says he's the baddest boy of all and *never* does what he's told.'

'Gosh!' Tina said inadequately. 'And *then* what happened – when you woke up?'

'Story time. Miss Taylor told us two stories and then she played some music on the gramophone. She said we was to play we were little flowers what were curled up on the floor asleep when it rained, only then the sun came out and it made us uncurl and stretch and be big, big flowers. Billy made a rude noise and Miss Taylor slapped him. He went ever so red but he didn't cry. He was still in the corner at goin' home time, only then his mammy came so he had to go to the cloakroom and put his coat on.'

By now, they were actually on the tram and Davy was having to raise his voice to be heard above the racket. 'Everyone's mammy calls for them, 'cept for me. I told Jacky you were me sister, but you'll have to pretend to be me mammy, Tina, 'cos Miss Taylor don't know about sisters.'

'Poor little blighter,' Arthur said when Tina

repeated her small brother's words later that evening. 'Davy can't remember Laura, of course, but I think of her often. I wish . . . but there's no point in wishing.'

The pair of them were sitting by the dying kitchen fire. Tina got up and went over to give her stepfather a quick hug and a kiss on the forehead. 'I think of her often, too,' she said softly. 'I didn't miss her so much at Manor Farm because she'd hardly ever been there, but coming back to the flat and the café . . . well, I've missed her dreadfully and it must be even worse for you, Uncle Arthur.'

'It's hard on all of us because your mam were a wonderful woman,' Arthur said sombrely. 'There's something you could do for me, queen, if you would. I never thought to ask you this, but it's for Davy's sake as much as mine. Could you bring yourself to call me Dad?'

Tina was surprised at the pleasure this suggestion gave her. 'Of course I could! After all, I don't remember my real dad and you've been grand to me and Tess,' she said. 'I see what you mean about Davy as well. It'll be a lot easier for him if we all call you Dad. Next time I write to Tess, I'll suggest she does the same.'

It was Christmas Eve and Tina, headscarved, booted and with two woolly jumpers on under her rather worn winter coat, was searching for stocking presents. Arthur had managed to get hold of an orange for the toe, and Tina had sacrificed some of her sweet ration to buy a quarter of a pound of jelly babies and a Mars bar. She had found a cartoon book depicting the adventures of Mary Mouse, much loved by Davy, and now she was searching for a toy vehicle of some sort, preferably a Dinky, which she knew would give her little brother hours of pleasure. Davy had inherited all Mike's toys, but these had been pretty battered, and a brand-new car for his collection could set the seal on Davy's Christmas.

Christmases had got leaner now that Tina was back in the city. When she had lived at Manor Farm, Mrs Brewster had insisted that she sent parcels home, and though she had usually shopped for small extras she had known that the bacon, eggs, butter and cheese which had been delivered to her step-father were a far more acceptable present than anything she could buy. Now, however, she had bought Arthur a pair of rather clumsy khaki gloves and Tess a beautiful headscarf, scarlet, with a pattern of yellow and green leaves. Neither item had been expensive or new but she had had to spend a whole Saturday afternoon searching the city, and thought she had done well to run to earth gifts which she knew would be greeted enthusiastically.

Her search for a Dinky car had led her all the way up to Scotland Road, where the bomb damage was still largely unrepaired. She was hovering outside a shop which looked like a hardware store, wondering whether to go inside and ask if they stocked toys, when someone poked her in the back and a voice she had once known well sounded in her ear. 'Well, I never did! If it ain't teeny weeny Tina! What's you doin' in this part of the world? Don't say you've moved back in with your Auntie Millie!'

Tina whipped round. 'Harry!' she gasped. 'What are *you* doin' here? Someone said you was in the Navy but I didn't think you were old enough so I thought you must still be livin' in the country. As for me, I'm Christmas shopping. I'm still livin' on Heyworth Street but I'm looking for a Dinky toy for my little brother and it seems as though there isn't one in the whole of Liverpool. I s'pose you don't know where I might look?'

'I might,' Harry said cautiously. 'Honest to God, Teeny, it must be goin' on for four years – mebbe more – since we last met. Look, I'll mug you to tea and a bun in Mrs Spellman's Tea Rooms, so's we can talk over old times in comfort. How about it?'

Tina grinned at him. Harry was a couple of years older than her but they had always been close. He had been evacuated to Hereford, along with the rest of his class, but had returned to Liverpool for Christmas 1939. She had meant to write to him to keep in touch, for she knew his address – he lived in Danby Street, opposite the school – so she had had no excuse for not doing so. Only life on the farm had been so full and she had had a great many letters to answer – letters from Tess, her mother and later her stepfather. And Mike, of course. Mike wrote to her quite often and had been very grateful when he had learned of her return to Heyworth Street: *It'll be hard on you in some ways, leaving the farm and all your friends, but knowing you you'll soon make new ones*, he had written. *It'll mean an awful lot to Dad, though, to have you back. You're a good girl, so you are, just like your sister!*

Following Harry into the tea rooms, Tina told herself that she had no reason to feel guilty. Letters are two-way things and Harry had never written to her, never sent her so much as a Christmas card. She said as much as they settled themselves at a small table for two. 'So if you didn't join the Navy, Harry, what are you doing? It were one of me cousins who said you'd joined up, but I reckon they got you mixed up with someone else.'

'No, whoever told you that was right,' Harry said. 'Only the ship I were on got torpedoed, crossing the Atlantic. I were picked up but we were shelled in the water by enemy ships and I were hospitalised for a couple o' months. It's all right, you needn't look so horrified – it were twelve months ago an' I'm right as rain now. I'm back on board ship, too; a battleship this time – bigger 'n' better than a destroyer, believe you me!'

'Oh, Harry, I'm glad you're all right,' Tina said. 'But what about your football and cricket, stuff like that?'

'Well, I'm still keen on them and play 'em when I'm ashore,' Harry said cheerfully. 'Liverpool's my home port, so I come home whenever my ship docks. But wharrabout you, queen? I was real sorry to hear you'd lost your mam and I feel guilty that I've not kept in touch.'

'I wish you had,' Tina said wistfully. 'It's all right now that I'm working in a proper job, but before, when I was at home looking after Davy, keepin' the flat nice an' trying to make meals, I were dead lonely.' She did not tell Harry that she had cried herself to sleep many a night, had simply longed for someone of her own age to talk to, and of course had missed her mother with a painful intensity.

But it seemed that Harry understood without words for he leaned across the table and patted her cheek. 'You're all right, kiddo,' he said gruffly. 'You always was. I reckon you had more guts than anyone else in our gang.' He would have continued to speak, Tina thought, but at that moment a waitress arrived at their table to take their order. Harry turned to Tina. 'Tea, or would you rather have lemonade, if they've got any? Or there's ginger beer . . .'

Tina smiled, realising that he was remembering her tastes from years past. However, it would not do to say so. 'I'll have a cup of tea, please, Harry,' she said demurely. She shot him a mischievous glance. 'I telled you I were in a good job and well paid, so if you buy the tea, I'll throw me gelt about and we'll have a couple o' sticky buns.'

Harry drew himself up. 'You ain't the only one with a bit o' money,' he said grandly. 'And when I asks a young lady to take tea wi' me, I pays the bill.' He turned to the waitress and Tina saw the elderly woman hastily wipe a grin off her face. 'A pot of tea for two, please, miss, and a plate of fancies. Gorrany cream ones?'

'Well, it's only mock, but it's real good: you'll scarce tell the difference,' the woman said. She was short and broad, with her grey hair cut in an old-fashioned Eton crop. She jotted down their order and waddled away, and Tina saw she was wearing down-at-heel shoes and remembered Arthur telling her that Mrs Spellman, who had kept the tea rooms for countless years, had been unable to find girls to wait on and was employing her older sister.

The place was beginning to fill up and Tina wondered how the older women would manage. She had never actually worked at the Restawhile as a paid employee but had often helped out whilst Davy had his nap in the old basket chair in the kitchen, and knew that speed was extremely important when a café was busy. She expected a lengthy wait, there-fore, and was pleasantly surprised when the elderly woman delivered their order after only a couple of minutes. To be sure she puffed and panted rather, and slammed the tray down on the table without ceremony, but she gave them a big grin as she did so. 'There y'are; gerroutside o' that little lot,' she said breathlessly. 'Us don't stand on ceremony in wartime so give us a shout when you've ate and drunk all you want, an' I'll fetch your bill. Them fancies is a tanner apiece an' a pot o' tea for two's a bob, so if you downs the lot there'll be three shillin's to pay.'

She left them and Tina, watching her retreating back, said thoughtfully: 'It's odd, isn't it? Before the war norreven Mrs Spellman would have employed a waitress who was over sixty and fat, but now they're

357

glad of anyone they can get and doesn't it just prove that they were wrong before? I mean, our grub arrived in half the time it would have took some pretty young thing years ago.'

'Aye, the war's teachin' us all to shake our ideas up,' Harry agreed. 'But I don't want to talk about waitresses, I want to find out what's been happening to you. Come on, spit it out!'

Nothing loath, Tina began a spirited account of her life since returning to Liverpool, for she guessed that this would interest Harry more than a catalogue of farming days, and presently, when their tea was finished, he got up and the two of them set out for a small shop where Harry thought she might well discover one or two Dinky toys.

Tina trotted along beside him thinking how nice it was to meet an old friend, but when the toy was purchased and Harry accompanied her back to Heyworth Street, she found that Arthur, though perfectly polite to Harry, did not seem too keen to encourage her old friend to visit again. 'There's a much bigger difference between fourteen and sixteen than there is between ten and twelve,' he said rather confusedly. 'Oh, mebbe not in the usual way, but there's a war on, remember? Harry must have lied about his age when he joined the Navy – he were always a big lad – and from what you say he's had a pretty bad time of it, so I reckon it's made him older'n his years. You've been down on that farm, living the sort of life a kid should have. You've never had to crouch in an air-raid shelter wonderin' whether the next bomb to drop has got your name on it. See what I mean?'

'No I don't,' Tina said baldly. 'He's me pal, that's all. If we go to the cinema it'll be to see the film, not to start messin' about in the back row. If that's what you meant, Unc— I mean Dad? 'Cos if so, you're barking up the wrong tree, so you are, and anyway I'll be fifteen come next April.'

'Oh well, don't say I didn't warn you,' her stepfather said wearily. 'I had young Davy in wi' me while you were gettin' the messages but Mabel's givin' him his tea in the Restawhile, so that'll save you a job. I thought you an' meself might have fish 'n' chips, seein' as you won't want to start cookin' when you'll be doin' Christmas dinner tomorrow.'

'Mabel? Who's Mabel?' Tina said blankly, and rather naughtily, since she knew very well whom Arthur must be referring to.

She watched with interest as colour blotched her stepfather's face, though he replied airily enough. 'Mabel? Why, Mabel Tasker, of course. I don't use her first name at work 'cos it wouldn't be businesslike, but we've known one another years and "Mrs Tasker" seems a bit formal outside of shop hours.'

It had never occurred to Tina that her stepfather might be lonely, might even consider remarrying, and she was not sure how she felt about it. She decided she would have to think it over when she was by herself, and headed for the stairs to the flat above. 'Oh yes, you're quite right. Only of course I've always called her Mrs Tasker, being so much younger. See you in about twenty minutes, Dad.'

Upstairs, Tina hung her outdoor things on the pegs and hurried through to her bedroom. She sat down in front of the mirror and surveyed herself earnestly. She had recently had her soft light-brown curls cut short because when her hair was shoulder-length it had to be tied back from her face at work and tendrils of it would keep escaping from the confining band. Besides, short hair was so much easier than long! She only had to run a comb through it and it looked tidy, and when she washed it, which she did every Friday night, she could do so using only a tiny amount of shampoo. It dried quickly too, so her new style was altogether satisfactory. But now she was examining herself for the first time as a young woman, which was what Uncle Arthur had somehow managed to imply she had become. Her small face was slightly freckled still from the summer sun and the light-brown eyelashes that surrounded her large hazel eyes were long and curled. She hated her nose, but now she saw that it was both small and straight, though she would have preferred it pert and retroussé like Jessie Matthews, the cabaret star's. She had never worn make-up, which was practically unobtainable anyway, but now it occurred to her that Tess kept a little jar of Vaseline in her dressing-table drawer, which she used on her long black eyelashes. She had explained to Tina that this made one's eyes look larger, but Tina dismissed the idea of borrowing some. She thought her eyes looked quite big enough in her small face and decided, as she turned away from the glass, that her stepfather was talking through his hat. Harry knew she was fourteen and she knew that he simply wanted her friendship and nothing more. Why, I haven't even grown any bumps on my front yet, she told herself, heading for the kitchen, and when Uncle – I mean Dad – heard me complaining that Davy was starting to call me Mammy and that folk would think bad things about me, he just laughed and said not to be so silly, 'cos everyone could see I were just a kid.

She went into the kitchen and got out plates and cutlery, laying the table for their fish and chip supper. As she did so, she began to consider the question of Mrs Tasker – Mabel – and her stepfather. After only a short while, she decided that such a marriage would be a very good thing for all concerned, particularly herself. At present, Davy was very much her responsibility. She loved him without being under any illusions to his devilment, for Miss Taylor the nursery teacher usually greeted her arrival to claim her little brother with considerable relief and sometimes with stories of his inventive naughtiness which caused Tina's hair to stand on end. She had resigned herself to looking after him for her father at least until the war ended, when, she had supposed, Tess would take over. Now, however, she realised that this was most unlikely. Tess was twenty, scarcely a child, and Tina had little doubt that her beautiful sister would marry and probably move away from Liverpool when the war was over. She imagined poor Arthur trying to do right by Davy with her own reluctant assistance and knew that his marriage to Mabel Tasker would be the saving of them all. Of course, he had not mentioned marriage, but the blotching of his face when Tina had asked who Mabel was had said an awful lot. I'll encourage him like crazy, because he'll need an awful lot of encouragement, Tina told herself, remembering how much Arthur had loved Laura, and knowing how much he still missed her. I'll tell him it's his duty to provide Davy with a proper mother, not just an older sister. And anyway, I'm real fond of Mrs Tasker; she's a wizard cook and a really hard worker and she's got a great sense of humour. But what's even more important is that Davy likes her. Yes, I'll do everything I can to get them together.

She went hopefully to the pantry and lifted the wire mesh cover off what proved to be a nice big slice of jam roly-poly. Good, they would have that after the fish and chips. She got a tin of dried milk off the shelf, along with some saccharin tablets and Bird's custard powder. Everyone hated the taste of dried milk but custard made with it was almost indistinguishable from the real thing.

She was making up the milk with water when something else occurred to her. Why should she not invite Mrs Tasker – Mabel – to share their meal? The older woman had been looking after Davy all afternoon and deserved a little treat.

Tina bustled round the kitchen thinking about Harry and how much she liked him. He was not her boyfriend, probably thought her too young, though perhaps if she acted more grown-up ... The girls who now worked beside her in the factory often played games in their lunch hour – hopscotch, handball and skipping – and Tina decided, regretfully, that she would have to opt out of such enjoyable pastimes in future. Only it would be so dull to cluster around the factory gates and talk about perms, nail varnish and film stars ...

As she poured the made-up milk into a small pan and carried it over to the stove, she decided that growing up would have to wait; Harry was her pal and that was enough for now. As soon as the custard was made, she would go downstairs and suggest that Mrs Tasker should come up and share their fish and chips.

March 1944

The crew of the *Flora-Dora* were about to take a week's leave. Tess, too, meant to go home, since March was a quieter month on the farm than, for instance, June would be and she was keen to see her little brother again whilst he could still remember her clearly. Danny actually wondered whether he should go to London and see a bit of life, something he would not even have considered had it not been for the awkwardness which still existed between himself and Phil.

Danny had made several attempts to get back on better terms but, contrary to all his expectations, Phil remained aloof. He truly does believe he's in love with Tess and perhaps he really is, Danny thought, but it's clear as daylight Tess isn't in love with him. I know she likes me, though, and I don't mean to see her hurt, and that's what will happen to anyone who gets involved with Phil. If only his cousin could settle down to his marriage with Sophie and forget he had ever clapped eyes on Tess. Danny was sure that Phil must have been in love with Sophie, otherwise why would he have married her? He could be kind, but Danny did not think that kindness would stretch to marrying a girl he did not love. What a mess it is, what a devilish mess. But I suppose it will all work out in the end; such things usually do, and in two days we'll be out of here – for a week, at any rate.

On the night before their leave started everyone had a meal in the cookhouse and then went straight to bed. Danny slept fitfully at first, and then, as the realisation that he need not get up at his usual hour made itself felt, more deeply. He shared a room with the bomb aimer, whose name was John Branch, though he was usually known as Twiggy, and the rear gunner. Once he had shared with Phil, but after the row Phil had changed places with Twiggy, which made things easier.

They were all very tired and slept the night away, but when Danny woke up and went along to the cookhouse for breakfast he saw no sign of Phil. He asked someone who shared his cousin's billet where he was. 'He's gone, old fellow,' the man replied cheerfully. 'He went straight off last night, soon after we returned to our billet.' He chuckled. 'He decided to steal a march on you, get himself an extra day's leave.'

'Oh, I see,' Danny said, and felt relief wash over him. It was nice to think his cousin was so anxious to get back to Sophie that he had set off for Herefordshire as soon as he possibly could. What was more, when they both left the airfield at the same time, they sometimes actually shared a carriage at some stage of the journey. The last time this had happened, Phil had ostentatiously perused a Penguin paperback, not looking up except when the train drew into a station, though Danny had noticed his cousin had scarcely turned a page in the two hours they had spent sitting opposite one another.

Danny had expected to catch an early train, and indeed he did so. Twiggy, a Londoner, suggested they might travel together, at least part of the way. 'Tell you what, Danny,' he said, when the two of them were waiting at the station for their train to arrive. 'Have you ever been to the Windmill? My sister's one of the dancers there and she can always get me a couple of tickets to see a show. Why not come along? I can't tell you exactly who's on, but they have all sorts – Ted Ray, Arthur Askey, Max Miller, they've all appeared on the Windmill stage at some time or other. We've got a spare room and you'd be very welcome. Why, my parents would love to meet you.' He chuckled. 'I've sung your praises often enough, Skip, and I've a little brother, Denis, who collects photographs of Lancasters and would be bowled over to meet a real live pilot.'

'Well, I'd love to come, but what about my parents?' Danny said dubiously. 'Mind, although they know I've got leave I've not told them exactly when it's to start and finish. I meant to ring them up when the train reached London . . . well, I suppose I could still do that. If you're sure, Twiggy.'

His friend grinned. 'Course I'm sure,' he said jubilantly, bending to pick up his kitbag. 'This looks like our train!'

When Phil arrived at his final destination, he was hot, cross and generally fed up. He looked round the large and bustling station disparagingly, then hefted his kitbag and moved to the entrance. Outside, he saw a great building, approached by many steps, guarded by stone lions and elaborately pillared. The pavement was busy. He had intended to take a taxi, because in his experience taxi drivers could always advise one as to the whereabouts of decent, cheap lodgings, but the queue for cabs stretched for thirty yards. Phil had not thought to provide himself with sandwiches, or a bottle of anything to drink, so he decided to ask a passer-by where he might get a meal. Come to that, he could also enquire about lodgings, though now that he came to look more closely at the passing crowd he realised that a large number of them were in uniform and probably had no more local knowledge than he himself possessed.

However, even as he hesitated, he saw a large woman in a headscarf and a shabby black coat approaching. She carried a heavy shopping basket in one hand, whilst the other was firmly clasped by a small and skinny child. Phil stepped forward. 'Excuse me, madam. I'm sorry to trouble you but I've only just arrived in Liverpool and I've not had a bite to eat since yesterday. Could you direct me to a café or a restaurant? Something cheap, if possible; is there a Lyons hereabouts?'

The woman stopped walking as though she were glad to do so. She patted her chest and replied in an accent so broad he had difficulty in understanding her. 'Eh, chuck, wharrever 'ave you been doin' then? I t'ought as 'ow dey fed youse real well in the forces.'

'They do, as a rule. Only last night I was flying a Lancaster over Germany on a bombing raid. We limped back in the early hours but I was too tired to go to the cookhouse so I went straight to the station and caught the first train I could. But cross-country journeys are hell – I'm on an airfield in Norfolk – so it's taken me, oh, a dozen hours to get this far.'

The woman tutted, eyeing Phil with respect. 'You poor young bugger,' she said cheerfully. 'Now in the old days I'd ha' told you to try a canny house, but they's all been flattened by bloody 'itler, or they can't get the grub. I reckon you'd best make for the nearest British Restaurant. They'll feed ya.'

'Aye, they will 'n' all,' the small child corroborated in a shrill voice. Her hair was pulled back from her face in two scraggy plaits, but she spoke out with enthusiasm. 'Me nan – this is me nan, mister – took me there yesterday an' we 'ad snoek 'n' mash; it were grand. Then we 'ad jam roly wi' real custard; that were grand, too.' She sighed deeply and pulled her plait round so she could nibble it. 'Wish we could have us dinners there every day,' she ended wistfully, '"cos I's always hungry.'

'Right; thanks very much. I'll go there,' Phil said. 'If you could just tell me which way . . .'

The old woman gave him concise instructions, rather to his surprise, and then added: 'What's youse doin' 'ere if you ain't gorra pal to give youse a meal? There's airfields around here, I don't deny it, but if youse was bound for one o' them you'd have fed there 'n' all. Free, what's more, though the British Restaurants is cheap.'

Phil grinned down at the oddly assorted couple. 'My girl lives near here. She doesn't know I've got leave, let alone that I'm in Liverpool, so I'm going to put up in a cheap boarding house, and feed myself for a few days,' he said. 'D'you know Heyworth Street?'

The old woman took a deep, wheezy breath, but it was the child who answered. 'Us lives there,' she said excitedly. 'Well, norron the street itself, but in Water'ouse, which is just off of it.'

'Oh,' Phil said, slightly taken aback. He had wanted to ask the old woman what the devil she meant by a canny 'ouse but had decided against it since he suspected that the explanation might be long, tedious and irrelevant. Now, however, he smiled vaguely at the child; had she said Waterbus? Or Waterlouse? But at least if they lived there they might know of a cheap lodging house in the area. He addressed the question to the old woman, but she shook a doubtful head.

'I dunno, lad. You see, them bloody Leftarther done so much damage in the May blitz back in 'forty-one that the cheap boardin' 'ouses 'n' that is full o' families what were bombed out. Why, there's folk livin' in gardin sheds, so they tell me! No, I can't bring to mind any lodgin' 'ouse what ain't crammed to the earbrows.'

Unexpectedly, the small child laughed. 'High-brows, Nan,' she said reprovingly. She turned back to Phil. 'Hotels ain't so bad, though. There's the Adelphi, an' the big 'un, the North Western Hotel, what you've just passed.' She began to tick them off on small, matchstick fingers. 'The Hanover, the Imperial, the Bradford . . . only they're all in the city centre.' Abruptly, she struck her forehead with one grubby paw. 'Wharrever is I thinkin' of? There's a real lovely hotel on Everton Brow, not far from Heyworth. It's called the Laurels. My mam worked there once, clearin' tables an' washin' up 'n' that. She said it were a nice place, didn't she, Nan?'

'Oh aye, so she did, and Annie's right, I reckon it 'ud suit down to the ground. It ain't been bombed, tharr I do know, an' so far as I recalls they'll do you b and b for six bob a night.'

'It sounds perfect. I'll go there as soon as I've had myself a meal,' Phil said fervently. He gave the child his most attractive smile. 'Where does your mam work now, dear? Is she still at the Laurels?'

To his surprise the child, who had been so chatty,

turned her head away, but the old woman answered after only the briefest of pauses. 'Me daughter were killed in the May blitz, chuck,' she said. 'And Annie's father went down wi' the *Hood*, which is why she's livin' wi' me.' She put a large hand on the child's head, smoothing the mouse-coloured hair. 'An' we's all right, ain't we, Annie?' she said gently. 'We gets on a treat, doesn't we, queen? An' now we'd best be off or we'll miss the next bloody tram as well as the one what just whistled past.'

Phil felt dreadful. He knew he had upset the little girl, and for the first time he noticed that the clothing the child wore was ragged and dirty. Her small feet were thrust into threadbare plimsolls and the ends of her little thin plaits were tied with bits of string. He remembered Tess saying that the poverty in Liverpool had been amongst the worst in Europe before the war and now he realised that was not just statistics, it was people. But for an accident of birth, baby Christopher might have been dirty, dressed in rags, and always hungry. At the thought, his heart contracted. From the moment of his birth he had adored his little son, and now he realised, with a pang of real distress, that he could have been at Hilltop right now, lifting Chris above his head, and kissing his son's round, rosy cheeks.

Abruptly he ran after the woman and child, digging in his pocket as he did so. He found a ten-shilling note and a couple of half-crowns and grabbed the woman's arm, hauling her to a halt. 'Here, buy yourself a decent meal or two,' he said breathlessly, and thrust the half-crowns towards the child. 'And you might get yourself some new plimsolls, or – or some sweeties.'

The woman accepted the note round-eyed but the little girl looked at the coins in her hand, then up at Phil's face, and shook her head. 'I's all right; you gorra pay a hotel,' she reminded him. 'They cost, hotels do.'

She held the money out and Phil felt tears prick behind his eyes. She had so little and he had so much! Firmly, he closed her fingers round the coins, then bent and gave her a kiss on one pale cheek. 'They pay us really well in the Royal Air Force,' he said gravely. 'Now off with you or you'll miss another tram!'

The small incident had given him a lot to think about and Phil walked slowly towards the British Restaurant, undecided as to what he should do. Had he come all this way for nothing? If so, the sooner he returned to Hilltop Farm the better. But he decided, as he joined the queue in the restaurant, that there was no point in trying to reach Herefordshire today. He glanced at the menu, chalked on a blackboard above the heads of the diners. He could have roast beef and two veg, followed by apple pudding and a cup of tea, for a shilling. Phil grinned to himself. No wonder the old lady and the little girl had thought so highly of this place; he did not know much about the price of food but he doubted if one could make a meal in one's own home as cheaply.

He picked up a tray, collected and paid for his meal, and found a space at a table already full of garrulous, friendly girls, their ages ranging, he thought, from fifteen or so to the mid-twenties. At home, he knew the girls would have continued to talk amongst themselves, glancing curiously at him from time to time but waiting for him to inaugurate a conversation should he wish to do so. These girls, however, were different. As he sat down, the nearest one grinned at him, then spoke. 'It ain't often as we gets roast beef at home,' she said cheerfully. 'This place is prime, and the beef's better'n what my mam manages to squeeze out of old Fletcher – he's our butcher. Go on, dig in; you'll enjoy it, I can guarantee that.'

Phil, taken aback, agreed that he was sure she was right and began to eat. He had hoped to spend the time considering his problem but his companions made even eating difficult since they fired questions at him non-stop, chattering away as if they had known him all their lives, asking him about the air force, what he did and where he was stationed. 'Walls have ears,' he said at one point, but they just laughed uproariously.

'You ain't told nobody nothing that they don't already know,' a short fat girl with acne and a nose so upturned that it could have been a snout remarked cheerfully. 'We all works at the munitions factory so we ain't likely to be spies in disguise.'

They all laughed again and Phil laughed with them, thinking what a friendly lot they were. Tess had lost a good deal of her Liverpool accent but some of it still remained, and hearing the talk around him made Phil think, wistfully, that he was in Tess country. He simply could not leave here without at least trying to get in touch with her.

Presently, he finished his meal, got directions to Heyworth Street from his new friends, and set off. He intended to book himself into the Laurels, just for one night. Tomorrow, he thought he would go to Heyworth Street and check on greengrocers there, find Tess and see what sort of reception he got. Back at Grange Farm, Danny was always with her so that he never got a chance to say what was on his mind. He should have better luck here with Danny out of the way.

He found Everton Brow and booked himself into the Laurels, paying for his room in advance and warning the proprietor that he might need it for a further night but would be unable to tell him until the next day. The man, middle-aged with a square, self-confident face, nodded and said he would save the room until two o'clock the following afternoon. He added that breakfast would be served at eight prompt and asked Phil if he would like to come into the kitchen and have a cup of tea with himself and his wife. Phil, with his stomach full of British Restaurant food and drink, did not feel sociable and said that he would go straight up.

In his own room he got ready for bed and climbed between the sheets, expecting to sleep at once, for he was very tired. His mind, however, was too active; it kept replaying the little scene outside the station when the fat woman and her granddaughter had stopped to advise him where to eat. Then he thought of the friendly girls at the British Restaurant and then his mind did a sort of double-take and he found himself thinking of Hilltop Farm and Sophie, and their little boy. Restlessly, he turned to peer at the luminous face of his wristwatch. It was nearly midnight; surely he should get to sleep soon? Then, infuriatingly, he began to question his motives in coming to Liverpool. Was he here simply in order to see how Tess would greet him or was there an element of spite in his actions? Was he simply trying to prove to Danny that, given the chance, Tess would choose him rather than his cousin? Several times he had almost decided to make it up with Danny, to admit that he had been in the wrong to try to claim rights over Tess. Was he seriously going to make a play for her with Danny many miles away and then tell him about it, gloat over what he had done? Suddenly, the whole exercise seemed unbearably shabby and Phil knew that he should not so much as walk up Heyworth Street, let alone go into a green-grocer's shop and ask to see Tess. He had meant to tell her he was visiting a friend in the city but now he acknowledged that she would be very unlikely to believe such a tale. Sighing, he thumped his pillow, turned to face away from the window and made up his mind. He had been mad to come here and would be even more mad to stay. He would go back to Hilltop on the first possible train tomorrow morning and he would make a point of visiting Danny at Manor Farm before their leave ended. He had heard himself described, by people who did not like him, as stiff-necked and unyielding and now he was forced to believe that they could be right. But he had come to his senses at last; he would apologise to Danny for his behaviour and tell him that Tess was simply a beautiful and charming girl who loved Danny and had never looked twice at himself. And by this time tomorrow, I'll be with my own little boy . . . and with Sophie of course, he told himself, and almost instantly fell asleep.

Tess reached home late in the evening to an ecstatic welcome. Tina was full of talk about her work and her friends at the factory, whilst Davy chattered on about the nursery and his new pals, but it was her stepfather's news that thrilled Tess most. 'Mike's managed to get leave,' Arthur said exuberantly. 'Of course he can't say definite what time he'll arrive home but he's settin' off at some ungodly hour tomorrow, so mebbe he'll be back in time for elevenses.' He looked shyly at Tess. 'I'll be in the shop, of course, and Tina'll be at the factory, but I thought mebbe if you've nothing better to do you might pop down to the station and see if you can meet his train. I told him there was a chance you'd be back but didn't give him no date nor time, so I reckon he'd be real thrilled if he arrived at Lime Street to find you waitin'. What do you say?'

'Of course I'll meet him,' Tess said. 'When did he get back from Tunisia? Oh, Dad, I didn't even know he was home! He's been awful good about writing but so many letters get lost that you're never up-to-date with what's happening abroad. Gosh, it'll be marvellous to see him again.'

Next morning, however, a good deal of her pleasure at the thought of seeing Mike had seeped away. She and Mike had not set eyes on one another for more than two years and she knew that the time lapse would be difficult to bridge. She had told him about Danny but had said he was simply a friend, explaining that they had been drawn together by the fact that she had known his parents, albeit briefly, whilst Tina had been living at Manor Farm. She had talked about other men too but had always ended her letters with the words *From your own loving Tess*, thinking this would reassure him that the men she mentioned were simply friends and nothing more. Her relationship with Mike had once been a far deeper thing, but that had been long ago. Looking back, she realised that she thought of their pre-war selves as just a couple of kids. They had been thrown into one another's company when their parents had married. From what she had heard from other people, she was pretty sure that after such a long separation she and Mike would meet as strangers, and would have to build their relationship from scratch.

So the mood in which she arrived at Lime Street station was one of uncertainty. She would recognise Mike, of course she would, as he would recognise her. He would be in uniform and no doubt tanned by the Tunisian sun, but he would still be the Mike she had once believed she loved. Hastily, she chided herself for the thought. She *did* love him; it was just that she had grown used to his absence, had not had time to prepare herself for seeing him again, was uneasy as to how he would react to her, for she had not been the only one talking of friends. He had mentioned impromptu dances with Waafs or local girls, trips to the beach and barbecues on the sand. Yes, she knew well enough that she had not been the only one to seize any chance of normality. And his job, though possibly no harder physically than hers, was far more mentally demanding. There had been occasions in her own life when there had been danger from the skies. Because they were so near the airfields, Tess and Sue had been strafed as they cycled across the flat marshes, and once a big American bomber had overshot the runway and crashed in the very next field to where she and the other girls had been working, hoeing between rows of young carrots. They had rushed towards the noise and had been literally picked up and hurled backwards by the blast as the fuel tanks had exploded. Tess knew she would never forget the terrible scene, would hear in her nightmares the roar of the flames, and other, worse sounds.

So now she entered the station concourse nervously and was dismayed to find the place positively swarming with RAF personnel. A train had clearly just arrived and men were piling off it, shouting, laughing, hefting their kitbags, whilst others pushed past them, anxious to get aboard and grab themselves a seat before the engine got up steam and started off on its return journey.

Hesitantly, Tess began to push her way through the crowd, then stood still for a moment, bewildered. Someone had shouted her name, or it had sounded like her name, but for the life of her . . .

A tall figure stood in front of her, cap on the back of his head, kitbag on one shoulder. He had grown. He looked enormous towering over her, blotting out the light. She said: 'Mike?' in a tiny, doubtful voice and then she was swept up in a hard embrace. Instinctively, she threw her arms round his neck, knocking his cap to the ground, and hugged and hugged while he muttered love words against her hair. 'Darling, sweetheart, oh, Tess, I've missed you so much! But what are you doing here, queen?' Abruptly, he held her back so that he could look into her face. 'Are you going somewhere? Meeting someone? I can't believe . . . it's like a dream come true . . .'

'I'm on leave and I'm meeting *you*,' Tess said, with a little catch in her voice. 'I – I meant to run into your arms like they do in films, but there are so many of you and you're all so tall, and I was still looking towards the train . . .'

Mike gathered her into his arms again, but loosely this time, gazing down at her. 'There's only one of me, sweetheart,' he said huskily. 'But I reckon I know what you mean. And now let's gerrout of here.'

*

Phil saw Tess the moment he stepped on to the concourse and was still pondering whether to go over and speak to her – for it seemed as though fate intended them to meet after all – when a great tall chap in air force uniform, with two rings on his sleeve and the coveted wings of a pilot on his breast, hurled himself towards her, took her into his arms, and began kissing her with the sort of desperate hunger which told Phil all that he needed to know.

For one moment longer he hesitated; ought he to go over, interrupt their meeting, tell the fellow that he was kissing Danny Brewster's girl? But it was a stupid question, because Phil had never seen Danny kiss any girl the way the tall, red-haired officer was kissing Tess. So he would not speak, but he walked past them so close that his arm brushed against Tess's. He murmured an apology and her eyes, which had been fixed adoringly on the officer's face, swung round to give him a quick indifferent glance, and Phil saw that she did not recognise him. Her eyes were starry, enlarged by tears of joy, and her whole mind was directed at the man in whose arms she stood.

Phil hurried on to the train, telling himself that of course she had not known him: the Phil Ryland she knew was far away in Herefordshire, along with his cousin Danny. Climbing aboard the train, Phil wondered why he did not feel pain, but then reminded himself that he had given up all hopes of Tess for himself the previous evening, when he had decided not to visit Heyworth Street. He was going to be sensible from now on and appreciate Sophie and the child. But he did wonder what Danny would say when he told him about the scene on Lime Street station.

By the time the train had deposited him at the end of the first leg of his journey, however, he had known that he would say nothing to Danny. How could he? It would mean admitting that he had behaved in a thoroughly deplorable fashion, for he realised now that coming to Liverpool, intending to have a crack at Tess, had been utterly despicable.

As he journeyed on, though, he began to think that his trip had not been altogether wasted. It had taught him some much-needed lessons. He had a wife and a little son awaiting him, as well as a loving mother and a father who bore pain and disappointment bravely. All right, so he, Phil, did not love his wife, but she was hard-working and sweet and he thought he might come to love her given time. Sitting squeezed up in a corner seat on a slow, smelly and extremely noisy train, he vowed that in future he would count his blessings. He *would* love Sophie, and he would make her love him, too. And he would tell Danny he had not meant any of the nasty things he had said.

He knew himself well enough to realise that it would be tempting to somehow let Danny know that his pursuit of Tess was useless, but he would sternly put such temptation behind him. He meant to be a changed person from now on. Satisfied, he tipped his cap over his eyes and settled himself to snooze until he reached his destination.

Soon, he slept.

Chapter Twelve

Sophie was spraying the apple trees in the long orchard, congratulating herself on the fact that she had actually managed to pick a calm and windless day for the task. It was a pleasant day for March, though chilly, the spray actually landing on the trees in a thoroughly satisfactory manner. Sophie remembered the first March after Phil had left and smiled a little guiltily to herself. She had been so green! She had decided they would spray the following day, and when it had dawned dry had congratulated herself on her foresight and marshalled her troops accordingly. Nigel, though his speciality had been the dairy herd, must have watched farmers spraying their orchards for years, and had tried to warn her that the day she had chosen was unsuitable, but she had simply ignored him. She had been uneasily conscious that as a farmer she was far from perfect, but could see no reason why she should not go ahead with her plans. Nigel had pointed out that he thought the wind was getting up but she had ignored him. She and the land girls donned overalls and headscarves and went out into the orchard.

There had followed the sort of day she was sure none of them would ever forget. By noon the wind had been so strong that the spray had blown everywhere except on to the trees and the girls were soon coughing and spluttering, wiping streaming eyes and shouting above the noise of the wind that Nigel had been right: today was truly unsuitable for applying any sort of spray.

Sophie had had to agree in the end, of course, particularly when the small herd of goats which she had recently introduced into the orchard so that they might keep the grass down had forced their way through the thick hedge, obviously considering that Sophie was a dangerous maniac from whom they must flee. When Sophie and the girls had retreated to the house, Matthew had stared at them with astonishment. 'Whatever were you doing, trying to spray on a windy day?' he had asked plaintively. 'I could have told you . . . whatever got into Nigel to let you loose in the orchards in weather like this?'

Naturally, Sophie could not let her father-in-law blame Nigel for what had been her own fault and had confessed to ignoring the other man's advice. Matthew had grinned and as she passed his wheel-chair had given her a consoling pat, causing a cloud of dust to arise which had made him sneeze. 'We all have to learn and some of us learns the hard way,' he had observed. 'I did the very same thing the first year I took over the farm, but it taught me a lesson. Never plan spraying even a day ahead; wait until there's a dead calm – and there always is if you wait long enough – then start the work early and keep on until 'tis finished.'

How right he had been! Not only had Sophie had

382

to wait for a calm day to re-spray the trees, she had also had to buy more spray. Then there had been the gap in the hedge which the goats had made in their wild flight; that had to be repaired and the goats themselves had had to be rounded up, though Sophie had not returned them immediately to the orchard but had kept them on another pasture until after their next attempt at spraying. Fortunately, it had been a cold March and the grass which the goats had been bought to devour had scarcely shown any new growth, so with luck, Sophie had thought, when the goats were returned to their original place they would not be eating grass contaminated by the wind-blown spray.

'Sophie, love, I've brought your elevenses out here since I know you'll want to get the spraying finished whilst the weather is calm, and I have a message for you.'

Sophie turned and smiled gratefully at her mother-in-law, standing by the mossy gate, a laden tray in her hands. Hilltop Farm was not on the telephone but Mrs Cantrip often rang Manor Farm from the box in the village, announcing her intention of coming up to Hilltop to see her grandson – and her daughter, of course – and Auntie Deb or Uncle John relayed the message.

By Daisy's side, Chris beamed up at his mother. When the weather was fine, he often accompanied Sophie when she was working in the orchard, and now he climbed on to the lowest bar of the gate and rested his chin on the topmost one. 'Mummy, can I have some of your elevenses?' he asked hopefully. 'You've got Nana's home-made biscuits and tea in a flaks and I've only got milk.'

Sophie smiled at her son. 'Better not, darling, and the word's flask,' she said. 'This spray is nasty stuff so I think you're safest back in the house with Nana and Grandpa.' She took the tray from Daisy and lowered it on to the grass, then turned to the older woman. 'Thanks very much. Those biscuits look delicious,' she said. 'I'll bring the tray back to the house as soon as we've finished here, which won't be long, I hope. In fact, I reckon we'll be done by dinnertime.'

'You are doing well, my dear,' Daisy said approvingly. She smiled at her daughter-in-law. 'Don't you want to hear the message?'

'Yes of course, though I'd hazard a guess it was from my mum,' Sophie said. She took a biscuit from the plate and bit into it. 'Fire ahead.'

'I don't want to say too much in front of you-know-who, but it was a call from a certain person's d-a-d-d-y,' Daisy said, and Sophie saw that the older woman's eyes were very bright and her cheeks flushed. 'He's on his way home! He hopes to arrive around teatime this afternoon.'

Sophie was surprised at the rush of pleasure which the news gave her, though she was aware that since Chris's birth she and Phil tolerated one another far better than they had at first. No, tolerated was too cold a word. They were friends now as they once had been, though there was nothing warmer in their

384

relationship. Still, friendship was better than antagonism. Ten months had elapsed since Phil was last home and that had only been for a forty-eight. She had read the newspaper reports of the huge waves of bombers which had attacked Germany and knew there had been many casualties. Indeed, it had been freely rumoured that had it not been for the American heavy aircraft, things would have gone ill indeed for the Allies. But Danny phoned home two or three times a week and Phil wrote often, just to let the family know that he was all right. Come to that, Sophie supposed, since both men flew in the same aircraft, Danny's phone calls must mean that they were both safe.

So now she smiled brightly at Daisy whilst the other girls abandoned their work and headed for their elevenses. 'That's wonderful,' she said quietly. 'But, as you say, best keep it a secret from you-know-who, just in case.'

'I'm you-know-who,' Chris said, turning an angelic face towards his grandmother. 'Who's coming to tea, Nana? Is it Nana Cantrip?'

Sophie saw Daisy looking hunted and decided to tell at least part of the truth. 'Well no, not today, but it is possible that your Uncle Danny might come back to Manor Farm for a bit,' she said. She turned to her mother-in-law. 'Isn't that so, Daisy? I know aircrews usually all get leave at the same time.'

'Yes, but Deb said Danny's coming home in a couple of days, because he's stopped off in London to see a show; a pal's putting him up,' Daisy said. 'He'll ring when he gets to the station, unless it's the middle of the night. But P-h-i-l should arrive this afternoon, if . . .'

'Daddy!' Chris suddenly screamed. 'It's my daddy!' He tugged excitedly at his grandmother's skirt. 'It's true, isn't it, Nana? It's my daddy what's coming home!'

Sophie laughed and rumpled her son's hair. 'Yes, darling, Daddy's coming home,' she told him. 'But we don't really know when he'll arrive because trains are so unreliable these days, so it might be tomorrow morning before you get to see him. That's why Nana and I thought it best not to tell you.'

'But I guessed right, didn't I, Mummy? I'm bright as a button, I am,' Chris said boastfully. 'Will he bring me a present? I'd like a box of soldiers or a toy police car. Sammy Reeve has a police car and a fire engine. Do you think . . .'

'No I don't, darling,' Sophie said, smiling at Daisy's shocked expression. 'Daddy's been far too busy flying his aeroplane and keeping us safe to go searching for toys. But if he's home for a few days, perhaps he'll take you into Hereford on the bus and buy you a little something.'

'Hooray!' Chris said, not mincing matters. Then he capered off towards the farmhouse, calling over his shoulder as he did so: 'Just going to tell Grandpa. He'll be as pleased as – as Christmas!'

The two women smiled at one another. 'I'm sorry, Daisy. I know you were shocked because he thought he might get a present, but he's only a child, after all.

386

He really isn't greedy. And to give Phil his due, he usually manages to bring something home for Chris.'

'I know it,' Daisy admitted. 'Well, now the cat's out of the bag, I'd best go and take a good look at my store cupboard. I'd like to make something special for supper tonight.'

Sophie turned back to the land girls. Nigel's wife, Patsy, was pouring tea from the large flask into tin mugs, adding milk from the smaller one. She finished her task, then handed a mug to Sophie. 'So your old man's coming home, you lucky girl you,' she said. 'Bet we shan't see much of you over the next few days.'

'I don't suppose you'll notice much difference,' Sophie said, rather regretfully. 'Farm work waits for no man, and no woman either. Still, Phil's very good and helps out in any way he can. In fact you'll probably see more of him than you bargained for. He'll be poking his nose in everything and probably telling us we're doing it all wrong.'

'I wouldn't mind a chap like that criticising me,' Maggie said. She was a tall fair girl, with a humorous face and a trick of raising her eyebrows one at a time. She did this now and Sophie laughed.

'Oh, go on with you, Maggie! But I dare say I wrong him and he won't criticise after all. Besides, tomorrow, we're planting out the onion sets and summer cabbage and I know how you love that job, so maybe we'd all welcome Phil's help.'

The girls laughed, crunching the biscuits and drinking the welcome tea. 'Now if there's one thing I love, it's planting bloody cabbages,' Blodwen said. She had been plump and soft-skinned – soft-spoken too – when she had first come to the farm from her home in the Brecon Beacons, but now she was tough and muscular and not at all afraid of giving her own opinions, even larding them with the swear words which she heard from the older men – Nigel and Mr Sampson – when something went wrong.

Sophie drained her mug and got to her feet. She glanced at her wristwatch, then up at the sky. The clouds, which had scarcely moved at all in the windless air, seemed lower and more threatening. 'Oh, damn. Let's get this finished off before the weather changes.'

They finished the orchard as Sophie had hoped they would, and were glad they had done so when a mizzling rain started. Despite having been warned that his father's arrival time was uncertain, Chris still accosted everyone who came into the kitchen with the words: 'Has my daddy arrived yet?' Telling him that Phil would go straight to the kitchen when he did get home brought no comfort, and had it not been for the nasty turn the weather had taken Sophie believed she would have dressed her son in his outdoor clothing and let him play around on the edge of Baxter's Piece so that he could watch the lane. However, the rain made this impracticable, so she and the other girls spent a very chilly afternoon doing the back-breaking work of setting cabbage plants, only stopping when the light grew too bad for them to see the furrow along which the cabbages marched.

Everyone trooped back to the farmhouse, had a good wash and some bread and cheese, and then began on the ordinary evening tasks such as milking and feeding. Nigel, who did most of the work necessary with the sheep, usually spent part of the night in the lambing shed, though Patsy liked to take over from him at around three in the morning. Sophie was very grateful to both of them, for though helping a lamb to get born was a job which made one feel that the work was truly worthwhile, it was better that she should get a decent night's rest in order to get on with other work the next day.

By the time Sophie returned to the kitchen, Chris had decided that his father must have missed the train. He wept, then had a tantrum when Sophie pointed out that it would soon be his bedtime, and was finally coaxed into good humour by his grandpa, who suggested they should play Pelmanism, a game at which Chris excelled.

'But bread and butter and a mug of warm milk first,' Sophie said firmly. 'Then you can beat Grandpa into flinders by finding all the pairs like lightning.' To her own surprise, she was beginning to feel not exactly anxious, but restless, and as soon as Chris was safely tucked up in bed, with Daisy sitting on the chair to read him his bedtime story, she decided to pop over to the lambing shed and check that there was nothing Nigel wanted. Then she would walk down the lane, the short way. Perhaps she would meet up with Phil, perhaps not, but the tension in the over-warm kitchen was beginning to get to her, and the way Matthew leaned forward and cupped a hand round his ear at every sound from the yard outside made her long to escape. Putting on her mackintosh and knotting a thick headscarf under her chin, Sophie had to admit that the weather seemed to be worsening. Once or twice she heard a roll of thunder, accompanied by a sharp spatter of rain against the windowpanes. 'Is this going to ruin the spraying?' she asked Matthew with some trepidation, and was relieved when he shook his head.

'No, that powder sticks like glue. The wind's pretty gusty, but not all that strong, and the rain's only mizzling.' He gazed at her, clearly noticing for the first time that she was wearing her outdoor things. 'What's up? Going to give Nigel a hand? Daisy packed him sandwiches and a flask and he's got plenty of cold water and a primus to heat a kettle on if he needs it. He reckons three of the ewes – maybe more – will be having twins.' He beamed at his daughter-in-law. 'That'll mean bottle-feeding, which will give our Chris something to think about besides aeroplanes and speedway riders. When I first came into farming I dreaded lambing but I liked having the littl'uns trotting around the kitchen and tugging so hard at the teat when you fed 'em that it was more like a test of strength than a feeding session.'

'Yes, I like the lambs, though I agree with Phil that sheep are the stupidest, most contradictory, disease-ridden animals any farmer can own,' Sophie said. 'Why can't the contrary beasts lamb during the day?

And why do they jam their silly heads through wire fences and never think to pull back when they realise they can't go any further forward? And then there's dipping . . . how I hate dipping sheep!'

Matthew chuckled. 'Well, I agree with you that sheep are a lot more trouble than cows, for instance, but financially they're a boon,' he said. 'We get a decent price for the wool and when we have enough lambs to sell off – which is most years – they fetch a good price too.' He cocked an intelligent eye at her as she crossed the kitchen and stood with her hand on the back door. 'But you're wearing a headscarf, boots, the lot; you generally just slip a jacket round your shoulders to run over to the lambing shed.'

'I'm going there first, but then I thought I would walk down the lane as far as the phone box to see if I can meet up with Phil.'

Matthew's face brightened into a smile. It occurred to Sophie that he looked not merely delighted but also relieved, and she thought for the first time that perhaps her in-laws saw more than she had imagined and guessed that her marriage was by no means perfect. If so, she was glad to have pleased her father-in-law, for though he had been no great shakes as a farmer – Phil had constantly complained of him in years gone by – suffering had changed him. Now, he was anxious to help in any way he could, tackling the mounds of government forms which had to be filled in and dispatched. He often worked long into the night with never a grumble and she appreciated the fact that he listened to every farming programme on the wireless, and read all the many pamphlets the Ministry of Agriculture sent him, in order to pass on any useful tips, though she knew such pamphlets bored him to tears.

So now she smiled brightly at him. 'It takes me about twenty minutes to reach the main road and forty minutes to get back to Hilltop,' she said cheerfully. 'That means I'll be an hour at the most and oh, Matthew, wouldn't it be nice for Phil to have someone to climb the hill with.'

Matthew agreed that she was right and said he would pull the kettle over the flame in exactly fifty-five minutes. With a sigh, he reached for the farm ledgers. 'But if the weather's too wild, just go as far as Manor Farm, then come home,' he instructed her. 'Phil won't thank me if he thinks I've sent his poor little wife out to become a drowned rat. Wish I could go myself, but that's been impossible for many a year.' He picked up his spectacles just as Sophie opened the back door and the wind blew in, causing him to grab for his papers and to command her, testily, to 'shut the bloody door before the wind turns all my work upside down'.

Sophie shot into the yard and slammed the door. Outside, she almost changed her mind as the wind tried to tear her headscarf off and rain sluiced down her face. But the thought of returning to the kitchen was not a welcome one and she set off across the farmyard. At this time of year, the big barn was converted into a lambing shed. She opened the little door at the side and went in, thinking how cosy it was compared to the farmyard itself. Nigel looked downright biblical, with a plaid blanket wrapped round his shoulders and a mug of tea steaming gently by his side. He had made himself an armchair of straw bales and it appeared that there was a pause in activities, though his eyes shot open as she closed the door gently behind her.

'Everything all right, Nigel? You look very cosy. It's a vile night out there and Phil still hasn't arrived, so I thought I'd just pop down the lane as far as the main road; see if we can meet up. If so, we'll climb the hill together and I can point out that we've set about a million cabbages in Baxter's Piece. Is there anything you need?'

'No, I'm fine thanks, Sophie,' Nigel said. He pointed to a ewe who stood near at hand, shifting uneasily from foot to foot. 'She'll be next, I think, but there'll be nothing doin' for an hour or so. I reckon Mr Phil will be right glad of a bit of company 'cos that hill's tedious steep for a feller what's had a long journey, an' even if he gets a taxi they won't come up this yur lane on such a night. Aye, he'll be glad of company.'

Sophie agreed and bade him good night then made her way, rather reluctantly, out of the lambing shed and across the blustery farmyard, but when she turned into the lane she found it was more sheltered between the high hedges and the rain seemed to have eased. Starting to walk downhill, she glanced up and saw the ragged clouds which were flying across the dark sky, alternately hiding the moon's pale eye and revealing it, caught in a web of stars. In the tricky moonlight, she saw the landscape now clearly, now half-hidden by racing cloud shadows, and felt a stab of pure excitement and exhilaration. It was grand to be out on such a night, with no beastly cabbages to plant, no tractor to be cranked into life, no wretched apple trees to be sprayed. And she was going to meet Phil, who was her husband, even though they had never slept together since that awful time in the hayloft. They would meet, perhaps exchange a chaste kiss, and then climb the hill together. Perhaps it would be the start of a better time for both of them.

As she walked, she considered what she had just thought: *Climb the hill together* . . .

Wasn't that a poem? She struggled with the memory for a moment, then smiled to herself: of course! It was that Scottish chap, Robbie Burns, and she had always loved the poem:

> *John Anderson, my jo, John,*
> *We climb the hill together;*
> *And many a canty day, John,*
> *We've had with one another:*
> *Now we must totter down, John,*
> *But hand in hand we'll go,*
> *And sleep together at the foot,*
> *John Anderson, my jo.*

Remembering the poem sent her thoughts winging back to school and to bus journeys, on one of which she had committed at least part of the poem to memory. Thinking back she remembered her English teacher's voice, translating the broad Scots in which the verses had been written into something more understandable to her class. She had explained that, in this context, 'jo' meant sweetheart, and that the hill the couple had climbed had been the hill of life. Was I thinking of that when I remembered the poem? Sophie wondered, then laughed at her own fancy. How ridiculous! She and Phil had not even begun the steep climb of a proper married life and the 'canty days', meaning joyful, happy ones, had been notable mainly by their absence. Still, she had resolved to try to grow fond of Phil and that was a beginning, surely?

At this point in her musings, the moon went behind a cloud and Sophie fished hastily inside her pocket and produced her little torch. In winter the lane became a stream here so that the soil was washed away, leaving large rocks protruding. A false step could cause a nasty tumble, perhaps even a broken ankle. So she flashed the torch, avoided the worst obstacles, and had just pushed the torch back into her pocket when she saw a figure approaching her. The moon emerged from its bed of clouds and she saw that the figure was clad in air force uniform. Phil! Unaccountably, her heart gave a tremendous bound and happiness flooded her. She had passed Manor Farm a while back and was now only a short way from the main road, which meant that she and Phil really would 'climb the hill together'.

She began to run, grateful to the moon for lighting

her path. She shouted, and Phil looked up, and then she was in his arms, burying her head for one blissful moment against his shoulder, laughing, crying, suddenly full of an emotion which she did not understand. He was murmuring, holding her tight, and she looked up into the face above her own, and it was Danny.

For a moment, she felt stunned, yet not truly surprised. Her mind had thought that the man approaching must be Phil, had to be Phil, but now that she was in Danny's arms she believed that her heart, and the whole of her eager body, not only had known it was Danny the moment his arms had closed about her, but had known when she felt such a restless yearning to leave the farmhouse and go down the lane that Danny was near. For a moment, they simply stood holding each other, gazing into one another's faces. Then Sophie said, softly: 'We had a message from Phil. I was coming to meet him. I didn't mean . . . only you held out your arms . . . did you know it was me?'

They had been careful never to be alone together since her marriage; in fact had only met half a dozen times. Now that she came to think about it, they had never exchanged even the most casual conversation. Yet now she knew, without a shadow of a doubt, that she loved Danny Brewster, always had, always would, and after this moment it would be idle to deny it, either to herself or to Danny.

'Of course I knew it was you,' Danny said. He was smiling tenderly down at her and any doubt she might have felt disappeared. 'Who else would be tearing down the lane and flinging herself into my arms as though the past years didn't exist? Oh, Sophie, I've never reproached you, never questioned you, because I had no right, but why did you do it?'

'Marry Phil, you mean?' Sophie whispered. 'They made me, my mum and dad. You were abroad and there didn't seem any choice.'

'But you didn't love him.'

It was a statement, not a question, but Sophie shook her head anyway, resting her cheek for a moment against his damp greatcoat, so that she shouldn't have to meet his eyes. 'No, I never did love him, but I love Chris, of course. And Phil doesn't love me, never pretended that he did. I think the truth is, darling Danny, that he was desperate to get away from the farm and wanted someone to leave in charge. If he'd managed to get hold of Nigel before . . . before deciding that I could do the job, I don't think he would ever have . . . well, you know. I don't think he would have made such a fuss of me, brought me up to Hilltop to help, taught me such a lot about farming.'

'That's incredible!' Danny gave a short laugh but Sophie could tell that he was angry. 'Tricking you into sleeping with him so that you'd accept his proposal of marriage, and then abandoning you so he could join the air force! If anyone else had told me such a story I'd never have believed them, but, thinking back, it fits in with things I've heard Phil say.'

'It's . . .' Sophie began. She had been about to say that it was worse than that, then realised that she could not possibly do so. Phil and Danny flew in the same aircraft and she had heard Phil saying, more than once, that in order to survive an aircrew needed to trust one another implicitly, each one willing to help the others in any way he possibly could, whether aboard their Lancaster or down on the ground. To tell Danny what Phil had done would be to destroy the bond which had always existed between the cousins. After the war perhaps, when this horrible tangle must surely be sorted out, she might tell Danny the truth. But for now, it must lie heavy on her heart; a secret which only she and Phil could share. But Danny was looking at her enquiringly, plainly expecting her to continue, so she said, rather wildly: 'It's the sort of thing that happens in wartime when you're very young and rather afraid, I suppose. And there's not a thing we can do about it, not now at any rate. We both know Phil doesn't love me, but if I walked out on him I'd be letting everyone down: his parents, Chris, and Phil himself. Oh, Danny, I know how fond you two are of each other, so I guess you must know that Phil thinks he's – he's irresistible. Right now it would hurt him dreadfully to realise that he isn't. Not to me, at any rate.'

'Well, you mustn't blame yourself, because I'm as much at fault as anyone,' Danny said, turning her so that they could begin the walk up the lane, though this time their arms were about each other's waists. 'I never asked you to marry me, never even suggested an engagement. Like a complacent fool, I simply expected you to wait, so if I've lost you, it's no more than I deserve.'

'But you haven't lost me and I hope to God I haven't lost you,' Sophie said eagerly, thinking how well their steps matched. She was a small girl and Danny only a head taller, whereas Phil simply towered above them both. 'I bet Phil hasn't been faithful to me, either, not with all the popsies and floozies and cuties one hears about, all eager to satisfy his every desire.'

She was half laughing but Danny, though he laughed too, shook his head. 'No, you're wrong there. Phil's behaved pretty well, by and large. We met a girl we both thought was special, but I never felt for her the way I feel for you; and I'm sure Phil simply enjoyed her company. It was just a friendship, really, because I suppose we were all lonely.'

By now they were level with the broad drive which led to Manor Farm, and Danny pulled her to a halt. 'I'm home for three or four days, darling,' he said. 'Is there any chance that we might get together? By the way, you said you were going down to meet Phil. He left the airfield before me and I stayed in London with a pal to see a show, so I'm a day late. Phil should have been home yesterday. What's he been up to; any ideas?'

Sophie shrugged helplessly. 'No, never a one. Auntie Deb – your parents told me to call them Auntie Deb and Uncle John – came up to Hilltop this morning with a message saying Phil would be home sometime today. We assumed he'd come straight from the airfield but I suppose he might have gone off on some business of his own. I'll ask him when he gets back, if you like. As for you and me meeting over the next few days, I – I couldn't do it, Danny. It's not just the scandal which would arise if someone saw us, it's such a horribly sneaky, underhand thing to do. Only I shall write to you and ring you at the officers' mess as often as I can, just to hear your voice. It's not as satisfying as being together, but it will have to suffice until – until we can sort things out properly, in the open.'

'I know what you mean and actually I agree with you,' Danny said. 'I was chatting to Mrs Cartwright, who used to work for the baker, coming back on the train, and she was saying her husband was taken by the Japanese when Singapore fell. He's been gone since the start of the war and she knows she won't see him again till it's over. She's never heard a single word from him either . . . imagine that! So if she has had to bear such a long separation, you and I are surely strong enough to bear being apart until the war ends? It can't be long now.'

'I can stand anything if at the end of the wait I get you,' Sophie said frankly. 'I keep telling myself the war can't last for ever . . . Churchill said, a couple of years ago, that the Battle of El Alamein was not the beginning of the end, but perhaps the end of the beginning. The war can't last much longer, surely?'

'The fellers are saying there's an invasion plan for

the summer, and that really *will* be the beginning of the end,' Danny said. As he spoke, he was unbuttoning his coat; then he leaned across and unbuttoned hers. She went into his arms, and he wrapped his coat about her. Immediately she felt warm and safe, and when he started to kiss her, excitement and desire thrilled through her and she clutched him convulsively, murmuring that she loved him, had never loved anyone else, wanted to belong to him, to shout her love from the rooftops.

Yet it was she who broke the embrace first, stepping back with a sigh and buttoning her coat once more, though with trembling fingers. 'That was lovely, and it will have to last us both for a long time,' she said as decisively as she could, though her hands were still shaking and there was a decided tremor in her voice.

Danny had buttoned his own coat and now he picked up his bag, which had somehow dropped to the ground, and Sophie saw his teeth flash white as he grinned at her. 'No way, sweetheart. Look, I'm going to walk you back to Hilltop. It would be a perfectly normal thing to do; you are my cousin by marriage, after all. And if you were to go down to the main road again, Uncle Matthew would wonder why on earth the walk had taken you so long. What we've got to do, my love, is to act normally.' He took her hand and together they began to climb the steep lane towards Hilltop Farm.

Phil had fully intended to spend his leave enjoying the company of his small son and trying to make up to Sophie for his past behaviour, but he had reckoned without the air force. Thanks to the vagaries of the train service, it was very late before he began the long climb up to the farm, and when he reached it the first person he saw was Patsy. She had just emerged from the back door of the house and was crossing the yard, carrying a large flask in one hand and what he took to be a packet of sandwiches in the other. He hailed her and she jumped a mile, then came over to him, her face wreathed in smiles. 'Phil! What a fright you gave me. I'm just going over to the lambing shed to relieve Nigel. He's been on since ten o'clock so he'll be glad to get a few hours' sleep. Sophie walked down to the main road earlier hoping to meet you, but no luck, of course. Do you want to just come in and have a word with my old man? Or would you rather go straight to bed?'

Phil went to the lambing shed, exchanged a few words with Nigel, and then made his way quietly into the farmhouse. It was too early even for the milking so he went straight up to the bedroom he shared with Sophie. Last time he had been home, Chris had slept in a cot in the same room as his parents, but now, it seemed, he had been moved out and the only person slumbering in the single bed under the window was his wife. The second bed had been made up, probably when they had received his telephone message, and Phil stripped and climbed between the sheets as quietly as possible, determined not to wake Sophie. She was lying on her side, breathing evenly, and he thought she looked rather sweet, her loose hair tumbled about her face and the fans of her lashes lying on her sleep-flushed cheeks. His last thought, as he sank into sleep himself, was to wonder where they had put Chris.

He awoke, at what felt like an incredibly early hour, when a weight landed on his chest, and a shrill treble piped: 'Daddy!' about an inch from his ear. He was still struggling back to consciousness when a wet and eager kiss landed in the middle of his cheek and an accusing voice said: 'Who's been sleeping in *my* bed? I sleeps in this bed when you're away, Daddy, but last night Mummy made me have the little pull-out bed in the front parlour. I liked it 'cos when I cried and said I'd be lonely, Nana said I could have old Nell to sleep with me. It was lovely. As soon as Mummy had gone upstairs, Nell climbed on to my bed and we cuggled each other all night. You are awake, aren't you, Daddy? Mummy wouldn't let me come up before but then the telegram boy came so she said I'd best wake you.'

Phil sat up and stared round the room. Sophie's bed was empty and his small son, now staring at him anxiously, was clad in blue denim dungarees and a scarlet jersey and looked, Phil thought, good enough to eat. 'Well, I am awake,' Phil said, giving Chris a hug. Then he asked the question which he knew his son was expecting. 'How much do you love me?'

'I loves you three,' Chris shouted. 'Only now I can count up to ten, so I 'spec' I loves you ten.'

Phil laughed, picked Chris up off his chest and sat him on the bed, then swung his feet to the floor. He glanced at his watch and saw that it was not yet ten o'clock. He was wondering why Sophie had not let him sleep on when he remembered what Chris had said. 'Did you say something about a telegram, Chrissy? Oh, hell and damnation, don't say . . .'

'Hell and 'nation, hell and *dam*nation,' Chris squeaked delightedly. 'The boy came, the one on a bicycle. He hates our lane, he said . . .'

The opening of the door cut the sentence off short and Sophie's head appeared in the aperture. 'Phil, I'm awfully sorry to wake you when Patsy told me you didn't get in until after three,' she said remorsefully. 'But there's a telegram. Your mum opened it because the boy wanted to know if there was a reply and we didn't want to wake you unless it was absolutely necessary, but it was from your Wingco; they want you back as soon as possible. No explanation, of course, but he said to telephone the airfield.'

Phil groaned and stood up. 'This is the first decent bit of leave I've had for nearly a year,' he said bitterly. 'Trust the bloody air force to muck things up.' Sophie had come into the room and Phil thought her expression was softer and less guarded than usual. 'Oh, Sophie, I meant to make a real effort to put things right between us during my leave, to show you I'd changed. But it doesn't look as though I'll have time to do anything but say hello and goodbye.'

Chris had been staring from face to face and now, to Phil's horror, the big blue eyes filled with tears and the little boy cast himself at his father, clutching his bare legs and beginning to wail. 'Not goodbye, Daddy. Don't go away – you've only just comed,' he cried. 'Stay with Mummy and me for a lickle while. I'll be good. I won't ask if you've brung me a present, nor I won't pester for a story. I promise, I promise I'll be good!'

Phil picked up the child and hugged him tightly, trying to hide his own emotion. He spoke thickly to Sophie, over their son's curly head. 'Danny's home too, of course, and I reckon he'll have had the same telegram. Oh, dammit, suppose I say I didn't get back until tomorrow, if you see what I mean. Only if they really need us . . .'

Sophie stared at him. 'If they've gone to the trouble of sending telegrams then I imagine they must need you quite badly,' she said quietly. 'As for when Danny got back, I believe Auntie Deb said he'd spent a day in London visiting a pal. Where were you, Phil? I'm assuming you and Danny started your leave at the same time.'

Phil stood the child down, feeling the hot blood begin to creep up his neck. If he was honest and told Sophie where he had been, it could ruin everything. He said dismissively: 'I've got friends too, you know.' He began to dress, pulling on his uniform trousers and going over to the washstand. There was cold water in the jug and he poured some into the basin, then started to lather his face and neck. He addressed Chris as he rinsed himself off and reached for the towel. 'I'm sorry, old fellow, truly I am, but at least I'll be here until tomorrow; I don't think there's much point now in my leaving today. I know it's not much but I'm afraid it will have to do. Tell you what, it looks a reasonably fine day so we'll get Nana to put us up a picnic and we'll take a couple of jam jars and a flour bag on a split cane and fish for tiddlers this afternoon. Would you like that?'

Chris gave a prodigious sniff then nodded, knuckling his eyes. 'It would be nice,' he said forlornly. 'Shall we go into town this morning so you can buy me a present?'

Sophie tutted but Phil shook his head. 'No, I don't think that's on, old man,' he said gently. 'I have to walk down to the village to call my airfield, and while I'm there I'll telephone the railway station to find the times of the trains tomorrow. Now you trot downstairs like a good boy and tell Nana I'll be down in five minutes and could she get me some breakfast please.'

'Why not use the phone at Manor Farm? It's not nearly as far as the village,' Sophie said. 'Besides, if Danny's already rung and made enquiries you won't need to do so. You can tag along with him.'

'I really ought to ring,' Phil said awkwardly. 'Danny and I had a bit of an argument – all my fault – so I'd rather phone from the village box. But I won't bother to phone the railway station. I'll pop into Manor Farm on my way back and tell Danny I'm sorry about the row, and then we can arrange to travel together.' He waited until the small boy had disappeared, then walked over to Sophie and put a hand on either shoulder. 'Hello,' he said softly. 'Do I get a welcome-home kiss? Just a little one to show that we're still friends even if you don't want us to be lovers.'

Sophie stood rigid for a second, staring up into his face, then she removed his hands from her shoulders but continued to hold them. 'I think we won't rush into anything,' she said quietly. 'We've a lot of ground to make up, Phil, and a lot of talking to do, before we go even a tiny step further. For one thing, I don't understand your sudden change of attitude. You've made no attempt in the past to get close to me and I've appreciated it, so why the change? Is it possible that some little Waaf has let you down or changed her mind about you?'

It was too near the truth for comfort, but Phil certainly did not intend to admit it. He began to button his shirt, avoiding Sophie's eyes, but saying impatiently: 'I told you I'd changed, though I can't tell you precisely why. I've realised how bloody lucky I am to have you to look after things for me, for a start. I know I'll have to come back to Hilltop when the war's over, but that'll be just a stop gap. You and I can build the place up together until it's worth a decent price, then I'd like to fly civil aircraft. And then there's Chris. He's a grand kid and God knows I've had little enough time with him, so it's your upbringing which has made him what he is. You could have taught him to hate me, or at least resent me, but you never have and I appreciate that more than I can possibly say.' He saw how Sophie's face had softened at the mention of their son and pressed on quickly. 'Every time the Lanc lumbers off the ground, I know all the aircrew get the same sinking sensation, the fear that this time we may be the ones who won't get back. Other men worry that their wives won't be able to cope, but I know that wouldn't be the case with you. You've grown strong and independent, and you don't need me at all. But the truth is, Sophie, that I want to be needed. Want to be missed, come to that. Oh, dammit, I want to be loved! I know it's a lot to ask and I don't mean to ask it, but I do mean to mend fences so that love might be possible one day. Can you understand that?'

Sophie nodded, but now it was she who would not meet Phil's eyes. 'You'll find love all right, Phil,' she said huskily. 'You're a very lovable bloke. But remember, one step at a time. And now let's go down and have some breakfast.'

Phil had rung his airfield, confirmed that they had already spoken to his cousin, and said that he would be catching the same train. 'When will Flight Lieutenant Brewster be arriving?' he had asked. 'Our homes are only half a mile apart, so we'll probably travel back to the airfield together.' The Waaf who had answered the phone, however, was unable to tell him anything other than that Flight Lieutenant Brewster would be back just as soon as he could the following day. Phil thanked her and replaced the receiver.

He walked briskly up the lane, telling himself that apologising to Danny should not be so difficult; he must have done it a hundred times, after all. Then he caught himself grinning at this flagrant redistribution of the truth. He *ought* to have apologised to Danny a hundred times, but thinking back could not recall one occasion on which he had done so. Oh well, if this was a first, he must make it a good one. He strode across the farmyard and entered the Manor Farm kitchen breezily, as though sure of his welcome. Danny was sitting at the table writing a letter. He was scowling and biting the end of his pen, but when he looked up and saw his cousin the frown cleared and a tentative half smile touched his mouth. Phil took a deep breath but Danny forestalled him. 'I take it you got the telegram this morning? I phoned the railway station first but there simply isn't a train today which would get us back in time for tonight's raid, if that's what they had in mind. But I've worked out a route which should get us in by teatime tomorrow. It'll mean five or six changes – bloody nuisance that – but it's the best we can do.'

'Thanks,' Phil said rather feebly. He had rehearsed his apology as he climbed the lane but now he realised resentfully that it had gone clean out of his head. 'Um, what time do we leave?'

'Not too early; eight o'clock. Dad'll run us down in Bessie,' Danny said. 'Better bring sandwiches, though I dare say someone will be selling drinks along the way.'

'Right,' Phil said. 'Danny, I came to say I'm bloody sorry for . . .'

'Oh, shut up; it's taken as read,' Danny said

gruffly. And if there was a touch of brusqueness in his voice, Phil thought it was well deserved. How like his cousin to spare him the embarrassment of a proper apology. He was beginning to say so when the back door opened and John Brewster, a couple of elderly farmhands, and three pretty land girls trooped into the kitchen. In the flurry of greetings and goodbyes, Phil promised to be at Manor Farm by a quarter to eight next morning, joined in Uncle John's cursing of the Royal Air Force with a good deal of vehemence, gave his cousin a friendly buffet on the shoulder and then said he really must be off since his time with Sophie and Chris was to be cut so short.

After Phil had left, the land girls and John Brewster drank tea and ate scones, and then abandoned Danny in the kitchen once more. Danny's mother, who had been doing the bedrooms, came downstairs, patted her son absently and made her way to the dairy. Danny sat at the table staring at the letter in front of him; then, with a sigh, screwed it into a ball and tossed it into the fire. He had been writing to Tess, but what was the point, after all? She would come back from her leave and they could talk then, though when he thought about it he realised he had little enough to say. Theirs had been a friendship, would still be a friendship, but if he were honest it had never been anything more. He realised now that, sub-consciously, he had been trying to fit Tess into the place in his heart that Sophie had held . . . still held.

He did not think Tess would be truly upset when he told her that there was someone else, but he also thought that to make such a declaration on paper was entirely unnecessary. One does not write a Dear John letter to end a non-existent affair, he told himself with a grin.

Having made up his mind, he stood up and stretched. It had been good of Phil to try to apologise for the row between them, and at one time, because of the bitterness he felt, he would have let him go ahead with it. It would have been a rare treat to see Phil humble for once. But when Phil had breezed into the kitchen, and Danny had guessed that his cousin had come to say he was sorry for the rift, how could he possibly have let him? He, Danny, had every intention of appropriating Phil's wife just as soon as circumstances allowed, so he could not let Phil apologise for something so minor in comparison.

It was odd, Danny thought, collecting up the writing materials he had borrowed and returning them to their place in the dresser drawer, how circumstances alter the way one thinks. Until the telegram had arrived, his leave had stretched before him packed with a hundred things he meant to do. Despite knowing that he must not attempt to be alone with Sophie, he had fully intended to go up to Hilltop Farm, ostensibly to see his aunt and uncle and his small nephew. He had avoided them since Phil's marriage, but had now decided that if necessary he would be the one to apologise for their row, or at least take Phil to one side and say they must sink their differences or upset their parents and make life difficult for everyone. Once he had broken the ice, he had been pretty sure that at least seeing Sophie would be perfectly possible. The two families had always helped one another and with Nigel busy with the lambing, Danny guessed that the Rylands would welcome any extra assistance that he could offer. The Brewsters had never kept sheep, their pastures being more suitable for cattle, so at this time of year he could well have afforded to offer his services to the Rylands. John Brewster was a very efficient farmer and would not grudge his son to Hilltop.

But now that he only had one day of freedom, that day seemed to stretch emptily and endlessly before him. The trips into Hereford to see old friends and to do some shopping, the expeditions up to Hilltop to play games with his nephew, the hours spent chatting to Uncle Matthew in the evening whilst secretly devouring Sophie with his eyes as she moved around the kitchen performing simple household tasks, none of these things were possible now. With only a day spent here, he could not thrust himself between Phil and his son. No point either in walking into the village and catching the bus into Hereford; such a trip would take most of the day and of course he could not possibly contact his various friends to let them know he was back. Even walking up to Hilltop Farm, he realised, would be an intrusion when Phil, like himself, only had one day. But he did not intend to hang around the farmhouse feeling sorry for himself. He would go and give his mother a hand in the dairy and ask whether there was anything else he might do to help.

Happily, Deborah had realised even before Danny himself that her son would be at a loose end until he left the following day, so when he appeared she suggested first that he should take the chestnut cob which pulled the trap for a bit of exercise around the fields. And after that he might go down to the hop yard. 'Your dad thought the Min. of Ag. would tell him to plough up the hops, and I think if they had done so he'd have been quite glad,' she said. 'But apparently they need good hops as much as ever, so two of the fellers and two of the girls are stringing up and clearing any weeds. The new growth will start some time in the next few weeks and they want to be ready. You could let the cob loose in the next pasture and give 'em a hand if you've nothing better to do.'

Danny's face, which had been sombre when he had entered the dairy, brightened at the suggestion and Deb watched him go thoughtfully. Lately, she had begun to believe that Sophie had never quite got over her feeling for Danny, even though she had married his cousin. That had been an odd affair, but like everyone else Deborah had simply accepted that Sophie and Phil had had a fling because Sophie had been stuck at Hilltop during that appalling January of 1940 and that Phil had married her to give their child a name and respectability. But even if you accepted that Danny and Sophie's had merely been a boy and girl friendship, it had been strong enough for the couple to continue writing to one another until Sophie's marriage. Was he avoiding Sophie now? Deborah did not think herself a particularly observant woman, but it would have been difficult not to notice that Sophie never introduced Phil's name into a conversation, which would have been odd had they been truly in love, yet whenever Deborah talked of Danny Sophie would smile, flush a little, and then quickly turn away, or change the subject. Now Deborah realised that perhaps she had been mistaken. Young love could also be true love, and if that was the case then her heart bled for Danny.

Tess had a wonderful leave. She and Mike were back on their old footing. The two of them visited cinemas and dance halls, but mostly they took a packed lunch and caught a bus heading for the surrounding countryside, got off at the terminus, and simply walked. Naturally enough, on such expeditions, they also talked and did a certain amount of kissing and cuddling. Mike, however, was determined that they should not 'go too far', as everyone put it. Tess agreed but sometimes wished that Mike's principles were not quite so high. He could have taken precautions, she told herself, but she respected his judgement and thought his attitude was probably the right one.

At the end of her leave, Mike saw her off at the station. They stood very close, feeling all the misery of the separation that was to come, and when Mike suddenly jerked her into his arms and began to kiss the side of her neck Tess let the tears form and fall, because she knew him so well now that she could guess what he was thinking. This might be all they would have and moral rectitude was all very well but it was a pretty cold bedfellow. So she was not surprised, once she was aboard her train and leaning out of the window to exchange a last kiss, when he said fiercely: 'Oh, God, I love you so much, Tess. If I get a forty-eight and come down to Norfolk, will you be Mrs Mitchell, just for one night? Not in Ludham, of course, but in Norwich.'

Tess laughed, though tears were running down her cheeks. 'I thought you'd never ask,' she muttered, as the train began to move. 'Of course I'll be Mrs Mitchell . . . oh, Mike, I do love you.'

Chapter Thirteen

All through the summer, Tess and her fellow workers slogged on the land and listened avidly to the BBC news broadcasts. Tess saw as much as she could of Danny, for the two had remained close friends despite Danny's telling her that he was in love with a girl back home, and Tess's prompt riposte that she and Mike intended to marry as soon as the war was over. Tess heard in dribs and drabs that Sophie had married someone else, that she and her husband had a small son and that she lived quite near Danny's parents' farm. 'But she doesn't love her husband; it was all a horrible mistake,' Danny had told her earnestly. 'We can't do anything about it until the war is over, of course, but then – oh, then we'll sort something out.'

Tess had been sorry for him because her own love affair was so simple, so wonderful. She and Mike had had their forty-eight, staying in the Bell Hotel in Norwich as Mr and Mrs Mitchell, and falling more deeply in love than ever. She thought, in fact, that their weekend had done Mike more good than she would have supposed possible, for their loving had smoothed out the lines on his face and given him an appetite for his food. His jerky movements had calmed and the twitch which he had developed whenever he talked of his next sortie disappeared. But for Danny, none of this was possible. His Sophie was someone else's property, no matter how you looked at it; there could be no stolen weekends for them.

In her own blazing happiness, Tess would have done anything she could to help her friend, and when he asked her to address his letters for him so that no one would recognise his writing, she was eager to do so. She had been rather shocked to discover that Danny's young lady was Phil Ryland's wife, but sympathised even more strongly when he told her how he and Sophie had been childhood sweethearts and how Phil had taken advantage of his cousin's absence to court and win Sophie.

Before the Normandy landings, Danny and his crew no longer flew nightly to Germany but concentrated on the railway lines, bridges and roads on the other side of the Channel, so that when the Allies landed the Germans would be unable to move their troops about the region, save on foot. Sometimes, Danny told Tess, he could see the sense of this, but at other times he grew angry, saying it was madness to destroy roads and bridges which the Allies themselves would surely need. Tess found herself angry for another reason. It was not as though the countryside was empty of people; French peasants were still trying to grow their crops and feed their beasts. It was all very well to say the bombers were attacking military targets, but bombs do not always land where they are meant to and Tess, labouring in fields, cow byres and orchards, hated the suffering of ordinary people which she was certain must arise from the raids.

In June, the Allied army had landed in France; with the troops still advancing July slid into August and August into September. She and Mike met whenever they could; their need for each other was so great that they took it for granted they would spend any leaves together. Mr Turnbull watched his corn grow gold and began cutting, and the young men from the RAF stations nearby came over, often gaunt and hollow-eyed, and went back to their billets the better for a day in the sunshine, thinking of anything other than war.

Danny and the rest of his crew had done their checks, and now the *Flora-Dora* was climbing into the night sky. The air force had pasted the French communication system until Paris had fallen, and now that almost all of Belgium had been liberated they were off to Germany to do as much damage as they possibly could, and to demoralise the Axis troops. The moon shone on the great mass of bombers, and way ahead of them Danny could just make out the pathfinder, the plane which would lead them to their target.

The heart of Germany was a long haul. The chaps used to joke that at least, if they crash-landed on arrival back home, there would be so little juice left in the tanks that the old *Flora-Dora* ought not to burst into flames, but it was little consolation for the nagging worry that one might run out of fuel over the Channel and be forced to ditch. Small chance of survival when you were bobbing in the sea with a little tin whistle and a tiny light your only means of attracting attention, and your Mae West perhaps keeping you afloat but not preventing the cold from claiming you.

No point in thinking like that, however, particularly when there were at least four hours of boredom ahead – though boredom was better than the stomach-churning fear which clutched you as soon as you got near to enemy territory. All the planes zigzagged wildly to try to avoid searchlights, radar, flak and enemy fighters, but the manoeuvre was not always successful. Still, it gave you something to do and was better than being a sitting target, for once radar and the searchlights found you it was only weaving and gaining or losing height which could save you from a devastating and probably fatal attack.

Danny settled himself in his seat. Radio silence was, of course, being observed and ordinary conversation was pretty well impossible above the roar of the engines. Automatically, he fell into the familiar routine of a long flight, constantly glancing to right and left to check that the correct distance between the Lancasters was unchanged and that there were no enemy aircraft in the immediate vicinity. Experience told him that as the flight continued he would grow colder and colder, and strange things might happen to the instruments as they, too, grew colder. His eyes flickered across the control panel even though it was too early for the air speed indicator to freeze up. It was a routine check which he knew he carried out constantly, almost without realising it. Their lives depended upon every one of them knowing exactly what each should do in any circumstance that might arise and everyone had to be constantly alert, though Danny imagined that the tail gunner, Ted, had to struggle against sleep, cut off as he was from the rest, with little to do until enemy aircraft came into sight. Danny's eyes slid sideways, checking, always checking. Smiffy, the wireless operator, a tall skinny Scot with a thin, anxious face, was bent over his radio set and did not look up. He was first rate at his job, but then the whole crew were good. Danny knew it, and felt a little buzz of contentment. Phil had pulled out the small canvas seat close to the pilot's and was already scanning the instrument panel in front of him. He had taken off his big leather gloves because he always said he could not concentrate on the trans-ferring of fuel between the tanks whilst his hands were muffled in gloves. He glanced up and the two men grinned at one another, then Danny turned back to his instruments once more.

His relationship with Phil was, thank God, back to normal and had been ever since that shortened leave. There was a tacit understanding between them not to mention the row again, far less the subject of it.

'Hey, Skip, what's in the sandwiches? If it's bloody fish paste I swear I'll take them back to the cookhouse and force them down the throat of whoever made them. Why can't they give us a change? Even Spam would be better than fish paste.'

Danny turned his head to grin at Smiffy, standing at his shoulder and unwrapping the greaseproof paper in which their sandwiches were wrapped. 'You can't be hungry yet, Smiffy! I reckon a decent breakfast, plus a chocolate bar, keeps me going until we reach the target. I save the sandwiches until I'm so bloody starving I could eat strips of carpet. You got breakfast, didn't you?'

Aircrews were always issued with a good breakfast, or a meal that was called breakfast at any rate, before a bombing mission. Each man was entitled to a couple of rashers of bacon, two shell eggs, not the dried sort, and a nice thick round of fried bread. But Danny knew that Smiffy, excellent radio operator that he was, suffered from pre-flight nerves on occasion and was unable to do justice to what Danny considered to be the only decent meal the cookhouse ever provided.

Smiffy looked hunted. 'I ate the eggs – well, one of 'em – and bit of the bacon, but the fried bread made me feel a bit sick,' he said apologetically. He had unwrapped the sandwiches and now his face brightened. 'Well, I'll be damned. Someone up there must love me,' he said, lifting a corner of the national loaf and peering inside. 'It's corn beef and brown sauce; that'll do me.'

Danny, who had been about to offer one of his own two chocolate bars, was relieved. As Smiffy turned to go back to his station, Danny said: 'In a way, it's sensible to eat the sandwiches early because the pressure makes them go dry and curl up anyhow.' He unwrapped a packet of chewing gum and popped a couple of pieces in his mouth and was immediately struck by a strange thought. In years to come, whenever I pop a section of chewing gum into my mouth I'll hear the steady thrum of *Flora-Dora*'s engines and see the stars above. And I'll be back, with the cold growing more intense and the fear of what's to come starting to curdle my gut.

'Crossing the coast, Skip,' Phil's voice said softly. 'Still holding formation?' Danny nodded, though the bombers had spread out upon reaching height. 'Good. Then we're in for a couple of hours of boredom, at least, before things start to hot up.'

Danny never dozed or lost concentration on the flight out, and tonight was no exception. His mind felt needle-sharp, and as the cold increased, so did his anxiety that both the crew and the machine itself should be in perfect condition when they neared their objective. It was when they penetrated the heartland of Germany and had to lose height for the attack that the worst danger would come. There were few bases in France, Belgium or Holland from which German fighters could now set out, and Danny knew the general opinion of his friends and colleagues was that Hitler was pinning all his hopes on the V2 rockets with which he had begun to bombard London and the south coast of England. The Doodlebugs had been bad enough: horrible, pilotless bombs which came over in droves. When their engines cut out they dropped to the ground, causing enormous damage, but also a sense of helplessness for the air force could do little against them. But the rockets came silently and, as Smiffy had once remarked, 'you didn't even know they was on their way till you woke up dead'.

The piece of gum in his mouth had lost its savour by the time they were approaching the target. Danny looked anxiously ahead and below, and then Smiffy shouted above the roar of the engines. 'Lights on the starboard side, Skip; searchlights too. Better get weaving.'

Danny grinned and began to manoeuvre the big aircraft into a series of zigzags, then turned to Phil. 'Fuel evenly distributed? Oil pressure OK? Good thing, since we can't be far off our target. Any complaints?'

'No; she's running smooth as my watch, all systems go,' Phil said. He peered out of the cockpit, then pointed down. 'See? That's an airfield, below, and I reckon the target's dead ahead. Glory, it's not going to be a picnic tonight!'

Danny, beginning to lose height, for they needed to be a good deal lower when laying their eggs, grunted as Phil turned and slipped back into his seat. And then it seemed as though one minute they were alone in the dark sky with paling stars above them and no cloud for miles, and the next they were in the middle of the action. Flak burst around them; searchlights combed the sky, suddenly lighting up the cockpit bright as day, and as suddenly, when

Danny jerked the big plane on to another course, dipping them into darkness. They saw a formation of Messerschmitts climbing rapidly up, presumably from the nearby airfield. Ted, on the tail gun, screamed into his microphone instructions which would bring him within firing range of the nearest one, and then Frank, the turret gunner, managed to fire a burst which must have been successful, for the enemy went into a steep dive from which, Danny thought, he would be unable to recover. For a moment he watched, fascinated, as the pilot struggled out and his parachute bloomed, caught for one moment in the searchlight's yellow beam, before he floated earthwards.

The noise was dreadful but above it all, through his headset, Danny concentrated on Twiggy's words. The bomb doors were open and Twiggy, as though they were peacefully practising the manoeuvre, guided Danny to what he considered the perfect spot and then pressed the bomb release button and launched his bombs. As always, the sudden loss of weight caused the *Flora-Dora* to leap into the air, making Danny feel like a cowboy on a bucking bronco. He knew they could gain as much as four hundred feet when the weight of the bombs suddenly left the fuselage, and so did everyone else. Phil, he noticed with a grin, braced himself in his seat and no doubt the others took similar precautions. Almost immediately, they realised they had hit the target. There was an enormous explosion, flames shooting up into the night sky.

'We've done it, we've done it,' Twiggy exulted, as Danny put the Lanc into a steep climb. 'Wingco said at the flight briefing that he wanted us to take out a factory which was making some pretty awful weapons of war. I reckon we just did it and smacked Hitler on the nose. Now let's get out of here.'

Danny was congratulating himself that they had got away with it when they overflew the airfield he and Phil had seen earlier. He was still climbing and was not surprised when he heard a burst of gunfire from Ted and then a curse. 'Missed him! Can you swing me a couple of degrees to starboard, and then maybe . . .'

They all felt the impact, knew the *Flora-Dora* had been hit, but Danny, sensitive to every slight change in the big plane's movements, did not think it was serious. Not flak, though: tracer bullets.

'Everyone OK?' he shouted. He could see Phil and Smiffy for himself, but Twiggy, Frank and Ted were not visible from where he sat. 'Ted? You all right? Frank?'

Ominously, there was no reply from Ted, though Frank said: 'I'm OK, Skip, but I think Ted may have been hit. That bloody Messerschmitt did another run past just now, straight across our tail. If Ted had been OK . . .'

'Ted? Are you all right?' Danny heard his own voice pitched above the roar of the engines and hastily switched on his intercom, repeating the question. After a moment, Ted answered.

'I've been hit. It's my arm. I'm half out of my jacket

425

and bleeding like a pig . . .'

Danny continued to weave but tried to keep the plane reasonably steady as Phil got to his feet, grabbing the First Aid box as he went. 'I'll try to stop the bleeding,' he said. 'I'll take over from Ted until things cool down a bit.' Danny, concentrating grimly on getting as far away from the action as possible, realised that the routine they had practised so often had come seamlessly into play when he heard Phil's voice over the intercom. 'Another one coming in at eleven o'clock; can you get me so I can get him? Twiggy's doing up Ted's arm . . .'

After that, things really hotted up. *Flora-Dora* took another hit, but the tracer bullets strafed the fuselage without, apparently, doing much damage. Danny jinked, wove, lost and gained height, but the Messerschmitt seemed to have decided that it would follow them until one or other was down, and Danny felt a sick sinking in the pit of his stomach. At a guess, the pilot attacking them must have been a pal of the flyer whose aircraft they had downed almost over the airfield and was determined upon revenge. Danny felt sweat trickling down the sides of his face, despite the cold, as he tried every trick he knew. Then there was a thump which rocked the plane and someone cried out, almost at the same moment as a burst of fire from the turret sounded simultaneously with a cacophony of voices which broke out as everyone spoke at the same moment into their intercoms.

'Got 'im! I've got the bugger!' That was Frank.

'Jeeesus. Can we gain height, Skip, and head

straight for home? I've used up pretty well all the bandage but Ted's still bleeding a bit.' That was Twiggy, his voice strained and anxious.

The last voice seemed very small, very thin. 'Danny? I – I think I bought that last one.' Danny looked round desperately, then gestured to Smiffy. 'Take over for a minute, Smiffy,' he said breathlessly. 'I just want to check . . .'

Smiffy, like Phil, had trained as a pilot and though to Danny's knowledge he had never landed a bomber, he was quite capable of flying her whilst weaving towards home. Besides, now that they had outgunned the Messerchmitt they might hope to get away without being attacked again. Danny waited until Smiffy had slid into the pilot's seat, then made his way towards Phil, crumpled forward over the tail gun. He bent over his cousin, noting the pallor of Phil's face and the sheen of perspiration on his forehead. 'Where did he get you?' he asked anxiously.

Phil's arms were clasping his waist; he was still conscious. 'Dunno. Felt as if I'd been punched in the belly,' he said thickly. 'Tried to stand; legs won't move.'

Danny looked wildly round. Ted was propped against the side of the fuselage, eyes closed, and Twiggy was straightening up still with the First Aid box in his hands. He caught Danny's eye and came over. 'What's up? Don't say that blighter got in another hit before Frank downed him.'

'He did. Can you give me a hand, Twiggy? Phil's

too heavy for one to move and he needs to get out of the tail before we can – can assess the damage.'

Wordlessly, Twiggy joined him and the two of them manhandled Phil out of his seat and on to the floor. Phil moaned once, then gave Danny a pallid grin. 'Sorry,' he whispered. 'Not going to be much use on the gun; tried to sit upright but I kept falling forward.'

'It's all right, old fellow; didn't you hear? You and Frank between you sent him spiralling down five minutes ago. With a bit of luck we won't be needing a tail gunner any more on this trip.'

Phil gave a tiny nod and Danny began to unfasten his cousin's flying jacket, but one glance was enough to show him that all the bandages in the world could not control what was happening to Phil. It looked as though the burst of tracer had practically cut him in half. Hastily, Danny rifled through the First Aid box until he came to the morphine. They all knew the drill, but when Danny prepared to give the injection his hands were shaking so violently that he knew he could not do it. Twiggy, still hovering, took the syringe from him and inserted the needle with an efficiency which Danny knew he could not have mustered himself. He wondered whether it should have been administered at all since Phil had not complained of pain, then thought of the bloody mess he had seen when he had started to open the flying jacket and shuddered. They had done the right thing, he thought, and took the marker from the box, drawing a rather wobbly M on Phil's wet forehead to indicate that morphine had been given. He was squatting back on his heels when Smiffy called, his voice urgent. 'Skip, can you come? She needs trimming . . .'

Danny gave Phil's hand a quick squeeze, then stood up and made his way back to his seat. A fat lot of good it would be to stay by Phil whilst poor Smiffy crashed the old *Flora-Dora*, killing the whole lot of them. But even as he took the joystick he could feel that all was not well. The port outer kept backfiring and was running decidedly rough, and it took all his strength to keep her steady. He began to check his instrument panel, then glanced quickly over his shoulder to where his cousin lay. Stomach wounds are always bloody, he told himself, trying for any sort of reassurance. And it might not have been a stomach wound. It could easily have been just a flesh wound . . . all right, a really nasty flesh wound. Wish I knew a bit more, Danny thought, as the big Lancaster droned on through the night. Wish I'd not let him take over as tail gunner . . . wish there was *something* I could do!

They crossed the coast without seeing any more enemy aircraft – or, for that matter, any of their own kites – and Twiggy, more experienced than Smiffy, took the controls so that Danny could snatch another quick look at his cousin. Phil was conscious, but he looked ghastly. His face was wet with sweat, his hair and eyelashes soaked, yet he was cold. Danny struggled out of his flying jacket and put it round the wounded man, but still Phil shook. Ted, propped up nearby, said that he thought Danny ought to make for the nearest airfield and get the *Flora-Dora* down as quickly as possible.

'That last hit was near the undercarriage,' he said, and Danny could hear that he was striving to keep his voice calm for everyone's sake, anxious not to let them know that he was seriously worried. 'If we have to do a belly-flop, better sooner than later.'

'Right,' Danny said absently. He bent over Phil. 'Did you hear that, old chap? We're going to make for the nearest airfield, wherever that may be, and I'll put her down as gently as a sigh, so we can get you out of this and into a proper hospital. Can you keep going for a bit longer?'

He was about to turn away when Phil's eyes flickered open and his hand came gropingly out from under Danny's flying jacket. 'Danny? Is that you? It's bloody dark in here.'

'Yes, it's me. And it will soon be getting lighter. The sun's about to rise,' Danny said, trying to keep his voice level. There was no cloud cover and the rising sun, scarlet as a sucked lollipop, was illuminating the cockpit, fingers of light stroking along the fuselage. But everyone knew that one's sight dimmed as life ebbed. 'Just you keep still; not long now.'

'No, not long now,' Phil said. His voice was small, almost a whisper, and . . . and thick, Danny thought. Oh, God, let me get him into hospital in time, don't

430

let all Phil's hopes end like this! 'Danny, is that you?'

'Yes, it's me,' Danny said again. 'Don't try to talk, old Phil. Save your energy . . .'

Phil gave a tiny, wheezy chuckle. 'For what?' he said faintly. 'God, Danny boy, I've been every sort of fool, but that's all over now. You'll look after Sophie? And the boy, of course.' He gave a deep sigh, and to Danny's horror blood suddenly brimmed over his lower lip and ran down his chin. His next words came out in an odd, bubbly sort of voice. 'I never thought I'd love a kid the way I love Chris . . . good coming out of evil . . . one hope of redeem . . . redempt . . . you'll take care of him? Tell him his daddy loved him, didn't want to leave . . . all my own fault, of course, desperate to get away, beyond the blue hills and into the real world . . . you'll tell him that? Didn't . . . want . . . to . . . go . . .'

Tears were running down Danny's face but he dared not linger by Phil's side a moment longer. Twiggy's voice came urgently from the pilot's seat. 'Danny? We're over the English coast . . . if you want to land at the nearest airfield . . .'

'Right, Twig,' Danny said. He gave his cousin's hand a quick squeeze, then bent over him. 'I'll look after Soph and the kid until you're fit again,' he said, and heard his own voice choked with emotion. He cleared his throat and spoke with an assumption of confidence he most certainly did not feel. 'Got to go now; got a kite to land!'

'Yes, of course. Danny, Sophie was always more your . . .' Phil whispered as Danny turned back . . .

just as blood gushed from his cousin's mouth and the fair head flopped sideways.

'Phil!' Danny said, and would have gone to his cousin save for Smiffy's hand on his arm.

'If we're going to have a chance you'd best get back in command, Skip,' Smiffy said, his voice clipped. 'There's something wrong with her port wing; it wants to dip. Come *on*, Skip!'

Danny cast another wild look at Phil, then returned to the cockpit and slid into his seat as Twiggy slid out of it. As soon as he touched the stick he was aware that this was his job, that it was more important than anything else, that it was their one chance of survival. In his heart he knew it was already too late to do anything for Phil, so he turned his total attention to the task of getting *Flora-Dora* down safely on to the nearest airfield. He gave the distress call: 'Hello Darky, hello Darky, can you give me a heading to land please?' Immediately there was a response and he turned on to the course given and, shortly, saw a runway in front of him.

And Ted was right: when he pulled the lever to lower the undercarriage the green lights which should have shone out to show that the wheels were down did not appear. Gremlins? A fault in the electrical system of the Lanc? Or a true reading? In normal circumstances, Danny would have aborted the landing and flown past the tower asking whether his landing gear was down, but this was a strange airfield, he had wounded men aboard and he doubted the *Flora-Dora*'s ability to go round a second time. Already, he was uneasily aware that a port engine was out and the usual steady hum from one of the starboard engines was interrupted and ragged. He had no option but to get her down while he still could.

There was noise all about. He could hear the tower saying something, giving him advice . . . Danny tried to ignore everything but the task before him. Gently, gently, as slowly as he dared, he brought the great plane down to the runway. For one frightful moment, he thought he had misjudged his where-abouts and was about to crash into a ploughed field; then, instead of touching the ground as lightly as a bird, she screamed and skidded along on her belly, came to a juddering halt. Instantly Danny released his straps and shot forward, bashing his head so hard on the windscreen that for a moment he thought he was going to lose consciousness. The smell of fuel was frightening and when Danny freed himself from the muddle of the cockpit and began to go down the fuselage to help the others he saw the first flickering of flames. Then it was no longer just flickering, but licking into the *Flora Dora*'s interior, and everyone made for the outside world at speed, Frank and Smiffy supporting Ted between them.

'Get a move on, Skip,' Twiggy gasped, as Frank and Smiffy wriggled through the door in the fuselage and thence on to the ground, turning to receive Ted. 'Lower away!'

'You do it,' Danny said. 'I've got to go back . . . Phil . . . I can't leave him . . .'

'No point,' Twiggy said brusquely. 'He's bought it, Skip. Get out whilst you still can!'

Danny hesitated, then found himself grabbed and literally hurled from the plane and hustled away. There was grass, a hedge, a great deal of noise . . . a ditch into which he fell just as *Flora-Dora*, with a *whump* and a roar, exploded. Danny's face was unceremoniously thrust into mud and water . . . and as he struggled free, he saw the scene lit up, hideously, in scarlet and gold.

Chapter Fourteen

August 1945

'Hold still, will you, Davy!' Tina was wielding a soapy flannel on her small brother's face whilst excitement buzzed through her. She and Arthur had been delighted at the government announcement of two whole days' holiday to celebrate VJ Day, though judging from the weather which she could see through the kitchen window folk were going to get pretty damp. There had been street parties back in May, to celebrate VE Day, but everyone was determined that this party would be the best of the lot. They would have today to prepare, and tomorrow to actually enjoy the celebration.

For Tina, however, VE Day had lacked a certain something because Harry had been halfway across the Atlantic. His ship had come into Liverpool once since then, but the turnaround had been so quick that he'd not even been allowed ashore. But his ship would dock again some time today and because it was a holiday not even the Royal Navy would keep all the men aboard. Tina beamed at her reflection in the small square of mirror above the handbasin. She and Harry would have a wonderful time together and for once she would not have to traipse Davy around with her, since Arthur, also on holiday, had announced that he and Mrs Tasker would join in the celebrations and take care of Davy.

The flannel, this time rinsed of soap, passed swiftly over Davy's small face and as soon as it had done so he opened his eyes and gave his sister an accusing glare. 'You put soap in my eyes on purpose, *and* in my mouth,' he said. 'You're horrible to me, Tina Collins, you're probably the horriblest girl in the world, even horribler than the horrible Japs. And why does I have to be bleedin' clean, anyhow? No one else is going to be clean. They's goin' to be havin' fun.'

Tina giggled. Davy always made a fuss when she washed him, much preferring his father's attentions which were of the 'cat's lick and a promise' variety. But now she towelled her little brother dry and then began to dress him in the clean white shirt, grey shorts and dark blue jersey which were his best clothes. 'You know perfectly well that Dad wants you to be a credit to him and Mrs Tasker,' she said reprovingly. 'Besides, you're going to *three* street parties, imagine that! First there's the one at the factory, this afternoon, then there's the Heyworth Street party tomorrow, and in the evening Dad's going to take you to St George's Plateau to watch the fireworks. And after that you'll come home here and all of us, me and Harry as well, will have bangers and chips. Aren't you the luckiest lad in the world?'

Davy grinned and Tina reflected that he wasn't a bad kid and never stayed miserable for long. 'Yeah, I s'pose I am goin' to have a good time,' he admitted.

'Only you mustn't say Mrs Tasker any more, not now she's goin' to marry our dad. He says I can call her Mam, or Auntie Mabel, whichever I likes best, so I'm tryin' them out in me head, whenever I remember.'

'That's sensible,' Tina said approvingly, kneeling on the floor to tie neat bows on Davy's shiny brown walking shoes. 'There won't be much happening this morning because of the rain, so I might go and help her in the kitchen – the café one, I mean. She's making a heap of little cakes for the street party an' I said I'd see if I can help her, but as soon as that's over I'm going down to the docks to see if I can meet Harry.' She held out a hand. 'C'mon, chuck, we'd best get a move on or Mrs Task . . . I mean Mabel . . . will think we've already gone off on the spree.'

'Can I come down to the docks with you?' Davy squeaked, as they descended the stairs and made for the Restawhile kitchen. 'I won't be no trouble and I won't blow raspberries if Harry kisses you, or tell him only sissies kiss girls.'

Tina sighed, realising that she had just fallen into a pit of her own making. 'We'll see,' she said guardedly. 'If the rain's beltin' down you'd do better to stay in the dry, but if the weather clears I might – just might – let you come along.'

Harry stood at the rail as his ship slid alongside the quay and was made fast. All the seamen would be eager to disembark but Harry knew from experience what a scrum there would be once the crew were down the gangway and on to solid ground once more. Everyone would be searching for their own friends and family, for that one particular face, and he knew it would be a lot easier to spot his Tina from up here, pinpoint her position, and then join her. Leaning both elbows on the rail and scanning the crowd, he told himself what a lucky blighter he was. He and Tina had been going steady ever since their first meeting after her return to Liverpool, and though his parents kept reminding him that she was only sixteen – he was only eighteen himself – he knew that, for him and Tina, age simply did not matter. He honestly thought he had loved her even when they were just a couple of kids in school, and now that love had deepened and turned into something which he was sure would never change. She was awfully pretty, with her mass of light brown bubbly curls, and the small, pointy-chinned face which always reminded him of a kitten. But it was not just her looks. She was quick and intelligent, always laughing, full of bright ideas. Sometimes he felt he floundered along in her wake, barely managing to keep up, but he told himself that this was because life aboard a warship was a serious business. Once he was demobbed and ashore all the time, he would be as carefree as she.

When he had first begun to examine the crowd it had still been raining lightly, and umbrellas had obscured many faces, but now the rain had stopped and umbrellas were being furled, and suddenly he saw her. She was alone and had just untied a dark headscarf – navy blue with splashes of red and green

– which had hidden her bright curls. Even as he spotted her, she must have seen him, for she began to jump up and down and wave the headscarf vigorously, an enormous smile spreading across her face. Harry's heart lifted. Forgetting all his resolves, he began to push his way towards the gangway, saying half apologetically as he wriggled and shoved: "Scuse me, mate . . . sorry, old feller, but I've just spotted me girlfriend, and I can't wait to give her a kiss.'

'Everyone gets a perishin' two-day holiday, but not land girls,' Tess said grimly. 'Mr Turnbull says harvesting waits for no man, holiday or no holiday. And there was I, planning to get on a train and zip up to see Mike, so we could celebrate the end of the war together.'

Sue pulled a face at her. The two girls were making their way down to the enormous wheatfield. They had harvested less than a third the previous day and hoped to finish the entire twelve acres today, since rain had been forecast for tomorrow and some of the clouds scudding overhead looked as though they might anticipate tomorrow's downpour at any moment. 'Catch a train? You should be so lucky!' she said derisively. 'The whole of Great Britain is having a holiday to celebrate the end of the war and that means no trains, no buses, no restaurants or cafés, no cinemas, no theatres . . .'

'All right, all right, I suppose we might as well get on with the harvest instead of hanging about doing nothing in Lavender Cottage,' Tess admitted grudgingly. 'They say the forces are being demobbed already but that they'll hang on to the WLA for ages and ages. After all, with half Europe starving we can't really expect imported food to start flooding into the country, so I reckon there'll be a good few months of managing on what we can produce at home before we get any help from abroad. But I'm telling you, Sue, once Mike is demobbed, we're jolly well getting married, whatever anyone says.'

Sue smiled gently at her. 'And now you can stop worrying and perhaps tonight we'll both get a decent night's sleep,' she remarked. 'I know it's nerve-racking when someone you love is in pretty constant danger – I worry over chaps I've known, of course I do, but I don't believe I ever have nightmares half the night and lie awake for the other half. You're too imaginative for your own good, poppet.'

Tess knew that her restlessness was partly her own fault. When she and Mike had become lovers, the worries had simply grown and grown, as though she were actually a part of Mike and he a part of her. She knew that if he died and left her she would be scarred in a way she would not have been had they never made love, and with this knowledge came the night-mares, the inability to sleep soundly and the perpetual nagging worry that no one should risk being as happy as she and Mike were when they were together. Ruefully, she acknowledged that Mike had known what he was talking about when he had tried to keep their relationship from deepening into intimacy. When it happened, of course, she had been deliriously happy; only afterwards did she realise how much more bitterly she would suffer if Mike was snatched from her.

So now she looked across at Sue and pulled a face. 'You're right. I'm sure I'll stop imagining the worst now that the war's over,' she said. 'I know dreadful things happen in peacetime, but they can happen to anyone. And now let's get on with the task of feeding Britain!'

Sophie had been truly tempted to give everyone a day off to celebrate the ending of the war, but when she had suggested it the girls and Nigel had looked at her blankly. 'What would we do?' Patsy had asked, in some puzzlement. 'No matter what happens, cows have got to be milked and fed, and Baxter's Piece will be smothered in weeds if we don't get going with the hoes. Tell you what, though, there's a cinema show in the village this evening, a special ending for the street party, so we could go along to that if Mrs Ryland does us an early high tea.' She turned to Sophie. 'They're showing *Snow White*, the Disney cartoon. You could take young Chrissy.'

Sophie thought this was an excellent idea and one which would combine duty with pleasure. Despite her efforts to see that Chris had the sort of life she thought he deserved, he had never been to a cinema and could not even go into the village to play with other children on the green, because getting him there and back would have added to the many difficulties of life at Hilltop.

Matthew had been needing more and more attention ever since Phil's death, though Sophie did not think his ill health was a direct result of losing his son. It seemed to her that the harder Matthew tried to do as much as he could, the worse he grew, and now Daisy spent virtually all her time nursing him and looking after Chris.

The girls were in the big barn, allocating the day's work, so after only a moment's thought Sophie smiled approvingly at Patsy. 'Yes, I think we'd all enjoy a trip to the pictures. We can cycle down as soon as tea's over and I'll take Chrissy on my carrier,' she said. 'I'm sure you agree, don't you, Nigel? Especially if Daisy can move high tea forward an hour or so, to give us a proper evening off?'

Nigel nodded.

'Right. Then we'd best get down to Baxter's Piece and start getting rid of those weeds,' Sophie said. The girls picked up their implements and began to make their way down the hill. Mr Sampson had died six months ago but Sophie thanked God for the old man's foresight every time she passed the field and saw the neat rows of vegetables flourishing there. They had had several arguments with the Min. of Ag. when the powers-that-be had wanted them to grow corn of some description, but in the end common sense had prevailed and they had been allowed to continue to grow vegetables and some soft fruit on the only suitable land they possessed.

Baxter's Piece, being the lowest land down the lane owned by the Rylands, meant that one was passing

Brewster land on one's right, and from here Manor Farm was clearly in view. As she always did, Sophie turned her eyes resolutely away from it and felt the familiar ache in her heart even as she did so. Only a year ago, she and Danny had met on this very lane one stormy night and had run into each other's arms. She had thought that things would be simple from that moment on, but this had not proved to be the case. The news of Phil's death, coming so soon after that meeting in the lane, had been like a hammer blow. At the funeral, Danny had come over to her and begun to tell her that Phil's last words had been of her, but before he was halfway through the first sentence a terrible and astonishing thing had happened. Chris had been standing pressed close against Sophie's side, clutching her skirt, his small face so white and woebegone that Sophie had questioned whether he should have been there at all. As Danny's uniformed figure had approached them Chris had looked up, and later Sophie realised that for a moment his expression had been one of incredulous delight. Then the little boy had screamed and attacked Danny like a miniature fury, biting, kicking and scratching, whilst tears had poured down his cheeks and he had shouted: 'Get away from my mummy! Leave my mummy alone! I want my own daddy!'

It was as though he sensed something between Danny and me, Sophie thought later, back in the calm of her own narrow bed. Or was it the air force uniform? Had Chris thought for one glorious moment that it was Phil coming towards them; that 'dead' didn't mean for ever?

She had soothed Chris, of course, until his screams had become sobs and his sobs had turned to hiccups. But Danny had said quietly that he thought he would not return to Hilltop for the funeral tea. He had said it not to Sophie but to Uncle Matthew, though Sophie, standing nearby, had heard every word. Next day, she had waited for him to come up to the farm to see his aunt and uncle and then, naturally, to see her. However you looked at it, she was the widow of his best friend, the cousin he had adored, and so, surely, should merit some attention?

He had not come. She had expected a letter but he had not written. He left Manor Farm the day after the funeral and had not returned to it since, or not to her knowledge, at any rate.

And with his absence, Sophie's feelings of guilt had rapidly multiplied. On his last leave, Phil had apologised abjectly for the way he had behaved, had begged for forgiveness and vowed to do better in future, to work on their marriage until it became the love match that everyone had thought it. She was glad now that she had not totally repulsed him, but the fact that she had had every intention of doing so at some point so that she and Danny might be together once more could not be denied.

So when Danny made no attempt to see her or get in touch, she guessed that he, too, must be suffering from an uneasy conscience. To Danny, perhaps it seemed worse to steal a woman from a man who could not fight back than it would have been to take her in what he might have thought of as a fair fight.

Many a night Sophie cried herself to sleep, telling herself that when the war ended and Danny returned to Manor Farm they would be able to sort things out, but VJ Day had arrived, men were being demobbed all over the country, and still Danny did not come. She longed to ask Auntie Deb and Uncle John what was happening but was afraid that if she did so they might realise that the question was not a casual one, and she dreaded anyone's guessing how she felt about Danny until she knew for sure that her feelings were reciprocated. There was also Chris to consider. He had always been casually fond of his Uncle Danny, but that had been before Phil's funeral. Since then, though he talked continually of his daddy, any mention of Uncle Danny brought a quick change of subject by Chris. Matthew remarked on it, saying uneasily that it was almost as though Chris blamed Danny for Phil's death, but Daisy had jumped in at once with a far more sensible explanation. 'Nonsense, Matt,' she had said briskly. 'This is a child of five you're talking about. He simply can't see why he has lost his father whilst his uncle remains alive and well. When he sees Danny back on the farm, in his old working clothes, he'll be as fond of him as ever.'

Meanwhile, the work on the farm continued. The sheep had been shorn and last year's lambs sold. The cows had calved and were milked morning and evening; the apples would soon be ready for picking.

Nigel and Patsy had been saving hard all through the war, and meant to buy a smallholding of their own as soon as something suitable came up. 'But we won't leave you in the lurch, young Sophie,' Nigel had assured her when he told her what he intended to do once the war was over. 'We'll wait till you've found another manager before we begin to look around. And I dare say the land girls will hang on for a bit longer as well. My guess is that fellers coming out of the forces with new skills may not want to come back to the land, which will make the girls indispensable for a good while yet.' He had looked at Sophie quizzically. 'I know it's a bit soon to say this, but I reckon you'll marry again. No matter what you and Phil felt for each other, it – it weren't like an ordinary marriage, were it? Why, in the past five years Phil hasn't been home more than half a dozen times, if that. And you've always been too busy to go and see him.'

They had been alone in the kitchen and Sophie had met his gaze squarely. 'I know what you mean,' she had said slowly. 'I've never been a full-time wife, not like Patsy and Daisy. And I expect you're right and I will marry again, one day. But I don't intend to make another – I mean, I won't make a grab at the first man who asks me, just for the farm's sake. You know Phil didn't intend to run the farm himself, I suppose? After the war, I mean.'

'Oh, I reckon that were just talk,' Nigel had said easily. 'He were carried away by the glamour of flying aeroplanes and wearing a uniform. He'd have come home and settled down. He must have loved this place really. Farming must have been in his blood, same as it is with Danny.'

Sophie had shaken her head. 'It's not at all the same: Hilltop Farm was like a millstone round Phil's neck.'

There had been a short silence while Nigel digested what Sophie had said, then he had asked, 'And what about you? I know damned well that farming isn't in your blood, though you've took to it like a duck to water. What would you do if there was no farm to run?'

Sophie had laughed and pushed back her chair. 'Well, I wouldn't be a blacksmith,' she had said lightly. 'I wanted to go to university, you know. When Danny and Phil and myself went to and from school together on the bus, we used to talk about the wonderful careers we'd have. Even Danny didn't mean to settle down on Manor Farm at once; he meant to get experience in other countries to see what farming methods are employed abroad. As for me, I rather fancied teaching, only even then I spent a lot of time helping on the farm and enjoyed it thoroughly. I guess I hoped I'd marry a farmer.'

But now, walking down the lane, a flash of movement in the Manor House farmyard caught her eye. She glanced quickly across and saw Danny, just emerging from the back door. She was carrying her hoe across one shoulder and before she remembered her resolve to let Danny make the first move she found herself flourishing it at him. He waved back, hesitated, then came towards her. Sophie told her feet to get going, to follow the other girls into Baxter's Piece, but they remained rooted to the spot. As Danny approached, she saw that he looked older and more careworn. His hair had grown rather longer than it had been kept during the war, and he was actually in civvies: a grey open-necked shirt, old flannels, and the wellington boots that were obligatory on the farm at most times of the year. He came slowly across to her, not hurrying, but he was smiling and his eyes shone very brightly. He held out both hands and took hers. 'Sophie! I was going to come and see you later. I was demobbed a couple of days ago but didn't get home till last night. How are you? And the boy, of course?'

'We're very well, thank you,' Sophie said coolly. 'You?'

Danny's smile faltered and he dropped her hands. 'I'm well too,' he muttered. 'But I've been pretty busy, with one thing and another. Look, we need to talk. Can you . . . ?'

'I've been pretty busy too,' Sophie said coldly. Just who did Danny Brewster think he was? He had neither written nor made any attempt to get in touch with her since Phil's death, yet now he seemed to assume that they might just pick up where they left off, so long ago. Well, he was jolly well mistaken. She had managed alone because she had had to do so, and she would continue to cope alone. She glanced behind her, then back at Danny. 'I've got to get on; can't let the others think I'm not pulling my weight,' she said briskly. She turned away, but Danny's hand shot out and grabbed her arm.

'Sophie, hang on a minute. I'm sorry I haven't been in touch before now, but as I said . . .'

'Yes, I heard you; you've been pretty busy,' Sophie said. 'Too busy to pick up a pen.'

She would have turned away but Danny retained his grip on her arm. He no longer smiled and his mouth was grim. 'Two can play at that game,' he said harshly. 'I've waited and waited for you to write; too busy, were you? I expected you to get in touch because it was scarcely fair to write to you at Hilltop when either Uncle Matthew or Aunt Daisy would recognise my writing . . .'

Sophie, furiously angry, cut him short. 'It doesn't matter. It's too late for talking,' she hissed. 'As I said, I've work to do.'

Two days after VJ Day had been celebrated, Tess got a telegram from Mike. It was quite brief. *Important we meet asap*, it read. *I'll be with you four or five o'clock tomorrow stop Ask evening off stop Mike.*

Tess frowned down at the little yellow form. The telegram had been sent that afternoon. They were still harvesting, sometimes until it was almost dark. But she and the other girls had worked right through the VJ celebrations; surely tomorrow Mr Turnbull would let her go early for once?

'Why not, my woman?' Mr Turnbull said when she put in her request some ten minutes later. 'You worked straight through that there public holiday,

449

and your young feller's got something to tell you I don't doubt.' He grinned at her. 'Invite the missus and meself to the wedding and we'll call it quits.'

So the next day Tess worked as usual, and wondered. She and Mike had discussed their wedding plans, the possibilities, what sort of life they would both enjoy. Tess admitted that she loved country living and would like a little place of their own in a village, or at least a suburb, whilst Mike vacillated between trying for a job flying civil aircraft or returning to engineering. A really good job in an engineering firm was quite possible, for Mike had not wasted his time in the air force and despite the fact that he had been a pilot and not a mechanic he had learned a great deal about aero engines and how to get the best out of them.

'The best pilots spend a lot of time with their flight mechanics, because if something goes wrong when you're several thousand feet above the ground it's the knowledge you've managed to pick up that will save your bacon, not some feller down below,' he had told Tess. 'I don't know that you'd get work on a farm once all the fellers are back, but there's other jobs in the countryside . . . yes, I reckon that one day we'll earn enough to buy a decent place and have the sort of life we would both enjoy.'

It would be hard at first, they acknowledged, smiling at one another with something that was almost pleasure at the thought of the struggle to come. They knew that hardship was a part of life, and they smiled because tackling such hardship together would be downright enjoyable after the time they had spent apart.

'But one day we'll have the sort of life we want,' Tess had said dreamily the last time they had met. Of course 'one day' was a long way off; at first they would have to do what all young married couples did – make do with what they could afford and save like mad – but they meant to be sensible. A family would have to wait until they could live on Mike's wages alone, though Tess knew they were luckier than most. Arthur would give them any help he could, and Mrs Turnbull had been teaching Tess to type on her ancient Olympic whenever she had time to spare. Things would turn out all right . . . so why was Mike rushing down from Lincolnshire to Norfolk? Why should they need to talk?

Much to everyone's surprise, Mike arrived just before five o'clock driving an ancient jeep. 'A pal lent it me,' he said vaguely, smiling at Mrs Turnbull and kissing the tip of Tess's nose. 'Come on, queen, I'll take you for a spin.'

Tess got into the passenger seat and the jeep coughed and wheezed its way out of the farmyard and along the lane, but as soon as he could Mike turned the vehicle into a gateway and cut the engine. Tess, who had been eyeing him covertly, thought that he looked rather grim and suddenly – foolishly – wondered if he had changed his mind, no longer wanted to marry, no longer wanted *her*. When he did not immediately speak she voiced the thought aloud.

'Mike . . . if you've changed your mind . . . want to

leave getting married for a bit . . . I suppose it has all been rather sudden . . . I wouldn't blame you, or . . .'

Mike gave a shout of laughter and flung his arms round her, squeezing so tightly that she gasped. 'Changed my mind? Oh, love, that's so absurd I'm surprised you can even think such a thing, let alone say it! No, the reason I didn't say anything just now was because I was trying to find the right words. Only I can't, so I'll just tell you what my dad said to me on the telephone yesterday . . .'

When he had finished explaining, Tess sat back, not knowing what to say. Arthur had announced that he was selling the greengrocery business and buying a small general store in Little Sutton, which he and Mabel could easily run between them. 'And he's looking to us to run the Restawhile,' Mike said gloomily. 'It's doing very well indeed, so it will be on a partnership basis, just until he gets the general store up and running – it's been let go, he says – and then he'll make over the whole business to us. I tell you, sweetheart, you could have knocked me down with a feather when he outlined his plans. I know he's always said that when the war was over he meant to sell the greengrocery, but it never occurred to me that he'd expect us to take over the café.'

'You could explain that we've plans of our own, I suppose, and don't much want to run the café,' Tess said doubtfully. 'I mean, you left the greengrocery business before the war even started, and I was desperate to do something other than waiting on. Don't you think he'd understand?'

'He'd try to do so, but he'd have to cancel his plans to move out to Little Sutton,' Mike said apologetically. His expression was still anxious, Tess saw. 'And he's not getting any younger . . . the war, and losing poor Laura, and even having to look after little Davy, have taken it out of him. But if you can't bear the thought of living over the shop again . . . though it would only be until we could afford to move on . . .'

Tess stared before her. Two lives, the one she and Mike had planned to live and the one which had just been suggested to her, danced before her inner eye. Liverpool, weary and bomb-damaged, people carrying on their lives under all the difficulties which would beset a country which had been at war for six years. Herself and Mike working a twelve-hour day just to keep the Restawhile running, the worries over staff, rationing, shortages . . . and living over the shop, presumably in the cramped little flat to which Laura had first taken them when Mr Mitchell had offered her the job of manageress of the Restawhile.

Then there was the other picture. A cottage with a long garden, a few fruit trees, currant bushes, a strawberry patch. She would keep poultry, a pig in the sty at the bottom of the garden, a cat to catch mice and to purr by the fire on winter evenings. She pictured Mike going off to do the work he loved and was good at, and herself getting a country sort of job, rearing a family in clean country air, visiting the city often . . . but not living there, not hemmed in by houses, people, and traffic.

Tess sighed and snuggled up to Mike, kissing the side of his neck as she did so. 'Oh, Mike, of course we'll take over the Restawhile. It was selfish and silly of me to suggest that we wouldn't. After all, we're young and strong and have all our life in front of us. And we'll be together!'

'You're a queen, queen,' Mike said lovingly, rubbing a finger along the line of her jaw. 'Tell you what, we'll tell Dad to let the chap who's bought the greengrocery have the flat, and we'll rent a little place not too far away, mebbe with a bit of garden. Just whilst we're managing the café, because as you say it won't be for ever. And when you've got some good young women working for you, I'll start back at the engineering works and before you know it we'll be putting the Restawhile on the market and moving out to the country, like Dad and Mabel.'

Tess saw that the look of strain and anxiety had left his face and knew a moment of pure happiness. What did it matter where one lived, after all? She and Mike might have to trim their ideas a bit, but she knew they would be ecstatically happy simply because they were together. She leaned back in her seat, then turned to him. 'We'll get a car as soon as we've enough money, so we can get out into the country Sundays,' she said. 'And I'll find up the recipe books and learn to cook all the things Mam did. It's a challenge, that's what it is!'

Mike grinned and hopped out to crank the engine into life, then climbed buoyantly back into the driver's seat, beaming all over his face. 'You're all right, gal Tess,' he said in a very passable imitation of the Norfolk accent. 'I'll phone Dad as soon as I get back to Digby and pass on the good news!'

'Come along, young man, it's time you were in bed,' Sophie said. It was September now and Chris had just completed his second week at the village school. It had been a novel experience to find himself suddenly thrust into the company of a dozen children his own age, but to Sophie's great relief he had responded well and set off for school each morning eager for the day ahead. However, he did get pretty tired and by bedtime he seldom argued the toss but obediently made his way upstairs, barely managing to stay awake for his nightly story.

Now, Sophie sat down on the end of his bed and reached for the book of the moment, which happened to be the *Just So Stories* by Rudyard Kipling. They were halfway through 'The Elephant's Child', a great favourite with Chris, though he enjoyed most tales. But when she began to read, her son waved an imperious hand at her. 'Not that one; Miss Bridge is reading that one to us in school. We take it in turns to play the parts and today I was the Elephant's Child. I had to hold my dose and talk funny . . . leggo, you are hurtig me,' he said happily. 'What about that one Daddy was reading to me, do you 'member? It were about Ratty and Mole and Badger, what lived in the wild wood. I did like that one, Mummy.'

Sophie stared at her son. She encouraged him to talk about Phil, to remember him with pride and affection, but she had never taken *The Wind in the Willows* out of the bookcase, thinking that reading the story, which had been one of Phil's favourites, would be too poignant. Now, however, she got Phil's old copy out and went and sat on the end of the bed once more. 'I can't remember where you were up to,' she said, trying to keep her voice calm and even. 'Would it be best if I started at the beginning again?'

Chris snuggled down in bed and stuck his thumb in his mouth, then removed it to remark in a sleepy mumble: 'Daddy left a bit of paper in to mark our place.'

Sophie began to read.

Downstairs, Daisy was preparing the evening meal whilst Matthew read his paper. Now that he was in school, Chris ate in solitary splendour at about five o'clock whilst the rest of the family had a later meal, and now, with Sophie and Chris out of the way, Daisy felt it safe to broach the subject which she knew was very much on both their minds.

'I had a bit of a chat with Deb last week, when I went down to Manor Farm to ask her for that knitting pattern she promised me,' Daisy said, keeping her voice low. 'And I asked her whether Danny had any plans to move on. I said he'd only been up twice since he got home, though I didn't add that both times it was when Sophie was out of the way. She said Danny doesn't talk much, though he has said he wants to go back to university and get his degree. After that, she thinks he'd like to travel. I said what about the farm but she said John has everything in hand and can manage without Danny for a few years yet. What on earth will we do, Matt, if Sophie marries some fellow and moves away? She'd take Chris, of course, and I know she'd mean to bring him back from time to time, but it wouldn't be the same. He's so like Phil was as a little boy and already the farm is his life. It would be cruel for a country boy like him to end up living in a city.'

Matthew snorted. 'And I suppose you imagine Sophie would be happy in a city?' he said derisively. 'You worry too much, woman. I don't believe Sophie would willingly leave the farm and she's never talked about remarrying, has she? So why assume she'll do so?'

'Because she's young and pretty and because I believe she and Phil rushed into things without thinking it through,' Daisy said, almost hesitantly. 'If you remember, Matt, it was always Danny and Sophie when they were young, whilst Phil played the field.' She glanced at Matthew, and when she spoke again her voice was apologetic. 'I wouldn't say this to anyone but you, but you know Phil wasn't a – a very stable sort of character when he was young. And though he loved Danny – they were closer than most brothers – he was jealous of him, always wanting whatever Danny had. I – I sometimes thought he married Sophie because she had been Danny's girl.'

Matthew grunted. 'He married her because she was pregnant,' he said bluntly. 'And if anyone let Danny down, it was Sophie, not our Phil. She wasn't forced to sleep with him, she chose to do it, so don't you go blaming our boy for that particular piece of mischief.'

'Oh, I don't,' Daisy said hastily. 'But I'm afraid Danny does . . . blame Sophie, I mean. That must be why he avoids her, and if they happen to meet by chance . . . well, you can feel the ice forming, I'm telling you. They really seem to hate one another and I was so hopeful that they'd get together again, now that Phil's gone. It would have been the perfect solution, Matt, and you know it. They could have moved in here and taken over the farm, and we could have retired to that nice cottage that John's had all done up and modernised. I'm certain it was done with us in mind – Deb even let me choose the wallpaper and the paint, and the lovely bathroom suite. Imagine having our own bathroom! Deb says we could get a sort of lift thing to get you into and out of the bath; you'd love that, wouldn't you?'

Matthew sighed, but nodded his head. 'I do miss having a proper bath,' he admitted. 'But if Sophie does go off, my love, then we'll put the farm on the market and retire to John's cottage anyway. We've got a bit of money saved, and we should get a decent price for Hilltop, so we shan't be too badly off.'

'Yes, you're right, and an awful lot of people are worse off than us,' Daisy agreed, trying to sound cheerful. 'But I'd like to see Sophie happy. She's been a wonderful daughter-in-law to us, Matt, and at one time I thought she and Danny were made for each other.'

'I don't see how you can say that; they were just a couple of kids when Danny joined the air force,' Matthew observed. 'And remember, old girl, you can't know what goes on inside someone else's head, and the more you try, the more confused you'll get. In other words, you can't live Sophie's life for her, though no doubt you think you'd make a much better job of it.'

Daisy smiled reluctantly and moved over to the oven as she heard Sophie's footsteps descending the stairs. 'You're right, of course, and it's early days yet,' she remarked, bending to remove a meat and potato pie from the depths of the Aga. 'Maybe something will happen, which we've neither of us thought of, to make things right again.'

Sophie ate her share of the meat and potato pie, drank two cups of tea, and began on the washing-up. Outside, it was a beautiful evening, and for a moment she considered walking into the village to visit her mother. However, Mrs Cantrip was a whist fanatic and Sophie remembered that on Fridays she cycled over to the next village with her friend and partner, Mrs Ellis, to compete in their weekly whist drive. Sophie's father would almost certainly have left the house and be comfortably ensconced with a couple of cronies in the snug of the Black Lion. If Sophie joined him there, he would buy her a soft drink and try to make her welcome, but the Lion was really a man's pub and Sophie knew she would not feel comfortable.

She finished the washing-up whilst Daisy dried the dishes. 'It's a lovely evening and not too late, so I think I'll walk into the village,' Sophie said. 'Mrs Bailey stays open for ages on a Friday and I've still got some sweet coupons left, so I'll pop in and buy some humbugs, if she's got any.' She turned to Daisy. 'Anything you want?'

'No thanks, but I've a good mind to come with you,' Daisy said, looking longingly out at the rays of the setting sun that lit up the yard. 'But I don't think I'd better. Suppose Chris were to have a nightmare and wake?'

Sophie laughed. 'He'd come down to the kitchen and cast himself at his grandpa,' she said. 'He's a big boy now, Daisy, and besides, he flaked out after only a couple of pages of his story, so I don't think he'll be coming down in a hurry.'

Daisy, however, shook her head. 'No, not tonight. It's your mother's whist night, isn't it? I'll walk down with you some other night, when she's at home.'

'Oh, don't be so daft, Daisy,' Matthew said. 'It'll do you good to get some fresh air; you've not been out all day. If you want to chat to someone, go down to Manor Farm and have a chat with Deb. And while you're there, ask her why her no-good son hasn't been up to see his old uncle lately.' He pulled a face. 'Nigel's all very well, but he thinks of nothing but the smallholding he's going to buy. I could do with some rational male conversation.'

'Well, if you're sure,' Daisy said. 'I haven't seen Deb since last week so I wouldn't mind a chat, and I'll pass your message on to John; to Danny himself if he's around.' She peered anxiously into her husband's face. 'Are you sure you don't mind, Matthew?'

Matthew, with a copy of the local paper spread out on his knee, cast his eyes up to the ceiling and groaned. 'For God's sake, woman, why should I mind if you nip out to see your sister for an hour? You never know, I might actually get to finish reading the newspaper without being constantly interrupted.'

Daisy laughed. 'All right, all right, you bad-tempered old bear, I can take a hint,' she said, and Sophie smiled at the teasing note in her mother-in-law's voice. Once, they had bickered and sparred their way through life, but the hard years of war had mellowed them and now they were as loving a couple as one could wish to meet.

'I shan't be long either, Matt,' Sophie said over her shoulder as she and Daisy let themselves out into the yard. 'Probably an hour at the most. Is there anything I can get you from Mrs Bailey's grand emporium?'

'I'll have a couple of your humbugs, if you manage to lay hands on some,' Matthew said, just before the door shut; he was fond of sweets.

Side by side, Daisy and Sophie strolled down the lane. 'Why don't you pop in with me and have a word with Danny?' Daisy suggested as they drew level with Manor Farm. 'You and he used to be such friends . . . well, the three of you were I suppose, catching the same bus to school an' all. You don't meet enough people your own age, Sophie. Besides, Deb might be glad of something from Mrs Bailey; you never know.'

Sophie smiled but declined. 'Auntie Deb's got the telephone and the use of the car, and lots of people to run her errands,' she said rather reproachfully. 'Besides, you're supposed to be asking Danny if he'll go up to Hilltop to have a chat with Matthew.'

'Well, all right then, but you can call in at the farm on your way back from the village and we'll walk back together,' Daisy said firmly, causing Sophie to shoot her a suspicious glance. What was her mother-in-law up to? But no matter how hard Daisy tried she would not succeed, because there was Danny to consider as well as Sophie, and whenever the two of them chanced to meet – always by accident now – Danny's whole attitude had been so antagonistic, so cold, that Sophie had had only one thought in her head, which was to get away.

So now she agreed she would call in at Manor Farm on her way back from the village and set off down the lane. Within a few yards, however, she changed her mind and when she reached the gate which led into the sloping pasture she climbed nimbly over it and set off towards the river. She would not put it past Daisy to send Danny after her under some pretext or other, and a walk into the village with a cold and silent companion who had been forced to accompany her against his will would be very unpleasant. However, if she followed the riverbank until it reached the stone bridge she would still get to the village, even though it would take a little longer. Resolutely, she set off.

By the time she had covered half a mile, she was seething with annoyance. She had not come this way for years and nor it seemed had anyone else. She had not realised how overgrown and neglected the path had become. Once, she and Danny and Phil had followed it often, fishing for tiddlers in the shallows, paddling, collecting the tadpoles which flickered in and out of the quiet pools. Then, reeds and rushes had not invaded the banks, cattle had not pocked the smooth turf and stinging nettles had not flourished in great intrusive banks so that one had to take a longish detour in order to get by. Over one pool a great many gnats hovered and Sophie was bitten on the arm, though the biter was immediately and vengefully swatted. God, I must be out of my mind, Sophie told herself. Peering ahead, she saw the stone bridge, though the bushes she remembered had grown up a good deal and now half obscured it. She would have to keep an eye open for Danny's head bobbing along over the top of the parapet as she scrambled up the bank to rejoin the road which led to the village. Then she looked down at herself and grinned ruefully, thinking that Danny was unlikely to even recognise her should he suddenly come into view. She had not bothered to put on wellingtons but still wore her old school sandals and was muddy up to her knees; the hem of her dress was draggled and filthy, and every inch of skin that she could see was scratched and stung. She put a hand up to her hair and hoped no one would see her before she got to the forge. She knew where her father kept the spare key, as no doubt everyone else in the village did, and would let herself in and have a wash and brush-up before visiting the shop. She glanced at her wrist-watch and realised she had made quite good time, despite the many obstacles; if she got a move on, she might actually reach the forge before her father set off for the pub.

She had reckoned without the bridge. In times past, it had been an easy climb and there had been a most convenient gap in the hedge which allowed access. Now the hedge had grown up, thick and prickly, but worse was the state of the bank. The village lads had turned it into a regular mudslide and Sophie groaned with dismay. She could, of course, walk to the very top of the meadow and then along to the nearest gate, but that would take ages and Mrs Bailey would have shut up shop long before she reached her.

Cursing her own stupidity in taking this particular route, Sophie began an undignified and painful scramble. At first she achieved a couple of feet only to slide back three, but then she managed to grab hold of the coping of the bridge. Feet scrabbling wildly, she pushed herself away from the mud, got the toes of her sandals wedged into the stonework, and hung there. She glanced down. Below her, the water curled lazily, the weeds waving beneath the surface. It wasn't deep, but it would be cold, and she dreaded to imagine what everyone would say if she walked down the village street drenched to the skin. Anyway, it was quite a long drop and the bed of the river would make a hard landing. Fruitlessly she struggled, but though her arms were strong she could not get more than a couple of inches higher and the stone of the bridge was hurting her hands dreadfully. Soon, blood would be added to mud, and a fine sight she would make!

She had almost decided to drop into the water when hands seized her wrists and a voice she knew well said abruptly: 'Trying to commit suicide, Sophie? I know the river's pretty full at this time of year but I don't think it's that deep. Wedge your feet against the stone as high as you can get them and I'll give a mighty heave.'

Sophie did as she was told and Danny, for it was he, gave a tremendous jerk. Sophie flew through the air, crashing her ankle painfully against the parapet, and then the pair of them were sitting in the road and Danny was laughing, though his face was anxious. 'Are you all right? My goodness, you knocked all the wind out of me!' He scrambled to his feet, then held out his hands and pulled her to hers, his eyes rounding. 'Sophie Ryland, what *have* you been doing? Mud wrestling is obvious, but why all the scratches and stings? My dear Sophie . . . oh, Sophie, my darling . . .'

One moment they were standing inches apart, the next she was in his arms, and in seconds all her uncertainty and misery had drained away. This was where she wanted to be, where she was meant to be.

However had they thought themselves enemies? Weeping dolorously into the comfort of his shoulder, his chin resting on top of her head and his arms tightly about her, she said, her voice muffled: 'I th-th-thought you h-h-hated me! Whenever we met, you were so cold and horrible. You hardly looked at me. Why, Danny? Do you still blame me for marrying Phil?'

'Oh, Sophie, as if I could blame you! For a start, Phil was here and I wasn't . . . but we've already been through all that. I thought it was you who hated me. You'd never meet my eyes and when you did your look was so cold that it froze me to the spot. Then there was the guilt. I desperately wanted to tell you what Phil said to me just before he died. But it seemed too cruel, and once time had passed . . . oh, I don't know, I began to wonder whether you thought it was my fault. I let him take over the tail gun, but you know Phil. I was busy keeping the old *Flora-Dora* aloft and Phil didn't exactly ask permission. Well, you know how he was.'

'None better,' Sophie said, and pulled herself free of his embrace with some difficulty. 'Look, I'm in an awful mess. Can we walk down to the forge? Mum's at a whist drive and Dad's at the pub, or at least I expect he is, so I can clean myself up and make you a cup of tea, and then we can talk.'

Danny agreed, and presently they were ensconced in the Cantrip kitchen, both sitting in the same armchair, with two cups of tea to hand. Sophie could not stop smiling and knew that Danny was in the same state of euphoria as herself. At last, at long last, they were going to sort things out, to talk without fear of interruption.

Danny started, telling her of the *Flora-Dora*'s last flight, and of how Phil had asked him, Danny, to take care of Sophie and Chris. 'Just before he died, he said: "You'll look after Sophie? She was always more your . . ."'

'Go on, what next?'

Danny shook his head. 'There wasn't anything else, sweetheart, because he – he died. But I think we could both make a pretty good guess at what he had been going to say. If he had been able, he would have said: "Sophie was always more your girl than mine." So you see, neither of us need feel any guilt. Phil was trying to give you back to me. I've always known he was twice the man I was – am – and I never blamed you for preferring him. He was a grand chap and I loved him, so I tried not to feel hurt when you married. But that's all over now and I feel we can fresh with Phil's blessing. Can you possibly same?'

course I can. I've always loved you, Danny. there's something I've been meaning to tell u . . .' She paused, gazing earnestly into Danny's ark eyes, so near her own. A hundred pictures stled through her mind: Phil, trying to make things right, regretting what he had done, Chris, round-eyed and innocent, Matthew and Daisy, proud of their tall, handsome son. And Danny himself, still looking up to Phil, admiring him.

But Danny was staring at her curiously, his dark brows rising. 'Yes? What have you been meaning to tell me?'

'Oh . . . that Phil and I married on impulse, in a great hurry,' Sophie said vaguely. She knew now that she could never tell Danny what had happened between herself and Phil, not if they both lived to be a hundred. Danny had loved – still loved – his cousin and love was far more important than self-justification, more important even than truth.

'I see,' Danny said dreamily. He sounded more than half asleep, Sophie thought affectionately. 'Well, no one could accuse *us* of rushing things. It's been years . . . oh, by the way – will you marry me, Sophie? Only I warn you, I'm a dull sort of a chap; if you say yes we'll likely spend our lives right here. I've no desire to go beyond the blue hills.'

'That suits me,' Sophie said.

* * *

'So you do understand, don't you, pet? And you[...] to love Danny as I do? I know he isn't your real f[...] but he loves you very much.'

Chris snuggled down in his bed clasping [...] teddy, then smiled at his mother. 'Course I unde[...] stand. My own daddy's gone to heaven, you said[...] Only – only I'll never forget him, Mummy, and I'l[...] always love him.'

'That's fine, pet,' Sophie said unsteadily. 'Go to sleep now.'

Chris waited until his mother's footsteps descending the stairs could no longer be heard. Then he slid out of bed and padded over to the window. He knelt on the sill and gazed out at the dark sky. 'My real daddy's up there,' he said conversationally to the teddy in his arm. 'He's flying his plane high among the stars like I will, one day.' Then he sighed and returned to his bed. 'Good night, God bless, don't forget to undress,' he said sleepily. 'I love you, Daddy Phil.'

Little Girl Lost

Katie Flynn

It is a cold night and Sylvie Dugdale is weeping as she walks by the Mersey. A figure approaches and, dodging aside to avoid him, she falls into the river.

Constable Brendan O'Hara, just coming off duty, sees the girl's plight and dives in to rescue her. He is dazzled by her beauty, but Sylvie's husband is in prison and the closeness that Brendan soon longs for is impossible.

Sylvie has to escape from Liverpool, so Brendan arranges for her to stay with his cousin Caitlin in Dublin until it is safe to return. There she meets Maeve, a crippled girl from the slums, who will change all their lives when a little girl is lost . . .

arrow books